DAIMONION

The Apocalypse, Book One

J.P. Jackson

Dati Amon wants to be free from his satyr master and he hates his job—hunting human children who display demon balefire. Every hunt has been successful, except one. A thwarted attempt ended up as a promise to spare the child of a white witch, an indiscretion Dati hopes Master never discovers.

But Master has devilish machinations of his own. He needs human-demon hybrids, the Daimonion, to raise the Dark Lord to the earthly realm. If Master succeeds, he will be immortal and far more powerful.

The child who was spared is now a man, and for the first time in three hundred years, Dati has a reason to escape Master's chains. To do that, Dati makes some unlikely alliances with an untrained soulless witch, a self-destructive shape shifter, and a deceitful clairvoyant. However, deals with demons rarely go as planned, and the cost is always higher than the original bargain.

Published by
NineStar Press
PO Box 91792
Albuquerque, New Mexico, 87199
www.ninestarpress.com

Warning: This book contains scenes of graphic violence, torture, and gore.

Print ISBN # 978-1-947139-36-7
Cover by Natasha Snow
Edited by Jason Bradley

Table of Contents

Dedication

To my husband Lonny, who has supported me through yet another wild and crazy adventure; thank you for everything you do, and everything you are. I love you.

To my own flock of Daimonion: Jonathan, Rachel, Brandon, Kim, Kari, Laura, Scott, Adrian, and David, you helped bring my demons to life, and for that I'm eternally grateful.

To the fantastic people at NineStar Press, and particularly Raevyn and Jason, thank you for giving my demons a home.

And finally to my first-round editor, Samantha Cook, without you, my dear, my magic was scattered, unfocused, and without purpose. You taught me how to cast far better spells and weave my will in dark and terrifying ways. Don't ever stop.

Deal with a Demon

DATI

Snow crunched beneath my taloned foot as I searched. My breath hung as fog around my face until the winter wind whipped it away. My padded soles were too tough to feel the iciness, but my mind was frozen numb, ignoring the guilt that came with the job. The drudgery of stalking the city streets was tiresome, and the possibility of attaining success depressed me.

I was just north of the city's downtown, where all the houses had been built during the war, and their age showed. Master had sent me to search there. Somewhere among these wartime houses, behind the cracked walls and beneath the peeling shingles, there was something that belongs to us.

I hunted a lost child: a dark child.

A thick blanket of grey wrapped the night sky as snowflakes landed atop trashcan lids, cars, and untrimmed hedges. The sight before me felt darkly ethereal. Perhaps it was because of my one scarred and injured eye, or maybe it was the snowstorm, but the night was hazy and blurred. Beams of light from the nearest streetlamp illuminated the snowflakes as if they were hundreds of thousands of falling stars.

Make a wish, I thought to myself. A silly human expression.

I wish I didn't have to do this. I wish I wasn't so lonely. I wish to be free.

Silly thoughts. Punishable thoughts.

The winter breeze soothed my skin and tousled the dark curls of my hair, which was just a little too long. I stopped on the corner of the street, just out of reach of the lampost's exposing brightness.

The snowstorm cocooned the neighbourhood, muffling the city under a layer of pristine, untouched innocence. The fresh snow made me feel comforted and safe.

With the street empty, I shook my wings out, sending a flurry to the ground before draping them back over my shoulder. My wings would look like a cloak to any human who might see me, but then it was late at night, and humans didn't see well in the dark. Besides, I didn't really want to be seen by anyone.

I was being cocky. Walking around with my wings exposed was technically against the rules, but my heavy clothes prevented me from tucking them away.

There were rules that must be obeyed. First, no human was to know what I was, or that we existed. Second, Master's orders were never to be questioned. Third, complete assigned tasks on time, and never, ever displease Master. They were his rules, and I was to follow them, for fear of retribution.

But I did not always obey.

I loved to watch humans: their relationships, the "busyness" of their lives, the drive and passion that sparked creativity and ingenuity, but mostly the kindness in them. Despite what some would say, they were inherently gentle in nature. And I confess I was a little jealous of it all.

But tonight, I didn't watch. Tonight, I hunted.

Walking down the ragged neighbourhood, the houses all began to blur together with the same small structures and stucco-faced veneers. Massive trees lined the boulevard with branches that reached high like outstretched arms as if to welcome the inclement weather.

I stopped at each structure as I passed by, analysing if only for a brief second to see if the beacon shone through the windows. The glow would be a cold colour, white but tinged in purple, a phosphorescent violet that could only be seen by my kin, the D'Alae. It emanated from all children who possessed latent demon blood. The result of a hybrid mating. Children who were still human and yet, in part, demonic.

We call them the Daimonion.

Hours passed by as I examined each house. And then, one abode, just slightly smaller than the rest but without the obvious need of attention, grabbed my interest.

The demon-light presented itself, glowing in slow pulsations of violet-white light from the furthest window from where I stood. Every time I found this light, my body reacted instinctually and involuntary. I hated my other self, the demon within and the dark violence that surrounded it, but hate wasn't strong enough to stop the fiend from emerging.

Adrenaline pumped through my veins. Closing my eyes, my head dropped as the change began. There was nothing I could do to stop it. My fangs elongated, my barbed tail stiffened, and my hands morphed from their human shape into the required rakish talons, deadly and sharp, elongated and pointed, with venom beginning to ooze from the base of the nails. Another night, another child ruined by my nocturnal visit.

But you have to do this, Dati. You have to ensure Master is kept happy, I reminded myself, repeating the last sentence like a mantra, trying to justify the gnawing ache in my stomach.

Within seconds, I found myself next to the window where the demon-light beckoned. With a quick push, the old window slid open, and I slipped into the child's bedroom.

There, beneath a hand-stitched quilt, slept my prey. Such a small boy, with auburn hair surrounded by small stuffed animals. He couldn't have been more than five years old. Toys littered the room and crystals hung in the window, catching the streetlight and casting prisms all around the room. A small nightlight shone from the corner, its warm yellow glow distorting my shadow across the room into a large ominous silhouette. From the boy, the ebbing radiance glowed fiercely.

I bent over the child and delicately pushed his scruffy hair off of his forehead. Freckles danced across his nose. His breath smelled and tasted of cloying sticky-sweet innocence.

I straightened myself up and stretched out my wings, cramped from the long night's walk, then held up my clawed demon hand, tensing it. The skin was black, like liquid ink, and the ebony demon flesh flowed up to my elbow where it faded back to pink. Veins of evil persisted up towards the shoulder.

Reaching over, I steadied myself to tear open the skin on the back of the boy's neck and inject the venom that would unleash the evil hidden within his body. I gently pushed the boy down into the mattress, ensuring there would be no struggle.

Just a hair's breadth away from making the incision, the cut that would change everything, I stopped. Guilt churned my stomach, making me nauseous, the same way it did for every child before this one.

The bedroom door burst open, and light from the hallway exploded before me. Standing straight and scampering against the wall, I raised a hand to shield my eyes from the blaring light.

A small stout woman with fuzzy slippers and a tatty nightshirt walked into the room and flicked on the boy's bedroom light, her flat nose and cheeks ruddy with anger. She was furious. How could someone who looked so unassuming appear so fierce, despite the jasmine and vanilla perfume that clung to her clothes?

"Back away from my boy, beast! He is not yours to take." Her voice was thick with an eastern European accent.

I had broken Master's most important rule. No human must know what I am. Remorse flooded through me, and my tail went limp as I came to one realization. I would have to kill her.

I lunged forward, faster than her human eyes should have been able to see, but before I was halfway across the room, she raised her hand and, with short, thick, but deft fingers, tossed a piece of paper into the air and spoke.

"*Відкрий!*" She spoke with specificity and authority. To my ears, it was harsh and unfamiliar. The air around her swirled, causing the flannel night skirt she wore to rustle around her covered feet. Her long hair, plaited, had been disturbed and shanks of dark blonde waved around her head like medusa's snakes. The piece of paper disintegrated before me, but the symbols and writing from the page hung in the air. With sudden quick movements, the writing encircled me in a spiral.

"*Злови!*" As she said the foreign word, the hanging writing vibrated with a high-pitched hum. Lines emerged from the tails and stems of the suspended script. Lines weaving and wrapping, growing into long threads.

"*Замотай!*" With the last word, the letters wound about me. Wrapping me tightly, the strings bound my feet and hands and looped around my torso, lifting me up off of the floor. This woman, in her bunny slippers, wearing threadbare clothes, had me ensnared, and all I could think was how Master was going to be angry with me for getting caught.

I had never met any human who could contain me.

I had no idea what to do.

I was a demon. I would unleash Hell.

As I glared at the woman, my eyes felt as if they were burning. I flexed every muscle in my body, straining against the magical spell, and released a howl so deep, so guttural that the walls of the house shook. The lights flickered, and the air became tainted with the smell of rot and death.

In response, the ropes wound tighter, cutting into my flesh and constricting my limbs so that there was no escape.

Very quickly rage turned to panic. This wasn't supposed to happen. Humans were supposed to fear us. This woman should have been weeping uncontrollably in fear, prostrating herself at my feet.

Looking around frantically, I tried to determine how close I was to the window and pictured myself hurling my body out of the opening.

As if she could read my thoughts, the window slammed shut.

"You are mine, creature." Her green eyes twinkled with pride at being able to restrain me. But her anger never left her face as she pursed her thin lips and locked her jaw, seeming to settle in for a fight.

I had no choice, and not wanting to do so, I went deeper and let my evil rush like a fevered virus through my body. Embracing its darkness, power surged through my veins. I could feel it. If a corpse could feel its body decaying, that was exactly how the dark felt as it took over. It was dreadfully painful and yet deliciously addictive.

My face became hollow and gaunt as the flesh wasted away, while my eyes sunk into my skull and skin tightened over my bones, turning it translucent and greasy. The bedroom light flickered and then dimmed as my pupils enlarged until the irises were all but gone, reflecting light and making them glow. My voice deepened and thickened.

Being in the presence of a creature from Hell turns most people's courage into a melted puddle of their own waste. This woman was beyond comprehension, standing there, waiting for me to finish.

"For how long will you hold me, woman?" I asked. The light in the room popped and crackled as I spoke, my bottomless voice cutting through the air, its reverberation causing her to grimace. The lines that held me fast tightened a little, and as they did, the skin on my talons thickened and each claw elongated further. My unrestrained wings stretched out, unfurling to their full span, but despite my obvious nonhuman form, I felt as scared as I imagined this human female was. I needed to escape my binds and then end this bitch.

"You will not have my boy."

"And if not me, then some other will come to claim him," I lied. There were no others like me within Master's territory. But I resorted to anything to get free. "If you know what I am, and how to do this—" I wrenched my arm, still snagged within the magical writing. "—then surely you know why I'm here." I glanced at the slumbering child.

That seemed to hit home.

"You lie, like all of your kind. You lie! I know, D'Alae, Bringer of Nightmares, I know."

I cocked an eyebrow as she spouted my namesake. My barbed tail lashed back and forth in anger. My lip curled, and through gritted fangs, I growled at her. The sound hung in the air between us, but I could smell the doubt she was feeling. Her uncertainty tasted like dirt and sweat. She wasn't entirely sure.

"Are you so confident? Do you know for certainty that tomorrow night another of my kin won't visit? There are others. My Master has many. I fail tonight, another one comes tomorrow. If not tomorrow, then another night, or perhaps we steal him away from you in a crowd, or we wait until one day when he goes to school and take him when you're not there to protect him. Tonight, or some other time—you can't be there forever. He is ours." I spit the last part out with as much hatred and darkness as I could. The shadows crept in closer, gaining ground on her light. My mind whirled, attempting anything so I could get free.

The script that ensnared me loosened, just slightly as she took a step back. Her squared shoulders, which had been braced and steady, eased slightly as she realized that she would not be able to have her child at her side forever. She knew that I, the demon, spoke a truth.

"But what if you spared him?" she asked tentatively.

"That is not an option."

She stepped towards me, her gaze intense and expression unreadable. "You don't understand. I will not lose this child to your side. So I ask you again, I beg of you, what if you spared him?"

"My Master has spoken. I do not act on my own. There are others who know of his existence." I looked at the boy. It seemed preposterous that this conversation was being held over such an insignificant human, and that the being could sleep through all of this.

"I can hide him from all others, but you must leave him be. I can't hide him from you. You have seen him," she pleaded.

"And why would I do that, even if I believed that you could hide his existence?" The nightlight in the corner suddenly burned brighter and brighter until the bulb could hold the energy no more. It shattered.

The woman closed her eyes at the tinkling sound of glass hitting the wooden floor and appeared as if she would cry.

"Because I will offer you my magic. I can heal any wound. I will keep you alive and healthy if you leave my boy untouched. You leave me his soul, and I will heal yours." She hung her head in shame as she whispered the next sentence. "And I will give you the name and location of another of your half-breed children." With that, the writing fell to the floor, freeing me.

"There is no healing my soul." I rubbed my wrists. It was true; my soul was beyond repairing. It didn't even exist in one piece. But now I was intrigued. The potential to bring two children back to the dark in one night would make Master most happy.

The woman reached forward and, with one finger, touched my face. She traced the line of the scar that ran down from my forehead, across the damaged eye, and ended at the lip. The scar tissue was a remnant of Master's unhappiness with my abilities.

As her finger passed over my face, calmness seeped into me. The darkness within subsided. I felt soothed but also light-headed and dizzy, warm and safe.

"Look." She wrung her hands and wrinkled her face in disgust at what she had just done.

I opened my eyes. She pointed to the mirror that hung on the boy's door. I peered at my image, and for the first time in a long time, my eyesight was perfect. The scar was gone, and the eye that had been damaged was healed, but the altered iris now shone a bright ice blue.

So she could heal and snare demons. Clearly this woman was more than just a mother of a boy who was Daimonion. My mind raced and schemed at the possibilities this woman had opened up. There was a glimmer, a sense of expectation, a betraying notion that perhaps Master could be bested by another. Hope that maybe Master's demands would never have to be executed.

But that was disloyalty. Master would destroy me for having such thoughts. But maybe...maybe there was hope that the wounds he inflicted could only be temporary. I was terrified, going against him, but something inside me had to break free, if only just a little.

I made the deal.

Marta, the pudgy, overprotective mother, hid her child from the rest of my kind using more of her words written on paper. She held in her hand a leather-bound book and found the page she needed, ripping it from the spine as she had done earlier.

"*Невидимий!*" As she spoke, a tear rolled down her cheek.

On a separate piece of paper, she wrote the address of a different child, the one who would replace hers.

And so that night, I became healed, found an alternate child, disobeyed my Master, and kept that dirty little secret hidden for a very long time.

A Night's Harvest

DATI

Regularly and without warning, Master would send me searching for one of our lost children. Each time, the information on where to go would be delivered without his presence. Sometimes a map with a section of the city would be left propped up against my bed pillow, other times something as mundane as a letter would be sitting on top of my food inside the refrigerator. Regardless, it always spiked dread within me. The hunt for another tainted soul had begun.

This went on for years. Nothing ever came of my deal with the Healer: no swift violent retribution, no punishing torture sessions for straying from my task. I had gotten away with betrayal and disloyalty, and I held those treasonous actions very close.

But regardless of what I wished for, and despite the seeds of mutiny that made my hands tremble each time my demon talons reached out for their next victim, the regular notifications continued to arrive, although the method of arrival always disturbed me slightly. It was a reminder that Master was ever present, even if he wasn't physically close.

A scratching noise came from behind me while I ate my dinner by candlelight. Dinner at the table—a ridiculous ritual on my behalf, a way of imitating the humans that I had become fond of. I carefully put my knife and fork down, nervous that Master watched me right then. He'd have some form of horrifying punishment ready if he discovered my affection for humans.

At first, I wasn't sure where the noise came from. I glanced over my shoulder, expecting Master to be standing right there, but found no physical being making the noise, which left me wondering if some of the Disembodied had crept into my abode. It wouldn't have been the first time.

But upon rising and turning around, the origin of the clawing sounds became evident. Street numbers were slowly being scrawled into the wall's surface behind me, and as the numbers were drawn, the lines ran red as if scrawls had been engraved into flesh instead of plaster.

I threw the silk napkin over my dinner, which was mostly uneaten, and sat down heavily, held my head in my hands, and sighed in relief. At least some bodiless creature hadn't penetrated my home, but the reprieve was stained with the knowledge that I had to steal the innocence away from another child.

I hate this.

The numbers completed themselves, and I took note of them, the address a familiar locale. Leaving my uncooked slab of meat behind, along with the flickering candles, I made my way towards the door.

I had lost my appetite.

I stood in a city suburb near the trunk of an old willow tree, attempting to hide beneath its numerous weeping branches. Each house in the neighbourhood was built at least in part with stone, and no two houses stood alike. Turrets flanked the corners of the home directly in front of me, with ancient ivies rambling up the stone, anchoring themselves with little tendrils as they wound their way towards the roof. I had been in this neighbourhood before, and in fact, within the house that I stood in front of.

My barbed tail twitched in anticipation of what was about to happen. I had grown to loathe this duty, the endless searching, plodding up and down empty neighbourhood streets attempting to find the beacon.

Looking up at the castle-like house in front of me, I could see the slowly pulsating balefire emanating from a bedroom window. Its radiant glow illuminated the lower half of my body as my tail swished back and forth. I pulled myself deeper into the shadows and away from the light. I grimaced, my heart ached, and my gaze dropped to my talon feet. My body reacted instinctually, transforming into a demonic beast from the human form I cherished.

"I'm so very sorry," I mumbled to the child from where I stood, peering out from behind the sagging branches. A slight gust of the night's autumn wind blew through the mighty tree, gracefully swaying its limbs. One gently brushed my shoulder as if to comfort me, as desiccated leaves tumbled down. So many years of this had worn me thin, and I despised the one who made me do it.

The family's teenage daughter had returned home late, far past her curfew, leaving the back door open for me. Slinking through the dark house, an unwanted intruder, I passed by the girl's bedroom. Her door was ajar, and she peered through the crack at me. Long hair hung on each side of her head, and her dark eyes were framed by furrowed eyebrows. She wore the tiniest of smirks. She watched me pass by and then quietly closed her door. I had harvested her years earlier. Now, it was her brother's turn.

Finding the boy sleeping in his small bed, I inspected his peaceful and tiny form, caressing his fine blond hair. I scratched the toddler, who couldn't have been more than three, on the back of the neck, slicing the skin open. The sticky venom dripped off the tip of my rakish nail and dropped into the wound I had opened. The flesh instantly blushed red, swelling in response to the foreign substance. In time, a cluster of freckles in the shape of a spiral would form, encircling the incision I had made. I took a moment to stroke the boy's hair, then quickly fled the scene.

From beneath the tree, concealed in shadow, the demon-light flared brilliantly. The quiet evening was suddenly pierced by the child's anguished shriek.

The last stage of the venom infection was now complete, releasing his inner evil. He called for his parents and sobbed. Guilt welled up inside me as my mind painted a picture of what was happening to him. Tears streaming down his face as the pitch-black venom coursed through his veins, making him slick with sweat and unleashing terrors deep within him, his parents rushing to his bedside to comfort the child. But tonight would only be the beginning of many in which night terrors would be the norm. Nightmares involving monsters who would taunt him from the shadows cast against bedroom walls. The closet would house a Pandora's box of fiends, beasts from Hell who were just waiting until the lights went out to feed his dreams. Gradually the demons would twist his mind into accepting darkness as the norm.

My venom had worked. His demon blood was now active. I felt dirty.

There was a small chance that the child would escape, that during puberty the hormones emitted with the maturation process would negate the venom. If this happened, then he would not darken. He would be spared from being one of my brethren. I hoped for that, for him. But then he would be Nephalem, one who could sense us, feel our presence, and sometimes even see us for who we really were. Once the venom courses through the blood, he could never truly be free, but perhaps he wouldn't be one of us.

But this is what I am bid to do. I am Dati Amon, a D'Alae, and we gather back the children who belong to us.

My task was finished for the evening. My limp tail wound itself around my leg, as if it was ashamed of me. I brought my wings in tight, slinging them over my shoulders like a cloak. The blanket of night's darkness would soon peel back, revealing all creatures under the blazing sun. I had no place there, so I made my way home.

Sleep is my only solace, when I fantasize that I am free, unbidden. It is darkness, a time of stillness in which there is no scorching brilliance of light to blind the eyes or disturb the mind. I find the pitch of night to be peaceful. In an unconscious slumber, there is a comfortable nothingness.

After harvesting yet another child, I so desperately wanted that stillness, that peaceful tranquility, which only comes with deep sleep. On that night, this feeling was disrupted.

In the deepness of my dream world, my mind perceived movement from the outer limit of the darkness around me. Was it a trick of the mind? Was it something I thought I saw but wasn't really there at all?

"Who's there?" I called out.

A source of light appeared at the far end of the room, a slow glow that revealed a robed figure, hooded, two eyes glowing ultraviolet, peering directly at me. He stretched out his hands. Whispers of smoke twisted along his fingers, smoke the same colour as his eyes. It swirled to his fingertips, then fell to the floor in an eerie waterfall of luminescent purple against blackness.

"Dati," the form hissed. It sounded like claws scraping steel.

The tendrils pooled at his feet, growing like vines and writhing along the floor towards me.

The smoke crawled across the distance between the robed figure and me. I was not sure that the tendrils were safe. Perhaps they were dangerous. I scampered backwards in an attempt to escape the smoke, but it gained on me too fast and began collecting around my feet. The tendrils wound around my legs, growing like wild creepers, wrapping themselves about my body, branching and crawling, covering my form. They enclosed me like wrappings around a mummy, until shoots coiled around my neck, and encircled my head. A wisp washed over my eyes, and I was blinded. I panicked, clawing at my face as my view changed...

I stood on top of a building. It wasn't high. Perusing my surroundings, it appeared that I was in an industrial area. The moon shone overhead. The corners of the building glowed, pulsating, the same violet colour as the robbed figure's eyes and smoke.

With a blink of the eye, my view changed again. I stood inside the building with a concrete floor, smooth on my bare feet. There was a table in the center of the room. All around there were other beings standing at random spots, in a trancelike state, empty and void of expression. Then it all disappeared.

An alarm clock screeched, yanking me out of my slumber.

I sat up in bed, rubbing my eyes. It had been months since I had dreamt. Remnants percolated through to my conscious mind as I remembered the robed figure, the purple smoke, a building, and the full moon.

"Shit!" I ran to the window and surveyed the night sky. The moon was low, but perfect and round like it had been in my dream.

Damn it. If I didn't hurry, I was going to be late. That hooded figure was Master. That little display was his way of summoning. I hadn't been called into his presence for months.

Without really thinking about it, I reached behind my head and scratched the back of my neck, feeling the sharp ridges of my scar. It was a habit I had whenever I thought of Master. There was a brand there, with a thick circle superimposed over top of a pentacle. Other mystical symbols had been marked into my flesh, tattooed, carved, and burned with both brands and blades. It was my hex mark. In the center, the flesh was black, lifeless. Little tails scampered out of the middle, one running up to each point of the pentacle. I always wanted to scratch it, my body's way of saying that the deadness there didn't belong. It was where Master had ripped part of my soul away from me, and how he ensured I obeyed his every word.

Master had done that to me when I was very young. It had been very painful.

And frightening.

By holding a part of my soul and threatening to destroy that essence, it meant I would never cycle. When I finally died, my life would end. No broken soul can reincarnate. Master held my existence in his hands, ensuring this would be my last. My last life was to be a slave to a psychopathic Master, as a miserable indentured servant. He had removed my hope of being free, in this life or the next.

This summon was for more than just myself. There had been others in the dream room too. This was very odd. Master didn't have gatherings.

As I sat here thinking about it, my time was running out. I needed to get going. Lateness was *never* tolerated. In the summons, the moon hung high in the night sky, almost at its apex. I would have to be at my destination before that moon was in that same position tonight. I had about an hour, maybe a little more.

I had a bad feeling about this night. Then again, whenever I had dealings with Master, nothing good ever came of it. The tasks he regularly set before me were filled with vengeance and blood. I held no hope of that ever changing.

I hated him with every fiber of my being. But I feared him just as much.

Wings in Flight

Dati

I ran my tongue over my canine fangs, checking to see if they needed a brush as I considered what area of the city would contain the building from my dream. But instead I found myself remembering the way all four of my fangs had drawn blood and squelched the lives of those who had displeased Master. I grimaced at the phantom sensation of my teeth sinking into the flesh of humans who had crossed him. A twisting knot formed in my stomach and my tail jerked, as being enveloped in his darkness always made me nervous.

Enough. I have to go.

I grabbed clothes, donning them as fast as I could.

There was one window in my bedroom that I had spent some money on—under-the-table money—for a custom job. This high up, no building would ever have allowed windows that open. I had an extra alteration made.

I pulled the window open, just like a door, then slid the remaining panels to the side. A breeze blew in, the night air cooled my perpetually hot skin. I took a deep breath, concentrated, and then flexed my shoulders forward.

The scars along my back stretched apart, starting just beneath the hex mark, unzipping all the way down to the base of my spine. As the scars splayed, bones covered in leathery skin extended through the slits of my shirt. Methodically, the skeletal frame of my wings unfolded, unhinging straight outwards. Once free of their protective sheath, they slid more to the sides. Joints opened, and then with one final shudder, the structure extended as far as they would go and unfurled, releasing enormous bat wings. I crouched down and gave them a couple of good flaps, stirring the loose papers on the bureau.

My wings—although huge—were lightweight and strong.

I took a couple of large steps forward and launched myself out of the window. With my body as straight as an arrow, I hurtled towards the street, letting several floors pass by me with dizzying speed.

The night breeze caught under the dark expanses of stretched skin as I spread my wings. I arched gracefully up towards the night sky, and as I continued up, I passed through the layer of smog lying overtop of the city, obscuring my body from the casual observer, and headed west, to the meeting destination.

I loved the way the air rushed past my skin, fluttering my clothes as the adrenaline of excitement sped throughout my body.

The advancing storm chilled the air. Lightning illuminated the way through the last of the city center. The tops of buildings changed from skinny downtown towers, like fingers reaching up from the ground towards the sky, to sprawling block-long roofs. Inspecting the world from above gives a very different perspective. Detail is lost, the little things become unimportant, but one can see so much of the bigger picture. A creature can feel small when compared to all the space that exists. I could see all the places I would like to go.

As I reached the industrial area, I began scanning the flat rooftops in search of a sign, anything that would indicate where the meeting was being held. The knot in my stomach twisted, as if a screw had been turned one more turn tighter. I glanced at the moon; it was nearly at its apex. My time was up. I needed to find the spot. Lateness would not be tolerated. Clenching my fists, I beat my wings a little faster, propelling me until...

I chanced upon one of my own, another creature of the dark, scuttling down an alley and making their way towards the destination.

Watching the figure as it slithered through the dark and dirty alleys, I glanced forward and saw the mark. A building two blocks up contained the sigil I was searching for, not that anyone of the human population would have noticed, though. Just like dogs could smell where other dogs have been, Darkening marks could only be seen by our kind. The cornerstones of the building pulsated, displaying a faint violet colour. This was the indication—the mark that I had been searching for. It was the same ultraviolet colour I had seen in the summoning.

The creature that I had been watching skulked into the front door of the building and disappeared. I wondered if it was Hemming; I expected to see him tonight. The creature moved like Hemming, with purpose and grace, hidden in the shadows and almost gliding through the dark. Agility and fluidity were attributes a Shape-Shifter excelled at.

I spotted an open window on the second storey. Flying upwards and circling once again, I aimed this time at the window, propelling myself towards it. I was quite agile when on the wing, and while aloft I had no need for human doors. An open window would suffice just fine.

Shifting the placement of my wings upwards, I backbeat several times as I closed in on the window. That backbeat always made the most incredible bass drum noise, and the more speed and weight that slowed the flight down, the more reverberation occurred. I loved that noise.

As the window came closer, I reached out to grab it with my bare feet, but I came at it far too fast. With quick adjustments, I arched backwards to curve myself away from the building, and in a slow circling motion, like an airplane coming in for landing, I made a second attempt.

The landing was met with deadly accuracy as I grasped the wooden windowsill with my clawed talons. Splinters from the window's ledge dug into my feet, but the tough soles protected me from any harm.

I launched myself from the windowsill towards the ceiling, unfurling my wings to their greatest extent. They formed a canopy over me and allowed me to hang in the air for just a second, but to anyone other than demons, it would have seemed that I was suspended. Folding my wings up and straightening my spine, I fell down onto the cold cement.

As my taloned feet hit the hard surface, I lurched forward from inertia, my palms slamming into the floor. I dug my talons into the concrete and left deep puncture marks.

I tucked my head under to avoid an impact. My wings followed and flew forward to cover my form just as the robed figure spoke.

"Finally." His voice was gravelly.

Dammit, I've done it again. I had already displeased Master. Nothing I did was ever up to standard.

All the hate I held inside welled up inside me as I folded my wings back and lifted my head. When that much fierce emotion is felt, the demon within takes over. The skin on my face pulled tight. Heat burned from behind my eyes, which meant that they were glowing red with rage. I snarled, releasing a small growl.

Master, his black suit draped by a flowing cloak, scowled at me and raised his hand. With a flick of his thick-nailed digit, I was thrust backwards, clambering through the air. For just a brief second, I flailed my limbs, trying to grapple on to anything to gain control. But the wall was too close, and Master was too powerful. With one wing sprawled out and the other tucked behind my back, I smacked the interior wall of the warehouse.

I heard the crack of a wing bone. Then I felt the heat radiating outwards, which quickly turned into burning pain as a force pinned me to the wall. Damaged wings don't heal well, and if they do, they never heal right.

"You forget your place!"

I attempted to wrench my shoulder up to pry my one wing free, but I was paralyzed, splayed out, vulnerable.

Master's image shifted, displaying a visage of anger that transformed his human face into a demented mask of outrage. His soulless eyes simmered violet, filling with anger. He hovered inches above the ground, his mantle fluttering around his feet and gently brushing the concrete slab floor. He sailed through the air towards my restrained position. Terror welled up from within me.

I closed my eyes and turned my head away in shame. I was going to die. This was it.

So be it. I'm so tired.

There was a small part of me that thought how nice that release might be. Death. No more punishment, no more rules. No nothing.

But my instinct to survive was strong.

For the love of all that is dark; I can't die, not now...

Master glided towards me, slow and steady. As he drew closer, I tried in vain to turn away from him. I didn't want to peer into his eyes. I struggled and writhed in a desperate attempt to break free. A whine escaped my lips. I was sure Master was going to end me. He would make a bloody example of me in front of the others.

The attendees watched from the table, some with nonchalant glances and others with morbid curiosity. I could smell the diverse emotions, which left different tastes in the back of my throat.

Please, no.

Master leaned in close and whispered, "Why do you constantly fight me? What good do you think it will do? You're such a stupid creature. If I didn't have need of you.... Look at what you've done to yourself." Master gently stroked the hair on my head, as if soothing a distraught toddler, like he cared.

He fingered one of the glass vials at his throat, which dangled from a bejeweled chain. It was my vial, the glass jar that contained my excised soul part. He caressed the vial, taunting me. I could smell the hate wafting off of him, and I was quite sure he could sense my hopelessness.

He released the vial, and then he held out his hand. I flinched again.

Maintaining his telekinetic hold on me, Master reached behind me, grabbed my pinned wing and pulled it forward, releasing it from its entrapment. The broken bones rubbed together and chewed up the flesh inside as the shards were jammed into soft tissue.

Through a sneer, Master raised his voice to ensure all heard him. "Even though you flout me, I still care for all of my creatures. But do not ever disobey me again!" He wrenched his arm upwards, extending my wing to its full expanse, shifting the broken bones once again. The quick action produced an upswell of pain, and I became light-headed. Vomit rushed from my stomach to my mouth. I swallowed the bile, muffling my screams. My cockiness, my inability to keep my emotions in check might have just ended any chances of flying ever again. Master was right. I was a stupid creature.

Master turned around and floated silently towards the table, returning to his original position while straightening his tie. Everyone cast their eyes downward. Without looking back, he waved a hand and released his telekinetic hold on me. I slid down the wall and fell to a heap.

"Assume your position, D'Alae. Take your chair," he said softly, but his words carried great weight.

With humility, and as fast as I could manage, I pulled myself up, cradling my broken wing.

I made my way to the long table. The walk of shame seemed to take forever. My face burned with humiliation. I found the empty seat and took my place, my head hung along with the others. I placed my broken wing carefully on my shoulder, hoping to brace it. It throbbed.

I hated him. Oh, how I hated him, and wanted to be free from him. But all of my kind, the D'Alae, are bound in servitude. It was tradition and it had always been this way. As much as I longed for freedom from Master and his brutality, I'm not sure I would know what to do without him. But I could imagine.

"Now, let us begin," Master said, holding out his hands like a priest towards his congregation, as if we were about to start mass.

Infection

DATI

The table was wooden and intricately carved with twining vines that criss-crossed around the edge. Ornate shoots radiated from the edgework in elegant spirals, darting across the surface in rounded curlicues to the center.

From the other side of the table, Hemming offered a look of sympathy for the broken wing draped over my shoulder. It throbbed and burned, and every other moment, a sharp pain would shoot up the bone and down my spine. My knuckles turned white as I gripped the chair's arms, bracing myself against the pain. Hemming grimaced, if only slightly, in empathy, and he cast a resentful glance down to where two missing fingers should have been. Hemming was keenly aware of Master's propensity for punishment.

Hemming had sharp facial features covered by a thick brown beard that was kept short at the sides and long at the chin. His mouth was slim, and his dark brown gaze darted around the table, scoping the scene before us as much as I was.

I gritted my teeth as another shooting pain—like a nail had just been driven into the bone—emanated from the break. I dared not draw any more attention from Master. I surveyed the other participants around the table. I had never seen any of them before, except for Hemming, but then business with Master was done on a one-on-one basis. I wanted no knowledge of any other horrifying actions that were being perpetrated on behalf of my kind. I had heard of the tasks others were charged to complete, set out by Master, and they had been as sick and twisted as the deeds demanded of me.

Sitting directly to my left was a young girl. She couldn't have been more than twenty years old, if that. She had pretty bright blue eyes and long blonde hair that curled at the ends. The tips had been dyed black, as if gathered together in clumps and dipped into inkwells. She wore a fuzzy pink sweater and tight slacks that ended in a wide cuff just below the knees. It was odd attire for demon folk as we typically preferred clothes that allow us to melt into the dark. She didn't smell like one of us either; her aroma was off, stale like swamp water that was turning green. We, on the other hand, have an acrid burnt stench to us, a smell that reminds me of burning plastic. I wasn't sure what she was or why she was there.

There were so few of us present, and yet I had seen, or thought I had seen, many others in my dream-state summoning. Master began to speak, his deep voice soothing when paired with a handsome face, so deceiving from what he could be and had been moments earlier.

"The time has come." He stopped, studying us, as if expecting acknowledgement and agreement. "The time is now to bring *him* here to be with us, so we can be in *his* presence, and *he* can rule over this luscious human domain." He beamed at the thought of Satan's presence. It was disturbing to watch.

I chanced another stealthy glance at the night's participants.

Beside the young girl next to me was a filthy bloodsucker of a Vampyre with alabaster skin. His lips were too red, eyes too vacant. Past experience had taught me these demons were capable of a bloodlust beyond what any Hollywood horror movie could ever depict. Their thirst was violent and insatiable. I'd only witnessed one massacre. My stomach churned at the memory of a room washed in fresh hot blood and the screams of humans trapped in that room with a monster that taunted them with their lives. Not that any escaped. They all died, slowly, painfully, and bloodily. You would have thought evolution would tailor the Vampyre to be precise and efficient hunters. In truth, their evolutionary path was more directed by the acts of violence they committed. Most often, Vampyres hunted in mating pairs, and the bloodier the stage, the more virile and fertile the mating, producing large litters. They truly were more animalistic than humanoid.

"And we will be the chosen ones to bring *him* into this realm." Master still slogged on about his Hellish paradise in the human world. What in Hell's name did he think he was going to do? Bring about the apocalypse?

"For years, I have researched and toiled to find a way to bring our king, the Dawn Bringer, to this realm, and I have finally found the path to do so. Lucifer, the fallen, cast out because *he* wanted to be a god. Why should we be restrained or contained for ambition, for reaching and striving to be more?"

An enormous amount of piety rolled off of Master in waves. The whole speech sickened me, and his viewpoint was one I certainly did not share.

"*He* can bring us to freedom, to create for us a world where our pleasure, our needs, our desires can be explored without being punished, banished, or destroyed. Imagine a world where humans are freely available to us for our use! Think how we could stretch and grow and come to understand our full potential.

"I have spent so many years in a desperate attempt to know why we were created, who we are and what our purpose is. Surely our existence is meant to be more than just living in the shadows."

It was true, in some measure. None of my kin held any favour with the other god.

"We are so much more than that! I have fretted upon the reasons behind my existence: if I have achieved everything I can, if I could have done more. And then I came to believe that freeing *him* from his entombment, destroying the bonds between our two worlds that restrict *his* passage, and bringing *him* here is my ultimate purpose because it serves us all." Master closed his eyes and smiled. His hands rested on the carved tabletop. He gripped it tight. When he opened his eyes again, they were luminescent, reminding me of a black cat whose orbs were reflecting moonlight in the dead of night. You couldn't see the cat, just the eyes, burning and piercing through the darkness. It was unnerving.

"Imagine when *he* sits here in the human realm. It will be a new world in which we become gods to the meager sapiens that we are now made to hide from. The filthy pit that we all once called home will be no more. The humans shall fall before us, and offer up their flesh and spirit. This is our reason to exist, to bring *him* here, and yet...we don't quite have the Daimonion needed for the task. There are unique creatures required to create that passageway, the door that will allow *him* to come through. It is not an easy task. There needs to be sacrifices." He stopped again. I could feel his stare, probing us all, gauging our expressions, looking for dissention.

"You six are not enough," he repeated, "but I have the solution."

With those words, Master lifted his right hand and I cringed. Typical demon custom is that the right hand delivers, the left hand receives. But then he lifted his left hand as well, and in it, he held his dagger. With a quick swipe of the matte blade, Master ripped open the palm of his right hand with the serrated teeth. Blood flowed freely, as red as the rubies embedded on the haft of his weapon, dripping onto the carved troughs that decorated the wooden table.

Where Master's blood touched the table, it began to move and ripple. Master walked around and placed a bloody handprint in front of each of us. He took up position directly behind me.

As each blood print brought the carving to life, he leaned in close and whispered, "Regardless of what happens, you will care for her." I turned as he nodded towards the girl with the pink fluffy sweater who smelled like stale, sour water.

The wood splintered and crackled as it came to life, writhing and growing, taking my attention away from the teenager and her black-tipped curls. The smooth tabletop became a slithering mass of wooden vines, which quickly grew beyond the surface, reaching towards us, and with snakelike precision, the vines struck out for us.

The Mindbender, a member of the demon species who were masters of illusions and deception, hissed through its jagged sharp teeth. Its translucent skin revealed the veins beneath the surface. As the vine grabbed its wrist, it tried desperately to wrench the ensnared appendage free—to no avail.

I was so caught up in the blood magic and the vines trapping the others, I hadn't realized that Hemming, the girl, and the Vampyre were also imprisoned with their left hand strapped to the table. Master still stood behind me, and the air was rife with his anticipation and impatience.

Only the Kasadya demon—a rare order—and I had yet to be ensnared. I had never seen a Kasadya, or Watcher demon, before, but I knew them by reputation. They always had an ostentatious style of dress, and this one was no different. Sporting a black-velvet top hat with a wide silver buckle serving as a hatband, made me think he had just arrived from the 1800s. A decorative mantle of raven feathers encircled his neck, and the black of the feathers seemed to melt into the inkiness of his topcoat. These Watchers, with their dark irises, saw into the past and futures, of probabilities and histories. If he had gazed into my eyes, he would have seen all the secrets I had kept from Master over the years. He was a dangerous creature to have so close by.

I glanced up to discover that Master had moved back to his position at the head of the table. He stared at me with displeasure again. I had already received his wicked retribution once; I wasn't about to test Master's limits or tolerance a second time this evening. I held out my wrist like an arrested criminal awaiting his handcuffs and let the vines do their job. Only the Kasadya was left untangled, and he avoided the vine strikes like a well-seasoned martial-arts expert.

Master watched the Kasadya, his handsome face contorting back to the snarl I had seen earlier. Master took a step, leaned over in front of the Watcher demon, and squeezed his hand. Fresh blood fell directly in front of the Kasadya. The vines thrashed at the taste of it, lashing out ferociously. The vine latched onto the demon's arm and strapped it to the table with a thud. One vine reared up like a cobra ready to strike, and with deadly accuracy, whipped forward, wrapping itself around the Kasadya's arm, piercing the forearm, burrowing straight through, and anchoring it to the table underneath. Blood flowed from the wound, thick and dark. The Kasadya screeched loudly.

Master let his hand drop to the table, blood still flowing from the wound. Like a squirming mass of worms, the vines wrapped around his hand and wrist. Seething and caressing his wounded limb, I could hear them sucking the blood that flowed, like spawn suckling at their mother's teat. With his unmarred hand, Master reached inside his robe and produced a flask containing a substance that appeared very much like liquid mercury. The substance swirled in its confines. It churned on its own in the bottle.

"I had to pay dearly for this." He lifted the flask to his mouth, bit into the stopper, and pulled it out. It made a hollow *pop* when the cork gave up its grasp on the bottle. "But I have faith that this will grant us exactly what we will require to be with *him*."

He tilted the flask and let the metallic liquid pour out.

It was viscous, too thick to be mercury. There seemed to be far more of the substance coming out of the bottle than what the bottle should have been able to hold, but it continued to gurgle at a slow and seemingly unending rate.

As the liquid hit the table, it pooled into a perfect circle. A carved indentation on the tabletop beyond the squirming mass of vines allowed the viscous substance to collect. When the flask was finally empty, the vines froze.

For just a brief second, all was silent. Everyone held their breath. Nobody moved.

Our limbs were still lashed firmly in place by the sinuous vines, but the tendrils gripped even harder, squeezing like a python constricts its prey. Veins popped out on my arm.

The perfect circle of thick goo began to divide into six equal but smaller ones. The reformed smaller pools began travelling across the surface of the table, repositioning themselves, one in front of each of us. The shiny substance glistened and vibrated in front of me. That knot in my stomach formed again; this didn't feel right, or good. I tested my D'Alae strength against the vines that had me confined. Being feral, we were stronger than most others, but there was no getting loose. The liquid began spinning all on its own, counterclockwise until it swirled apart into another four equal fractions, which then changed from liquid into hard little silver balls. The balls rolled around for a bit and then settled.

Metallic spines emerged from the smooth surface, grew long and folded, then felt around until they touched the tabletop. Each sphere hoisted itself up on silver spidery legs. The spheres morphed and changed, elongating into metallic beasts, and inched their way towards our trapped supinated hands.

The closest silver monster scurried over and crawled up onto my palm. The tiny pinpricks of the spine legs punctured the skin and left little wounds, which welled up with blood. I glanced up and chanced a quick view of the fiends around the table. The same thing was happening to the others. I pulled my arm frantically, trying to wrestle it out of the grasp of the table's vise grip.

In retaliation, the creature speared me with one of its sharp legs in the fleshy part of the forearm, sending more shooting pain through my body. Using its legs and teeth, it began ripping up the flesh on each side of the wound. I yanked hard, panic taking over for a second time that night as I frantically tried to break away. I moved my free hand to beat the little terrors away from my wounded arm, but the vines on the table lashed out and ensnared my right hand. All I could do was sit and watch.

I gritted my teeth and let out a growl as the first scaly creature held up skin flaps as a second bug crawled into the wound. The girl beside me screamed *no* over and over as she experienced the same thing. She too attempted to rip her arms out of the vines that held her tight.

Master came behind her and stroked her long blonde hair as if to still her, then grabbed a shank of her hair and pulled her head back. He stared into her eyes and whispered, "Be good and be quiet, or I'll pour another flask right in front of you." Tears were streaming down her face. She bit down on her lip and closed her eyes just as tightly.

The bugs burrowed into our wounds. The pain was excruciating, but I dared not let any noise out. It dug its way up my arm under the skin. Just as I thought I might be able to bear the pain, the third and fourth bug followed, each of them tunneling their way up the underside of my flesh, creating a bulge under my skin. I threw my head against the back of the chair, trying desperately to maintain consciousness and composure.

There was so much pain, I couldn't hold back. The growl became a roar as my primal nature took over, my body morphed into its demon form. My hands, still lashed to the tabletop, changed into their claws. The skin at the fingertips merged with the fingernails and hardened. The tips slowly turned black, like rot crawling up each finger, hardening the skin as it went. The black continued until it reached my forearms, the veins carried the black pitch upwards, creeping from the back of the talons and continuing to the shoulders.

The girl next to me screamed again. I couldn't blame her. Even I couldn't believe the amount of pain I was in. I could feel all four of the silver creatures in my arm, digging, moving. As the first one crested my shoulder, a bulge grew under my shirt, which inched forward as they continued their journey, over the shoulder and down the side of the ribcage.

Hemming lost control of his human form. His ears morphed into points and sprouted with fur, but a moment later, they were leathery flaps. His face became a snout, fangs protruded from his lower jaw, and then he was Hemming again.

Through the torture, Master spoke.

"You've all now been, for lack of a better term, infected." Master let out a little hum of satisfaction. "My diminutive creations will reside in your bodies and survive off your blood until you find adequate hosts for each of them. By ingesting your blood and therefore incorporating your essence into their bodies, they become little transmitters of your unique physical traits and talents. Once you find a suitable host, my creatures will inject themselves into your subjects, passing along your genes and forcing the transformation of humans into various forms of Daimonion, but they'll be far more demon than human. I have specific targets in mind, and some of you will be instructed whom to get close to. The minions will do the rest. You have three months to complete your task. If you fail to find suitable subjects in that time, my parasite helpers will destroy you and then return to me. I have no need for those who can't perform."

I would have been shocked at this revelation, of what the parasites had been created to do— the making of demons outside of Hell was impossible. Daimonion, the children I hunted, were turned to the dark side once my venom was injected into them, and some even exhibited psychic abilities after puberty. But this...this sounded like Master was creating something more than just Daimonion.

The pain of the monsters as they dug deeper into my chest cavity, burrowing under my ribs...it burned as they tunneled. The girl beside me had passed out. Hemming's eyes had rolled back and foam formed at the corners of his mouth. His head bobbed—he too was losing consciousness.

"Don't disappoint." Master stood there for a moment, surveying the carnage. Blood splatter was everywhere. As he watched over us, a smile spread across his face, and the charming humanlike side beamed bright. Black smoke rose from his skin, tiny wisps at first, until there was so much you could barely see his chiseled facial features until a small hiss like steam could be heard, and then, he was gone. Evaporated.

The vines released our captured appendages. Creaking filled the room as the wood returned to its former solid state, a carved relief entwining the edge of a large table. The smooth tabletop was a mess of bloodstains.

I let my head rest on the edge of the table for a minute. The digging continued, and the little bastards moved around, jostling and jockeying for position. I let out a sob and then pounded my right fist on the wooden table several times in an attempt to release a large amount of anger, pain, and frustration. The wooden vines broke and splintered as I pounded, wood chips flying in all directions.

I was exhausted, bloody, and broken. Once again I felt used, worthless, and dirty. Master would make me brutalize more humans, creatures that I had grown to cherish and yet become jealous of. I had no desire to drag any of them through my darkness, or worse, help bring the underworld to the human realm.

I lifted my head, checking out the room. Perhaps I had passed out for a while—everyone was gone except for me and the unconscious girl.

A large incision and two loose skin flaps, bugs living in my gut, and a broken wing was my reward for showing up for the summons. That and instructions to ensure the safety of a very human-appearing girl. She wasn't one of us, but I felt sorry for her, passed out on the table with blood smeared across her face and sprayed all over her clothes. I couldn't leave her, and Master had made it clear she was mine to care for. She had fainted early and had not heard the last insidious speech from Master. She had no idea what was in her, or why it was there. She deserved, if nothing else, a fighting chance.

I shifted my wing, gritting my teeth as bolts of stabbing pain flared down my back until the wing was immobilized and draped across my shoulder. I grabbed the girl's chair, pulled it out, and caught her as she fell forward. I slid my hand around her waist and picked her up, cradling her close to my chest.

It was going to be a long walk home.

Retreat

Dati

I walked through the grimy and shadow-filled alleys, carrying the blood-smeared rag doll girl. My wings were wrapped around me and the girl like a cloak, my shoulder braced my broken appendage. I needed to find my way back home, on foot and quickly, without being seen by any humans.

Every block was an obstacle course, and I was exhausted, dirty, and—judging from the girl's complexion—I was running out of time. She had lost a lot of blood during the summoning, and Master had instructed me to look after her. If she died in my care, I would be next.

The sun peeked up from behind the cityscape, but home was just around the corner.

The elevator ride to the top floor was quick, and I lowered the girl down as gently as I could before my front door, my aching muscles complaining angrily at the exertion. But my body failed me and she crumpled to the floor. She didn't so much as twitch. How was it possible that she could have been passed out for this long? My heart raced. Maybe she was already dead?

Bending down, I listened to her—no. Her breathing was shallow and short, but it was there.

After patting down my body for the familiar feel of keys, it dawned on me that I had leapt out the window. Seriously? Fuck. I was locked out.

I rolled my eyes and shook my head. Master was right: such stupidity. There was only one way left for me to get in.

With a flash movement, I rushed the door with the shoulder that wasn't trying to support a broken wing, aiming as close as I could to the inside of the doorframe, nearest to the hinges. I hit the door and the metal fittings groaned. The door bent under my weight, the hinge pins snapped as they gave way, and the door clattered to the ground.

I stood quietly for a second, making sure that I hadn't disturbed anyone.

To my relief, the hallway remained quiet and empty. The last thing I needed was unwanted attention from a nosy neighbour. With care, I dragged the girl inside and quickly propped the door back in place. It would do for now, but I would need to have that repaired as soon as possible.

After a minute to catch my breath, I lugged the girl onto my leather sofa. Her clothes were ripped and stained with gore and filth after the night's events. What a completely bizarre outfit for a summons by Master. She appeared as if she was going to a sorority meeting, not a demon summoning.

The slash on her arm still seeped blood and needed to be bandaged. I was no Healer, but the least I could do was clean her up and prevent the wound from bleeding further. I left the sleek modern lines of the chrome-and-black leather living room and headed down the hallway towards my bedroom where supplies to bandage her arms would be in the master bath.

Two Shishi statues sat at the foot of the bed, one positioned at each of the front bedposts. The Shishi were good-sized marbled stone figures of Chinese palace dogs, but these were the demon version with pointed ears, slits for irises, and a maw full of razor-sharp teeth. The tails were long and barbed on the end, just like mine. Their flat pushed-in faces held many skin folds, which allowed them to trap scents, making them excellent trackers as well, but their main job was to guard temples and shrines. The Shishi only guarded places that housed great darkness.

I stopped momentarily and contemplated whether or not I should wake them, and came to the conclusion that it was better to be safe than sorry. I went to the Shishi statues and petted the head of each one.

"Wake up. I need you."

The stone eyes blinked a couple of times, and their gazes focused on me, glaring menacingly. They always awakened like this, as if challenging me for disrupting their sleep.

Within moments, colour spread through their bodies like a rapidly growing fungus. The stone on their backs cracked and crumbled off, turning into dust as it fell to the floor. In its place stood short wiry fur, though it retained the same marbling that the stone had shown. The creatures were not pleasant to look at. Little bowed and misshapen legs held up stout bodies, and the barbed tails curled and bent forwards over their backends. As soon as the transformation was complete, they sniffed the air and stood at attention.

"Guard the front door. Nothing goes in or out except me, and no one else gets close to the girl," I commanded. They trotted off down the hallway. Their movements were reminiscent of the stone that had cocooned them, so stiff and unemotional.

I continued on to the bathroom, gathered the gauze and tape I would need, and then walked back to the living room. The girl was still out. Good. Hopefully she would stay that way for a while.

I hastily washed her arm, clearing away the dirt from our journey home and the gooey blood that tried to coagulate to seal the gash. Once I had her somewhat clean, I wrapped the dressing over the jagged laceration made by the silvery minions and taped the whole mess up. It wasn't a good fix, but hopefully it would stop the bleeding. I threw a blanket over her and took a deep breath.

There was only one person who could help me out of this mess with the pallid girl lying on my couch and also with my own gash and broken wing. And that one person was Marta, the Healer.

As I walked out of the apartment, grabbing a long black trench coat hung near the door, I made sure the Shishi were in place. They sat on either side of the door and had already formed back into stone.

The sun was well up into the daytime sky by the time I was on my way to Marta's, wearing my coat to conceal the busted wing. Considering my disheveled appearance, with dirt and blood smears, I would be easily mistaken for someone who lived on the streets.

Perception and assumption ruled the human thought processes, and in their minds, they saw what made them comfortable. I was a homeless man and therefore ignorable. Before I could make eye contact with anyone in particular, either begging for spare change or creating a scene, everyone was just as happy to leave me alone.

I rounded a few corners, ending up on a slightly less-trafficked road.

Further down the street, I spied the bookstore I was after. It wasn't just a regular store. It was a new-age neo-pagan shop that sold a little of everything for the "white" witches of suburbia and urban downtown high-rises. Little did the patrons know the owner was much more than just a shopkeeper. She was, in fact, one Hell of a Healer.

A bell tinkled as I walked inside, its tone soothing as if casting a blessing. It always sent shivers down my spine.

The air was heavy with the smells of dust and incense, and as if to validate the heavy scent in the air, incense burned on the cash counter. Plants crowded the lobby: an aloe; a spider plant that teemed with little clone babies swinging from the hanging pot like circling helicopters; and, of course, the compulsory pothos sat on the counter, climbing up the wall and along a string that had been pinned into the ceiling tiles.

Despite the bookshop's welcoming appearance and scented greeting, there was no one behind the cash counter. Marta was always trying to aid some witch find the latest book to help her coven cast better circles, or invoke the spirit of… fill in the blank. I'd met only a handful of true witches in my time, and most were dark. The energy they could control was powerful, and power corrupts. Humans seemed to corrupt quickly and easily.

Witches were humans who could take pieces of life force and reshape that energy so that their will was done. That life force only comes from one place: their own soul. Every time a witch cast a spell, they lost a little more of themselves. Of course, they could always replenish that life force, but that meant taking it from someone else.

Most witches I'd known were broken creatures. Smart, quick, ill-tempered, and disjointed, and if you thought about it, that made sense. Piecing together a soul that came from various sources was bound to give you a fragmented outlook on life.

Those who figured out they could alter their own energies quickly learned the repercussions, and often choose never to cast unless absolutely necessary.

Healers were witches with a twist. Healers could bend and manipulate the life force of the participant and redirect it to speed up the healing process. It was rare talent with little to no consequences for the caster.

I stood on my tiptoes and glanced around the shop. I couldn't see anyone, but I could hear breathing and smell an odour of musk mixed with cut apples.

I walked past the cash counter, which housed all sorts of crystals and tarot decks, and walked into the first aisle of books. The shelves were heavily stocked with tantalizing reads and tomes of all sorts and descriptions, aptly organized with placards indicating various topics. As I turned to go down the next row, I stopped dead in my tracks.

At the end was a human, his gentle breaths loud in my ear and the smell of cut apples strengthening with each step I took towards him. The aroma was enticing, somewhat sexual and it made me conscious of my appearance. I brushed the dust and dirt from my coat, as if that would do anything to alleviate my disheveled appearance.

The human male was young, maybe twenty, light brown hair with a little red to it, average height, in shape but not overly muscled, bearded, and deeply engrossed in some book. He knelt in the aisle, which pulled up his tight khakis, exposing colourful socks above his hiking boots. The sleeves were turned up on his red plaid shirt.

It was his aura that captured my attention. I don't usually see auras, but when I do, it's more than likely a warning. All around the boy was a swirling mist of phosphorescent violet with pink highlights, about the same colour I would expect to see from a darkening mark, a lavender Aurora Borealis wrapped around him like a cloak. The luminous radiation was so thick it almost appeared tangible, and its movement caressed his entire body. It kept me enthralled and hypnotized as thin ropes spiraled down his arm and then around each finger. Each spiral of light and colour sent a warm tingle through me, drawing me in, arousing and mesmerizing me.

I took a deep breath.

He must have heard me. He turned around, saw me, and smiled a warm and sensuous grin that had just a hint of mischievousness.

"Hi, sorry, I didn't hear you come in. Can I help you with something?" The male stood up. He was just a little shorter than me and didn't seem to notice my current condition, the stress lines on my face from the last twelve hours of Hell, and clearly hadn't noticed the trench coat covering a broken leather wing.

"I...ah...well, I," was all I could manage before three things happened almost instantaneously.

One, his swirling aura immediately disappeared, which left me with a clear view of his tantalizing good looks. He had the lightest green eyes I had ever seen. They were darkly outlined by a heavy band of black, and highlights of golden-yellow hidden in the light green. His beard was full and thick, his jawline strong and masculine, his voice was musical and made me feel light-headed. The auburn shadings in his hair and beard gave him a glow, as if embers burned within and he was perpetually warm.

Next, the silvery demons residing just underneath my ribcage twisted, sending a sharp, gutting pain across my ribs. Was this their way of informing me I'd found a suitable host? I placed a hand over the little bulge below my sternum, a sense of dread washing over me. It couldn't be, not him, no way. I surmised right then how the minions would leave my body—they would rip themselves from where they lay.

The third thing was a hand on my arm, yanking me around to face a pudgy old woman.

"What are you doing here? In the middle of the day! Are you out of your mind?" she hissed at me through thickened words that implied her heritage. It was Marta. Where the Hell did she come from? She had a firm grasp on my arm and pulled me around the corner and down the aisle away from the most handsome creature I had ever seen, and that aura. I strained my neck back to have another glimpse. He looked at me with an amused grin. When our eyes met, he winked.

My heart fluttered. I returned the smile instantly, despite Marta tugging me away. Momentarily, I had forgotten about the searing burn of the broken bone or the sharp piercing of the silver spines in my gut. All I could think about was his face, until Marta had me in the lobby. She grabbed my face and made me look at her.

"I said, what are you doing here?"

I snapped out of it and stared at her wrinkled little face. "I'm sorry," I said, shaking my head. I tried to ground myself and focus on the task at hand, but his green eyes were still held fast in my mind. They were so beautiful.

"I need your assistance." I started to take my coat off and, for just a brief second, exposed my limp wing, which hung off my shoulder.

"Not here!" Marta crossed herself and mumbled a prayer under her breath. Christian signs in a pagan store? "Just stand there and don't move."

She disappeared the way we had come and spoke low to the young man, telling him to look after the store a bit longer. I was a special customer that she would be working with in the back. There was a smile in his eager response to help out, his words sending shivers all over my arms.

Within seconds, she reappeared and grabbed me again by the arm, moving the broken wing. This time I yelped at the twinge of pain. She glared back at me with disgust.

She took me through beaded curtains that hung behind the cash counter and partitioned off the storefront from her offices in the back. It wasn't the first time I'd been in this portion of Marta's store, but it was definitely the only occurrence when I'd been there during store hours. Marta stomped off through a hallway with me in tow. I imagined seeing little puffs of smoke coming out of her ears she was so angry.

She took me into the back room, which had an entire wall filled with an assortment of jars and vials containing all kinds of potions and ingredients. After pushing me onto the fainting couch, Marta sat at her desk with a furrowed brow. Her gaze was so fierce I felt it necessary to sit very still. Her lip curled at one corner as she seethed.

"Marta, I need your help. I'm wounded and a…" I struggled with the next word. Who was the girl in my apartment? "Friend." What else was I supposed to call her?

Ignoring Marta's ire and her glares, I removed my trench coat, exposing my naked upper torso and the damaged, lifeless wing.

She still fumed at me.

"Honestly, Marta, what the Hell? I need help, and you have to…"

"You promised! You promised me you'd stay away from him! You promised you'd never go anywhere near Alyx!"

And then it hit me, and I understood why Marta was so pissed off. The young man, that undeniably gorgeous creature with the vibrant phosphorescent aura and stunning eyes, was Marta's son. I hadn't seen him in many years—at least fifteen or so.

"That's your son? Marta, I'm sorry. I didn't recognize your boy. It has been many years since I saw him." Except now he was a man. But I didn't say that, and the minute I had uttered the apology, Marta relaxed, visibly, and exhaled.

"Ugh, tsk," Marta chastised me, then twisted up her nose after she took full stock of my blood-streaked dirt-ground clothes and my body odour, having sweated so badly from carrying the girl halfway across the city. She grabbed a shawl that was draped over a desk chair and spread it on the settee she used to treat patients.

"Here, lie down, face-first," Marta said. She was familiar with all my body parts: wings, tail, bone spurs, hairy chest, busted nose. You name it, she had put her hands on it and healed it; there was no room for modesty.

She grabbed my busted wing as I flipped over and placed my face down on the fainting couch. I crinkled my nose, as it smelled wretched. Marta stretched the wing out so that she could examine it. She ran her hands along the main bone, and I flinched as she reached the spot just before the break.

"It is broken, and the tissue inside is ripped. This will be difficult." Marta pulled her chair closer to me and brought the busted wing very carefully into her lap. She placed a hand on the crushed bone on top of the wing, and the other in the same spot under the wing. She closed her eyes and murmured, but I couldn't make out what she said. I'm not sure I really cared. The minute she started, warmth bloomed in the area of the break, and the heat radiated out and grew in strength, and I swayed with the magic.

I was dizzy and sleepy, and around me, white light shimmered and pulsated. The light was pearlescent and beautiful and warm.

Just as I fell asleep, Marta spoke. "What have you been up to, beast? There are some things I cannot heal."

But I was comforted, warm, safe, and utterly exhausted.

"And stay away from Alyx," she reminded me.

"I promised to stay away from the boy, and I will," I mumbled softly as I stifled a smirk, thinking of the fully grown man I had just met. The demon in me does come out to play once in a while. I would definitely be finding a way to see Marta's grown son again.

Meditation

ALYX

Mom dragged what had appeared to be a homeless man into her consultation office. I couldn't help but think that after a good scrub-down, the homeless guy would have been pretty hot. It was close to the end of my shift, but I wasn't going anywhere until I'd had a chance to interrogate Mom on the arrival of her sudden "guest." And those eyes! I'd heard of people with two different-coloured irises, but I'd never seen it in person.

After selecting an old clothbound book from the pagan gods section, I plopped myself on the stool behind the cash register and read several chapters. The book wasn't that intriguing, so being a little bored, I walked around the store, tidying up, and glanced out the shop's window to see if anything interesting was happening out front. The streets of downtown always had something going on. Except now.

I waited some more, then glanced at the time on my phone, gave up, and read a few more sections of the book.

What on earth could she have been doing for so long in the back with...whoever that man was?

The shop had been extremely quiet since the appearance of the stranger. I was flipping through the pages of my chosen book when Mom startled me with a touch to my cheek. I glanced up at her and smiled.

"You were in there *forever*," I said, dog-earring the tome. I jumped off the stool and scratched at my cheeks, digging through the beard. That always felt good.

"A complicated issue," Marta said. "But never mind now. It is done."

"Who was that, Mom? I've never seen him in here before."

"Never you mind. You forget you saw him."

At this point, the topic was over. Mom could be stubborn at times.

"Okay," I lied a little. "Do you need me to do anything else? Lydia has tickets to a play for later tonight. I need to run home and get ready to go out."

"You go. Have fun." She patted my cheek and then frowned. "And shave this off."

"Never, no way." I had grown the beard so that I didn't look like I was twelve years old, and besides, it was a great beard. Just twenty and my facial fur was thick—much fuller than any of the other guys. And it got me dates *and* stares from both guys and girls.

I was particularly interested in the stare from the guy who had gone back with Mom. His eyes were crazy cool, one icy blue, the other a steely grey. The clothes he wore were trash, but I could tell he was muscular. His coat was tight around the arms. His scruff was almost as thick as mine. And those shoulders, man, he reminded me of a linebacker. And the way he stared back at me…. Wow. If he wasn't as into me as I was to him, then I had no idea how to pick the gay guys out.

Even though Mom had said I should forget about him, that was the last thing I planned to do. I had to find this guy again.

I was late getting home, much later than I had wanted to be. It was supposed to be a fun evening with friends from my Religions of Antiquity class, but my mind had been completely absorbed with the dark-haired man who had visited the bookstore earlier in the day, the guy with peculiar eyes and goofy smile. Just before the play started, Lydia asked what was going on with me. I told her briefly about the stranger.

There was something about him I couldn't put my finger on. He was handsome, but that wasn't the right word. Maybe striking, or enigmatic? None of those words seemed to do justice to how I felt whenever I thought of him. Even when we stopped at an underground bar for drinks and my friends started discussing their favourite parts of the play, my mind kept wandering back to him.

That's when I spotted him, on the other side of the bar near the dance floor. I left our table midconversation and crossed the room in hopes of saying hello, but as I forced my way through the throngs of dancers who were gyrating to the bass-filled music, I bumped into a drunk Goth girl who flailed about out of time with the music. By the time I untangled myself from her and turned back to where he had been standing, he had disappeared.

Lydia came up to me.

"What are you doing? Why did you leave us?"

"He was standing right here," I shouted over the music.

"Who was?" she asked, squinting at me like I'd lost my mind.

"The guy I was telling you about, he was here."

"Really? What does he look like? Maybe we can find him." Lydia was always too helpful and a little too eager to see the guys I dated. But despite her enthusiasm, neither of us spotted the stranger with tousled hair and strange eyes.

It was more than just a simple physical attraction. There was this electrical energy that seemed to well up from inside of me and threaten to burst out whenever I thought of him. I felt nervous. Never had I been uneasy around other guys, so why this one?

And what was even worse, I had no really good way of finding him. It's not like Mom kept computer records at the store for sales and services; she still did everything by pen and paper. Totally old-world. But despite what Mom had said, I would find him.

There had been a couple of ways I had thought of, each a desperate hope of potentially reliving the chance meeting from this morning. I mean, I could have waited until the guy came back to the store. But in all the years I've been helping Mom out, this was the first time Mr. Blue-eye-muscle-man had entered the store on my shift. Mom obviously knew who he was. He had been in before, and I had missed it, so I was likely to miss him again.

I could try to pry information out of Mom, but I'd attempted that strategy in the past with other things, to absolutely no avail. She was horrifically stubborn when she wanted to be.

That really only left one other way, and from the get-go, it was the least reliable idea I could come up with.

Magic.

After all, I had been working in a pagan witch store for years. Surely all those books I'd read and all the hours that had been spent doing spells, incantations, and meditations had given me an extra boost!

Mom was a Healer and had abilities, like lighting candles with no matches when she thought I wasn't watching, and I would swear it never rained on us when we went outside—for anything. We never had a need for Band-Aids in the house. As a kid, scraped knees only lasted until I got home to Mom. But special abilities must have skipped a generation, because anything I'd tried was never successful. Except for the last few meditations, those had finally proven fruitful after years of practice.

In the last two months, I had finally managed to create my safe place: a beautiful lush and temperate woodland forest glen. Not only did I believe I was physically there, but I could smell and hear the babbling creek, feel the moss between my fingers, and see the bright greens and mottled browns, which were too vibrant and alive to be anything but real.

And then there was the appearance of the Satyr, which had been unexpected to say the least. He was much taller than I, powerful and animalistic, covered from the waist down with tawny goat fur and jet-black hooves instead of feet. The bridge of his nose was flattened, his cheekbones were high and scruffy with whiskers, and his eyes glimmered violet. Massive curved horns grew out from the corners of his forehead and swooped back. The animal had been very friendly.

Maybe, just maybe, I could glean some help, a clue or a hint as to where I could find the handsome stranger, in a meditation. There were numerous spell books for finding lost items and making love potions, but after racking my brain all night long, I couldn't remember any spells or incantations that would find an unknown person.

I could improvise, though.

I stuck around with my friends long enough to have concocted a new spell, and then I made my excuses so I could head home.

Tiptoeing down the hall past Mom's bedroom, I bypassed several floorboards that always creaked when anyone stepped on them. I made my way as silently as the old house would allow. It was entirely possible that Mom had heard everything, but it had been a couple of years since she bounced out of bed when I came home late. After all, I was twenty and an adult.

I closed the bedroom door, peeled off my clothes, and searched for the comfy baggy sweatpants I wore around the house. They were hiding in the corner of the room, near my bed.

Pulling on the worn-out fleecy garment, I noticed how thin and hairy my legs were. I wouldn't have called them chicken legs, but I bet that Mr. Blue-eye-muscle-man had thick stocky legs.

The old sweats, which had holes in the knees and a rather revealing rip in the crotch, felt comfortable once they were on. Many people who practiced magic did so skyclad. I just couldn't get comfortable enough to do it, and without being comfortable, meditations always failed. With these on, as grungy and old as they were, I had a sense of home and comfort that enabled me to go further than the couple of times I had tried it naked.

But I was quite comfortable bare-chested and barefoot. I cleared out a sizeable area in front of the bed. Once the spot was ready, and the laundry hamper was stuffed full of discarded clothes from the floor, I stepped towards the dresser. In a couple of the oversized drawers, I had, over the years, accumulated a large amount of paraphernalia from Mom's store. As I rummaged through the unsorted items, memories came flooding back while seeing specific objects. All of them good recollections, usually times spent with Mom in the shop. But there were certain items I was pretty sure would help me get what I was after, and it was those objects I was searching for.

In my head, I constructed a list of items for my improvised spell. I grabbed a light-blue candle for the meditation work, a minty-green candle for good luck, some charcoal, the little bronze cauldron, a piece of parchment, a silver marker, the wand, some incense, and some extra candles. That should do it...maybe. I honestly wasn't sure.

I lit the incense, its smoke beginning an upside-down cascade towards the ceiling. The cardamom gave off a smoky, earthy aroma, calming me as the scent enveloped my bedroom and washed around my head. I lit each of the candles and thought intently of their purpose as the wicks caught the flame. Four candles were aligned with the compass points, the light-blue and minty-green ones in the middle of the space, just next to the cauldron. Then I set the charcoal to burn and placed that into the brass pot that sat in the very center of the work area. I waited for what seemed to be an eternity until the charcoal was red hot, and then I began.

Picking up the wand, which was an old gnarled piece of hemlock with Norse runes etched into the shaft, I pointed it towards the north candle. While chanting, I moved clockwise in a circular motion and passed each of the compass points that were lit up by candles until I came back to the northern one.

"I call upon you, gods of old, to come to my safe space and lend me a helping hand. I call upon you Guardians of the East, come to me with your gifts of intellect, knowledge, and wisdom, guided through the air." A little gust of air made the eastern candle flame flicker and sway.

"I call upon you, Guardians of the South, come to me with your gifts of power, light, and burning energy, guided through fire." The charcoal in the cauldron hissed.

"I call upon you, Guardians of the West, come to me with your gifts of emotion, dreams, and passion, guided by water, and I call upon you Guardians of the North, come to me with your gifts of fertility, growth, and grounding, guided by earth. I call to each of you, be with me, assist me, as I am your child, a child of magic."

I placed the wand in the middle, near the cauldron with the red-hot charcoal. Sitting cross-legged in the circle, I reached for the piece of parchment and the silver marker. I held both items in my hands and closed my eyes. Visualizing Mr. Blue-eye-muscle-man, complete with the black trench coat that fitted him just a little too tightly and his scruffy bearded face, I recreated the scene from earlier that afternoon when he had appeared in the bookstore.

I took the marker and wrote on the paper: *The handsome man who saw my mom at the store today: Help me find him.*

I folded the paper in half, and then again, and one last time. I held it tight in my right hand and pictured walking down the street, bumping into this enigmatic stranger who I desperately wanted to find. I pictured myself working in the bookstore, turning around suddenly to be face-to-face with the unearthly eyes of the stranger. I pictured myself naked and held tight by those thick muscled arms, with my body pressing against his, enveloped in a quilted blanket.

Okay, that last thought maybe shouldn't have crept in there.

I was done. I had visualized this to death, and was afraid of what else my mind would come up with, although I was pretty sure I already knew that it would have been wildly inappropriate.

I dropped the paper onto the hot coal in the cauldron, and as it started to turn black and burn away at the edges, I whispered softly, "Come to me."

I sat back and closed my eyes again. The smell of the incense, still heavy and thick, and the twinkling light from the candles all around me made my head feel weighty.

Let me go to my safe place.

I sat there for several minutes breathing deeply, calming every muscle in my body, relaxing my mind. No random thoughts, no strange images. I just wanted blackness and then falling into the blackness, with no reservations or fears, eager to begin the journey to the forest glen.

Drifting, I swayed, falling into thin air and then through dense clouds, and finally coming to rest on my feet. A swirling fog enveloped me. As I took a step through it, the mist dissipated.

I walked for several feet, and in my mind's eye, shapes began to appear: a small pine tree, a bush, a tall tree with winding and snaky roots that exposed themselves by twisting out of the ground. Moss-covered trunks and stones. It was damp there, deep in the forest, and the smell was rich and overpowering with the scent of rotting leaves. It was natural and soothing.

Beams of sunlight poked through the canopy of deciduous trees and highlighted a small bed of ferns off in the distance. Clear water trickled along a shallow creek that ran the course of the woods. The gush and gurgle of liquid through the cracks and crannies of the river rock added to the relaxing sensation of the cool air in the forest. Birds chirped overhead, and on the other side of the glen, a squirrel chattered and ran, bounding across the forest floor, in an expedition for food.

I sat on a monster rock that was conveniently flat and situated in the middle of everything and, looking around, discovered there was nothing but endless forest surrounding me. It was as if I had found a secret druidic haven. This was my place, and it felt good to be there, although I had not been often, and was still all new but exciting.

The air was cool, both to the touch and my lungs, and it tasted like wood. The smells were delicious. The green was extra green, the muted brown of the roughened and wizened trunks made them appear alive. I was positive they were hiding nymphs in them. Out of respect, I sat, quietly pensive, and soaked up this place.

I loved it there.

I glanced down at my hands, and to my astonishment, the piece of parchment with my message was there, unburned. I unfolded it, inspected it, and turned it over, eyeing it carefully. It was the piece of paper I had thrown into the cauldron.

Acting on instinct, I held my hand out, palm up, and said, "From you to me, if it is your will, so let it be."

The piece of parchment folded upwards on its own, reminding me of butterfly wings. In response to my thought, the folded squares of the parchment rounded into oblong spheres, just like a butterfly. The ink from the message morphed, blackening and spreading as it turned red and white and evolved into a monarch butterfly, perched quietly in the palm of my hand. Launching itself into the forest, it fluttered left and then right, rising over a branch, ducking under a leaf, and then it was gone, out of sight.

I sighed. This place was completely exquisite. I closed my eyes and sat there, unmoving, thinking of nothing and listening to everything and nothing, and became completely lost in the sounds and smells and feelings all around.

And then there was a finger tapping me on the shoulder. I jumped off the rock and threw myself amongst the moss and leaves on the ground. To my amazement, the Satyr was in front of me, gazing down with wide violet eyes, his ears twitching frenetically. His cheeks were blushed through the scraggly beard, long hair tied back with raffia. His horns appeared to twist back in perfect symmetry from his hairline.

The Satyr looked down on me, wide-eyed, ears twitching. He reached down, his forearms covered in hair, human hair, but the nails of his hand were long, thick, and yellow. The creature was extremely muscular, and despite his ruffian nature, the groin was very human and overly developed. The hooved hindquarters were covered in goat fur, and a twitchy tail shook occasionally just like his ears. He was handsome if not bestial.

This wasn't the first time I had seen him. The Satyr left his arm outstretched towards me, offering a hand up off the forest floor.

"Silenus, you scared me," I said, taking the hand.

"Alyx, I'm glad you came back to visit." Silenus yanked me up to my feet without so much as a grunt, pulled my almost naked body close to him, and held me against his muscled and furry form. I rolled my eyes and smiled. I could feel Silenus getting excited, and in turn, it was sort of turning me on too.

"I so enjoyed our last visit. I was hoping you'd come back soon." His warm breath brushed against my cheek. It was sweet smelling—like cinnamon—and it made me feel at ease, even though something in the back of my head said trusting this creature would be a bad idea.

"Alyx." Silenus twitched his head and bent it to one side. "You sent me a wish, so I came to see you." Silenus's voice was lyrical and deep, very masculine. He stole a kiss from my cheek.

I giggled out of nervousness. "Okay, Silenus, okay." I kissed Silenus gently on the lips before pulling away.

Silenus pattered his feet on the forest floor in excitement, and from the pressure against my hip, it was obvious that the creature was fully aroused. I pulled away, and Silenus let me go but leered at me with lustful, glowing eyes. I had never seen such a colour of iris before. They were mesmerizing.

"Oh, Alyx, you do know how to tease. That makes me excited and happy. You really must come see me more often." He tilted his head the opposite direction and peered out from behind long hair that had fallen forward. "Now, about this wish. Who have you lost? Who do you seek?" He twitched his head in different directions with each sentence. His actions were so inhuman, and yet, he was so manly.

I returned to the large rock where I had been originally and sat cross-legged, trying to cover my somewhat excited private parts, if only just a little. I was still bashful in front of Silenus, even despite his last visit.

"Um, well, Silenus, you might be a little jealous..." I stammered slightly, unsure how the beast would react.

"Nonsense, my brother of the forest! I share well. There is another that you lust for? You need to find a lost lover?" Silenus inquired. He was so comfortable with all of it and in his own skin. He was confident and unashamed of his bestial looks.

"Well, sort of, yes. A man came in to the shop my mother owns. And I've never felt this way about another person. I'd like to find him, but I have no way of doing so. Can you help?"

"Perhaps," Silenus said quizzically. "If I help you find him, do you promise to come back to see me?"

"Of course! I love it here, and, well, you're fun." I blushed.

Silenus smiled sensually at me and then canted his head in a quizzical manner. "Come, Alyx, come here and let me hold you. I want you to think of your new friend. Think of every detail, every nuance of this man, the colour of his hair, his eyes, his build, and frame. I want you to picture every detail, and then once you have that image solid in your mind, think of him standing in front of us. Share him with me, Alyx; share him with me so that I can see him too."

I did as he had instructed. I let the Satyr embrace me as he gently turned me forward, hugging from behind. It felt safe and warm, and I quickly relaxed within his strong arms.

Without much effort, I thought of the man in the shop, everything about him, his steely grey eye and his icy blue one, the tousled black hair, his strange attire, and the goofy expression on his face when he realized that I had been looking back at him. A smile crept across my face.

Silenus's presence announced itself as pressure building inside my head. The image of the beautiful stranger became crystal clear and sharp, and if I had just reached out towards it, I would have been able to touch him.

Silenus exhaled calmly. "Alyx, look. Is this the man you wish to find?"

I opened my eyes and, in front of me, stood the dark-haired man I had thought about all day. I couldn't speak. I was awestruck and had that nervous feeling in the pit of my stomach. I simply nodded. Silenus nodded in unison.

"Alright, Alyx, shall we see where this man lives?"

I nodded again. Silenus moved his hand over my body, sensually, slowly, softly. From my thigh, he moved his meaty, callused hand over my groin, up my lower abdomen. It made the muscles in my stomach twitch from excitement. He continued up and over my chest, over my beard, across my lips and nose, over my eyes, and then onto my forehead, where the yellow-nailed hand stopped, warm, pressing my head gently into the Satyr's furry chest.

I was no longer in the forest. I had been transported downtown, not far from Mom's shop. In front of me stood an apartment high-rise. Although I had never been in the building, I was definitely familiar with it. And then my vision changed and I was in the elevator and heading to the top floor. The mechanisms ground to a halt and the doors pulled back. The hallway was dark, and a light in the ceiling flickered. I walked down the dimly lit corridor, then stopped and knocked on what appeared to be a broken door.

Silenus murmured, "Come back soon, forest brother."

I opened my eyes again to find myself in my bedroom. The candles had gone out, and it was almost morning. The incense had long extinguished, the smell only faint in the enclosed space.

I smiled.

It had worked, just as I had hoped it might. I cleared away the paraphernalia about my room and put the magical instruments back in the dresser. As I finished packing away the items, I noticed a fern leaf frond lying near my bed. I picked it up and examined it closely. It was from my forest glen.

Well, now. I put the last of the items back into the drawer. The Satyr had proved to be quite helpful again. *I think another visit to see the old goat is most definitely in order.*

Back in the forest, the beams of sunlight faded and the shadows grew dense. As the light receded from between the trees, and the safe place became dark, the butterfly flittered down to sit in the palm of Silenus. The Satyr's face was cast in shadow. He formed a maniacal grin, and his orbs glowed with their ultraviolet colour. He squinted in obscene pleasure, as his hand contracted around the butterfly and crushed it in his viselike grip.

Bound

DATI

I woke up with my nose smushed against the worn and threadbare upholstery of Marta's fainting couch. The lingering odors captured in the weave of the furniture's fabric made my stomach churn. My head was foggy, like I was coming down from a chemical high, and my body ached. I pushed myself up with both hands but stopped suddenly as the whole room spun. I let myself rest back on the chaise, when I noticed the note.

You'll feel sick when you wake up. Don't rush, or you will be sick. Rest much, and don't move the wing. The longer you keep it still, the better and faster it will heal. There's ointment in the jar for your friend. Leave through the back door.
Remember your promise.

Alyx.
The boy protected by the promise, with freckles that danced across his nose, was gone. The man Alyx, with the dazzling peridot eyes, remained clearly emblazoned in my memory.

I thought back to that brief moment in which we exchanged all but two sentences. Well, one sentence. I had done nothing but stammer and look like an idiot. His smile was so alluring.

To my mind, Alyx embodied everything I desired in a man, but his aura was the darkest thing I had ever seen in a human. When flares erupted from a body like that, it was a warning for me to stay away. It was danger, an alarm that signaled the creature was more powerful than I. But Alyx was human; the dancing lights attracted me—pulled me in closer. I felt flush thinking of that mischievous smile, and then it dawned on me that I had dreamed of Alyx, standing in a forest, while fast asleep from Marta's healing.

My dream of Alyx had been fluid, restless, and intangible. Despite the fact this was Marta's son. I needed to see him, the man, again.

For now, I needed to get home to the girl who I had left in my apartment and tend to her wounds with Marta's special liniment. After all, Master had been clear: she was my charge. Truthfully, I hadn't done a good job of that so far. Hopefully the bandages I had applied to her wrist had stopped the bleeding.

I attempted to get up again. My stomach lurched and bile rose in the back of my throat. Stumbling out of Marta's office, I glanced at the mirror that hung on the back of the door. I looked pathetic. Marta had splinted and bound the wing, and there appeared to be a poultice embedded in the bandaging. I grabbed my coat from the hook on the wall and gingerly let it cover me, tucking the ointment into my pocket.

Streetlights greeted me as I stepped outside and, for a second, blinded me too. I had slept the entire day. The girl would have been trapped in my condo with the Shishi guarding the place and blocking her exit.

Night noises came from all around me. Rambunctious laughter and talking filled the air, the late-night bar patrons spilling out of their watering holes and stumbling into the main streets, their voices bouncing off of the old historic brick buildings.

As I reached my apartment door, there was giggling and laughing in a high-pitched girl's voice. I carefully moved the busted door to one side. The scene before me stoked my ire past the point of control.

On the couch, where I had left the girl, was a smiling and cooing uninjured teenager. She wore a pair of my sweats and a shirt, both of which hung off of her like a child who had played dress-up with their parents' clothes. The sleeves hung longer than her arms, the waist was cinched and tied in a knot at the side to keep the track pants on her slender hips. A Shishi sat beside her, wagging its tail and pawing at her playfully, while the other was rolled over on its back as she rubbed its tummy. At her feet were bones from the steaks that had been in the fridge. She had fed them my food.

Two nights of pain, humiliation, infection with demonic parasites, with strict orders to ensure a little human girl's well-being, and subjecting myself to white magic had me on my last ounce of patience. Seeing that same little girl now awake on my couch—who had decided to *help herself* to my clothes and then feed my guardians like puppies—it pushed me past my limits. The sight before me unleashed all my anger.

But this time the evil was ready for battle, and along with the sunken rotting face and the uncomfortable pain of having the skin pull tight over my body, my fangs grew extra long. My gums ripped as the teeth protruded farther than normal, filling my mouth with blood, which spilled down my chest and splattering on the floor. My hands morphed into their demon black talons. Thickened vocal cords produced an unearthly growl that filled the room. The lights crackled and sizzled, and the shadows around me grew thick and dense.

"What have you done?" I snapped.

The Shishi immediately went into guard mode, as their round little bodies stiffened and their gazes locked on me. Their mouths elongated and stretched, baring their rows of razor sharp teeth, warning me to stay where I stood. They were protecting her.

"I hope you don't mind, but I—" she began, but as soon as she spotted me, her face registered fear and confusion. Her eyes welled up, and a tear slid down her pallid, rounded cheek.

"I brought you here on orders, and you act like you own the place and turn my guardians against me? What did you do to them?" I glowered. I took a step closer to her.

The young girl stood up. Her eyes were wide, her gaze darted in every direction, searching for an escape route, and her mouth was tensed with panic. She made a lurch towards the doorway but stopped, realizing that I had her cornered. There was nowhere for her to go.

And then it all went to Hell, so to speak.

The girl splayed her fingers and raised her hands out towards me. Her face stilled as a corner of her mouth snarled upwards. Her eyes, unblinking, turned milky white as if cataracts grew over the orbs like some fast-growing tumor.

In some way, shape, or form, she was dark, but I still didn't know what she was. I waited as her clouded, dead orbs flooded with blood. Her lips parted and she started murmuring, but I couldn't make out what she said.

Light from the lamps that she had turned on dimmed, and the corners of the room became lost in shadow. I couldn't tell if she had emanated darkness or if she had sucked the existing light into her, but either way, the room was cast in cavernous shadows and the temperature dropped dramatically. My breath lingered in front of me as I let it out in short, angered puffs.

"From the dark," she hissed. And with those three words, the shadows started moving; things were alive in the corners of my room. I hunched my back and crouched, ready to spring.

"In the shadows, where vile things creep, bind his hands, bind his feet," she whispered. Her voice, which had been perky and bubbly before, was now harsh and raspy.

With my nerves on edge, the room became deadly quiet. Until the sound of bare feet pattered behind me. I spun around. A black foot in the shape of a shadow disappeared into the dark corner. From my other side, something brushed my leg; a hand of the same substance dissolved back into the shadow from under the chair.

"In the shadows, where vile things creep, bind his hands, bind his feet."

A wind raised her long hair so that it was all standing on end, straight up. The flesh around her eye sockets sunk as she spoke and black veins crept out from the corners of her bloodied eyes and ran in random patterns across her face and down one cheek.

At her feet, one of the vile things from the shadow emerged, just half of it, and clung to her leg, sharp little claws on the end of tiny little hands. No facial features were present on the creature, just a corporeal form. A distorted little grotesque body that was reminiscent of a child. A toddler.

Within seconds, there were several around us, one clinging to the girl's leg, another crawling out from an impossibly tiny space under the chair, and one more peering out from behind the couch. The shadow creatures' movements were broken and jerky.

And then she screamed, "In the shadows where vile things creep, bind his hands, bind his feet!"

The sound of fabric tearing came from above me, and I glanced up. Dark veins of shadows snaked their way across the ceiling as if the roof itself was being torn open. The darkness above me grew and oozed downwards. Before I could react, tiny hands with sharpened fingers formed out of the glob and grabbed my shoulders and pulled me up to the ceiling. More grabbed my wings and pulled on them, like children who rip the wings off of a captured insect. I screamed in pain.

I was bound, just as she had commanded.

I scanned the girl's face, which was no longer human. Her skin was white, her face sunken and gaunt and covered in little black veins. Her blood red eyes had no irises or pupils.

The Shishi guards remained stone-like, watching me, never breaking their stare, ensuring I didn't move from my position. I struggled, tensing my muscles and summoning all of my demonic strength, but to no avail. I was held fast. The shadow minions might have appeared to be children, but they were supernaturally strong.

Just as I thought that this little human girl might have been the end of me, a strange thing happened. The girl's hair fell gently around her shoulders once more. The black veins sprinted down her neck and shirt, scampering like the little feet from the twisted toddlers. I could see the same pattern of spiderweb veins beginning on the palms of her hands.

She was losing control.

Within seconds, the mass of shadow children began to swarm the girl, crawling up her body, their claws tearing at the clothes, leaving scratch marks on her flesh wherever there was exposed skin.

She screamed as her summoned creatures turned on her. They pulled her down onto her knees.

The creatures on me were more cautious. I might have been pinned, but I was full of energy, and I was much bigger than the girl.

She screamed again, and then she said in a hoarse whisper, "Help me."

The words gurgled out of her as small appendages pushed their way into her open mouth and started pulling her jaw open and reefing on her tongue. It appeared as if they were trying to find a way to pull her apart. Tiny hands wrenched on her ears, yanking her limbs, poking fingers into her blood-red orbs. The distorted infants hissed and wailed in excitement.

At that moment, the Shishi turned from their stone guard stance into full-on protection mode. With teeth snapping, they went after the shadow creepers. The Shishi had changed into the menacing demon guards they had been created to be.

The guardians snagged the creatures one by one with their teeth. How they managed to bite into shadow is beyond me, but they were capable.

Screeches of terror filled the room. With each bite from the Shishi, the shadow forms would dissolve, their childlike screams fading as their corporeal forms dissipated.

My guardians kept at it until the girl was completely free from the horde, until she lay on the floor motionless, facing away from me on her side and barely breathing. The shadows retreated back into the corners, letting go of me all at once.

I fell face-first onto the floor with a thud.

My living room was completely destroyed, broken glass covered the floor from the coffee table, the lamp was bent in half, the leather couch ripped. Black remnants of the veining evil of the incantation stained the walls and ceilings where the shadow had grown and expanded, then ultimately receded. The apartment was completely ruined.

Great, a door that needs to be replaced, and now I have to get this all fixed too. I hauled myself up off the floor and crawled over to the girl, while the Shishi growled in warning. Clearly they were no longer mine, and contrary to their purpose, they were guarding a person, not a place. Exactly what the Hell had she done to them?

I pushed the girl over so that she lay on her back. She was wide-eyed and staring at the ceiling, but even though her eyes had returned to their normal blue colour, there was no blinking. She looked dead, pale skinned with her face frozen in shock. Her eyes had huge bags under them, and although the veins had receded somewhat, they were still present in the creases around her eyes and the corners of her mouth.

"Where the Hell did you learn to do that?" I asked.

I grabbed her wrist and felt for a pulse. It was definitely there, and in fact, it was racing.

She mumbled something.

Fantastic. I brought her home in an attempt to keep her alive only to drive her to cast a spell that made her go mad. Well, one thing was clear. It was obvious what I had dragged home. *D'Alae, meet Dark Witch.*

I inched closer and the dogs bared their teeth. "I'm trying to help," I said to them. They relaxed a little but were still on point.

"Come on, get up." There was nothing, no movement from her at all, just the same mumbling, her lips moving but nothing coming out. The girl had drained herself to the very edge of death.

"Well, you certainly smell like one of us now," I said aloud as I picked her up, placing her on the couch. That acrid burnt plastic smell wafted off of her. "And just who taught you a spell that you can't control? Your creator should be flayed. You sure as Hell aren't ready to be casting anything that complicated."

Most newly darkened spent a lot of time with their creator, learning everything they could. The human world rules no longer applied; you had to learn to walk again, in demonesque skin, so to speak.

Her face had aged. The skin was wrinkled and sagging. She appeared to have matured several decades in only a few minutes.

"What happened?" she asked. "What did I do this time?" Her lips were cracked at the corners from the shadow creepers, and a little blood wept from the wound. She was a mess, and she would need to replenish the life energy she had just spent.

"What do you mean, what happened? You called forth a little army of shadow creepers to protect you against me," I said, somewhat alarmed she had no memory.

"I'm sorry. Did I hurt you? You scared me," she said.

"You mean to tell me you have no idea or memory of what just happened?" I asked, still slightly annoyed with the whole situation.

"I'm sorry, I'm so sorry, it happens every time I get mad or scared." She sobbed. "I think you really must have scared me good. I've never felt this bad afterwards."

"You look like shit."

A tear rolled down her still rather unnervingly still face. She reached for the side table, where at one point a houseplant had been sitting. After the destruction of the living room, the plant was now on the floor in a pile of dirt, surrounded by broken pot shards, but a single stem, a twisted little piece of vine, had broken off, still green, resting on the table.

With her touch, it curled, turned black and died. She had absorbed the life force out of it.

"You're going to need a lot more than just a leaf from a houseplant after what you just did. We'll have to find you an adult human."

This was turning into a whole lot more trouble than I needed or wanted.

Her eyes were once again blank and vacant. She was a mess. The borrowed clothes from my bedroom had been shredded by the shadow creepers.

Walking into the master bathroom, I grabbed a washcloth and wet it, and then I found her another set of clothes, which wouldn't fit any better but would have to do for now.

I hadn't left her alone for five minutes, and when I returned, she was gone. I peered around the corner into the kitchen: nothing. I dropped the clothes and washrag on the kitchen counter, and walked towards the front door, which was moved to allow entry into the hallway of the apartment building.

There she was, floating down the corridor.

Literally floating, like a ghost, a couple of inches off the floor, her hair swirling behind her from some unknown wind, like Medusa's snakes. She hovered off the ground and moved from door to door, the Shishi at her feet.

I was amazed. Where was she finding the energy for this? Clearly she was still capable of casting spells, and I wasn't in any physical condition to bear the brunt of another one. I followed her with caution.

She became ghostlike, pale and gaunt, the black veining adding to the ghoulish appearance, hovering above the floor with her shredded and tattered clothes hanging from her.

She had stopped in front of each apartment in the hallway and lightly touched the doors' wooden surface with her fingers. Black veining rot emanated from her touch, and then she turned and went to the next. She repeated this until she came to the last in the hallway. She stared vacantly at the entrance. Then she reached out and touched it, and the door swung open.

She disappeared into the condo, the dogs following along behind her.

And then there was a scream.

I rushed into the neighbour's apartment after her.

On the floor lay a woman, in her late thirties, her face frozen in fear at the sight of the floating girl.

The ghoulish pale-faced girl took one finger, placed it over the woman's lips, and made the motion of shushing her, then moved her macabrely white digit from the chin of her victim who remained wide-eyed and still.

The girl moved her finger down the woman's throat, over her chest, and to just above her groin. As her finger moved, the clothes ripped in half and the flesh underneath peeled back, exposing sinew and ribcage and gelatinous insides that glistened with fresh blood. The woman screamed in pain as red gurgled down her body and pooled atop the hardwood floor. She sucked in fast breaths until blood filled her mouth, gradually suffocating her and ceasing the screams.

"No!" I yelled.

Her face whipped around towards me with an evil glare, warning me to stay away.

The ghostlike witch floated above her victim, took her hands, dug them into the fresh wound, and then peeled it back even further. The woman was still alive and continued to choke on her own blood, convulsing as she was held down.

She moved her maw closer to the chest cavity where the woman's beating heart would lie beneath the ribcage, and she inhaled.

Tendrils of light floated out of the body, like steam rising from a hot bath, emanating mostly from the victim's heart. The light was white, tinged with wisps of yellow, and it wafted up towards the mouth and nose of the hag. It continued to swirl around, until she took another deep breath, inhaling it in. She was sucking the life force out of the woman.

I stood there, disgusted, watching the murder of not only a life, but of a soul. The woman stopped moving after losing so much energy. She was done. Even if the heart continued to beat, however slowly, she was gone.

The witch pulled in every last little bit of light with deep inhales, until there was nothing left.

Finally, she plunged her hand down into the ribcage just beside the heart. Bone shattered with audible cracks, as the emaciated fingers disappeared into the chest cavity, and then emerged, holding her prey's heart. It had stopped beating, but her hand was covered in viscous deep-red blood. The heart was plump and full.

The witch's jaw lowered and unhinged like a snake, and then she placed the entire heart into her mouth and chewed. Blood ran out her mouth and down her chin.

Her expression that of pure satisfaction.

Beside the now dead body, a side table had been prepped with a glass of wine, a couple of pills, and a remote. The TV mindlessly spouted out voices. Several bottles of wine were scattered across the kitchen counter, a bottle of pills nestled between them. This apartment held the right contents for a personal party—a last party.

The hag's face slowly disappeared, and the young girl that I had originally seen at the Master's summoning table reemerged, innocent, young, and perky, no traces of black veins, no gaunt cheeks or hollow eyes, but from the dead unblinking stare, I could tell she was still catatonic.

I was angered by what I had just seen and yet, very hesitant to do anything about it. Interrupting her feast might have provoked another attack on me, which in turn would have caused her to require another meal.

This constant need to treat humans as food, held by demons and other creatures of the dark, repulsed me. I had spent so many years watching the human species. They had more value than a simple meal. They felt the fear and terror my kin imposed. It was cruel to treat them as we did.

She floated towards me. I moved out of the way as she and the Shishi went out the door she had entered, turned towards my apartment, and floated back down the hall.

I followed, but not closely, and as I reached my door, I found her lying on the couch, eyes opened but staring at the ceiling with hands resting on her chest like a body at a funeral. Her expression finally appeared rested and serene, while her chest rose and fell slowly. She was fast asleep.

Well, so much for having to look after the girl. Clearly she was quite capable of doing that herself.

The Shishi were back in statue form, and they were both sitting directly in front of the couch, protecting the girl.

I sat down carefully in the chair on the other side of the living room, making sure I didn't crush the splinted wing, and kept an eye on her. If I had to, I'd sit up all night, but there was no way I was going to sleep. I didn't trust her, and she was clearly powerful enough to bind me, kill a human, and eat their soul.

No, there most definitely would be no sleep tonight.

Repression

DATI

The girl on the couch shifted her position and let out a soft sigh. It was hard to resolve her propensity for death and wickedness with the soft face and pouty lips that slept so peacefully. Sitting in a chair throughout the night gave me plenty of time to examine her, as she slept away her murderous feast. I still didn't even know her name.

A witch. She wasn't exactly human anymore, but her blood wouldn't match that of a demon either. Her soul, however, had to be as dark and twisted as any demon in order to command the spell she cast last night. It was only a matter of time until the rot of the dark side seeped from her spirit into her human flesh.

The Shishi had reverted back to their stone façade. They sat in front of the couch, waiting for her to arise and bid them their next set of orders. I had lost them to her.

I stared at her. She was such a tiny person. Long gone were the black spider veins of leeching darkness. She was full, both physically and psychically, but her childlike demeanour and guise of innocence was misleading.

Only a few hours had passed since she returned to the couch. My eyelids were heavy, and I found myself straining to keep them open.

So what, if anything, should I do about the woman down the hall, split open from chin to belly, lying in a pool of her own blood with a missing heart? It was yet another mess I would have to clean up, and it would have to wait until the morning.

I yawned. I was so damn tired.

My tired mind drifted to Alyx and the dream I'd had the previous night. I remembered a woodland, deep in nature, where green moss flourished and ferns littered the forest floor. I ran my hand across old tree stumps whose roots stuck out, making the glen knotted and gnarled. Near my feet, odd little mushrooms poked their heads out from underneath the leaf debris, showing their unassuming little caps.

In the middle of it all stood Alyx. Simple and beautiful, his auburn hair a tousled mess, with leaves stuck in his mop and beard and a smear of dirt across his nose. His body was wrapped in that violet swirling aura. It danced around his neck and spiraled around his shoulder, then came back under his arm and across his chest.

I wanted to reach out and touch him, but hesitated. Alyx smiled and I smiled back, feeling silly, unsure of myself. I glanced away from him, embarrassed. Alyx took a step forward, autumn leaves crunching underneath his foot, and I leered at him, devouring his image, saving it in my mind to enjoy over and over. I reached out to take his hand.

A searing pain in my gut startled me awake. My eyes opened wide and I stood up quickly, then doubled over, wrapping my arms around my midsection and sucking in a deep breath.

The silver monsters living in my gut rolled, poking my insides with their sharp spines.

I had fallen asleep. But thinking of Alyx had stirred the minions, just as they had jostled me when I met him in Marta's store. There would be no way I'd let Alyx go through some demon infection and drag him into the pit of despair I lived every day. I had to find a way to get these things out of me.

I decided that I would find a way to rid myself of these without harming anyone, despite the fact that the very of thought of it was mutiny against Master.

The couch was empty. The Shishi guardians were gone as well.

Shit.

I scanned the room quickly, my thoughts racing through all the options of where she could have gone. A rustling noise came from the kitchen. I tiptoed towards the sounds.

As I poked my head around the door, I discovered her surrounded by plastic bags and placing items into my fridge. The Shishi were at her feet, tails waggling as they curiously watched her.

I breathed a heavy sigh of relief. She was still there and in one piece, and not about to cast her next apartment-destroying spell.

"What are you doing?" I asked.

"Oh my God," she said shrilly, dropping the juice bottle she held onto the ceramic tiles. The plastic bottle bounced a few times and then spun like a top and skittered off across the floor. "Don't sneak up on me like that!"

"What's with the food? And where did it come from?" I asked.

"I'm starving, and when I woke up, you were sleeping there in front of me. Creepy, I might add, and so I came into the kitchen to get something to eat, but the only thing in this fridge is raw meat. So I, um, 'borrowed' some money from your coat pocket and went out to find some food." She smiled warily.

So she was a witch and a thief, but at least she was honest. I groaned and rolled my eyes.

"I have a lot of questions for you, so fix your food and come back to the living room. We have things to discuss."

She seemed disappointed, concerned, and confused all at once. "Oh, okay. Do you want any?" She pointed to a crate of eggs.

"No."

The young witch did as she was told, eventually anyway. She brought a large glass of orange juice, a huge plate of scrambled eggs with cheese and a few pieces of toast piled on top, and sat down on the couch that she had called home for the last couple of days.

She piled the eggs and melted cheese over top of the bread and shoved it into her mouth. A cold shiver went down my spine. I had a hard time watching humans eat.

"Who are you?" I asked bluntly.

"Oh, yeah, I guess we never did that part, um, sorry. My name is Jenae," she said through a mouthful of food, all perky and happy. Putting the plate of eggs to the side, she wiped her hand on my sweatpants, then held it out in typical human custom. "What's your name?"

"My name is Dati Amon." I shook her hand, somewhat reluctantly.

"Say again? Da...what, I'm sorry, how'd you say that?" she asked, shaking my hand. As she touched my skin, she seemed to flinch a little, as if she somehow knew that the hot demonic flesh was not to be trusted.

"Just call me Dati."

"Okay, Dati it is. That's an unusual name. I've never heard that before. What is it, like French?"

"Actually, it's Babylonian," I said. It meant Bearer of Dreams, but for the children I marked, it meant Bearer of Nightmares.

"Yes, right, of course it's Barbarian." She had a blank look on her face, and I made the assumption she had no idea what Babylon was.

"What do you remember from the past couple of days?"

"You mean, like, the very last couple of days? Well, then not much, except I've slept a lot, but I'm still tired. I've been tired for days, like I just can't get enough sleep, and this hurts," she said, raising her bandaged forearm.

"But I remember the dream," she piped up again in between bites of scrambled cheese eggs, "where Master appeared and told us to come to that warehouse, and I remember finding it and thinking it was so cool that I could see that glowing purple around the building."

Well, that was interesting. Master was able to communicate telepathically with demons, but apparently that extended to witches as well.

"So what's with him anyways? He was so nice to me, but now he's just an asshole. Where does he get off stroking my hair like that and making that table pin us down while those things ripped us open? I don't like him." She sighed. "He used to be so nice to me when I was with Mira. He would show up when I was visiting her and promise me all kinds of things, and he would bring me cool stuff and sometimes give me money. But he was just a complete asshat at that meeting with the way he treated you when you burst in through the window, which was totally freaking awesome!"

I wondered when she would run out of breath.

"Oh my God, I forgot, you have wings! I've never ever seen anyone with wings. What are you? And then I remember all those others at the table and that thing that sat on the other side of the table..." She dropped off. "I don't remember too much after that," she snapped, and I could tell that was a lie. She must have known more, but whether or not she wanted to remember was another thing.

"Keep going. What else?" I wasn't going to let her squirm out of anything or not talk about something just because it made her uncomfortable.

She studied me cautiously but then started up again.

"My wrist. I remember those fucking bugs digging into my arm and the pain. I remember there was a lot of pain...but I don't really remember anything else. Everything is kind of a blur after that." She held up her bandaged wrist and forearm. "Did you do this? And how'd I get here? And what were those silver things? And..."

"One step at a time. I'll answer what I can, but I still have questions for you." I shifted in my seat and leaned forward. "Do you know what you are?" This should be good.

"What do you mean?" she barked back. "I'm a girl. What are *you*?"

"No, I mean, yes of course you're a girl. What I meant was, sitting around that table, you saw lots of things most other humans have never seen or want to see or even want to know exist. So, if you were brought to that meeting, that means that you're one of us, but I want to know what you are."

"Well, Mira said I was special and that she would show me how to do magic and get people to do what I wanted. In fact, she said that anything I wanted, I could make happen. So I don't know, like a witch, I guess."

I cocked an eyebrow. She actually got that right.

"So where's this Mira? How'd you meet her?"

"Oh, Mira, yeah, well um, she's dead. At least she was dead when I saw her last. I don't know, it was *really* weird, and the whole thing freaked me right out." She stopped short again.

"Keep going," I prompted her, needing the information but already regretting the inevitable onslaught of words that would follow.

"She was always on the same bus with me when I was on the way to school. And then this one day, she sat next to me and was all friendly and started talking to me, but she smelled bad. She was kind like a grandmother, and I never really had one, so I thought she was kind of cute, and then she showed me this little magic spell between us right there on the bus, and she lit the end of her finger on fire—which blew my mind—and then she had this really cool little lizard in her purse."

Jenae said the whole speech in one breath.

"I've never seen a lizard like that before. It had like little wings on it—so cute! It ran out of her purse when she opened it and up her arm onto her shoulder and perched behind her ear and stared at me, flicking its tongue out just like a snake. It sort of looked like a little baby dragon, and Mira said I could have one too, if I did everything she asked me to do. Then she asked to see my left hand, and she read the lines on my palm like a psychic and showed me the little star I have on my hand." Jenae lifted up her bandaged hand and showed me the star that was still outlined as if in ink.

"Yeah, that won't come off now," she said as she rubbed the ink.

"Then Mira gave me some cookies from her purse, and I thought she was really friendly. So I agreed to go visit her after school. She gave me her address, and then she got off the bus. I went to school that day, which was a total waste because I couldn't think about anything other than going to visit her, and then I went right to her house after last period. Her house wasn't very far from my school. I went there, and she was happy to see me and said her grandchildren never visited her, and she was happy that I came. I felt bad for her."

In went another scoop of breakfast, thankfully the last.

"Her house was a bit of a mess—I think she needed help—so I told her I would come see her and help her as long as she showed me how to do all that cool stuff. There were books everywhere and all kinds of jars with stuff in them. Some were cool and some were gross. Anyways, she made me sit with her on the couch, and then we had some cookies as she showed me a book of spells she had and told me how very special it was, and it had all kinds of really neat symbols in it that I've never seen anything like. Oh except for the runes, I'd seen them before.

"She said that she would help me make a book just like hers. So every day after school, I would go to her place but only for like an hour so that my stupid sister and mom wouldn't know where I was, and then when I was visiting, Mira would teach me things, and that's when I met Master." She stopped briefly, inhaled, and glanced at me. I sat there, somewhat wide-eyed.

She took a deep breath, recovering from her spiel, and then continued.

"Master said to me that I was extra special and Mira had found a miracle when she discovered me. Master promised that he would come and visit every now and then and that I was to do everything that Mira wanted. He promised me all kinds of things.

"Mira would always make tea for all of us when Master visited and bring out cookies—she always had cookies. Master had the most interesting purple irises, and then during the last visit, Master was there and, I don't know, I don't remember everything. I just remember having tea and cookies and then them saying that they thought I was ready, and then I must've fallen asleep or something. I mean, things are kind of fuzzy after having tea and I don't really remember anything, but when I woke up, I was on the floor and I was naked, which totally freaked me out—"

That was it, that's what I had been waiting for. So they had drugged her and then started the transformation. She continued.

"—I found my clothes folded on one of the chairs, but Mira was just lying in the hallway. So I got dressed and then went over to wake her up, but that's what totally blew my mind because she wasn't breathing. She was stone cold, so I guess she was dead. I couldn't stay there, so I ran out of the house."

I was shocked at how young she was and somehow seemed unaffected by her encounter and transformation into the world of the dark. She was completely disjointed in her thought. After everything she had been through, she was still perky and bubbly, despite the fact that such horrible things had happened to her. I would have expected her to be withdrawn and scared.

She trusted me—a total stranger—with far too much information.

"It was late at night, so clearly I had been asleep for a long time. I went home where I would get total shit for being late. When I did get home, my mom was totally drunk again, so she was an out-of-control bitch, and my sister was standing behind her and was yelling at me too, and then…. well, I kind of blew up and then I don't remember anything…and then I must have fallen asleep again, but I woke up in the kitchen, and the house was a complete disaster and neither my sister or my mom was around. And so I went to my room and packed up my stuff, and left. Screw them."

Sounded to me like she had cast another spell and feasted on her family.

"Jenae, how old are you?" I asked.

"Eighteen," she said immediately, another lie. I didn't even need to smell the difference. It was that obvious. But still, her pulse had quickened, the heat off her body grew, and her stench hung thick in the air. Spicy metallic oranges, mixed with that burnt acrid smell.

"Jenae, how old are you really? And don't lie."

She rolled her eyes. "God, you're as bad as my sister. Okay, fine, I'm *sixteen*, but my birthday is next month, so I'm close to eighteen."

I wasn't sure how to follow that bit of logic. So she was really sixteen, which explained the immature moments but also the rare brief instances of an adult brain working.

Master and Mira were obviously in league with each other and, for whatever reason, saw potential or special abilities in Jenae. Perhaps the little old lady had drugged her with the food or drink and then had done whatever witches do to transform humans. I had no idea what that entailed, as I'd never witnessed it, but it sounded like the old lady didn't survive the process.

Transmorphing a human had never been down topside. In the pits of Hell, warping human souls was a common occurrence, but demon flesh housed the morphed soul. That morphing process varied for each species, but it always took a lot of energy and time. If it wasn't done right or the soul wasn't selected carefully, the transformation would fail. I didn't really understand the biology of witches, but in the old woman's case, it sounded like she didn't have enough life left in her to survive creating a new witch. Again, I found this kind of odd. Mirabelle sounded like she was a well-experienced witch; she should have known what she was doing.

"Do you remember anything else?"

"I don't know. There was shit everywhere—in Mira's place—things were broken, and the walls had all these weird marks on them. Actually, kind of like the walls here. It looks like black mold or something, but there were also a bunch of symbols written on the walls all around where I woke up. The same kind of wriggly writing I saw in Mira's big book."

I guessed that the script Jenae referred to were invocation sigils that would have aided in her transformation. The black rot, well, that could have come from the girl and one of her uncontrollable spells. I wondered if Jenae had inadvertently killed her maker.

"Okay, my turn!" She put the empty plate on my coffee table and put her feet up next to the plate. I grimaced a little as her human toes clung to the edge. "What are you? I mean, you look human, sort of, but your eyes are so cool and you have the wings! What's with the wings? Can I touch them?" The gravity of the situation clearly had not sunk in.

"Jenae, you really sound like a nice girl. I don't think...no actually, I *know* you don't understand how much trouble you've got yourself into," I said, and she rolled her eyes again. I swear she could flip them into the back of her head.

"God you sound like everyone else. I'm not stupid, you know." She appeared hurt.

What had the old woman been thinking with turning this child? She was a bit bratty, but there was something else about her that didn't sit right. She was in deep trouble getting involved with anything that included Master, but she was so young she didn't seem to understand the gravity of it, or didn't care. It was like she was incapable of thinking any further than her next thought. She went from raging against her family and seemingly depressed and rejected to wide-eyed and excited that she was sitting with something that was obviously not human. I was certain that Master had elicited a new form of revenge. My actual punishment for disobedience and tardiness at the summoning wasn't the broken wing; it was the perpetual headache in the form of a yappy and clueless witch.

"No, Jenae, I don't think you're stupid. I don't think you understand what has happened to you."

She frowned, casting a sideways glance towards me. "Okay, then if you're so smart, you explain it."

"Well..." Where to start. "That old woman, Mira? She was a witch."

"Well, yeah."

"Not a nice one, Jenae, and I think she tricked you. I also think the food she gave you was drugged. Once you were drugged, she changed you. It's a process called transmorphing. Our kind do it to human souls who have descended and have special abilities or show affinities... a propensity for being evil. I've never heard of it being done here."

Jenae gazed at me with a vacant gaze. "So what? She turned me into witch. She said she was going to teach me how to do magic."

"Yes, Jenae, you are a witch. A bad one. I assure you, the old lady was right in one regard, you definitely have a talent for it. You cast a spell on me last night that could have killed me, but you lost control and the creatures you summoned almost killed you instead."

The Shishi snuggled in closer. They understood everything.

"Those 'dogs' are guardians created to protect palaces and shrines that house evil creatures, spirits, weapons, and artifacts. They are not protectors of individuals, so I'm not sure what you did, but they switched loyalties last night from guardians that protected my place, to protecting you. When you lost control last night, they saved you."

"They guard evil places?"

"Yes, Jenae. But now they guard you."

"So, I'm evil," she said, with a touch of incredulity. The girl wasn't stupid; the wheels were turning.

"Yes. Anything you do will be for evil, not good, and there is a cost," I said. I really wasn't the one that should have been having this conversation with her. I didn't really know that much about witches, at least not enough to raise one.

"What's the cost?" she asked.

"The cost is your soul, or at least pieces of it. A witch is a human who has the ability to take energy and reshape it to do what she wants. Sometimes that's summoning creatures, and sometimes that's changing the weather. I don't know much more than that, because I'm not a witch. But every time you cast a spell, you use a piece of your soul, and if you use enough of it, you can die. You almost did that last night. Every time you deplete that much of your soul, or life force, you have to replace it."

"Okay, how do you do that?" she asked. She was tense. I could tell she was sort of braced for my answer, and I think she already knew the truth.

"You take it from another human."

"I don't understand. What do you mean? How do you take someone else's soul?"

"You kill them and then you absorb their soul," I said.

She stared at me with a blank stare and saucer eyes, and then she went a little pale.

"You know what I'm talking about, don't you? Do you remember what you did last night?"

She violently shook her head, but I couldn't tell if it was an answer to my question or if it was in defiance of her memories.

"No, no, I wouldn't ever do that. I *couldn't* do that." Her eyes were wide, and her face was now completely ashen.

"I watched you do it last night."

"You watched me murder someone and 'absorb' their soul. Yeah, right, you're so full of bullshit!" Her fists clenched as she crossed her arms in defiance.

"Well, I sure as Hell wasn't going to stop you after what you had done to me moments before. Okay, come with me. I'll prove it to you." This wouldn't be pretty, but there was some reminiscence lurking beneath the surface of her mind. Maybe a good shock of viewing the corpse down the hall would bring everything to light.

I grabbed her hand and pulled her up. Jenae fought back by attempting to wrench away from me, but I was too fast and too strong. I dragged her out the apartment, down the hall, and to the dead woman's abode. I could smell the stink of death from in the hallway.

"Jeez, let go of me!"

No chance of that happening. I wanted her to see the dead woman, and I wanted to see if it would trigger anything.

I turned the knob on the neighbour's door and pushed it open, then walked into the main area, trailing her behind me. The body was still there, and the blood-soaked area around the body was shiny; it had gone gelatinous. The smell of copper was heavy in the air.

"Jenae, look. You did this last night. Bring back any memories?"

"No!" The body in its grotesque display made her start to heave. She was going to throw up.

I threw one hand over her mouth and pulled her close in to me, then turned her away from the sight of the body. I couldn't risk her vomiting. The heart that she had consumed was essential to keep her fed and alive. It needed to stay down.

"Do you remember what happened here last night?" I asked.

She shook her head and sobbed, before shrugging her shoulders and nodding ever so slightly.

We walked out of the apartment, shut the door behind us, and went back to my place. As soon as we got inside, I let her go. She fell to the floor, sobbing and crying. I helped her to the couch. As soon as she calmed down enough, we got down to the business of discussing what had actually happened in all of its gory details.

It was a tough few hours for her. Most of what she did remember was hazy, like she recalled a bad dream. We spent the better part of the day and early evening reconstructing the last few weeks of her life. The end result was that she admitted her mother and sister were dead; she had fed on them. Jenae also thought two, maybe three, of the metal parasites had crawled into her arm.

We had no idea how she had been transformed or what had happened to Mira, the old woman. Jenae had just finished making herself tea and sat back down on the couch when there was a knock on the door. I glanced quickly at her, wondering who was at my door and if the unannounced arrival posed any danger. She looked back at me and shrugged.

"Expecting someone?" she asked.

"No," I said. The Shishi were alive again and on guard. "Tell them to hold off. I don't need any more body parts to clean up."

Jenae patted each of their heads and calmed them down, but they continued to watch intently.

As I walked over to the door, the knock came again.

Hemming stood on the other side, except standing wasn't quite the right word. He was bent over and holding his midsection with his hands. The clothes beneath his hands were shredded and bloodstained, and his hands were covered in the slick dark-red liquid.

"Sorry, Dati, I.... I needed somewhere to go." And with that, he slumped towards the nearest wall and slid down. His breathing was fast and shallow. I hoisted him up and brought him over to the couch, gesturing for Jenae to move. She was wide-eyed again, then pointed and remembered.

"You were at the summoning," she said, then smiled, proud of herself for remembering.

My couch was becoming a convalescence bed. After lying Hemming down, I took a closer inspection of his wounds. There was blood everywhere, another reoccurring theme.

It looked like Hemming's midsection was ripped open, but I couldn't really tell with the bloodstained clothes. The shirt needed to come off. Hemming was mumbling and trying to talk, but it was incoherent.

"Jenae, down the hall there's an office. On the right-hand side of the desk, there are several drawers, and in the top drawer of the desk, there should be a pair of scissors. Go get that and bring them here."

Jenae disappeared.

"Hemming, what happened?" I asked, shaking his shoulders a little to try and get him to focus.

"Three at once. I may have provoked them a little. But yeah, I had three guys come at me..." He trailed off into a mumble I couldn't understand. Jenae showed up with the scissors, which I used to cut open his shirt.

Hemming grabbed my hand, and I almost sliced his fingers on the blade of the scissor. "Dati, they ripped themselves out of me, flew through the air, and embedded themselves into the bellies of each of them."

His intense gaze drove fear into my heart, but not as much fear as the words he said. I took a moment to fully understand what he said because I didn't want it to be true.

It was only a matter of time before the metal demons within us ripped their way out, just as they had done to Hemming.

Hemming's eyes rolled into the back of his head.

"Hemming, stay with us, come on..." I shook him again, and he peered up at me, his eyes losing focus. "Where did this happen? When did this happen?"

Hemming garbled something and passed out.

I sent Jenae for other items: hot water, a bucket, and some towels, gauze, and bandages. I wasn't Marta, but we needed to get him cleaned up to see how bad the wound was.

As I cleansed his midsection, a sharp silver spine poked out of the wound, warning me to keep my distance.

Perhaps I could take him to Marta. I had no idea whether or not she would help Hemming, but I didn't see any other option. But I couldn't possibly move Hemming in this state. I'd have to bring Marta to my place, to Hemming.

Jenae, who had been blissfully quiet, stared at me. She visibly crawled back a little further into herself as she said, "This is going to happen to all of us, isn't it?"

I nodded. I understood her retreat; it was the same retreat I had made a hundred times after Master had delivered punishment. It was a retreat into the corner of myself, where I thought I might be safe, but knew I had lost, had been beaten. It was the knowledge that Master ruled over me, and controlled everything about me.

Transmutation

ALYX

I had been tending Mother's shop all Sunday, and with almost no customers, it had been boring.

So out came the spell books. Again.

First I'd attempted an incantation from an old book Mom kept in the back—a short little rhyme that was supposed to change the weather. Except after reading it several times, it remained bright and sunny outside. No change at all.

I had stacked up several books with various spells that I'd tested out in the past with no success. After that last meditation, I was damned if I wasn't going to make at least one of these spells work. The entire afternoon I spent thinking about the man with the eyes and working my way through the pile of books with no success.

The final book contained a Voudon ritual for summoning fire. I scratched several symbols onto a piece of paper in front of me and then set a small metal bowl in the center and waited.

It was supposed to erupt in flame.

There was nothing. Not even a sizzle.

I gave up.

So then what had happened during that meditation? Why had that been successful? Was the Satyr real? Was the information I had been shown about the man of my dreams just my subconscious' way of dealing with my own obsession? Would it really hurt to go look at the high-rise?

I glanced up at the clock.

Five minutes to five.

My heart felt like it would beat right out of my chest. I giggled to myself. It was time to clean up the cash counter, stuff any receipts into the deposit envelope that would wait in the back office for Mom to reconcile, grab my coat, and head out. Time to lock up the shop and leave, and then maybe walk past the building—that's all—just walk past it, just to make sure that it really is still standing there.

Flicking the lights off, locking up the door, I headed out of the shop.

Here we go.

I can't believe I'm doing this.

No one would be waiting at home for me. Sundays had always been Mom's day to get together with her girlfriends and do whatever women of her age did when they went out in small gaggles. I imagined it was shopping or cards or trying out a recipe at someone's home. In the end, I really didn't mind. It gave me time to myself.

I hadn't turned the right way for home; instead, I went to go see the high-rise. And it really was only a few blocks up the street. *I'll just go take a quick peek.*

Rounding the corner, sweat dripped down my back.

"Geez, Alyx, get nervous much?" I said out loud to myself.

I rolled my eyes at myself. This was so silly.

Within a couple minutes, I was across the street, counting the storeys of the high-rise. It wasn't even close to the tallest building in the downtown core, and certainly not the newest, but the windows reflected the partly cloudy, slightly cool sky of late September on the prairies.

Without really thinking about it too much, I walked into the lobby of the high-rise. Ornate marble floors, black leather couches, and a faux Persian rug off to one side created an elegant sitting area, where the concierge's desk could spy on the inhabitants and keep them in line until the upstairs tenant came to retrieve their guest from the foyer.

But it was Sunday, and there was no one behind the desk.

I went over to the enormous bureau and inspected the front panel plaque that had a listing of all the apartments in the tower and the last name of the tenant who occupied the suite. Next to the name was a call button, and an intercom speaker was next to that.

I had no idea which apartment number to look for, nor did I know the name of the resident.

At this point, I lingered in front of the roll call of residents, with sweat still dripping down my back and my usually hot hands turning cold. A sure sign that I thought I was doing something wrong.

Damn it, this is just asinine. What the Hell am I doing?

Honestly, a fucking Satyr gave me this information—stop and think about that little fact, Alyx. I repeated in my head all the arguments as to why this was a stupid idea in a vain attempt to talk myself out of walking over to the elevator.

But I was already there, and within a second, I had pushed the call button for the elevator and the whirring of the mechanical gears and machinery became audibly noticeable. The elevator sped quickly down to its summons on the main floor, and when it reached its destination, the doors opened wide and I peered inside.

It all seemed sort of familiar, but weren't all elevators kind of the same? This one was no different, studying the panel of numbers, as the doors slid close. I swallowed hard as my finger traced the right column of numbers. 3...6...9, my finger continued all the way up to the top, 27, and then I pushed it—hard—probably a little harder than was really necessary.

The elevator took forever to reach the top floor. I readjusted my backpack, still feeling stupid and really uncomfortable—until finally the doors opened.

Left or right, which would be the correct way to the broken door? With only a fifty/fifty chance, I swung to my right and proceeded down the hallway. All the doors were the same, but after only a few steps, I could see the end of the corridor. There it was, the apartment at the end on the left-hand side of the corridor, and the door was ajar.

My heart skipped a beat, and my stomach sat tightly in my throat. *What the Hell am I doing? Following up on information that a Satyr gave me. A Satyr, Alyx, a Satyr.*

I had almost convinced myself to turn around and go home when I noticed that the door on the left-hand side of the corridor wasn't ajar, but off its hinges, and did that mean broken?

And there were voices coming from inside the apartment.

Leave, right now. This had gone from silly to creepy, and now I was slightly more afraid than I was giddy. Was this actually happening? These were the signs that Silenus had shown me; the building, the top floor, the broken door—was the vision that the Satyr had shown me coming true?

A tiny voice from deep within my subconscious screamed at me, *Of course it's real, and it is exactly what you wanted to have happen, and this is exactly where you need to be!*

As I took a couple more steps forward, I could hear a girl's voice talking and then a man's as well.

Well, see right there, this clearly was all wrong. There was a girl, and there shouldn't have been any girls. And yet, that male voice made my insides quiver.

It had to be him.

I knocked.

What the Hell did you do that for, I scolded myself.

There was immediate silence from inside the condo. I was just about to turn and run.

If it wasn't the right apartment, I could always just say that I had been given incorrect information and thank the resident and apologize for inconvenience. After all, that wouldn't have been far from the truth.

A pretty young girl's face appeared in the crack.

"Hi, can I help you?" she said. She wore an oversized T-shirt and a pair of sweats that were huge on her. Wow, talk about your Sunday lazy lounge-around-the-house clothes.

Crazy thoughts swam through my head. Maybe this guy was straight after all; maybe I had misinterpreted his stare. Maybe he was doing this chick?

A small part of me really did not like that idea at all. If he did girls, at least he could have chosen one his own age.

"I...um, sorry, I was just expecting a guy," I started, when suddenly the girl shoved the door to the side.

"Sorry, this thing... can you give me a hand?" she said.

I dropped my backpack and helped the girl slide the door to the side, just enough so that either my skinny form or her lean petite body would have been able to get past it.

"Thanks, there, that's better," she said, and then she turned around and went back into the apartment. "Dati, there's a guy out here asking for you."

Voices came from inside the apartment, not really an argument, just sort of tense words, and then there was silence. It was weird.

I stood just sort of on the threshold of the apartment, and now I felt beyond uncomfortable and stupid. My hands had gone ice cold. I cupped them and blew hot breath to warm them up.

That's it, this is over, it's time to leave—but I didn't want to be rude. I didn't want to just disappear on the girl. I poked my head around the corner. "I'm sorry, you know, I clearly have some wrong information. I'm sorry to bother you. I'm just gonna go."

By the time I had half of the sentence out, I had craned my neck to discover a living room that looked like a tornado had gone through it, with walls that had the weirdest paint job I had ever seen. It seemed as if the place was rotting, and there was a guy lying on the sofa who was pale and bloody.

What the Hell have I got myself into?

And then I saw him.

It was him.

All of him, in loose sweats and tight T-shirt that showed exactly how muscular he was, with his bearded face and black tousled hair. All I could do was stare. A smile crept across my face.

Silenus had done it; Silenus had led me right to him.

Holy freaking crap, that magic shit really worked!

He spoke for the first time—a deep baritone voice.

"Alyx! You can't be here, what the...how the Hell did you—" But he stopped abruptly. That gorgeous man's face went ashen white as the colour drained out.

His face contorted into a grimace.

I saw why.

Dati's stomach exploded with blood.

The girl screamed.

I started to move towards him—to help—but before I took a second step, something hit me in the gut. I glanced down and put a hand where something hit me, like a baseball had come hurtling out of nowhere and smacked me right in the gut.

A sharp pain like the blade of a knife drove into my belly.

I glanced up to see Dati falling onto his knees.

I didn't understand what was going on, but the pain was excruciating. I ripped up my shirt in time to see the spikes of a silver bug boring its way into my midsection.

I felt hot and feverish, and my hand instinctively went towards the bug to try and pull it off me, but I had become so dizzy.

My eyelids fluttered, and the scene before me went hazy.

Then Dati was there, and he had me in his arms, and he said something, but the ringing in my ears was so loud I couldn't hear a thing.

And then...darkness.

Cocoon

DATI

Hemming slept, but his rest was punctuated by bouts of flailing arms and the occasional flying fist. His sudden jarring movements were going to undo whatever first aid I had patched together. I hoped my poor curative skills protected him enough so that the wound wouldn't fester.

Hemming had once been human, that much I had learned of his history. Master had rescued him from his self-destructive tendencies, binding a deal with him when he had been a young gambling addict who drank too much and didn't know when to stop wagering. That contract landed Hemming with a primeval Shape-Shifting skeleton, a demon's anger, and a sudden lack of people who were searching for him and his funds. However, Master owned him.

On the rarest of occasions, Master would pair me with others within his band of fiends. A long time ago, he'd sent Hemming and me out to track an errant demon, one who never should have escaped the boundaries of Hell. After a couple of months searching for the creature and trying to capture it, we applied a limited scope of trust on each other.

When dealing with demons, one always wants to keep an ace up their sleeve.

It had not been easy to find the beast. It enjoyed taking up residence within children. Getting the demon back to its rightful place was costly. Most of the children it had possessed didn't survive.

Jenae squeaked out the tiniest noise of empathy from behind me. When I glanced back at her, she immediately quietened and turned tight-lipped, her eyes watery with impending tears. The silence was short-lived.

"Is he going to be alright? It looks so painful," Jenae asked in a small voice.

"He'll heal faster than a human." I was more concerned about the bugs twisting inside my guts, waiting to tear a matching hole through me.

Jenae's hand was pressed up against her midsection, and her gaze hadn't moved from Hemming's wrapped belly.

"I can't do this."

"I don't think you have a choice," I said.

"Take them out of me right now. I'll get you a knife from the kitchen; just get those fucking bugs out of me!" She clawed at the oversized shirt she had borrowed; bunches of fabric gathered in her hands. "I can feel them moving inside of me. I don't want them there for another second."

"Jenae, I'm not cutting you open, and frankly I can't imagine that the creatures are going to let me pull them out of you. I'm afraid you've just been exposed to the cruelest thing Master has ever done to us. As sick as it is, welcome to the club."

She hung her head low in defeat. "There's got to be a way. I can't stand the thought of them in there," she mumbled, tears running down her cheek.

"I'm not wasting time thinking about it right now, but if you come up with a better idea than trying to cut them out of yourself, let me know. Keep an eye on him," I said, pointing to Hemming. "I'm going to clean the blood off my hands."

If I was honest with myself, I felt the same, but I held no confidence in Jenae to circumvent Master's devious plan. Now if I had the soul vial that held my dismembered spirit, then that would open a few doors of possibilities, none of which ended well for Master. Until then, I would do as I was bid, suffer through Master's torment, and likely put others through pain and misery.

I washed my hands in the bathroom sink, staining the white porcelain bright red, until Hemming's blood washed away and swirled down the drain.

A knock coming from the front door, and then Jenae's voice.

"Hi, can I help you?" Jenae said, perky and friendly, apparently over her panic attack.

What the Hell now?

"I...um, sorry, I was just expecting a guy."

I froze. The voice, where did I know that voice from?

"Sorry, this thing...can you give me a hand?" By the scraping coming from the other room, Jenae must have been moving the door out of the way.

"There, that's better," she said, and then called out. "Dati, there's a guy out here asking for you."

My hands were dripping over the sink as Jenae spoke out to me. For a second, I didn't know what to do next—wipe the water on my sweats, grab the towel, or just run towards Jenae.

I didn't have visitors.

Where had I heard that voice? It gnawed at me, and I felt this undeniable sense that something had gone horribly awry, like watching black clouds gather on the horizon—knowing a bad storm was coming.

Jenae came around the corner and met me halfway down the hallway.

"Who is it?" I asked with concern.

"I don't know, just some guy asking for you," she said in an irritated tone. "Like, do I have a list of your friends and know them by name? Geez, it's just some guy!"

"I don't have any friends," I replied quickly.

"Yeah well, maybe if you did, then your mood would be a little less snarly and abrupt."

As I stepped around the end of the couch where Hemming lay, the visitor standing in the front entrance of the apartment came into view.

It was Alyx, the most beautiful creature I'd seen in hundreds of years, and he stood on the threshold of my home.

How the Hell had he found me?

The silver demons squirmed to life. Sharp spines pushed on the underside of my skin.

My hand instinctively covered the spot where Master's minions resided, as if that would stop them. I took a step back to put distance between myself and Alyx, but Jenae was directly behind me and my talon stepped right onto her bare foot.

"Jesus, Dati!" She pushed me forward to get me off of her foot.

Dread filled me as I stumbled forwards, the silver bugs twisting inside, pain flashed white hot through my chest as I held my hand out. "Alyx! You can't be here, what the...how the Hell did you..."

Except Alyx didn't know what was going on.

Alyx gleamed up at me, his bright aura suddenly danced to life, phosphorescent swirls illuminating his body.

With ferocious speed, pain seared through my midsection, the flesh shredded as a silver demon ripped itself out of my gut and flew through the air.

Alyx never even saw the oncoming danger. It hit him with a thud as he stepped back. The bug tore through his light-coloured fall jacket and his plaid shirt, then burrowed into Alyx's abdomen as if it was all layers of tissue paper. Alyx pulled up his shirt to see the last of the minion as it wriggled and tunneled its way inside.

The contortions of pain began to show on Alyx's face, and then all at once, his fantastical purple swirling aura retreated into itself and disappeared.

I couldn't catch my breath. The shredded flesh burned. My hand became slick with blood, and I tried to catch the steady stream of liquid as it wept from my abdomen, soaking my clothes.

Summoning up as much determination as I could to overcome my own pain, angry that Master had put me in this very spot and distraught that I had shattered my own promise that Alyx would never be dragged into my world, I rushed over to him.

Those gathering dark clouds of doom I had felt just moments earlier were now a violent thunderstorm unleashing its fury within the confines of my house.

I caught him just as he started to list sideways. As he fell into my arms, he stared at me and smiled for only a moment before his happiness was replaced with a grimace. He writhed in pain in my arms.

"Alyx, listen to me. Alyx!" His eyes were glassy. "I'm so sorry. This wasn't supposed to happen. I'm so sorry. Don't fight the pain. Just relax and let it happen. I'm so sorry."

I had failed. I felt heavy inside, knowing my promise to myself and Marta had instantly been killed.

Alyx's body went limp.

Jenae stood beside us with her mouth agape.

"Seven Hells! Don't just stand there, help him!" I screamed at her.

"Like what?" she yelled back, her eyes as wide as I'd ever seen them.

I scooped him up off the floor and rushed him down the hall. He mouthed something, but no sound came out. I gently lay him on my bed and pushed the hair out of his eyes, something I had done so very long ago.

"Don't worry, Alyx, I will look after you." I removed his clothes and inspected the entry point. Thankfully the wound was a little more than a hole the size of a dime.

But the transmutation had already started. The silver minion had released my blood into Alyx's body. The surrounding tissue had begun its transformation from human to demon.

Alyx arched his back. His fingers contracted as he clutched at the bedspread, his hands curling inwards like he was having a seizure. His mouth gaped open then closed, and his eyelids fluttered.

Tiny black crystals were growing in the skin around the wound. The human flesh was decaying as the demon fluids introduced itself into the body. The skin near the entry point reminded me of a scab. A shiny crystalized scab, which started to spread, creeping along the surface of his white skin. Alyx moved his hand to his stomach where his fumbling fingers tapped the growing coating and the hardening skin.

His eyes had rolled into the back of his head, and his mouth still opened and closed.

I grasped Alyx's hand and squeezed it. "Remember, Alyx, I'm going to be right here."

The blood from my wound still leaked out and dripped onto the bedroom floor. I ignored it, concentrating on Alyx. Watching him go through this was torture. The one human I didn't want to have any part of this was now irrevocably immersed in this Hell, his life forever changed—there was no such thing as "un-transmorphing."

And all at once, I felt far too human—this was all my fault.

I put my hand on Alyx's chest, measuring his fast, shallow breathing and his arrhythmic heart rate. "It's okay, Alyx. I won't go anywhere, I'm right here."

His heart calmed into a regular beat.

Crystalline spots now appeared on his sides and up on his chest. Like a cancerous tumor, it spread. A spot appeared on his shoulder and started growing up his neck, expanding rapidly, faster and faster.

Alyx stopped breathing. I held his hand and squeezed it tight.

Remembering the last pod I had witnessed in its formative beginnings, this next step was the hardest part. The growing corruption had taken over his lungs. Alyx's body convulsed, the seizure taking a hold of his whole body.

Alyx's lips curled back exposing his teeth and gums. I could see a black film inside his mouth.

Several minutes went by as he spasmed. Each muscle contraction sent pangs of guilt through me. As his body finally relaxed, he settled back onto the bed.

His human life was gone—forever.

The glassy rot crawled down his arms, encasing his limbs. Most of his face was covered. Smooth black gemstones sparkled as the whites of his eyes were replaced.

Within minutes, what once was Alyx was now a crusty, somewhat shiny, crystalline body lying on my bed. Any facial features that would have suggested Alyx was in there were gone. You could hear the crystals forming—*tinkling*—creating a death cocoon.

Everything in the last three days had gone horrifyingly wrong.

"Oh my god, is that what's going to happen to all of them?" Jenae said from behind me. I hadn't heard her come into the bedroom.

She pressed her hand to her belly, and if I wasn't mistaken, she gagged a little as well. The sight disturbed me, but the smell of the transmutation process was even worse. This was the smell of the pit: decay and death. In time, that smell would change to the burnt plastic odour we all carried.

"I've never seen this here, ever. But yes, or at least something similar. Every species is slightly different, but the process is the same," I said.

"What's happening to him?"

"The demonic matter from me is taking over, changing him from human to demon. Everything will be affected. The only thing not saved is the human blood. It's removed, and the new body creates demonic blood as well as other... *features*," I said, as I glanced over at my still bound and healing wing.

"Oh my god." She was mesmerized at the growing cocoon. And it was getting quite large. Tendrils were building and attaching themselves to the headboard of the bed, the floor, and the ceiling. I wasn't sure I'd have any room to even sleep on my own bed once it was done.

Jenae moved over towards it, her gaze still locked on the cocoon as it grew and changed. She reached out towards Alyx's crystalline envelope and was about to touch it.

"No!" I yelled at her and grabbed her hand.

"What? I told you, don't startle me like that. Geez, I'll end up doing some creepy magic shit on you again."

She had a good point, but I had pulled her hand back for her own safety.

"If the cocoon senses more human tissue, it will attempt to grow into it," I said, "and as it already has Alyx's body, you would disrupt the process. Don't touch him."

"But I'm not human. I'm a witch," she said with impunity.

"You're a human witch, girl. You are different. I don't know much more than that, and I tend to stay away from your kind. You're all unpredictable and dangerous." And as I said the words, she seemed hurt that she wasn't demonic like me.

"So, what happens now? Does he hatch?" she asked quietly, rubbing her hand.

"That's the basic idea."

"How long does that last?" She pointed to the black shiny pod.

"About a week, maybe less, maybe more if he fights it, but if he fights it too much, then the whole thing fails." I said the last part quietly. I wasn't sure how I felt about that. I didn't want Alyx to go through this and so a failed transmorphing would be his freedom.

"And if it fails?" she asked, already knowing the answer.

"He dies."

We stood there in silence for a minute, watching the cocoon grow, but it was slowing. The tendrils that were stabilizing the cocoon's position were the last bits of movement.

It was exceptionally quiet in the room, and the only noise was the soft clinking of building minerals.

"Maybe we should look at that." She pointed to my T-shirt, which was torn in the middle and soaked with blood.

"Yeah, maybe." I had blocked it from my mind, focusing everything on what I had done to Alyx. Somehow, I would make this up to him. Somehow, I would make good of this.

Jenae grabbed my hand. She was cool to my hot skin, and it was almost soothing.

Blood

JENAE

I couldn't stand to stay in Dati's apartment. I had to get out, for a bit anyways. Besides it's not like he would miss me. He was so attached to that gross cocoon. All he'd done for the last two days was sit in his room and gawk at it. It hadn't moved. It didn't do anything. What was he staring at anyways?

On the other hand, the Shishi were totally adorable. They followed me around everywhere and waited desperately for me to sit on the couch so they could plop themselves beside me and nuzzle my hand, begging for attention. They were just *so* cute. What a fuss the two of them had made when I started to leave the apartment. I tried to leave quietly. They wanted to come, but I couldn't take them with me. Someone probably would have made a stink about dogs being on the bus. I had convinced them to stay at Dati's instead.

"If you two settle down and stay here, I'll give you a treat when I get back. Please?"

They both sat instantly, obeying my wish, side by side. Slowly their marbled furry coats changed back into stone, resuming their guard positions.

This whole witch-thing was cool, and I totally loved the rush when casting a spell. The energy that shivered through my body made me feel all tingly inside, and for hours afterwards, I'd just float. Sometimes lights glittered all around me as if a disco ball spun above my head. Once fog and mist appeared, swirling around my feet, but during the last spell, I had made the whole apartment go dark with shadows. That had been the coolest thing yet.

But the magic was a little scary too. I couldn't remember everything. About halfway through a spell, the whole world would turn black—kind of like I had passed out. But then, I think I'd rather not remember having some creepy shadow babies trying to rip me open and gnaw on me like some kind of chew toy.

As I walked down the street, making my way towards Mirabelle's house, an orange tom cat came out from the trimmed hedges that lined the property. The tabby wound its way in between my legs with its tail straight up in the air, rubbing his chin against me.

"Oh my god, you're so cute!" I bent down and picked up the friendly little beast with rings around its tail. "But you're orange. Who makes a cat orange? You would look so much better if you were jet black."

I petted the furry critter. It stretched out in my arms and began to purr. It obviously loved the attention, just like the Shishi. As I stroked the animal, its fur changed from orange to black. Wherever my hand brushed, the creamsicle colour disappeared under inky black. I dropped the kitty in surprise. He landed softly and sat in the middle of the sidewalk, blinking at me as if disappointed the affection was over.

I *had* sort of lied to Dati. Well, not really lied, just maybe not told the whole truth. I'd said that I'd only done a couple of spells, but in reality, I've done lots. But nothing big, just stupid little stuff. And it usually just sort of *happened*.

Like the cat.

All this magic was a little freaky. Not to mention Master's summons and the pain that asshole had put me through. Thankfully I'd passed out. At least Dati had helped me. That's the only time that anyone has ever bothered to help me.

But I didn't get that either. He was supposed to be some kind of demon, with wings no less, who like—what? Harvested children? I would have thought he would be totally bad-ass, but instead he had been kind to me, given me a place to stay, and fed me.

He had also helped me understand a little bit more of what the Hell was going on.

Then there was that cocoon. Fuck, that was gross, and the smell of it had made me gag.

But then I felt so bad for Dati. He was really upset when it happened.

I checked to see if the cat was still there. But I couldn't see because *they* were in the way. I rolled my eyes at them.

Sis, Mom, and the woman from down Dati's hall stood in the middle of the sidewalk. They were always around and trying to talk to me. But only trying, they never actually said anything out loud, and most of the time when their mouths opened, the only thing that came out was goo. They were awful, covered in blood, with their chests split open, Mom and Sis with their eyes sewn shut with long straight pins. But the other woman's eyes were wide open, and they were milky white.

Ugh.

I picked up a pebble on the sidewalk and threw it at them. The tiny stone sailed through each one, making a little *puff* of white smoke as it passed through.

None of them were really there. I'd put my hands through them many times.

I shivered. Yuck.

Clearly no one else could see them. They had been sitting on the couch with me at Dati's before Alyx had shown up, before Hemming spilled his guts everywhere. The three bitches sat on the end of the couch and gaped blankly at Dati and me.

Dati never said a thing about them, so obviously he didn't see them.

There was a small part of me that thought I should feel bad—they were a constant reminder that I had killed each of them and absorbed their soul for my own use. See, this magic thing was totally gross.

But it felt so good when casting spells. So deliciously good, and all I wanted was to feel those tingly sensations, sensing the power as it moved through me just before the darkness made me black out. Plus, *they* disappeared when the spells started.

I turned around towards Mira's house, but Sis had moved and stood right in front of me. Her head was cocked to one side. I could feel her staring at me even though her eyes were shut tight. I didn't care. I kept walking. As I moved through her, she vanished in another bigger *puff*, only to reform again beside me.

I pulled a scarf out of the backpack Dati had given to me. I was currently decked out in a pair of sweats, an old T-shirt, and a hoody of Dati's, which were way too big.

I looked so unfashionable.

I felt worse.

It was late September. The leaves had already changed and were falling, and the breeze was cold. I had stopped in the coffee shop and grabbed a caramel macchiato with money that Dati had given me for food and things. The scarf I found had been draped over the back of a chair. The little brunette who had put it there never noticed it was gone, and besides, it was all the wrong colour for her.

The wrap was thin, but it provided a little bit of protection from the wind. I was still cold. Slinging the backpack over one arm, I hugged myself as I walked on to Mirabelle's place. Mira, actually—the old woman had said to just call her Mira.

So after everything that Dati had done for me, I figured I should try and help. Dati wouldn't cut out the bugs that were in my stomach, and there was no way in Hell I would let one of those things bust out of me. Fuck that. So, in order to pay back Dati for his kindness and to see if there was any way I could find something to get rid of these things, I had snuck out of Dati's place and gone to Mira's.

There *had* to be something at Mira's that would help heal Dati and Hemming, or maybe get the bugs out.

They needed to be gone.

I wondered if this was what it was like if you knew you had cancer. Knowing that something was inside, hurting you, and all you wanted was to have someone cut it out.

I dug the spare key out from the flowerpot and let myself into Mira's house. The three dead bitches trailed behind me, never far.

Maybe I could find something that would get rid of them too.

The smell inside the house was putrid, and black mold grew everywhere. The whole house was decaying.

Mirabelle hadn't been the best housekeeper. There was stuff everywhere. Jars of slime, dried herbs hanging from the window, books opened to various pages, and pots with stirring spoons sat abandoned on the stove. It was a gloomy day outside, so the inside of the house was cast in grey as well. I searched for a light switch and flicked it on. Nothing happened.

"Great. Well, I'm not doing this in the dark." I glanced around and found a candle and some matches. Once that one was lit, I went through the entire house, lighting as many candles as I could find.

I lit some incense too. I would have burned a hundred incense sticks if that would have gotten rid of the stench.

There was a small table in the living room up against the wall that had all kinds of magical stuff on it. If I remembered right, Mira had called it her altar. It had a caldron, a pentagram etched into it, crystals and candles, and more incense. There was a wand over to one side, and a little carved dragon sitting at one of the points of the pentagram.

Just cool shit everywhere. If it wasn't for the stink, I would have spent all day there.

But I had things I was supposed to be trying to find. Anything that might help Dati and Hemming, and maybe something to get rid of *them*. As I glanced over my shoulder, there *they* were, standing in the kitchen, eyeing me.

Shudder.

I stepped away from the altar and went down the hall towards the bathroom and bedroom. Mira lay in the middle of the hallway, still dead. But her shriveled old body was bloated, and the smell of rot was really heavy and stuck in my nose. I pinched my nose closed as I stepped over the dead body and went into the bedroom, except I misjudged and my shoe stepped on Mira's hand. The flesh squished away and fluid spurted out of the arm.

"Ugh god, that's disgusting. Honestly, girl," I said. I giggled a little. It shouldn't have been funny, but actually, it was kind of a little funny.

I had never been in the bedroom before.

I opened drawers, trying to find anything I thought might help. I really didn't know what I hunted for, but surely there had to be something. *Something more magical than oversized granny panties.* I held up a pair of Mira's undergarments.

There was a big old dusty bed, which despite the grubbiness of it seemed all too comfortable, a dresser, with more knickknacks scattered over the top of it. I ignored it all. I opened the closet, though, and squealed with delight.

For an old woman, there were some cool clothes hidden in the back! Most of it was old lady stuff, but there was a top with really intricate ruffling down the center of the shirt and at the sleeves. I took it off the hanger and held it up to my body. Looked like it should fit. After several minutes, I had found a few items that were retro funky and decidedly Goth.

I stripped and tried on a few items. The zombie girls stood there, the one watched me with her dead orbs as I removed my clothes. That made me feel a little weird. They were standing on the other side of the bed. I turned my head so I couldn't see them.

"Fuck them."

The clothes fit perfectly! How awesome was this? The old woman actually had clothes that I could wear, and on top of it, they were kinda cool.

At least I wouldn't have to be wearing Dati's old hand-me-down stuff that hung off of me like garbage bags.

I decided to go with a long flowing black skirt, the ruffled blouse with the bat-like sleeves, and a short bolero-style vest that was maybe just a touch too snug. It certainly accentuated my boobs, and I didn't really have much there, so this made me appear more chesty, and older. I also found a cloak with a cowl hood that would be better to shield away the wind than that frilly old scarf from the coffee shop.

On the dresser, thrown in among the assorted items, there was the most spectacular necklace that was strung out on a black metal chain with a huge raw chunk of amber.

I put it on, gently caressing it when it hung right on my neck.

I judged my new outfit in the mirror.

Now that looks like a witch. Sweet!

The old gal had taste after all. Funny, I had never seen her wear any of this stuff; she always had on oversized grandma muumuus whenever I had visited, even if that had only been a few times.

Other trinkets cluttered her dresser: rings, a couple of pairs of earrings, one of which I popped in to my earlobes right away, little dragons which dangled down, making them appear as if they were flying around my head, and then took the other clothes from the bed and stuffed them into the backpack.

It was just a few things, and it was not like Mira would be using them.

I went back out to the living room in search of bug removal...things.

This time, I studied the altar again a little more carefully. Surely there had to be something that could help.

That's when I saw the old leather book sitting on a shelf by itself, just under the altar. All kinds of symbols were carved into the front, although I only recognized the pentagram. I ran my fingers over the cover before sitting on the carpet with it on my lap. It flipped open totally by itself.

The pages were blank. No writing, just yellowed sheets of paper. This couldn't be right. Maybe I had the book upside down? I flicked through to the entire book. Nothing—just empty pages.

This was just stupid.

Shit. I slapped the book in frustration.

An odd sensation began, like a baby animal sucking on my fingertips.

I tried to pull my hands away from the book, except I couldn't move my hands—they were stuck.

I brought my hands together, clenching the book closed, and then saw why.

The leather binding had melted. No, that wasn't the right word, but the leather of the book was crawling up my fingers, swallowing my hands. I tried shaking the book, but it was fixed.

"Let me go!" Nothing happened with that either.

The leather looked like it had eaten all of my fingers. My thumbs were still free, but the fingers were glued in tight. There was no way this was coming off.

I felt that tightening in my chest and small beads of sweat forming on my forehead as I started to panic. What the Hell?

That's when I screamed.

Pins pushed against my skin. The needle felt fat, like the end of a pencil. On each finger, points were pressing down harder and harder.

The pain was excruciating. Spots appeared before my eyes, and I began to swoon a little. The pain reminded me of Master's summons, but my body held on. There was no passing out. Tears rolled down my cheeks, and blood trickled across the back of each hand.

But then the book whipped open on my lap, my fingers still attached and the pain in each digit growing intense.

I clenched my jaw as the book began to write out words and symbols on the very first page.

The symbols were strange and overlapped. They would appear and then disappear being replaced by new signs. I recognized none of them, but one word ran across the front page. I could read that word:

GRIMOIRE

The book itself was alive, pages flipping back and forth, writing ancient spells and incantations in red ink.

Blood-red ink.

My blood.

The pages welled up with pictures, words, and symbols emanating out from the center of the spine, until every single page held charts, tables, diagrams, and everything a witch would need to cast hundreds and hundreds of spells.

Tears rolled off my cheeks and blurred my eyesight by the time the book finished writing itself. Some dropped onto the book's pages, staining them, and making the fresh blood scatter as if splashing on a water-colour painting.

It took forever to finish. But as soon as the pages were full, the book spat my fingers back out.

The three vacant bitches hovered in the dining room. I could tell they were judging me for crying.

"Fuck off!" I screamed at them and threw the first thing my hand could find, which was a throw pillow. The pillow went right through Sis.

I wiped my face off with the sleeves of the ruffled blouse. Inspecting each of my fingers, I discovered holes in each, large enough to stick a toothpick into.

My hands throbbed. I felt a little light-headed after donating so much blood.

"Fucking thing." I kicked the book. Like what the fuck?

I knew what a grimoire was. It was a witch's book of spells. Why would Mira have kept this from me?

But despite the brutal introduction and the fact that Mira had never shown me the tome, a little voice inside my head told me it was exactly the place to look for help to heal Dati and get rid of the bugs inside of me.

I picked it up with one hand—I was never going touch the thing again with both hands—and I put it on my lap. There was a faint red tinge to it now. The book appeared burnt red.

"Not impressed," I scolded it.

Annoyed with the stupid thing, I opened up the book.

Beside me an opened mouth screamed. "Jesus fucking Christ!" That scared the Hell outta me. It was the first time any of them had made anything other than a mumble or gurgle. I glanced sideways, and Sis's face hung inches away from my ear.

I shook my head, ignoring them, thumbing through pages and pages. There was tons of crap in the book. I could have spent hours going through it and still not find anything useful.

Some of it wasn't even in English. Hell, most of it was scribbled in symbols. Besides, it's not like it had a table of contents. Or did it?

I fumbled my way past the grimoire page. It was a spell. Ha! And a good spell at that! "How to Make Him Love You" was the title.

"I just want to find something to heal those wounds!" I yelled at the book.

Pages rushed forward, falling still a moment later. The title simply said, "Staunching."

"Okay, um....Thank you?"

It was just a single page with a list of ingredients and some instructions.

Well, this had to count for something. Maybe this would work. I studied the list of ingredients and instructions:

➢ Shredded raw potato
➢ Cinnamon
➢ Sea Salt
➢ Vinegar
➢ Blood from dead flesh
➢ Fresh rain water

Stir together ingredients after the sun has set, churning counterclockwise for exactly nine minutes. All the items must be thoroughly mixed in that time.

In cheesecloth, take fistfuls of the matter and squeeze all fluid until mostly dry.

After washing the wound, pack it with the poultice and let sit for six hours. Remove, wash, and repeat two more times. Then leave the wound to heal on its own.

Well, that was fairly simple. I could get almost all of those things at the grocery store around the corner from Dati's apartment. I guessed the book was coming along with me. After all, it was written with my blood.

Should I really be taking these things? I guess Mira was supposed to have been alive, and she was supposed to have taught me all the witchy bits that Dati had told me about. And it wasn't really Dati's responsibility to get this all right. That should have been Mira's job. And clearly she wouldn't be doing it. I could see Mira's feet from the couch. They were sticking out from the hallway.

Another wave of shivers trickled down my spine.

This place was getting really creepy. I needed to grab stuff and go.

There was a little carved dragon statue sitting on the altar next to a wand with a blood-red crystal on the end. Powerful magic maybe? Which one should I take? I decided to take both even though the wand was long, almost too long to fit in the backpack. I had to stuff it in sideways, and even then, the zipper wouldn't completely close.

It was a cool wand, though, completely wrapped in copper wire, with swirls and whirls up one side of it. The handle was wrapped in black leather, and it had a strong smell coming from it, earthy and woodsy. I liked it.

And so, with a plan in mind and several items in tow and now dressed in a new retro outfit with a full backpack, I blew out the candles. No sense in letting the place burn to the ground.

I stood over Mira's body. It seemed wrong to leave her behind like this. I took the afghan off the back of the couch and covered her body with it. That made a surreal image. With the blanket draped over her old, decaying body, it looked like she was taking a nap in the middle of the hallway.

The final nap. And with that, I left the house.

The vacant zombies waited with me at the bus stop. I pulled the cowl up over my head so I couldn't see them.

God, I hope they don't start screaming on a regular basis.

The autumn night was cold. I was happy to crawl onto the stinky public transit vehicle. The new skirt and cloak billowed out from behind me as I moved down the center aisle to the last seat on the bus. No one even glanced at me, no one cared.

More importantly, no one knew who I was or what I was capable of doing.

That made me smile an evil little grin.

Trapped

Alyx

I peeled my eyelids open through a layer of gunk only to see a grey, dusky world like when you first wake up in the morning and the sun hasn't come up yet. With every blink, grit shifted further into my dry eyes. My hot breath clouded beneath my nose and smelled of rotting meat. Was I under the covers?

My thoughts felt thick and foggy, as if I had drunk far too much last night. I couldn't really think right. A dull thud like a hammer smacking my head accompanied every beat of my heart. This was one Hell of a hangover. I swear I could hear my blood moving, and it was far too loud.

My stomach lurched and heaved. Bile rose in throat, its bitter taste stuck in my mouth. My tongue had disappeared; in its place was a dry dishcloth. I attempted to lick my lips, but the rag inside my mouth only rasped over chapped lips that were cracked and sore.

My whole body begged to be scratched, like that summer I had accidentally rolled in poison ivy. I was sure I could feel the angry welts and pus-filled blisters covering me.

I tried to reach up to rub my face.

I barely moved an inch before my hand hit something hard and rough. I couldn't move, but then, I was so groggy and exhausted…

My next conscious thought was the sight of purple eyes, the irises morphing into purple butterflies that shimmered and danced in front of me. My body still itched all over, although my stomach had settled. Eyelids fluttered open. I lay still, staring directly in front of me. But there was nothing but dim shadows. I didn't feel quite as woozy, but I wanted to dig my nails into my skin; my flesh wanted to be rubbed and scratched.

The muscles in my legs were aching. They needed to move.

But I couldn't move. The covers around me were hard, not like bed sheets at all. I was trapped.

A stabbing pain erupted from my stomach, arching up my spine and exploding into my head. My brain was on fire.

Panic surged through me. My breath quickened as I broke out in a cold sweat. I opened my mouth and screamed, trying to bang my head against the barrier that kept me hostage.

The more I moved, the more intense the fire burned. My skin was melting; my hoarse shouts and pleas for help went unheard.

Eventually I tired. My throat burned from yelling, and my voice was nothing more than croaks. I gave up. My thoughts wandered, and I remembered standing in the threshold of the apartment I had been sent to by Silenus. The man with two-coloured eyes was there, warning me...

My knees had buckled under me, but as I collapsed, strong arms had grabbed me and held me close. My head spun, and the room swirled before me.

Gazing into two strangely coloured eyes, I could feel he was hot. Even through my clothes, his body heat soaked into my skin.

A deep, reassuring voice whispered, "I will look after you."

I awoke again. Still there was nothing but darkness.

Before, I had felt the need to itch, to dig my fingers into my flesh and scrape. Now a thousand knives stabbed at me. My hips ached all the way down to the bone, the pain throbbing and radiating to the base of my spine.

I tried to roll over to take the pressure off of my backside. Maybe lying on my side would alleviate the pain.

Except I still couldn't move. Something hard and rough was all around me, like I had been buried in dirt or rocks.

Something flipped in my brain. All I could feel was panic.

My stomach tightened into a knot.

Goosebumps erupted on the surface of my skin from fear. A cold dread burst into a wildfire of confusion. I wanted to run, to bust out of where I was, to be free.

I gathered all my strength and jerked my arm. It moved a fraction of an inch, followed by what I was sure was a long blade piercing through the flesh, travelling between the bones, pinning me. I let out a shriek, but the tomb in which I was covered muffled the sound. It angered me. I felt my eyeballs grow hot. I growled.

Breathe, Alyx, just breathe. Don't panic.

A lump formed in the back of my throat as the flames of fear consumed all thoughts in my head. Bolts of energy ran through my body as I strained all my limbs against the thing that held me hostage.

Swords ripped through each limb in retaliation to my motion, but I was still encased.

I sobbed. Tears ran down my cheeks.

Another dagger pierced my throat, punishing me for the sounds I made. Every time I moved, pain rippled through my entire body. Breathing became a laboured task, trying to catch enough air to fill my lungs, but it felt like a foot crushed my chest and kept me pinned down.

My breath quickened again.

Dati said he would look after me.

I inhaled as deeply as I could, over and over, slowly filling my chest with air.

I can survive this.

I just had to relax.

My stomach dropped, and the blades that inflicted the white-hot pain faded as the ground melted from under me. I fell through the darkness until layers of smoke—clear, white, wispy mist—swirled around me. Mist clung to my skin and covered me like soggy clothes. My toes touched the moist, cold ground.

A babbling brook gurgled through the glen, and small river rocks sparkled where the moonlight beamed its way through hundred-year-old trees with gnarled trunks and roots.

I sighed in relief.

I wasn't dead, or if I was, I had at least come to my glen—my safe place. This was calming. This was familiar. I immediately made my way over to my favourite rock. The flat surface was comfortable and gave me a wide view of the lush forest before me.

As I sat down, I noticed I was naked again.

I hated that. My thin body had always been a source of personal embarrassment.

But I also saw a little round opening in my gut, right below the ribcage. Torn flesh hung around the wound. The inside appeared black, leaking a thick substance that oozed and flowed, matting the hair on my belly. It didn't hurt, though. If anything, it was numb. I stuck my finger into the squishy hole; quickly it became covered in the viscous and foul-smelling liquid. I pulled it out immediately when something from inside pricked my finger.

Silvery spiny legs pushed out from inside of me.

The legs flailed a little and then scampered back like a spider retreating into its webbed tunnel.

I wasn't sure what I was supposed to do. Whatever was in me had to come out; I flicked my hands in disgust.

I glanced around the glen to make sure it really was my safe place.

The green was still green, the river still ran, the squirrel wasn't around, but that wasn't too unusual. He wasn't always around.

Did it seem darker than normal?

Ignoring the horrific sight of my stomach, I walked through the glen.

The trees were still grandiose: thick and tough and endlessly tall. My gaze followed their towering spires all the way up, past the canopy and towards the sky, but the sky seemed too close. It was black and shiny, sparkling like the inside of a geode.

Past the scarred and knotted trunks—ones that were so rough you could make faces out in the bark—was the same black, sparkly night sky.

As I peered through the trees, I spied a crystalline wall tucked behind the first layer of the forest. I reached out to touch it, cautious and uncertain. Finally feeling brave enough, I ran my hands over the surface. My fingers found scales... No, it was lumpier than scales. It felt like a scab.

I extended my hand with my fingers coursing over the wall's bumpy surface. I followed it and ended up walking in a circle.

I was completely domed in. Was this the protective circle I usually cast before I came to the safe place? Why hadn't I seen or noticed this before? And if I was truly encased, where was the moonlight coming from?

I retreated to my favourite rock, unsure of myself, my surroundings, or what I was even supposed to do next.

I fidgeted, uneasy and hyperaware of the dim forest. The glen was very quiet.

A sudden gust rustled the hair on my head. I shivered and hugged myself to retain warmth. I needed shelter.

But I was tired, *really* tired, and sleep became more important than feeling unsafe or the fact that I was trapped in a scab of a dome with a silver spider having taken up residence in my gut. I needed to lie down and sleep.

My droopy eyelids drifted to the bed of ferns. The leaf-littered floor felt dryer, and I laid myself down, the curve of the ground cradling my back.

It was comfy. I reached out and grabbed a few large fern leaves from the forest floor and used them as a makeshift cover, a blanket of sorts. I gripped one very tight in my hand and then slept.

Silenus sauntered up to the black crystalline dome and peered inwards with a fist clenched. His eyes twinkled violet and that same maniacal grin spread across his face. He knew the boy was in there. It pleased him.

As he unfurled his fist, a crushed monarch butterfly dropped from his hand. It landed on the forest floor by his scarred and chipped hoof.

Wishes, after all, have a cost.

Agreements

DATI

Alyx's cocoon reminded me of shifting sand dunes. Little mounds would bubble up and then contract in on itself. The crystals tinkled when the pod expanded. The process would have been mesmerizing, perhaps even interesting, if it had not been Alyx trapped inside.

I could not imagine what he went through mentally, being a hostage inside the pod. However, physically I was aware what the process entailed. Human flesh dissolves from the bones, and even the bones would shift and change, organs would rearrange themselves. Alyx was under construction. He would be reborn as a demon, one of my kin.

I promised myself repeatedly...to protect Alyx. Whatever life I had ripped away from him, whatever chance there might have been for a productive human existence, I had to do everything within my power to guarantee he would have as close to that dynamic of existence in his new form.

That was, of course, *if* he would have a new life. The corruption could just as easily wither his heart, trapping him inside the cocoon forever.

I couldn't think of that possibility. I just couldn't go there.

I had been perched beside Alyx's pod for hours. I needed to move.

Pushing myself up off the floor, mindful of my laceration, I wondered if my wounds were healing. I pulled up the fresh shirt, and as expected, the cut was clean and it wasn't bleeding anymore. The surrounding skin was still angry and red and tender to the touch.

Maybe some food would make me feel better.

"I won't be gone long," I mumbled, knowing he would never have heard me.

Loud snores rumbled from the spare room, reminding me of my other guest. Hemming's wound would have been three times what mine was. At least he rested.

I flicked on the kitchen light and grabbed the top pack of raw meat out of the fridge, tearing through the cellophane with a sharp fingernail. If I had been feeling better, the raw, bloody steak might have actually been enjoyable, but right now, it just seemed like another task I had to do.

I sank my teeth into the cold raw flesh and ripped off a piece. Blood from the steak dripped onto my chin. I wiped it away with the back of my hand. *Yuck.* Cold. I never did like it cold. A minute in the microwave would be enough to take the chill off.

I had just swallowed the last bite from one of the steaks in the packet when Jenae clattered through the front door, already yapping away.

"No way! You got the door fixed! Way better. Where are you?"

I was taking a large bite of the second slab when Jenae rounded the corner. The Shishi dogs immediately broke from their stone form to scamper at her heel. That really pissed me off; it had taken me the better part of seventy years to get those damn things trained, and within a day, she'd undone all of that work.

"Oh. My. God. Do you have any idea how disgusting that is?" She gawked at me with a wide mouth and an I-did-not-just-see-that expression.

"Do you mind? I have to eat too," I said, somewhat annoyed, and tore off another hunk with my teeth. Jenae really could be an intolerable brat.

"Go ahead, eat, but do you think you could cook it first?"

"I can't eat cooked flesh. It has to be raw." I ripped off another bite. *There! Have that.* "Warm and freshly torn off the body would be better. Do you know how long I had to search to find a butcher who would cut this off a live animal? I can't eat it if the flesh comes from a corpse," I added the last part just to be an ass and gross her out some more.

"Just please tell me that's a beef steak. And fine, do whatever you need to do. I think I might have something that could help you and Hemming get better!" Her eyes widened with excitement, and she grinned eagerly. Perhaps it was a maniacal smile. I was not entirely certain either way.

I had apprehensions that she would have found anything that would assist Hemming or me. That's when I noticed the new clothes and the new outfit and the very full backpack.

"Care to tell me how the rest of your trip went?"

"Yeah, okay, so she was dead, and she was decaying, which really made the entire house stink, and there was black mold everywhere. It was gross, so I lit some incense—actually a lot of incense—and then looked around."

She ran her hands down her sides to indicate that she had scavenged some clothes along the way.

"And then I found this book!" She unzipped her backpack and several things burst out, spilling onto the kitchen countertop.

She held out a very large and ornately carved leather book. The hair on the back of my neck stood straight on end and my hands began to morph into their black talons. I took a step back. I knew exactly what it was, and I didn't want it in my house.

"And look what it did!" She showed me little puncture wounds on the tips of her fingers, completely unaware of my reaction to her book. "It freakin' bit me and drank my blood. Sick. But the book was blank when I first picked it up. Once it drank my blood...ta-da!" She flipped through hundreds of pages that clearly now had writings and inscriptions. Hesitantly and from a short distance, I peered at her opened tome.

"We really need to find you someone who can teach you how to use *that*," I said. I didn't know much about grimoires, but I did know they were powerful witch instruments and not to be played with. I was quite sure Jenae wouldn't understand the subtle implications or consequences of any of the spells in that book. Magic, of any sort, had a cost, and the price was nonnegotiable and usually less than clear about the amount owed.

"And what about the clothes?" I asked. "Where did you get the money to buy them?"

"Ha! See, you think I stole them. I didn't. Well, not really. They were Mira's! Can you believe the old woman would have had clothes this cool! It's not like she's going to need them." She did a little turn, making the dress flare out as she spun. As much as I hated to admit it, the outfit was a Hell of a lot better than my tattered old sweats and T-shirt.

"I'm going to check in on the others," I said, backing out of the kitchen.

"Okay. Is it okay if I use some stuff here in the kitchen? I want to mix up this stuff like it says to in the book so I can help heal you guys." She appeared convinced that whatever she had found would work. I didn't want to tell her I was already healing up rather nicely.

"Yes, fine, just don't do anything crazy and make sure you clean up when you're done. Leave my kitchen in one piece." And with that, I left her banging around in the kitchen, doing whatever it was she needed to do. It would keep her occupied and out of my hair for a while.

I went down the hall to see Hemming. To my surprise, he was sitting up. He glanced from his cell phone as my presence hung in the doorway. His tired eyes were still deeply set in his head, but his handsome angular face was far more cognizant than it had been and his swarthy complexion was back.

"Hi. Can I come in?"

"Did you switch species? Do you require invitations to enter a room, Vampyre?" He bowed his head and arched an eyebrow, indicating his permission. Hemming's voice was deep, but it had a lilt to it.

I sat down on the end of the bed. "How are you doing?" I half expected a smart-ass response and was doubtful he would tell me the truth. I suppose it was the polite thing to say. Polite. That was funny. Since when were demons polite?

"I'll live, I think." He inspected the makeshift bandages, tugging at a loose end that flapped uselessly. "This is some first aid mastery. Did you do this?"

"Well, if I didn't do it, Jenae was going to. And I'm not convinced that would have been any better."

"Hmmm, yes, thanks. Who is the sorority sister with the bad dye job anyways? We didn't really get a lot of time to do the get-to-know-you parts."

"Well, if you're up for a talk," I said.

"I can't sleep anymore. Please, something to amuse me," he said, arching an inquisitive eyebrow.

"You remember the summons, and the...hmm...infection, for lack of a better term?"

"What? You think I could forget Master's latest rampage of terror, bloodletting, and mass destruction?" Hemming huffed.

"Jenae sat beside me."

"I remember seeing her in that pink fuzzy sweater." Hemming rolled his eyes.

"That was her. So out of place and seemingly innocent, and she smelled...*human*."

"Exactly! How odd."

"Master instructed me to care for her, so she came here. I scared the Hell out of her, she scared the Hell out of me with a spell, and the Shishi have decided she's better than I am."

"Ah, so she's a witch. Never did trust them, spooky bunch and unpredictable. They like the icky things." Hemming faked a gag, sticking out his tongue as if he was going to throw up.

"Yes, agreed. Anyway, Jenae managed to kill the neighbour as well. Haven't cleaned that mess up yet. From the look of the neighbour's apartment, though, there was a lot of pills and liquor. I think the neighbour was a bit of a mess and that might buy us some time before anyone comes looking for her." I glanced at Hemming to see if my comment had registered any reaction.

It had been the wrong thing to say; pills and liquor and the neighbour being a mess. But I got no acknowledgement out of Hemming for sticking my foot in my mouth. After all, Hemming too had once been an alcohol-soaked mess.

"Jenae has no recollection of what she's done. The minute the spell got too intense, she blacked out and everything else happened on autopilot," I continued on. Obviously my comment hadn't offended Hemming.

"Great. I'm bedridden in a house with an out-of-control witch and a D'Alae who acts like a Vampyre. Sounds like she needs to go back to her creator and learn a few things. This is fucked up, Dati." Hemming grimaced deeply as he rearranged his sitting position.

"When Jenae *woke up* as a witch, she found her creator dead. See, there's another odd thing. She's been surrounded by death and has killed more than one human in order to feed, and yet, she doesn't seem bothered by it. She shows no remorse, or guilt—nothing! She killed and ate her sister and mother too," I said, attempting to make sense of Jenae's scatterbrain psyche. "There's something just not quite right."

"Sociopathic? Or just plain dark like most of our ilk? Imagine that, Dati." Hemming's dry wit laced with sarcasm was meant to be funny. In reality, his statement was more than true.

"Maybe. Or dissociative. I don't know. I just don't get it. Either way, she is in the same boat we are in, with these bugs in us. How many do you have left in you?" I asked.

"I think three more. But I have to be honest, I'm not entirely sure. I passed out too during Master's meeting. What about you? How many you got left?" he said, and pointed to my midsection.

"Same, three more," I said, "and I'm not looking forward to the other three coming out. I'm quite certain that there's no way Jenae would survive this. First of all, she's not demonic. She's still human, just a witch. At least we heal fast."

"See, there you go again—being nice. If I didn't know any better, I'd swear you were turning human. You've gotten soft over the years."

Hemming shook his head at me, as if he had raised a finger and waved it at me, scolding my behaviour. "If she's a little crazy and can't control her magic, then so what if she explodes in the process?"

"Hemming, if she dies and doesn't create her brood of witches, what do you think Master is going to do to all of us?" The retribution would be epic. He'd kill the lot of us.

Hemming's upper lip quirked into a sneer.

"Hadn't thought that far ahead." Hemming dropped his head and shifted the blankets around him nervously, glancing at me from underneath his eyebrows. "But now that you mention 'creating your own little brood,' I'm afraid I'm going to have to ask: I need you to do something for me."

I peered at him, squinting, and then shrugged my shoulders. "What's the need?"

"Collect those pods of mine. I should be there playing mother hen to them. They will be ready within a couple of days." Hemming grimaced again. "I know it's a lot to ask, but do you think you could bring them here? Once they emerge, we'll leave, and I'll be out of your hair. But if I don't get to them before they are ready, I could lose them, and if that happens, then we're back in that same predicament with Master. If I can't present Master with a little herd of Shape Shifters, he will kill me, potentially all of us, or worse."

"A Master irate with one of us is a Master irate with all of us. Even if I didn't know you as I do, I'd still agree to help you. Tell me where they are."

"Thanks." Hemming seemed to relax, his body slouching slightly as if tense muscles were finally letting the stress wash away.

"But I need to know," I asked. "You know Master has that soul vial of mine hanging around his neck. There is no worse Hell for me—I'm living in Hell right now—but what does he have on you, Hemming? How are you bound to him? Why do any of us continue to put up with his barbaric treatment?" Hemming's relaxed slouch shifted as he became uncomfortable with my questions. He turned ever so slightly away from me, and his gaze moved to the foot of the bed.

As my train of thought continued, I pointed at Hemming's midsection. "And what the Hell were you thinking, going out somewhere in public knowing that this might happen? Where did you go and what did you do that made three guys attack you?"

Hemming, ashamed, turned his head and stared at the wall. Then he looked back at me with resignation. "We all have shadowy secrets, no? I've never told anyone."

"Then don't," I said.

"No, it's just that… I…well…there was this girl. You know, demon meets girl, demon loses girl…" Hemming picked up his cell. He tapped it a few times and then gave it to me. On the phone was a picture of a young male child. "This is my 'Hell'. Somehow, Master knows I have a son. He sends me pictures of him every now and then, just to make sure I stay engaged in his tasks. 'Dog with a bone,' if you will."

"Does your son…?" I started, but Hemming cut me off.

"My son knows nothing. He doesn't know his four-legged father, but I send his mother money. She's human, and all she knows is that I'm mixed up in things that may not be of a 'legal nature'. So to keep her and the child safe, I steer clear. But apparently I peed on too many fire hydrants between them and me. Master has never said anything to me. He just sends me pictures of him, through the mail, through my phone, even through my dreams. So I toe the line, because I'm afraid of what he might do if I don't. I don't want my son involved or knowing about any of this. It's bad enough that one of *your* kind might still find him and mark him." Hemming pulled the comforter up around him. I think it was an attempt to hide everything he had just exposed.

"How old is he?" I asked.

"Four." And that was all he said. In fact, Hemming's eyes became distant, and he picked imaginary lint off of the comforter that was wrapped around him.

"You know, Hemming, I'm the only D'Alae in the area. I would be able to pass on him, if I knew who he was. It's not like I haven't done that before. I could do it again," I said, thinking of Alyx. In the end, that hadn't worked out well.

"You'd do that?" Hemming said with a hint of surprise and hope.

"I could," I said. "There are enough children to mark that Master isn't going to know if I've missed one."

"I would be indebted to you, man. Seriously." I had never seen Hemming so genuine before. I'd known Hemming for fifty-odd years, and that was through Master's tasks. So, Hemming was only revealing the current ties that bound him to Master. There had to be more, but for now, Hemming had shared this, and for now, that was enough.

"Let's forget about who owes whom and just agree we're on the same team?" I said. "But that's not going to prevent anything happening to him if Master already knows about him. We may have to get creative to spare your child." I glanced over my shoulder towards my bedroom where Alyx lay entombed.

"Alyx? He's your son?" Hemming inquired.

"No! Seven Hells, no. But at one point, I had made a promise... All I'm saying, Hemming, is that we can try to keep your son safe. But Master is vicious."

"Yeah, you don't really need to remind me of that," he said, indicating his wrist and midsection.

"So then we'll do what we can. But right now, there are some more immediate concerns. For instance, where are those pods of yours, and how did you manage to have three guys come at you at once? How did that happen?"

Hemming explained. "I got instructions on that too." Holding out his phone again, he showed me three pictures that had been sent to him. "Directly after the summons, this was sent to me. And stuffed into my coat pocket was this old T-shirt. So I went out on the hunt."

"And by hunt, you mean...?"

"Yeah, wolf form—cold wet nose and all. I found the one that belonged to the shirt and then corralled him and his friends into a back alley, and the minute we got close enough to each other, the bugs burst forth and did their job."

"So, where are they, Hemming?"

Hemming gave me a good description of where the event occurred. Hopefully, no one had found them. Hemming had tried to camouflage the pods as best he could, but same rules applied. Touching a pod while the transformation took place was never a good idea.

"I'll go soon. It'll be better if I do this when it's completely dark. That should be in a couple of hours or less, but I will, Hemming, I'll get them back here for you. We'll get us both through this, and your son." I put a hand on his shoulder. Hemming studied me with an I'm-not-sure-I-can-trust-you expression, and rightfully so; trust was not something you did between creatures of the dark. Instead he nodded ever so slightly.

"Alright, rest. I'll be back soon." As I turned to leave, another thought crossed my mind.

"Oh, and don't let Jenae do anything to you. At least not until I get back?"

Hemming let out a little laugh at that. "Agreed," he said. "So, you and Alyx?" He cocked an eyebrow.

"That's complicated," I said, and left it at that.

"It always is, Dati. It always is."

I left his temporary recovery room and went down the hall to my room where Alyx lay trapped.

I leaned over the pod as the crystals sounded ominous little chimes. "Alyx, I have to go out for just a little while, but I will be right back. I promise." I wanted to place my hand on the tomb, an act of reassurance, and actually reached out my hand to do so, but I stopped short. No contact; I couldn't touch him.

I backed away, feeling hopeless.

Bringing home Hemming's pods wasn't going to be easy, and I wouldn't be able to touch them either, so I needed something to keep the surface away from my skin, and the best I could come up with was several large bed sheets. So I grabbed the few I had and then went out to the kitchen. I needed my backpack, and that meant I had to take it back from Jenae.

I rounded the corner into the kitchen. Jenae had made a complete and total mess of the place. Bowls with white pasty thick gruel were scattered around the kitchen counter. She was busy, slopping the sludge into a towel and ringing it out over the sink.

If nothing else, she was determined. I'll give her that. But the smell from her 'cooking' was horrific.

"Well, you've made yourself at home. Just remember you need to clean this all up too," I said, with a bit of discontent and while examining one of the closer bowls. The mixture really did appear like lumpy gruel. I put my finger out to touch it.

"I wouldn't maybe do that," Jenae said.

"Why?" I pulled my hand back to my side quickly.

"I don't know. That batch turned out weird. Look what happens," she said, and then put her towel down on the counter. White liquid leaked out from the towel, ran across the counter, and dripped onto the floor. I sighed. Such a mess.

Jenae leaned over the bowl, examining it, and then reached her fingers out to it. And as soon as her hand was over top of the bowl, strings of the liquid started reaching towards her hand.

"That's not supposed to happen."

"Do not under any circumstances put any of this on anyone. That means Hemming or yourself. Do you understand me? I do not need to be cleaning up any more messes, or dead bodies," I said with as much authority as I could muster. Jenae, being the typical teenager, would most likely do the exact opposite of what I told her. "I mean it. Nothing until I get back."

"Yeah, okay." She put her hand back over the bowl, watching the strings form again. "I don't know why this isn't working. I'm doing everything it says in the book!"

I shook my head and walked over to the cupboard, pulled out a box of garbage bags, taking several out. My backpack sat abandoned on the kitchen counter. "I need this tonight, so if you don't mind?"

"Um, yeah, sure, just dump it out on the table."

As I went over to the dining room table the Shishi watched me carefully. I pulled the items out of her bag and placed them on the surface where I was sure they would remain for quite some time. Jenae wouldn't be putting them away, and that left another mess. Her presence in the house was getting on my nerves.

I shoved the garbage bags and the bed sheets into the backpack, and then walked towards the front door. It would be another hour or so until sundown, but I had one more task I needed to do before I could go retrieve Hemming's pods. I had to get rid of the body down the hall.

Rot

It took me far longer than I had anticipated, wrapping up the dead neighbour and hauling her out of the building without any witnesses. I travelled several blocks away from my home with nary a deep breath. The strenuous activity didn't rip open any of my wounds. That could only mean they were healing.

I ended up in a cavernous alleyway, and at the very end of it stood a dumpster that was already fairly full. So I pitched the savagely battered, pill-and-liquor-soaked addict into the bin. Good riddance.

I stood up straight and flexed my muscles, careful not to stretch out the still-bound wing. My back popped. It felt good. Actually, it felt better than good. There was a certain sense of relief that came with knowing that, even though this woman's body would eventually be found, it would take the police a long time to trace this to the same high-rise I lived in.

I made sure that identification of the corpse would be difficult. The small bag in my hoodie pouch contained the ends of her fingers—which meant no fingerprints—and the woman's face and teeth. As gruesome as that was, identifying the body would be almost impossible. All the police would have was a sack of meat.

Hemming's directions led me to a seedy area of downtown, and as promised, there was the river in front of me. I reached into my stuffed pocket, grabbing the gruesome contents of my hoodie, and unceremoniously pitched the squishy human bits into the waterway, but not before I had placed a good-sized rock into the bag so the damn thing would sink.

After a scramble up the riverbank and a quick jaunt down a side street, I came across the bar Hemming had described.

It was a shameful joint. The clientele that walked in and out of Mila's Pub made me think twice about ever going in. Combinations of meth addicts and prostitutes, gang bangers and miscreants ensured a lively group that could best be described as the dregs of urban city life: a group of people who had made a lifetime of bad decisions.

But, as promised, around the corner from Mila's was the empty parking lot that Hemming had described, flanked by an immense dilapidated building.

I cut across the parking lot to the warehouse. The first-floor windows were all boarded up as if the entire base was wrapped in a big bandage.

Behind the ramshackle monstrosity, I saw stacks of old forgotten wooden pallets. Another large dumpster was also tucked into the back, and in the corner, right beside the bin were three dark shapes.

I had only ever seen pods from my own kind. The whole transmutation process was a relatively secretive matter amongst the various demon ilk. I wasn't sure what to expect.

The cocoons were considerably different than Alyx's pod. These were amorphous—jet black and velvety. Round, sort of. They moved too. A blob bubbled up, distorting the surface, and then it disappeared. A bulge appeared on the other side of the sphere, and then the pod was round again. Whatever was in them was pushing and pulling the walls from the inside. Luckily, there were no filaments or strands anchoring them to their spot, which would make the task of moving them a whole lot easier.

"No skin contact," I reminded myself before slipping on some gloves and pulling out the bed sheets from my backpack, spreading out one of them in front of the first pod.

Hushed whines came from the pods as I knelt down and touched one with my gloved hand. A skeletal hand pressed against the surface from the inside, and a garbled moan erupted from the pod. The noise deteriorated into wet rasps and a click of teeth.

The hair on the back of my neck rose as I listened to the unearthly noises emanating from what was inside.

I placed my covered hands on the pod and attempted to roll it towards the center of the sheet. It barely moved. It was also far heavier than I thought it would be. I pulled on it again, with a little more force, but I was so unsure how much would be too much.

Again there was a push from inside the pod, almost resistance, and the noises were increasing. This was going to take all night.

I pulled a third time, hard.

A rip, like the sound of tearing flesh, halted my actions.

I stopped and inspected the pod carefully. Running my fingers over the top of the cocoon, I couldn't spot any tears. With my feet dug in, and on my knees, I gave the pod another good, hard tug forward.

The whole front ripped open.

Black coagulated blood flowed out in a torrent, over my arms, and pants, spilling out onto the cement. The half-formed demon Shape-Shifting body floundered and panicked out of the pod, scampering on top of me.

The corpse was covered as if it had been dipped in tar, except it was more bone than anything else. Long strips of flesh hung off of the skeleton. There were some patches of sinew and muscle, but mostly it was bare.

The scalp had bits of hair poking out in decayed tufts; black ooze matted the hair to the thing's back. Its face was missing. There were no eyes in the socket, and the inky tongue was swollen with rot.

With the skull only inches from my face, it started to shift. Bones rearranged themselves, flattening out and stretching. Its jaw lengthened and teeth fell out as the tongue rolled. In the creature's half decayed state, it reached out a bony arm towards my face and tried grabbing for me. The noises that had been coming out of the pod before were now hissing from the gaping maw, and halfway through its scream of torment, its jaw fell off.

This was a morph that had not taken. The body still alive inside had rejected the demonic blood, or vice versa, and the human form was still in agony over being ripped apart and half rebuilt.

I grabbed its head and squished the skull, crushing it. Bits of bone fragments and grey matter exploded in all directions. What was left of the body flopped to the ground, dead.

The odour was overwhelming. Mixed remnants of decayed human flesh and shifting demon bits clung to me like lumpy porridge. My stomach churned. I turned my head and vomited repeatedly.

The viscous liquid from the pod was sticky. I opened and closed my fingers as the liquid formed strings between them. The fluid had soaked into my flesh, reeking of death, and now staining the crevasses of my hands and colouring black lines deep under my fingernails. Evil just does that; it wedges its way in.

At least the creature no longer suffered. I couldn't imagine how much pain and torment it had gone through. I immediately thought of Alyx and swallowed hard.

Hemming would owe me big for this.

Hemming...how would I tell Hemming that one of the pods didn't take? What was Master going to do with Hemming? What would Master do with all of us?

My mind raced through several scenarios. All of them had Master torturing us in bloody ways. An uneasy feeling gnawed away at my stomach.

I grimaced at the other two pods. I really hoped they remained intact.

Wiping myself off with the bed sheet, I approached the next pod. I attempted a very gentle roll forward. Again, I felt something inside press up against my own hands. I braced myself before rotating it towards me.

Within a few minutes of very careful manoeuvring, the black velvety case sat in the middle of the sheet. I gathered up the ends and created a sack.

Round two began. Same trial, just as difficult, but eventually I had two satchels of velvety, ebony evil. There was no way I was going to lug two of these creatures across the city with a wounded midsection, and I couldn't very well make the trip twice.

I had to borrow a car, sort of. I moved some pallets around and slid the wrapped-up pods in behind, concealing them with crates.

I hung out across the street from Mila's, concealing myself in the doorway of a closed-up business and waited for patrons to leave. The little alcove smelled heavily of urine.

I waited and waited. A few people had stumbled out of the bar and staggered down the street, some of them accompanied with entertainment for the night, but none of them wandered over to the line of parked cars.

To my surprise, another dark creature walked out of the building. The eyes are the tell: they reflect light differently than humans. This demon had a human with him. I had no idea what kind of demon it was, or why the human was a tag-along, but regardless of the situation, it wouldn't end well...for the human.

Eventually, a patron came out, one who'd had one too many, and stumbled over to the parked cars. That's when I moved in, quickly.

"Hey, buddy, you can't drive," I said.

"Fuck off, asshole," he slurred. Okay. Fine. He wanted to be difficult. I could be much more difficult.

He fumbled with his set of car keys. He stopped, wrinkled up his face, and then said, "Jesus, man, you fuckin' stink."

I wound up and landed one swift punch to the drunk's head, just above the ear. He fell to the pavement. The keys clattered as they tumbled under the car.

I glanced around. No one was within sight. Perfect. I bent over, fished the keys out from their landing spot, picked the drunk up, and stuffed him into the passenger side.

Within minutes, I had loaded the pods in the trunk and was driving home.

I couldn't stand the smell of myself. I was tired and wounds all over my body were screaming out for rest. Hopefully it would come soon. I turned the corner, and the drunk rolled and smacked his head against the passenger-side window. It made a hollow sound.

Pulling into the back of the high-rise, I parked the car beside the back-door entrance, which I had left propped open just for me.

I turned the car off and then pulled the interior lever to pop the trunk of the car. I threw the keys at the drunk, not really caring too much about him, his recovery, or if he even found his car keys when he finally did wake up.

With great care, I hauled the pods into the condo and gently set them down in the front entrance of my apartment. Hemming walked out from the kitchen, his face whitening as his gaze darted from one pod to the other.

"Please, no. Where's the third, Dati? What happened? Where is the third pod?" His voice wavered. He had a wild look of panic on his face.

"Hemming, I'm sorry. I really am. I moved it, and it split open."

"No..." He staggered back, clutching his bandaged wound. He shouldn't have even been up and walking around. "No," he said again. "You should have been more careful." He spoke curtly. The colour in his irises flickered, sparks of amber flared. "You should have been more careful!"

"Hemming, it wasn't my fault," I started before Hemming dropped to his knees.

"He'll go after him. I know it. He'll go after him, and I'll lose him to all this." He slammed a fist into the floor. Tears ran down his face.

Jenae hooked a brow up in confusion. As usual, she was incapable of understanding.

"Hemming, listen to me. The pod didn't take. It was rotting on the inside. Can't you smell it on me? It wasn't my fault, Hemming."

He glared at me, golden yellow eyes flamed violently. "Does it matter?" he growled. "There's now one missing. What am I going to do? He'll go after my son, Dati! My son!"

I needed to diffuse this situation, quickly. I had already started to back up, giving Hemming some space, and I didn't want to say another word. If Hemming didn't rein in the emotions, he was going to shift.

Too late.

As if on cue, a deep guttural sound rumbled from within Hemming's chest. His glowering gaze sized up Jenae and me.

His bones snapped and popped as Hemming howled in pain. His body shifted into inhuman shapes, making his clothes rip and fall off. The pink of Hemming's skin darkened, turning a sickly grey. Hair sprouted, forming small patches of dense fur. His bare feet elongated, and toenails thickened into giant claws. His hands contracted and shook as claws burst out of the first knuckle. Blood dripped from his wounds.

"Jenae, get behind me, now," I said quietly. The girl's attention was fixed on Hemming, watching him change. I grabbed her arm and pulled her behind me.

Hemming jerked his head back. His skull flattened, his ears grew furry and pointed, and the muzzle pushed forward. The noise of the bones reshaping disturbed me, despite the fact I had seen this before. Human teeth fell out of Hemming's mouth, and in their place, sharp fangs ripped through his exposed blood-red gums.

Hemming wasn't there anymore. In his place stood a demon wolf.

The wolf was terrifying.

Saliva oozed out in strings from between the teeth and pooled onto the condo floor. It growled at the two of us and crept its way forward.

I backed up and edged off to the side, trying to put myself and Jenae into the kitchen area, where we might have a chance to get down the hallway and into a bedroom. A closed door wouldn't keep Hemming's wolf out for long, but it would buy us some time. I grabbed Jenae who, despite my stink, was directly behind me and standing very, very close. I shuffled slowly, one step at a time.

The wolf watched us and took a few more steps forward. His yellow eyes seemed to fill the room, along with the snarls and guttural growls.

And then the wolf slinked its way towards the two pods that lay just within the apartment's entranceway.

We kept our movements slow and steady towards the kitchen.

Hemming the wolf sniffed the pods, glanced back at us, and then swung its head towards the closed door. It uttered a low growl that reverberated throughout the room.

From behind me, a wide-eyed and unbelievably quiet Jenae finally broke her silence and whispered, "Dati, I think the dog wants out."

She was right. The demon wolf pawed at the door a couple of times, leaving long claw marks on it.

I cautiously made my way over to the door. I was stupid to put myself so close to the wolf, but I believed Jenae was right. Hemming wanted out, and before the two of us ended up shredded by wolf teeth, I thought it best to give the dog what it wanted.

I slid my hand over to the doorknob and slowly turned, releasing the locking mechanism and allowing the door to open a crack.

The wolf barked at me. Its lips curled back, exposing its teeth. I edged the door open a little more.

Without warning, the wolf lunged at me, knocking me down. The weight of the creature hitting me was like I'd been hit with a sledgehammer.

Jenae screamed. The wolf's claws pierced the skin on each of my shoulders, and its jaws snapped inches away from my face. Drool splattered as the low throaty rumble continued.

It backed off of me, then sauntered its way out the open door and disappeared down the hallway.

"What do we do now?" Jenae whispered.

"We don't move until we are sure he is gone," I whispered back.

"Then what?"

"We wait for Hemming, not the wolf, to come back."

We waited for several minutes, listening carefully for any indication that the wolf was in the hallway, waiting for us. But there was nothing: no movement, no wolf growl, no snarling, no yellow eyes.

Hemming had gone.

Jenae breathed a deep breath. "Jesus fuckin' Christ!" She clutched her ruffled shirt in her tiny hands.

She spun round and glared at me. "And oh my god, you stink!"

Release

J ENAE

"I can't do this," I said, standing behind Dati after hours of waiting for something, anything to happen to the pods that were scattered around the apartment. Hemming's hairy shells were totally creeping me out with all their scratching, moaning, and whining.

"Can't do what?" Dati's gaze stayed fixed on his cocoon.

"I can't sit here any longer and just wait. It's been two days. I'm bored out of my mind." I crossed my arms.

I had no television, and I had read my grimoire cover to cover more than once—well, read what I could. So much of it was in other languages.

Hemming was still playing hooky, so of course I ended up egg-sitting. I had no idea when his velvety cocoons were going to split open, but if one of them so much as cracked even a smidgen, I was done, gone—out. There was no way I'd stick around to watch another Shape-Shifting mess. Gross.

The zombie bitches floated around Dati and hovered near the cocoon. The dead neighbour was staring Dati directly in his face. Dati didn't flinch a bit.

They were now whispering things to me, things I was sure were other people's thoughts. As they circled Dati and the cocoon they said together in quiet hushes; *"He wants him. He needs him. He only thinks of him."*

Their voices felt like tiny mouse paws running across my skin: dry, scratchy, and barely there.

Dati seemed completely obsessed with Alyx. Obsessed, I wondered, or in love? Could a demon love?

"What are you even doing?" I flung my arms up into the air in frustration.

"Watching," Dati finally said, not breaking his gaze from the pod. I thought he was peering through the black crystals, trying to see what happened on the inside.

"What's to watch? It hasn't moved or grown or done anything since it formed!"

Dati said nothing. He just stared at Alyx.

"Ugh, you're impossible. I have to go out. I can't be here anymore."

"Do not get into trouble," Dati replied without moving or glancing in my direction.

Maybe I would leave and just never come back.

"Fine." I spun around and left him alone with Alyx.

"Fine," Dati said.

But it wasn't fine.

And I was sure nothing would be fine ever again.

I filled the borrowed backpack with the grimoire and other items from Mirabelle's closet, including the little dragon statue, the wand, a ring, and the necklace with the big chunk of darkened amber. If I wasn't coming back, there was no way in Hell I was going to leave all this cool stuff just lying around Dati's apartment.

I caressed the stone and decided that it would be better hanging around my neck, not stuffed away. It was rough and raw, sort of burnt orange in colour until the light hit it, then it would glow an ominous yellow. The wire wrapping around it had spirals and other shapes that reminded me of the runes I had seen in the grimoire. I recognized the symbol in the center of the stone. It meant fire.

"*Do this, don't do that...*" I muttered to myself while shoving a worn but soft leather jacket into the knapsack. It was getting pretty full.

The whole situation at Dati's was awkward. I felt like I constantly intruded, as if I was walking in on Dati and Alyx *in the middle of something.*

"I can't believe he's even letting me leave. Probably doesn't care about me anyways. Nobody else does. Why should he?" I zippered up the sack and slung it over my shoulder.

I stopped and peered around the scarred and blackened apartment. Damage I had done.

I sort of felt bad for wrecking the place. Dati could have retaliated, but he hadn't. He could have ripped me apart if he had done it quickly enough. But Dati had never laid a single hand on me—unlike all the other adults: Sis, Mom, and the never-ending stream of Mom's boyfriends—they had all smacked me around or done worse things.

The backpack was heavy. I let it slide off my arm and onto the couch.

I took out several items of clothes to lighten the load and left them in a pile on the living room floor.

"I'll come get them later if I find somewhere else to stay."

I wanted to go back to school. Actually, I wanted to go to my locker and retrieve my iPod that had all my music on it. Dati had warned me—again more orders—to stay as far away from other people as possible.

I left the apartment in more borrowed clothes from dead Mirabelle's closet. I liked them. Most of the items were black, some trimmed in lace, and the whole collection was disturbingly pretty. The bodices were tight, and I liked the feeling of being strapped in. It made me feel secure, like having the Shishi constantly guarding me. They were just so damn cute, despite the slobber that drooled out from between their rows of sharp fangs. As soon as I walked to the front door, they wanted to follow me out.

I had to promise them more treats when I returned.

As the bus drove away, students scattered all around, most loitering around the doors of my old school.

The smokers were hanging about the fire hydrant, which was off of school grounds.

"Well, look who decided to finally come to school? It's shit-face," a female voice said from the group of smokers.

I closed my eyes and gritted my teeth.

It was Meaghan, a bully who had made my existence at school a living Hell.

She had arrived at my school in grade four. Isa, Lori, and I had always hung out together, and we were excited to see someone new. But within days, Meaghan had turned both Isa and Lori against me. The three of them were tight from that day forward and not far from each other. I was never part of their group, and neither was anyone else.

Meaghan had force-fed me dog shit in grade six—hence the nickname. All of them publicly humiliated me on the playground in grade eight by ripping the front of my shirt off, exposing my newly purchased training bra. Meaghan had snatched off my bra too, exposing my rather small breasts to the entire school.

Meaghan's torment was a daily routine. I had been tortured, slapped, beaten up, and humiliated.

Meaghan had no idea how much I had changed.

The taunt from Meaghan and her posse fueled a fire in my chest. For once, I was actually angry at them, instead of terrified of them. The thought of my grimoire, safely tucked away in my backpack, helped me conjure up evil possibilities. I could finally ruin Meaghan forever if I wanted, and *oh my god* was that tempting.

The trio of dead women silently huddled in close to me. Their vacant expressions changed as they focused their attention on Meaghan. Their mouths moved as they whispered more decaying words of poison into my ears. *"Kill her. Eat her. Destroy her."*

"Fuck off, Meaghan," I said quietly, unsure whether she could hear or not.

I turned and started to walk away from Meaghan, Isa, and Lori. The last two sported the same haircut and similar outfits to their leader.

My locker was closer to the rear of the school, a long walk across a half-empty parking lot. Scared that Meaghan might have actually heard me, I could feel a thin layer of sweat begin to bead across my back.

I wanted to distance myself from this bitch, get my stuff, and then get away from the school.

My hands shook as Meaghan gasped. "Did you just hear that? Did she really just tell me to fuck off?"

Oh Christ, she heard me.

I continued towards the parking lot. Not quite in a run, but it was definitely a quickened walk.

My heart beat loudly in my chest.

"Kill her, eat her, destroy her," the zombie chorus repeated over and over.

I could feel the words in the grimoire running over my tongue and slipping out my lips. Murmurs of such devilish words started a swell of power in my chest.

Which words, which symbols, how can I turn this around?

Should I give into temptation?

I glanced behind me.

Meaghan and crew were catching up. They were coming up behind me in a fast trot. There was no way Meaghan was going to be told to fuck off and let it go without a fight.

She reached out her hand, caught the edge of my Victorian lace collar, and pulled me quickly around, then pushed me to the ground.

I hit the grass hard, scraping my knees.

The fall pissed me off. My cheeks flushed hot with embarrassment and anger.

Everything Meaghan did was to piss me off. Anger and hate coursed through me as I spat, "You shouldn't have done that."

Meaghan laughed hysterically. Her hand flew towards me fast, slapping me across my face.

I didn't flinch.

"And what the Hell are you going to do about it, shit-face?"

I wasn't exactly sure which happened first.

I could feel the rock around my neck start to pulse. It was warm.

Licks of heat ran across my chest.

Then I felt the sharp spines of one of the parasitic minions inside my belly start to poke through my skin.

Oh no, no way in Hell.

There was no way I would let this bitch be my first morph. I wasn't going to transform Meaghan and have to be responsible for her, not a chance in Hell.

So I did the only thing I could think of.

I closed my eyes, let my mind go completely blank, just as it had said in the grimoire.

Raising my right hand, I drew the symbol for fire in Meaghan's direction.

"Ustrina."

As I said the word, I imagined Meaghan engulfed in a large ball of fire, melting, skin falling off the bones, eyes bursting from heat.

The copper wire that formed the fire symbol on the amber stone hanging around my neck glowed red hot.

Meaghan and her two friends stared at each other and started to laugh, a lot.

What is going on? Why isn't this working?

Another sharp pain in my gut made me grab my stomach and double over.

No, no, this can't be happening, not like this.

I gathered all the rage inside of me, the heat from my cheeks and all the years of feeling belittled and humiliated.

"Ustrina!"

The word fell out of me, but I didn't recognize my own voice. It had changed. It sounded deeper, more confident, and the word felt like it filled the air between us.

Fire erupted from the stone around my neck and wrapped around my waist.

The sharp spines of the minions retreated.

The dead bitches chanted in unison, *"Ustrina, ustrina, ustrina...."*

Meaghan's shirt edge burst into flames.

Meaghan stopped laughing.

She patted the little flames, trying to put them out. Her two friends frantically tried to help.

None of them were paying attention to me, but I wasn't completely there anymore. It took me a moment to realize I no longer stood on the grass.

I hovered an inch off the ground, and my hair billowed out behind me. My vision blurred as if I looked at the world through old warped glass. My lips kept forming the word against my will, and the voice coming out of me, which I didn't recognize, kept repeating "Ustrina."

Flames erupted everywhere. Fire spun in circles in the grass. On the hood of one of the nearby cars, heat melted and singed the paint. The ends of Meaghan's hair curled and disappeared in the heat. The air around us became unbearably hot, and crackling sounds popped like dry wood spitting sparks from a campfire.

Isa and Lori, unable to stand the heat, backed away and watched me as I hovered above the ground. They stood there for about half a second and then fled, terrified, running at a full pace towards the school.

The edge of my vision blackened. I was about to pass out again.

Fire burned intensely across the parking lot. Everywhere I could see there were scorch marks.

Meaghan shrieked like a little girl. She sunk to her knees on the grass.

I floated over towards her, bent over, and leered into Meaghan's eyes, which were locked on me in terror.

The last thing I remember was pointing directly at Meaghan's face, and saying, "Ustrina."

Then everything went black.

I floated over the burnt and smoking body. The fires around me all at once burned out as I punched a fist through the smoldering corpse's chest.

I was so hungry.

Meaghan's singed and smoldering form appeared suddenly to join the dead chorus. Her face was pasty and vacant just like the others.

Death Date

Dati

The door slammed, causing the apartment to shudder. I glanced at the clock and realized only a couple of hours had gone by. Sounded like Jenae had returned from wherever she had gone.

She had been right. Nothing was happening, and I was starting to have doubts that Alyx would ever emerge.

I left Alyx's cocoon and crashed into Jenae, who was running down the hallway towards me. Scorch marks were smudged all over her, and she smelled like singed hair.

"What the Hell happened to you?"

"Nothing!" she screamed at me, tears welling up in her eyes. Before I could stop her, she had wrapped herself around me and sobbed uncontrollably.

I had no idea what to do.

I held my hands outwards, a little revolted at the uninvited human contact. "Ah, okay, Jenae, what's going on?"

"I went back to school to get stuff from my locker, but instead I ended up setting Meaghan on fire, and I think I ate her, and the zombie bitches made me do it, and now she's one of them. I hate this! I hate her! I don't want her following me around like the others."

Just as I was about to ask for clarification, which I already knew would be the wrong thing to do, the front door of the apartment swung open with a bang. Somebody was walking into the condo.

"What the Hell now?" I peeled Jenae's arms off of my midsection. She stood there, slump-shouldered in front of me, obviously very upset. I had to move her off to one side so that I could squeeze past her.

As I entered the living room, I was surprised to see the Kasadya demon from the summoning in my house, where he had just deposited, rather roughly, an unconscious Hemming. Hemming was filthy and naked.

"I brought him here as I believe he belongs to you?" the Watcher said with a crooked eyebrow.

The Watcher demon's head dropped, and the arched brow shifted to a furrowed stare. "And we are all about to die."

"What are you doing in my apartment? And where did you find him?" I said, irritated.

The Kasadya inspected me with a long uncomfortable stare.

It felt like his gaze could burrow holes into my brain. He shifted his head to one side as he spoke at me. "I can see you do not understand. Yes, clearly you are confused; you are ignorant. Everything I see shows us all, most of us, perhaps just us here now, dead within a week, unless we change what is happening."

"One week?"

It was almost impossible to comprehend a Kasadya. Their clairvoyance gave them the ability to see everything around them in timelines, possibilities. They spoke of the here-and-now but also the what-could-be.

Deciphering their speech was a chore, like trying to sleuth out the Sphinx's riddles.

The Kasadya flittered closer to me. His black tailored shirt was so tight I could count each one of his ribs. The silk tie remained perfectly still as he moved, the tie's tail disappeared behind a black crushed-velvet vest. The demon's movements were ethereal as he moved without a sound towards me.

"Yes, there are more—more than just us. Several, in fact, *a horde*. A band who are also infected. The Master's plan is not what you believe it to be. And your—" The Kasadya paused, then shifted his head to the other side. "Your obsession—the one who is here... no, he is not here, not yet. He is the cause. Others will need him. He will need others. He is not complete—and you will lose him. He will destroy everything, including you. But what is certain is that we all die within the week unless we institute changes. These must be extracted," he said, pointing at his gut with long bony fingers.

Hemming made some strange half-human noises.

"What did you do to him?"

"I did nothing, and everything. I watched. He fed—devoured the human in every instance I watched. I watched some more. He shifted to human and then fell to the ground and slept."

"Wait, Hemming fed? On what? What did he eat?" I asked with growing alarm.

"A human male, adult." The statement was matter-of-fact. It had no emotion attached to it.

"Oh, Hemming." My stomach sank with disappointment and regret, knowing Hemming would berate himself for the wolf's actions.

Hemming's eyelids fluttered, but he was still unconscious.

I grabbed the Watcher by his overly fancy and tightly fitted outfit and pulled him in close. The muscles in his chest stiffened as I spoke. "You will say nothing to him about that, or I will kill you here and now." I stared at Jenae. "And that, young lady, goes for you too. Nothing. You will say nothing to him about what you just heard."

Jenae's eyes were large and round, still full of tears, mascara running down her cheeks. She nodded.

Hemming would never take another human life unless forced into doing so. It just wasn't something he would have done. But then, anyone under Master's control did things they wouldn't have normally. We did them to survive.

Hemming had always gone to extra lengths to ensure that his food was always four-legged, and never another human. The thought of cannibalization would have destroyed him or sent him out drinking again. I needed Hemming to concentrate on being present, sober, and capable when his pods hatched. I would have enough to do once Alyx emerged; I couldn't risk having Hemming out on a bender.

I released the Watcher. His gaze darted back and forth, determining which outcome would be the best of all the possible timelines.

Hemming groaned loudly. "What the Hell..." he said in a shaky voice, and his eyelids slowly peeled open.

"Dati? Oh man, am I in your poorly decorated apartment?" Hemming's eyes focused and looked around at the marred walls. "I'm naked again, aren't I? Dammit." He hunched over, attempting to hide himself and spotted the Watcher demon. "Who's the human-sized voodoo doll?"

"Just take it easy. Looks like you've had a rough couple of days," I said. "Jenae, go get him a blanket."

She stared at me, dazed and unmoving.

"Now, please," I said with emphasis. She disappeared down the hall.

Hemming grabbed one of the cushions from the back of the couch to cover his midsection. He sat upright, one hand holding his head.

I turned to the Kasadya. "What do you see?"

"Death." The word fell from his lips with gravity. The demon's eyes were glassy. His head tilted as his gaze narrowed, squinting at something no one else in the room saw. I assumed he watched another timeline play out.

"Specifics please?" I growled. I was starting to lose my cool.

The Watcher eyed me suspiciously, weighing his options, and cautiously continued. "I don't know what else I can—or *should*—have said that will make any *difference.*"

"How about how we die?"

"That depends. Which scenario of the fifteen possibilities I can currently see would you like me to recall? Remember every time you speak, those likelihoods change."

I sighed. This was going nowhere.

Jenae reappeared and tossed the blanket at Hemming, being ever so careful not to look at him, obviously embarrassed by his nudity.

"Alright, screw it. What are you proposing? We can't just knife ourselves and remove these ... What exactly are they anyways? Minions? Parasites?" I said. A part of me hoped that was exactly what we needed to do.

The Watcher frowned. "No, that won't—*can't*... they will not let that happen. Instead we must, *should* consider seeing the only being I know who can—will remove this infection without doing irreparable damage to us."

"Who? What is this being?" I demanded.

"She is an Elementalist. But she does not live close. It is, and will be, a long journey to see her, and there will be a cost, of course."

"Of course," I said, deflated. "How long a journey, exactly?" If this journey was going to take a month, only to find out that this Elementalist wouldn't do anything for us, we would have far less time to deal with the bugs living inside of us.

"Roughly fifteen hours northwest of here, unless we wait too long. Then the snow happens, which will extend the amount of time required to get to her," the Watcher said. He studied Jenae very carefully. "You, girl, you almost lost one today, but you held it back. And it is angry and seeks its retribution against you." He pointed at Jenae's belly accusingly.

"What?" I said. "What happened today, exactly?"

"I tried to tell you! You didn't listen," Jenae spouted, somewhat indignant.

"We were rudely interrupted," I said, staring at the Watcher as my lips curled up with distaste. I returned my glare to Jenae. "Again, tell me!"

I had lost almost any patience I might have once had.

She was still upset, and her pretty eyes were stained with tears. Her face was marred with ruined makeup and scorch marks.

She started with a quivering voice, "I left here and went to my old school. Meaghan was there, and she tormented me like she has every single day of my whole goddamn life. I accidentally lit her on fire, sort of."

"You did what? In plain sight of everyone? Are you insane?"

"It wasn't in front of everyone, and besides there's nothing really left of her."

"But, child, you haven't...you need to tell the rest of the story," the Kasadya offered up. "The silver spine came out of your stomach."

Jenae looked a little sheepish. "Um, yeah, that happened too."

"What does he mean? Did you lose a bug?" I asked.

"No, it tried to come out, but there was no way I was going to let that bitch Meaghan become like me! I wasn't going to look after her."

"But none of us have been able to suppress these things." I considered quickly how I would have prevented this from happening to Alyx. "They do their own thing, so how did you do it?" I demanded to know.

"I don't know how!" Jenae's flung her arms up. "I could feel a horrible pain in my midsection, and then I was so angry that everything else became I blur. I don't know what I did." More tears streamed down her face, and her wide eyes revealed that she was scared.

"I see what did and should have happened. It was the stone." The Kasadya offered up a hand towards his own neck, indicating Jenae's necklace.

I stared at the pendant and walked over to Jenae, inspecting its strange rough cuts and eerie dark shade of sunrise. Reaching out, I tried to grab the stone to study it closer.

As my hand went up, the stone glowed in response. With my fingers almost touching the rock, the stone erupted in bright light that bathed Jenae but burnt my fingertips.

So the stone had protected Jenae, just like the Shishi dogs, which were currently sitting at the entrance to the living room, watching her intently.

"Nice," I said, blowing on my fingers. "Where'd you get that?"

"Mirabelle's house." She turned her head away, unable to look at me.

"I see. Well, I think that's probably the smartest thing you've stolen. That stone protected you, and I imagine will continue to do so as long as you keep it on."

Jenae retreated back a few steps from me and pretended to pick lint off of her sleeve.

I gave up with Jenae. There was no controlling her.

I sighed to the group. "So, do we trust this and agree to go see this Elementalist?"

"Trust me," the Kasadya said with pure clarity. His jet-black eyes were dead and completely fixed on me. "Your impatience and anger is understood, but it will also be the end of you."

"Is that a threat, Kasadya?" I snarled, and the heat radiating from my eyes indicated they were glowing.

"Simply an observation that each potential destination I see right now ends with your anger," he said darkly. "Now isn't the time for this. You have other concerning events that are about to occur..."

Hemming, Jenae, and I stood there, staring at the Kasadya.

There was a dead stillness. No one said a thing.

"And?" I said impatiently. "What is going to occur?"

"Wait."

An audible rip ended his last word.

"Now," the dark Watcher flicked his head down the hallway.

That same ripping sound had occurred only a day before.

"I will return in eight days. We will leave then." The Kasadya turned and seemingly floated towards the outer wall of the apartment, and just before he hit it, he drew a symbol in the air.

The mark grew in size and shimmered. The air around it rippled in response. The Kasadya stepped into the hex symbol and disappeared.

The rest of us watched in shocked silence. I'd never seen any demon-kind do that before.

Another rip punctuated the room, followed by a wet squish like thick liquid hitting the floor.

"Hemming," I said without turning around, "they're opening."

Emergence

DATI

The velvet pods had split open at one end.

The wet contents from inside gushed onto the floor. The rancid smell in the room made it difficult to be present, but worse yet was the sight of a monstrous being coloured the same grey flesh tone as Hemming's wolf. Its spine was covered in sparse bristly black hair. It lay on the floor, quivering in the middle of the sticky black puddle. The demon was certainly no wolf.

The pod collapsed, having released the fiend, who slowly started to stir. It rolled to one side and, with shaky unsure muscles, righted itself. Four massive paws, each displaying thick sharpened claws held the being upright. It was hunched and the body was thick with muscle.

The other pod squelched open. A thin limb stuck out, unresponsive and unmoving.

"Geez, Hemming," I said. Hemming glared at me and motioned to be quiet. The beast responded to my voice and swung its enormous head towards us.

Jenae who had followed us rather quietly into the room, took a hesitant step towards the monster. She was transfixed by the massive creature.

Sharp teeth protruded from the elongated muzzle that ended with a large leathery nose. A ring of straggly hair surrounded the head and petered out as it ran down the neck and over the creature's breast. Two rounded ears rotated, attempting to hone in on the position of my voice and Jenae's steps. Its obsidian eyes, apparently unable to focus, blinked several times. It sniffed the air as one massive paw thumped towards us.

Jenae took another step closer.

Hemming hissed at her in warning. Jenae spun around quickly to face us. Her eyes were white as snow. She raised one hand, palm out, towards us.

An invisible force pushed us up against the bedroom wall, pinning both Hemming and me.

The audible thud of our bodies hitting the wall made the monster's head shift towards us. A guttural snarl reverberated in the room as its lip pulled back, exposing more sharp teeth.

Jenae returned her focus to the monster, held out her hand, palm exposed, and edged in closer.

The creature breached the gap between the two and put its muzzle in Jenae's open hand. Jenae patted the side of the beast's head.

Without warning, it convulsed and dropped to the floor.

The three of us were stunned to silence as muscles contracted and seized.

Bones cracked as they began shifting internal structures. And for the first time, the creature experienced the process of becoming human from demon. It sounded very painful.

Within a minute, a young pink-fleshed male lay naked before Jenae, covered in patches with the sticky tar that had been in the pod.

Jenae crouched down and pulled the massive body onto her lap, cradling the man. She lifted up his head, pushed the hair out of his face, and hugged him as he slowly came around.

The second creature still struggled to remove itself from its casing.

Hemming moved over to the second pod, reached in through the slit that had opened at one end, grabbed hold of the internal contents, and with strained muscles, wrenched the monster towards him.

I instantly recognized the animal.

It was gangly and leggy, the face flattened and elongated, but again, the skin was taut over the muscles. Unlike the first animal, this beast appeared incomplete. There were places where the stark white of bone could be seen. Ligaments were visible attaching one bone to another, some disappeared under flesh. Each of the four legs were almost total bone past the knee, but the limbs ended in large black hooves.

It was a horse.

Hemming, covered in rot, retreated and let the stallion attempt to stand up on its own.

I whispered carefully, "What was the first one?"

"Bear," said Hemming. "Jenae, you're lucky he didn't rip you apart."

"Caleb wouldn't have done that. Not to me."

"Caleb? You've named him?"

"No." She sneered at me with contempt. "He told me his name."

"When? I didn't hear anything," I said.

She just stared at me with an expression that implied she hid something. That she had just said something she shouldn't have.

I ignored her and turned to Hemming. "A horse and a bear... Isn't that sort of an odd combination? I mean, how much ferocity does a Shape-Shifter have when they turn into a horse?"

The bear, I understood. The claws on it alone would disembowel anyone, not to mention the amount of inherent strength an ursine creature could summon.

The horse still struggled to maintain its composure on wobbly legs when it made a strange strangled noise, like it was in pain. Hemming had a concerned expression on his face.

"He hasn't started to morph back to human yet. That's not good." Hemming had already lost one pod from a failed morph. He couldn't afford to lose another.

"What's the risk it won't make it at this point?" I asked, not knowing anything about how Shape-Shifters were born.

"Low, actually. You're right too. I've never heard of a Shape-Shifting man-horse. What the Hell do you do with that?" But as soon as Hemming said it, his eyebrows furrowed. He had come up with something.

The horse dropped onto its front knees and whinnied a second time. The muscles along its back were convulsing and rearranging. It appeared as if it was going to morph into human form, but then tissue started to grow.

"Oh, wow, that's why," Hemming said. I gave him an inquisitive glance, and he said, "It's not done. Look, it's not just a horse."

The shoulders of the horse changed, growing bones in a very familiar form. Within seconds, a full skeletal frame for wings had emerged. Tissue crept across the bones, spreading outwards and filling the structure until there were massive leathery wings.

"That makes the next step unbelievably more difficult," Hemming stated, with an exasperated face.

"The next step?"

"In order to solidify the shift, to engrain the body's memory of the beast inside, their first meal will have to be the animal they morph into. They have to eat the whole beast. A horse and a bear would not pose that much of a challenge, but I'm fairly certain that I haven't come across a horse with—what would you call those? Bat wings? That's not going to be available at the first fast food joint we drive up to." Hemming groaned. "We will have to leave within the hour as they'll be hungry."

"Oh." My eyebrows rose in surprise. "Yeah, I'm not sure what to tell you. Pretty sure I've never seen one of those before either." I pointed to the horse. It was finally complete and pawed the floor with its hoof, leaving deep grooves in the wooden planks.

"Can we borrow some clothes?" Hemming had a blanket wrapped around his waist. Caleb was still completely naked, which Jenae did not find embarrassing at all, oddly.

A *thud* sounded behind us as the horse dropped to the floor, gradually morphing back into a man.

"And your bathroom. We'll need to use your bathroom too," Hemming pinched his nose and fanned his face. The stench was pretty strong in the room.

I groaned, but it wasn't like I could very well tell them no.

"Yes, go ahead." I pointed in the general direction of the master bedroom where they would find everything they needed.

"Where's Parker?" The tall horse-man said as he hugged his legs to his chest, sitting on the bathroom floor. He still shivered uncontrollably. His smooth, lean body was slick with sticky goo, the remnants of the demonic pod.

"What's a Parker? Actually, before we go there, who the Hell are you?" Hemming asked, and then spun around. "I know your name, Caleb."

"That's my asshole brother Riken. Parker is his boyfriend and just about as much of an asshole as Riken," Caleb said. Turns out the bear was in an equally foul mood. His voice, though, rumbled out of his big barrel chest. Even in human form, it wasn't too hard to see that he was a bear of a man. Hemming made a note to himself not to piss the bear-man off. "There was three of us that night when you sharked us on that pool game and then ran."

"Yeah. So, about that part. Sorry. I had a job to do, and it got done."

Riken leered at me, suspiciously. "What do you mean, job?"

"Sorry, boys, you were targeted and marked. My boss texted me pictures of all three of you. I found you, and well, the little beasties inside me did what Master said they were gonna do," Hemming explained.

"What?" Riken said, his mood was foul.

"Look, we don't have a lot of time for me to get into details. I imagine you're both hungry?"

Riken glanced at Caleb, and in unison, they nodded.

"Right, so, you're hungry because you've been trapped for five days in a cocoon that has completely changed you. You might look the same, but you're not." Hemming pointed to Caleb. "You can Shape-Shift into a bear, and you—" Hemming swiveled and pointed at Riken. "You, you ornery shit, are a horse with wings." Hemming shook his head and rolled his eyes. "That is going to make our next step damn near impossible. We need to get you your first meal as a Shape-Shifter, and that will have to be the same animal you change into."

Riken glared Caleb with a snotty can-you-believe-this-guy expression plastered on his face.

"Don't believe me, huh?" Hemming, who'd been able to change into a wolf for a very long time, focused on shifting his face and, more specifically, his snout.

Bones cracked and popped, but the boys watched, partly fascinated but mostly horrified as Hemming's face elongated and human teeth fell out, quickly replaced with a row of sharp canines and protruding fangs.

"Holy shit!" Caleb said. He was more fascinated. Riken gaped as if the carpet had been ripped out from underneath him.

Hemming let his face return to human form—which oddly enough, always took less time.

"Please don't try that at home or by yourself," Hemming said in his own snotty way, and then rubbed his face. Shifting always hurt. "No shifting until I teach you what you need to know. Now, please, get showered and cleaned up so we can go get you the appropriate food."

"Cool," Caleb said, and immediately went to turn on the shower.

God, he's hairy. Hemming grimaced.

Riken, who was still regaining his composure, managed to find balance on his gangly long legs, and then glared at Hemming.

"You still haven't answered my first question. Where the Hell is Parker?"

"He didn't make it."

"Christ, man, give me a straight fucking answer!" Riken balled his hands into tight fists.

Caleb chuckled.

"What the fuck are you laughing at, you goon?" Riken leered at his brother.

"You said straight."

Hemming tried very hard to suppress a smile.

"That's not funny. Where is he?"

Hemming sobered up from wanting to giggle at Caleb's remark. He glanced at Riken with as much sympathy as he could muster. Gay or straight, no one wanted to find out their significant other was dead.

"I'm sorry, Riken. Parker didn't survive the morphing. His pod rotted. Parker is gone."

Riken's eyes registered a number of emotions—panic, anger, loss. He lost his footing again and slumped to the tiled floor.

Caleb was at his side instantly. Sibling rivalry aside, it was obvious Caleb cared for his brother.

"Shit, Riken, man..." Caleb said.

"Just don't! Leave me alone." Riken pushed Caleb away. Turning back to the shower with his head lowered in defeat, Caleb crawled in to wash off the sticky slime.

"Fuck!" Riken shouted and hit the wall nearest him with his fist, leaving a huge hole in the plaster.

Well this is gonna be fun. Hemming wasn't sure what the Hell to do with Riken. Caleb should be easy enough to deal with, despite his size. Riken was going to be a handful.

Jenae and I waited in the living room, not saying much of anything as my thoughts drifted off to Alyx, wondering when he would emerge.

Three men, all cleaned up and clothed, appeared before us.

Hemming had found some clothes that I had kept from ages ago, quite literally, a century. He wore baggy pants, with a musty old union jacket adorned by brass buttons. A black T-shirt was underneath. The two boys had a mishmash of things on.

Hemming and I were close in size, but he was skinnier than I was. There was nothing that would have appropriately fit Caleb, nor the other young man, who was as tall as Caleb, but lean and wiry.

"Caleb and Riken, this is Dati, whose clothes you are wearing and whose bedroom you just destroyed. Say hello, boys." We made some awkward uncomfortable acknowledgments of each other's existence. "And this is..."

Caleb cut him off. "Jenae," he said with an expected deep, rumbling voice.

Jenae approached him. Caleb opened his massive arms and enveloped her as she came within reach. Jenae nestled and melted into his huge frame.

"Okay, yes. Well, I guess that's, um, yeah, awkward," Hemming said. "We need to go."

"I'm going with Caleb," Jenae announced.

"That, you icky little witch, is not a good idea," Hemming said with a frown.

"I don't care what you think. I'm going with Caleb."

Hemming gaped at me as if to ask for help. I returned the glare with a you're-on-your-own stare.

"Jenae, they need to feed. This isn't going to be safe, or pretty," Hemming said, crossing his arms and glaring at her.

"I couldn't care less about safe and pretty, and I can look after myself. And in case you've forgotten, I bust open people's chests and eat their hearts. I'm pretty sure I can handle whatever Caleb has to do. I'm going." She squeezed Caleb's hand, and he returned the gesture by pulling Jenae in closer to his side.

I was utterly shocked. Jenae had had a moment of witchery lucidity.

"Alright, I'm not fighting with you." Hemming turned his glance to Caleb. "This is your responsibility. Do you understand?"

Caleb nodded.

Riken rolled his eyes, but he was noticeably quiet, even shy.

"We have to be back here in four days, right? And then it's 'off to see the wizard'?" Hemming asked, confirming our plan.

"Sounds right to me," I said.

"You're going to be okay with Alyx's pod?" Hemming nodded his head in the direction of the master bedroom, knowing I'd be by myself.

"I think I can handle it," I said with confidence. In reality, I wasn't sure.

"Then we're off. Let's go."

"Wait!" Jenae said.

Everyone stopped. She let go of Caleb's gargantuan hand, disappeared down the hall, only to reappear a moment later with a cloak under one arm and her backpack slung across her shoulder. Caleb smiled when she returned to his side.

"Okay, now we can go."

Hemming stared at me again, silently begging for help. I shrugged my shoulders.

The four "humans" left, and the Shishi trailed behind Jenae.

As the door closed behind them, I realized that, for the first time in a very long time, I was alone.

The apartment was quiet—deathly quiet.

The place was ruined. The walls had black stains from Jenae's dark magic; the air reeked from the hatching of Hemming's pods; and rips and tears in the furniture were signs that the Shishi had been where they had once been trained not to go.

In my bedroom, Alyx's pod lay, faintly chiming as the crystal continued growing.

The stench was noticeably thicker down the hallway, cloying in fact, as I passed the spare bedroom where Hemming's egg sacs lay, concave and empty. They would disintegrate and decay now that their purpose was completed.

Part of me wanted to clean it all up, but there was more drive to go sit and wait for Alyx. I settled onto the floor, got comfortable, and waited.

Alyx should be ready to come soon. I hoped.

Crack

ALYX

My eyelids popped open. My lips curled back, and a growl erupted from deep within my chest. Heat like flames danced around my eyelids and across my brow.

I tried to move, but something blocked my efforts.

And then I remembered everything: the forest with a Satyr, the high-rise apartment, stabbing gut pain, black crystals, entombment within a rock-hard scab, buried alive for days, my flesh being ripped from my body, and then growing back.

I could feel wet stickiness around my hands and against my back.

And I remembered the cocoon growing spikes that pierced through my bones and skull.

I was still trapped.

A wildfire of anger flared inside, blazing forward until it could go nowhere else but into a howl of rage.

I wriggled in the tight space and slammed my hand against the enclosure. To my surprise, after several hits, the crystalline structure broke. Shards of jagged crystals brushed past my fingers as they fell into the interior of the shell.

Hope flooded throughout my body in a furious wave of anxious energy. *There is a way out of this*!

I thumped my fist again and again. The crack grew bigger, expanding until light crept into the dark recesses of the cocoon.

My fingers poked through the hole. An influx of fresh air rushed into the coffin, bringing with it new smells that were cleaner than the rot I smelled within.

That was all the incentive I needed.

I would get out of this cursed entombment if it took me days to pummel out of it.

Hatchling

DATI

In the three hundred years I had been alive and the numerous years I had spent with humans, I had never had time or circumstance to experience what it was like to know someone intimately.

Everything had been for Master.

Too many questions tortured my brain. What would it be like to have someone to rely on? Was it possible that one person would always be there? Who could trust me that deeply, no matter what? Could Alyx be that person?

A howl cut through my forlorn questions. It echoed from within the capsule.

Thump, thump, thump.

The rapping cut through the room, muffled and deadened, echoing from inside the cocoon.

I hunched over the crystalline pod and listened.

Thump, thump, thump.

And then, *crack!*

A thin talon finger poked through the hard casing. The blackness of the cocoon faded into a translucent mesh. I could see a body inside.

"Alyx!" I was so excited and nervous. I desperately wanted him out.

I looped my finger around his. He responded. His finger latched onto mine.

Alyx's muffled cries seemed to me like shouts for help. The casing should have broken away easily.

I climbed on top of the pod, no longer caring about my skin touching the structure, letting my fists pound frantically. Despite the crack, the cocoon wasn't going to give up its contents without a fight. I summoned all my demon rage. Heat flushed my face and the skin of my hands turned ebony. I continued to hammer at the spot where the crack had started, and after several strong blows, chunks of shattered crystal fell away like broken glass.

With a few well-placed smashes, Alyx's hand broke free, and I grasped it in mine.

"Alyx, I'm here! Don't worry. I'm going to get you out," I yelled, and his hand tightened around mine. Being as careful as I could, I pulled my fist back and eyeballed a spot halfway up his arm. I beat the crystal until it exploded in all directions.

Tar oozed out from the pod. The stench, thick and caustic, assaulted my nose. Another punch and the pod collapsed further, exposing his chest.

Alyx's talon curled into a tight fist, and he beat the casing around his head. The mineral broke into large chunks. Alyx should have been able to do this on his own, but I wouldn't let him exert himself to death, trying to break free.

Furiously, I pulled away shards from Alyx's face. His chest heaved, and after wiping away the viscous slime and shards, Alyx's face emerged.

Despite the filth, he was still the same handsome young man who wanted to help me in Marta's bookstore. My heartbeat quickened.

Alyx sucked in the fresh air with a quick and raspy inhale. The gurgle churning in his lungs was audible.

I raised both arms, focusing all my strength into my fists and plunged them down onto the remaining crystalline cocoon. Ingots of grey shards flew in all directions as the last of the pod exploded.

Alyx lay amongst the debris. Glassy cocoon fragments littered his body, which was coated with a thick layer of sludge.

He was finally free from his entombment.

Alyx's hair had turned a deep auburn with streaks of copper and crimson. When his eyes opened, the emerald green I remembered was gone. The irises shone bright lime, circled heavily by a black edge. Yellow hints of yesterday now blazed gold.

Muck glued his new leathery wings to his back. A shiver rippled through his body, jarring the fixed appendages and spraying pitch all over me and the walls.

Alyx choked, coughed, and then vomited while I held him, a vile mire flowing out of his mouth and nostrils. He repeated that several times, gagging and heaving in between bouts.

He breathed deeply again. For a brief moment, I thought he was done, as his body went limp from the exertion of ridding his body of the putrid liquid within.

And then without warning, his entire form went rigid. I felt the reverberations of his chest as a warning growl escaped. Alyx's head turned towards me. His lips curled back, exposing his new and very sharp canines. Before I could pull back, Alyx opened his demon maw and chomped onto the fleshy part of my forearm, his long fangs piercing the flesh deeply.

With a fighter's instinct, my talon made contact with Alyx's forehead as I pushed him away while pulling my arm out of his mouth. I grasped the puncture wound, putting pressure on the bite. Dark blood welled up from the wound and spilled onto the floor. Little rivulets ran down my forearm onto the back of my talons.

Alyx, free from my arms, scampered away from me and hid in the shadows of the bedroom corner. He coiled himself into a defensive stance and hissed at me.

The irises of his eyes flickered, as if on fire, slowly erupting until they were burning bright red.

"What did you do to me?" he demanded with evil ferocity, his voice filling the room.

I braced myself for a potential fight while still grasping my arm.

"Well, that's a complicated question. You didn't have to bite me. Damn it, Alyx." I pulled a pillow off the bed, ripped the covering off, and tore a strip, winding it quickly around my arm and bandaging the punctures.

Alyx remained frozen in the corner. Strings of ebony slime drooled off of him. He watched my every move with fierce intensity.

I hadn't expected a physical retaliation from Alyx. I had conjured up several scenarios where he had been angry with me for stealing his human life and turning him into the demon. I was somewhat taken aback by his current naked and afraid form, cowering in the corner of my bedroom.

"Come here, Alyx. It will be okay. I promised I would look after you."

Eventually, the bright red irises subsided back to green and his body seemed to relax a little. He didn't, however, move any closer to me. His face contorted. I thought he was about to start crying.

I was crushed. My broken promise had such ugly consequences.

Alyx's head bobbed around in an awkward manner, not surprising when you consider that he hadn't moved in days. He brought his hand up to his face and tried to wipe away the sticky pitch that clung to his body. As he did this, an object dropped from his hand.

Slick with the pods gleaming stringy pitch, it appeared to be a plant leaf.

This was curious. There should have been nothing left in the pod but Alyx's human form.

"Alyx, can you stay there for just a second? You dropped something. I want to see what it is." He swayed forward a bit and croaked out an acknowledgement.

I inched closer to Alyx, keenly aware that his rage could bubble forth in an instant. I stooped over the dropped item, inspecting it, and sure enough, it was a long frond. I shook my head. That was beyond strange. Where had the leaf come from?

Alyx threw up again and groaned.

"What is this stuff?" he said, hunched over and heaving.

"You don't want to know," I said, without really thinking about how to delicately explain

Alyx, still dripping sticky strings, glanced at me with a questioning expression on his face.

"Come on, let's get you clean."

I offered my hand to him, a gesture of peace. He sniffed it, cautiously, then shook his head while coiling himself tightly into the corner. The disappointment crippled me. Instead I simply pointed in the direction of the bathroom.

Alyx skulked towards it, never taking his gaze off me for very long, until he saw his image in the bathroom mirror.

I had completely forgotten about the massive mirror that hung over the sink.

Alyx gasped at his reflection. His eyes widened.

"Oh my god, what the Hell..." He reached for his face, his fingertips exploring the new demon form that seemed like the old Alyx, but with improved musculature, senses, and talents. His back muscles flexed instinctively, and the large wings flapped uncontrollably, spraying goo up the bathroom tiles.

His face had a week's worth of red stubble on it, and he ran his hand over his huge pectoral muscles.

"What happened to me? What is this, this...gunk? My eyes...they are so different." He whipped his gaze around in my direction. "What did you do to me?"

A guttural snarl escaped his throat, and the sound ricocheted off of the mostly stone bathroom. It took him by surprise, erasing his anger.

"Alyx, I have a lot to tell you, but first, let me tell you I'm so sorry," I said. "I promise I will guide you and teach you everything you need to know. I didn't mean for this to happen. I didn't want this to happen, not to you."

"Why am I so angry?" Alyx glanced around, confused.

"That's a side effect. It will lessen with time, but never completely."

"I don't understand. What happened to my body? I'm *huge*." Alyx ran his hands over his torso.

The demon blood had taken Alyx's thin frame and amplified the musculature. He was now athletic, bulky, and ripped. Ready to fight if needed, capable of tearing apart most other creatures, human or otherwise. As D'Alae, we had wings, and we had strength.

Alyx turned his attention back to the mirror. "Oh my god, I have a tail." He arched his back and flicked his new muscles. "And wings." He glared at me. "You did this?"

"Unintentionally," I said, but with guilt.

"You're the same?"

"Yes."

"What are we? What am I?" Alyx's face was portraying panic, the scent of it permeated the air as well. Panic, fear, aggression. The stronger the emotion, the more we could sense them.

"Why don't we get you cleaned up first? And maybe get you some clothes?" I suggested.

His chest moved rapidly. He breathed heavily, excited, panicked, and unsure of everything.

"Alyx, I promise I'm not going to hurt you, and I will try to make sense out of all of this." I purposefully stood away from him, giving him space. His mind raced; his gaze darted back and forth, weighing the options, thinking quickly. We stood there, unmoving. I let him process the situation. His head hung slightly, a motion to me that signaled some measure of acceptance.

There was a slight sob.

I stretched out my hand a second time, trying to imply help, kindness, my willingness to make all of this better.

Alyx ignored it.

"I can do this myself," Alyx said sternly and just loud enough for me to hear.

It felt like someone had sat abruptly on my chest, the weight was so heavy. Alyx had rejected me.

I grabbed him a fresh towel and placed it on the bathroom counter, then left him to clean himself up.

I had utterly failed.

Walking back out to the living room, I found the condo was noticeably too still. After the whirlwind of demons, animals, and witches, the quiet of sitting alone with my discarded affection was isolating.

Damage permeated every corner of the condo. The black stain of Jenae's shadow creeper spell marred the walls, and gouges in the ceiling marked where I had been held against my will. The leather furniture had been ripped from the Shishi's claws. Blood stained the convalescence spot Hemming had taken up and splattered on the carpet from where I had stood when the parasite ripped free of my body.

I leaned my weight to the side and slid my barbed tail out from underneath, waiting patiently for Alyx to emerge from the bedroom.

Maybe there was something I could say, something I could do that would change his current mood. Perhaps the morph to demon had clouded his brain so thickly with anger that this was just a reaction after hatching.

Glass shattered.

The door to the bedroom door slammed shut.

In one motion, I went from sitting to leaping over the back of the couch and ran down the hall. I opened the door to the master bedroom to discover the curtains billowing wrathfully as cool night breezes infiltrated the room.

Broken glass shards caught what little light there was and gleamed back at me from the carpet. No water was running in the bathroom. The towel I'd lain on the counter was wet and lying discarded on the floor near the busted window.

Alyx was gone.

The Hunt

ALYX

The wind ripped through my thick hair as my talons pierced the concrete exterior of the high-rise. I had flung myself out of the building in hopes of flying away, but I scared myself shitless and instead ended up clinging to the side of the building. It was through this flight and fright scenario that I discovered my new demon talons, and damn, they were tough. Tough enough to pierce through the building's exterior.

This shit is cool.

Small chunks of concrete crumbled and fell to the ground far beneath me—and I could actually track their fall for the entire distance, too. I felt electric, like thousands of tiny buzzing sparks of energy were coursing through me.

Scaling down the building, my new tail and wings flapped in the breeze.

A very small part of me felt really guilty for leaving Dati. He seemed to care. No, I know he cared, but the constant rage I felt overrode any guilt I might have felt.

How the Hell could he do this to me?

On pure instinct, a growl rumbled through my chest. I could feel my ribcage vibrate with the noise. Bursting with rage, I plunged my talons into the side of the building and a small explosion of concrete erupted. I stopped my descent and marveled at the sharpness of my fingertips and the rippling musculature that kept my body hugging the vertical structure.

Oh god, what is Mom gonna think?

What the Hell am I going to do now? Waltz into her shop and say hi?

Ugh, that is not going to be a good conversation.

I immediately resented Dati. Hate burned inside of me again. Just thinking about what Dati had done made my lips curl back, exposing my freshly formed fangs.

I should crawl back up there and rip him apart for doing this to me.

I inhaled deeply and snorted out a gruff harrumph in disgust. But breathing in the night wind awakened something else in me. The evening was full of scents, ones I'd never noticed. One aroma in particular refocused my attention towards the ground, and it intensified as I scampered down the building towards the street. The prevailing aroma was one of the sweet smell of meat. Rotting garbage was also wafting heavily. I sucked in the night air and was overwhelmed with refuse.

Eww. that is just gross.

With a few storeys left, I leapt off the side of the building and unfurled my wings. The air rushed underneath and billowed them outwards. I seemed to know exactly what to do with them, flapping them enough to maintain some buoyancy. I glided gently downwards.

Hmph. That wasn't so hard. I should try flying again.

I scrutinized the wall of the building I had just repelled and followed the tall structure all the way to the top floor. Damn, that was tall.

Attempt to fly again? Hell yes, but maybe not from way up there.

I hadn't stayed in the shower long enough to clean off all the pitch from the cocoon. Gobs of the sticky goo clung to my skin, occasionally dropping and making a splat as it hit the cement. It reeked, adding another unpleasant odour to assault my nose. But despite my own stench and the rotting garbage, that enticing allure of meat kept me intrigued as I followed what I was sure to be a meal. The pleasing whiff rose above the refuse and made me forget about the city waste.

Food. My belly growled loudly at the thought.

From the end of the alleyway, my peripheral vision caught movement. Whipping my head around, I spotted a homeless person scavenging through the trash bins in search of new treasures.

My mouth became wet with saliva, and my heartbeat quickened. The flush of anger returned, giving me goosebumps as my taloned feet gripped the solid alleyway; the stone was cold and moist on my bare but rough skin. I inched a few deathly silent steps closer.

I sucked in a deep breath and could smell him from where I stood. My eyes rolled into the back of my head from the pleasure the scent triggered. I hunched over and inhaled deeply, filling my lungs to their capacity, trying to smell every little morsel of the delicious aroma.

Where are you? I can smell you...

It was musky and spicy. Drool ran over my chin as I crouched down, catlike, and slowly inched forward.

I could see his stink before me, drifting yellow wisps of smoke like the tendrils of a snuffed-out candle but gleaming phosphorous, and not sooty black. The smoke swayed and ebbed on the tides of the airwaves. I took another deep breath, savouring the odour. Pleasure flooded my brain, easing the anger that pulsed within me like an alarm.

Like an idiot, my clawed toes knocked a discarded metal can and sent it scurrying towards the hapless man. I stopped dead, trying to meld into the darkness of the alley.

The man peered up, greasy hair falling out from underneath his toque, which was pulled down over one side of his head at an odd angle. His face was crystal clear to me in the dark. Dirty and wrinkled, he scowled as he surveyed his surroundings, searching for the source of the sound. After several minutes of paranoid scouring and unintelligible mutterings, he returned to his dumpster diving.

I decided to take a different approach. From my crouched position, hiding in the shadows of the back alley, I scaled the wall beside me and crawled over it sideways towards the trash bin.

I positioned myself directly overtop of him. The smell of his human flesh thickened, and the excitement it generated from deep within made me purr with satisfaction. The rumbling noise echoed through the stone and pavement of the back lane.

The drifter stopped his searching and glanced around again. This time, his face wore no scowl. This time his eyes were wide as he focused on my demonic form clinging to the building from above him.

A new scent caught my attention, and the hair on the back of my neck spiked. Shivers ran down my spine, exciting me, not frightening me, as the odour grew stronger. I leered at my prey as the man's eyes became wider, viewing my evil form clinging unnaturally above him. It was fear. A maniacal grin spread across my face, exposing my canines. I could feel them extend as the spicy odour of flesh became complemented with the hints of citrus—that was fear.

My eyeballs burned hot as another growl of satisfaction escaped from me. Unable to retain or mask my emotions, the new demonic body's primal instincts took over as thoughts of violence and savagery swarmed my brain.

I pounced with my talons outstretched. I grabbed his greasy slick coat, wrapping myself around him, positioning myself so that I was behind and grasping him in a bear hug. My talons pierced through soiled clothes into his soft flesh and he screamed in pain.

My maw opened. I found a bare spot at the base of his neck and punctured the skin with my teeth.

Blood welled and flowed into my mouth as my teeth hit bone. Hot and sweet, the liquid left a sticky residue that clung to the inside of my mouth and the back of my throat. It was delicious but not what I wanted most. The feel of the flesh on my tongue was satiating me, the soft, squishy human flesh. I ripped what I could from the neck, and my ill-placed bite and rolled my tongue over the small morsel, flipping it around my mouth, playing with my food, until I swallowed it.

It was the best thing I had ever tasted, the tenderest meat I had ever chewed.

"Dear God, save me..." the homeless man whispered so quietly I almost didn't hear it. It was a desperate attempt at prayer.

His call for help...to *that* being. It made me want to shrink away. For just a brief second, I loosened my grip on my prey.

Sensing the release, he struggled and yelled out. But all that happened was a muffled gurgle as blood erupted from his mouth—the thralls of a panicked man attempting to escape.

Oh no, no you don't.

With no god in sight, my momentary lapse disappeared. I bit the man a second time, this time into the top of the shoulder where there was more flesh and less bone. Ripping the meat from his body with a quick jerk of my head, blood flew in all directions as the man continued to scream.

I didn't care.

I ate the larger chunk of flesh, chewing it, savouring every bite until it slid down my throat.

My prey desperately tried to wrestle free of my grasp. It was useless. He wasn't going anywhere, but at the same time, his thrashing was becoming more and more annoying. I moved one talon up to his face and began to squeeze. I held him until I felt some bones snap. They made a sickening *pop* sound. The stranger stopped squirming as he took one more ragged breath.

I sank my teeth into the other side of his neck as his last breath railed out of his filthy body. He was dead as I ripped another chunk from his body and delighted in its savoury tenderness.

With no fight left, I released him and ripped the clothes away from his torso, exposing his chest. Using my razor-sharp talons, I peeled off a slice of his thin underdeveloped pectoral muscle. Blood oozed to the surface, but without a heartbeat, the blood didn't flow with the zest of a living person.

With great delight, I stuffed the piece of chest muscle into my waiting maw and started to chew.

I stopped. Instantly. The flesh had turned. It was like acid in my mouth.

I spat it out violently.

I snarled at the dead dumpster diver as if he had done this to me, had tainted my meal. But through the anger and unsatisfied hunger, it dawned on me...he wasn't breathing...he wasn't alive.

My food wasn't alive. What did I just do? I just *killed* someone...

What the Hell did Dati do to me?

A scream of frustration burst out of me. The resulting howl echoed through the backstreet and bounced off the nearby buildings. Every muscle in my body tensed as the yell poured out of me. My wings extended themselves, and my spiked tail stood out, erect. The wail lasted for several minutes. And then, it was over.

My head dropped, wings slumped, and my tail looped itself around my leg.

Closing my eyes, dark thoughts simmered through my mind. Frustration turned into strength. Hopelessness morphed to anger and revenge.

I would *hurt* Dati for doing this to me. He had no right to change me. I didn't ask for this.

As my head lifted, another growl rumbled through my chest and down the alleyway. My eyes burned hot again.

I kicked the corpse lying at my feet; its limbs flailed as it was flung away from me.

Fine then. I'll have to find another meal. I'm going to need the strength anyways.

I launched myself out of the bin and, for the first time, realized that I had left Dati's apartment completely naked. I couldn't walk around the city searching for my next meal completely nude with a fish hook for a tail swinging about.

I jumped back into the bin and removed the filthy clothes from the dead body. His pants were way too tight. I fought to get them on and had several minutes of awkwardness trying to get my tail tucked into the back comfortably, and there was no way I could button them up at the waist. But the garment at least covered up the dangly bits.

The shirt he had worn was ripped to shreds, but the jacket remained relatively intact. I slipped that from the dead body and found it equally as challenging, trying to slip that garment on while managing to contract the wings. It didn't work.

After fighting with the coat, I eventually discarded it and flopped my wings over my shoulder. Oddly enough, I decided they kind of looked like a loose trench coat, as long as no one studied me too carefully.

Leaving the back alleyway and the dead homeless man, I ventured out into the city, intent on finding an appropriate dinner.

The hunt was on, and the juicy smell of victims saturated the air.

The city was just one big fast food restaurant, and all I had to do was fly into the drive-through.

Mother Witch

DATI

Two cops shuffled out of Marta's shop as I neared the store, keys and cuffs clinking against their heavy utility belts. They hurried past me and into their cruiser without giving me a second glance. Although I wasn't surprised that Marta had resorted to involving law enforcement—it really introduced a complication I didn't want to deal with.

As I crossed the threshold into the store, the familiar fairy-bell chime sent shivers running down my spine. The gentle tinkling was a blessing to those entering and leaving the premises. One day, I would get rid of that bell.

"For you, my shop is closed today," Marta said from behind her beaded curtains. She pushed them aside and stepped into the storefront, crossing her arms in defiance. Her eyes were red and the flesh around them puffy, her cheeks wet with sadness.

"Marta, I know I'm the last person you want to see…"

"Person, ha!"

"Okay, I deserve that."

I hesitated for a moment, thinking of all the things that had happened to Alyx since he had arrived at my apartment door. Marta would be thinking a lot less of me with the conversation I was about to have with her.

"Marta, it's about Alyx. I need your help finding him."

"You think I haven't already been looking?" Marta waved her hand over top of a map and scrying crystal. "I can't find him. He is nowhere. They can't even find him!" She pointed to the cop car that was just driving away. Marta's face glowed redder and her accent thickened as she became more flustered and irritated. "Wait. How do you know he is missing?" She came at me, jamming a finger into my chest. "What do you know, beast? Out with it." Her lips were pursed so tight a clamshell would have been easier to open.

I turned towards the entrance of Marta's establishment, flipped the lock on the front door, and spun the Open sign to Closed.

"This is going to take time, Marta, and you won't like what you hear."

"More demon lies. What do you know about Alyx?" she demanded.

"Marta, please. I made a promise to you, and I've kept that promise. I never harmed your boy." I sighed, long and deep. I was exhausted and exasperated. I had been on the hunt for Alyx, but finding him in the city was a futile search. There were far too many dirty alleyways, shadowy haunts, and sleazy bars where any one of us would have normally hid. Alyx hadn't been in any of them.

Marta was my last chance. I had hoped that she could do some white healing magic that would help us find him. Apparently, she had already used that.

But then I considered that her efforts would never work. Marta was searching for the human Alyx. That Alyx was no more. The demon Alyx, however...

I carefully planned my words to make sure they counted. "Your young man made a foolish and ill-timed decision to find me. How he did it, I have no idea."

"You foul creature. You twist words to make me think you're some good beast? Trying to help me? I knew I couldn't trust you. I knew my deal with a demon would come back to haunt me. It always does. Is this then my payment? My Alyx? I should've known better..." Tears streamed down her face as she clenched her tissue closer.

"Marta, how many times have I come here for your help over the years? It's been a rare occurrence when I've darkened your doorway. Other than your talent for healing, what have I ever asked of you? Nothing. I kept my word. Alyx was safe. But Alyx grew up and began making his own decisions. You have to know I did nothing. But if we don't work together, we will both lose him, if he isn't lost already."

"What do you mean lose him?" she sobbed through tears of frustration.

This wasn't going to be easy.

"Alyx isn't human anymore."

She shook her head. "No, no, no. No!" Marta yelled at me this time while slamming her fists into the shop's counter. I had to show her.

I lifted up my shirt and displayed the red jagged wound that was healing nicely. It would eventually form a scar crisscrossing just under my ribs from where the silver minion had extracted itself.

"My master infected his small horde with…I don't know what they are…parasites maybe? Our instructions were to find hosts and… well, it's complicated."

Marta's lips hadn't changed, but her face was scrunching up and turning into a scowl full of rage. She wasn't hearing any of this, but I had to keep trying.

"These parasites transfer demon blood into suitable human hosts, which turns them into…well, us. Your Alyx was infected with my blood. He's been missing for a week because he's been trapped inside a cocoon. His body morphed into…into one of my kind."

"What are you saying?" Marta spit out the words with hatred. Little droplets of saliva flew out of her mouth as she spoke.

"I'm saying that Alyx found me on his own. He got too close to me, and one of these bugs decided that he was a suitable candidate. The thing ripped itself out of me and bore its way into Alyx. That started the process of changing Alyx into a D'Alae, like me."

Marta backed away from the counter, distancing herself from me. "No, it can't…" She screamed at the top of her lungs, turning away from me, and gripping the sides of her head. "I was supposed to keep him close, keep him on the right side." Marta was blithering. "I did *everything* to ensure that. You were never to take him."

Marta slumped to the floor.

I rushed over and caught her, not wanting her to pass out or bang her head on something.

"Up you go." I hoisted her up, but her knees were still buckling. So instead of attempting to get her to stand, I scooped her into my arms and carried her to the office in the back of the shop. This time, she was the patient on her fainting couch. I sat in her swivel chair.

I gave her a few moments to compose herself while I fiddled with a wand that was lying on her desk. I dropped it abruptly when its crystal point touched my skin and burnt me.

I shook my hand, trying to alleviate the pain, and noticed the blister beginning to form. "Marta, I don't know what I can do to prove that I have no desire to hurt Alyx or you. If anything, I want to protect him."

"Well, you didn't do a very good job of that now, did you?" The words stabbed deep with the truth of it.

"No. I didn't." I let my head hang slightly. The guilt I felt weighed like a bag of rocks that pulled me under unseen waters.

Marta sniffled as she watched me. Despite her anger, her anxiousness from not having seen or heard from Alyx for days, she put that aside as I struggled with my own inner imps of failure.

"Alright, beast, let me see."

Marta grabbed my hand. Her tender human flesh felt warm and secure until her light magic wrapped around my hand as energy tendrils trickled, sparks igniting randomly.

Her spell continued to gain in strength, encompassing more and more of me until a wall of light pushed me up from the chair where I sat and pinned me against the wall of Marta's office. A wave of nauseating brightness penetrated through me and burned deep, searing into my eyes. It felt like shafts of sunlight were stabbing my head—but it was Marta's fingers, digging through my brain for memories.

I felt her firm touch but was aware of her soft skin. Marta's perfume, an aroma of jasmine and vanilla, overcame me. Her odour was oppressive, but I did not sense it through my nose or skin. It was deep within me. I could feel her inside my head, searching for something hidden within my memory. The truth.

The night Alyx showed up at my place.

Jenae crossed the hall to tell me a friend had arrived. I told her I had no friends. Hemming lay wounded on the couch. Alyx entered into my apartment, an unknown and uninvited guest. I warned him to get away, but instead he took just one step too close. And then it was done. The parasite sailed through the air, I leaked blood, and Alyx collapsed as the minion bore its way into him.

The black crystals swarmed out of his wound quickly, covering him in his entombment. Glassy pillars anchored him to the ceiling and walls of my bedroom where I laid him gently to rest during his metamorphosis.

The memories of the past week flooded through me, right up to the point Alyx shirked away from my outstretched hand—the heavy guilt I had from not having kept him safe and the stabbing rejection as Alyx refused me. I was so sure that he and I would...

As suddenly as it came, the wall of light receded and I was left reeling. My hands grasped for something to steady me.

Marta caught me and helped me sit down. I had become the patient again. Once settled, she patted my thigh.

"Okay, demon. I see what you know. Memories do not lie." She might have been kind to me, but there was still grit in her voice, a tenaciousness that hinted at the lengths she would go to for her boy. "Who is the girl? I have seen her before…" She wiped the tears away from her cheeks. "Wait…I think…"

Marta went to one of her filing cabinets. There were several in the back room, each holding any assortment of items, the least of which were files. She pulled out a large plain envelope from the one silver cabinet next to her desk and dumped the contents. Scattered in no order were a number of pictures.

Marta fingered carefully through the old photos; most were losing their colour. As she did, her fingers appeared reticent, as if these were memories that were too hard to touch.

"Here." She held out a photo towards me.

I took the photo cautiously, eyeing her while I grasped the image. She nodded and urged me to look.

It wasn't a good photo. A little blurry even, but I was stunned. It was a picture of Alyx and a very young version of Jenae…

And Master.

"What the Hell is this?" I did not like the uneasy feeling that swirled in my gut. My brain threading together connections that I was unsure I wanted to know.

"That"—she pointed at the photo—"is Alyx's father. He was the one who tricked me, who made me believe that I could overlook your evil and live a happy life. That I could love one of you… I was a young, foolish witch. But from that unthinkable relationship, I had Alyx. The only thing that kept me living with my choices, from ending everything, was Alyx. I was so young and so stupid."

"That's Alyx's father?" My stomach lurched.

"Yes."

"That is my Master. He was the one who sent me to your house when Alyx was a child. He wanted me to harvest Alyx."

"Well, of course he did, you idiot." Marta stared at me incredulously. "He wanted Alyx by his side, and I wouldn't let him anywhere near. It took everything I knew to shield Alyx. Everything. But it is almost impossible to hide a father's flesh and blood or from any eyes who had seen Alyx. If Silenus had never laid a hand on his son or never had him in his sights, I would have been able to steal Alyx away from him forever. More mistakes I made."

"How is Jenae with them? What is she doing in this?"

"That is Alyx's half-sister. After I sent Silenus packing and barred him from ever entering this house, he returned repeatedly but only once with the girl in tow. He hoped that with another child in hand, claiming she was Alyx's sister, I would succumb and take them both in. I met them in the park near the house, and I let Alyx play with the girl. But it was a short visit. Only enough time to ensure that Silenus knew he was never to come calling ever again. A neighbour took the photo—not that I was aware—and she gave it to me shortly after.

"I know how to drive him back to his damned world. And if I had, he would never have gotten back out."

I caressed the edge of the photo. Alyx's father was my Master. The overwhelming ties and subtle manipulations that Master had machinated over the years left me speechless. Worse, I wondered how much of my feelings towards Alyx were my own. Had Master somehow spoon-fed me in ways that I hadn't discerned all in an attempt to get his son back close to him?

"It damn near killed me to turn her away," Marta continued, "knowing that he would get his grip into the child and twist her. I've lived with a lot of heavy burdens over the years to bring up Alyx as far removed from the dark as possible. I made sure Alyx had access to the knowledge in my store, but I fed him full of the light and all the power that comes with it.

"I knew one day he would have to fend his own battle. I didn't realize it would come so soon. I wanted him to have a life before any of this reared its ugly face."

A very loud *thump* came from down the hallway. It almost sounded like a car had hit the stone wall in the back of Marta's shop.

Then from the front of the store, the sound of breaking glass filled the room. The big picture window must have shattered.

As soon as the sound of tinkling shards had stopped, the light in the room Marta and I sat in dimmed, and the shadows grew very long, very quickly. The air grew dense and thick, and an uneasy feeling fell over me.

"Hello? I smell a demon and a white witch in here! Where you at, sweeties?" a musical voice filled the room, and the smell of cherries and honey saturated the air.

"Oh shit." I turned to Marta, "Listen to me and listen quick. I haven't seen this one in a very long time and she's..."

"Hush, D'Alae. I know a Succubus when I smell one."

Killing

DATI

The shadows in the dark corners of the room elongated and reached for the ceiling. We had seconds before the beast would show in the doorway. My hands morphed into demon talons, and the skin on my face tightened. I was ready for what was coming. Marta, on the other hand, was calm and still, and her eyes were closed. Around her, a faint glow emanate, almost like a halo.

The aroma of cherries intensified, and a sticky honey scent lingered after it. Staccato clicks echoed, growing louder with each step. Long slender fingers wound around the edge of the doorframe, the nails painted a deep red.

The demon was very tall and lithe, and she slinked out of the pitch black of the hallway, entering into Marta's office. I crouched to fighting stance, ready for battle, claws raised.

"Well now." She leered at me, her gaze sultry. "It has been a while, hasn't it, Dati?" She walked over to me, hips swinging suggestively, her tight black dress enhancing every curve of her body. The outfit was split from the waist to the floor, and the ends of the dress puddled behind her. Black leather stiletto boots encased her shapely thighs. She bent over and, with puckered lips, placed a gentle kiss on my forehead, despite the fact I was hunkered, postured for a fight.

She giggled manically and then wiped her lipstick off of my skin. She dragged one long sharp nail down the side of my face and under the jawline, up to my chin.

"I like the beard, honey. It suits you."

"Alicia, it has been a long time," I spat out between clamped teeth. "A very quiet and uneventfully long time without you around."

"Now, now. Don't be petty. It doesn't do your body good. All that pent-up negative emotion causes stress. Don't worry, hon, I had more than enough fun while I was away. But Master asked me to come back. Special assignment. How could I resist?" Alicia flicked her head and long tendrils of thick dark curly hair bounced across her shoulders. The simple gesture revealed two shiny black horns, hidden in the voluminous hair that any woman would kill for. And several had.

"Hanging out with white witches now? Hardly demon-ish of you. And drop the war-stance, sweetie. It's not gonna get you anywhere anyway. What's the line? 'I'm a lover, not a fighter'?" Alicia rolled her eyes, then leered at Marta, who stared down at the floor of the office, doing anything and everything possible to thwart what would have been an instant attraction to the Succubus if she so much as glanced at Alicia. Whatever calm meditation or spell she attempted before Alicia's entrance had long since evaporated.

"Oh, sweetie, don't worry. I'm not gonna lick you in places you've never thought of. You're not my type. But I might want to watch you squirm just a little."

Marta grimaced.

"See, Master brought me back for some specific reasons. I learned all kinds of things while getting fucked by the old goat. Turns out the old boy's still got it, and he's thick. I like 'em thick." She held out a cupped hand, indicating a size, and smiled devilishly. "Know what he told me? He said you were a good lay back in the day, huh? Liked it a little dirty, too."

"Alicia, please. This is not really necessary," I said as Marta's cheeks reddened.

"Such a prude, Dati." Alicia whipped her head around towards me. Her pupils morphed into slits like a snake ready to strike. Her irises burned and shimmered topaz colours. "Really, put the claws away, D'Alae, or she will pay."

Alicia leaned in, and despite her original promise, a forked tongue lashed out and licked Marta's cheek. Marta whimpered but held fast and kept her eyes tightly shut.

Now we were in trouble. Succubae were female demons who used sex, pheromones, and human desire to get what they wanted, creating chaos in their wake. Alicia was by far the most devious, mean-spirited bitch I had ever met. Once her eyes shifted, there was no turning back. She had turned on all of her charm and was coming at us with hormones racing at full tilt. I could smell her musky scent of rage underneath the permeating stench of cherries.

Against my better judgement, but wanting to keep Marta safe, I suppressed my demon, leaving us undefended.

"Never did understand why you turned all this down." She ran the palm of her hand over the front of her breast, which I was quite sure would make a fleshy appearance by bursting forth from the skimpy attire. "But then, I had no idea you liked the little boys. And as it would happen, I've found one for you. In fact, I think you already like this one."

My mind reeled, thinking of my missing Alyx. I took a step towards Alicia and snarled in the process.

Alicia, unfazed by my warning, bent over and whispered in my ear, "Tell me, is he tight? He looks like he would be." She leaned back to stare me in the eye before calling, "Oh, boys!"

Heavy footsteps stampeded in the hallway as an assortment of male demon ilk and human men, all dressed in black, filed in around Alicia.

A couple of shadowy figures formed in the darker corners of the office where we stood, while a flock of crows erupted from behind her. The bird's wings became a flurry of feathers, and the squawking drowned out all noise as the fowl flew together and coalesced into a mass, morphing quickly into a monster of a man that stood behind her and guarded her. The demon's hair was jet black and long, and seemed to be made out of the birds' plumage. His eyes were solid white.

A thundering crash came from the back door as it was blown open, and the sound of more footsteps stormed from the hallway that led to the alley out back. The tips of my fingers slowly turned sharp and black as my talons returned, anticipating a fight—but I was trying very hard not to lose control.

Along with the cacophony of footsteps, I recognized the sound of something being dragged. I controlled my breathing, hoping that it wasn't what I feared.

Seconds went by, and we were surrounded by Alicia's male-harem, each of them decked out in shadowy clothing, tough boots, and sporting overdeveloped muscles. Each man displayed the same red scar mark on their necks: a circle with two vertical slashes near the top. It was Alicia's hex mark. That scar told every other demon that these men belonged to her.

With my D'Alae strength, I would have outmatched any of them one-on-one...except for maybe the crow man. He was huge. But with all of them surrounding me, I was significantly outnumbered.

As Alicia's sentinels came into the office, they split, circling us. One hung back. He was another huge monstrosity, whose face was more bull than human. He sported an earring in each lobe and a large link of chain through his nose. He came into the center of the room, directly between Alicia, Marta and I, and dumped a body at Alicia's feet.

The prisoner's wings were sprawled out and pinioned with a thick brass ring that pierced through the reddish leathery skin. His arms and legs were hog-tied.

Alicia grabbed a shank of his red hair and lifted his head up.

"Alyx." I might have been relieved to finally have him in my sights, but in the current situation, there was no room for relief. I was actually terrified. Alyx was in danger. My lips curled, my eyes went hot, and another snarl rumbled menacingly in my chest.

The men in black nearest me took a step forward, closing in.

"Please...leave him," Marta begged, her chest heaving with sadness. Tears streamed down her face. "Take me. Do whatever you want to me, but leave my boy alone."

Alyx responded to our voices. His gaze was wild, the irises glowing hot and red, just like mine. Froth formed at his mouth, his teeth chomping down as if trying to bite his way out of his binds. He must have bit his tongue as he was thrown in front of us because blood had sprayed across near our feet. The front of his coat and chest was also covered in blood, both dried and fresh. Some of it—I could smell—was from Alyx, but most of it was not his. That told me Alyx had been feeding on humans.

Marta's grief overcame her as she reached out for her boy. Before she reached him, Alicia's minions held her back.

"Marta, I'm sorry." I reached out for her, but she shrank away from me.

Alyx whipped his head around in my direction. His violent behaviour escalated. His limbs contracted and flexed, pushing against the ropes that held him. His body lurched in my direction, wings flapping uselessly, maw open, and teeth lengthening. His jaw snapped with violent rapidity. He snarled and howled, the skin on his face shrinking and tightening. He appeared to be a lot less like Alyx and a whole lot like the demon he had become.

Marta ripped herself out of the hands of her detainers, reached one hand, and placed her outstretched palm on her son's forehead. She said one command.

"*Втихомирся!*" Her homeland's word in the mother tongue fell from her lips, and the air between her face and Alyx's shimmered. As the air wavered, it began to glow, and the spell grew quickly. It surrounded Alyx and covered him, and the light intensified. It grew so bright that Alicia's men had to take an extra step back.

Alicia wound up and smacked Marta across the face. The loud crack of palm-meeting-cheek filled the room, and the glow from Marta's spell vanished.

"That's quite enough of that," Alicia said.

"Mom?" Alyx relaxed his grimace and morphed into the handsome man I had seen in his mother's bookstore. But now his expression was laced with fear, a sour aroma that wafted off of him and hit me with guilt.

"It's okay, Alyx, I know. I saw. Dati showed me. No anger, no more. I brought you up better than that, better than this…"

"That's it, witch, you're done." Alicia raised a hand, summoning one of her legion towards her, and with her other hand, reached out and grabbed Marta's neck. Alicia's sharp red nails dug into Marta's neck. "You've ruined my fun. Time for something else." She squeezed Marta's throat, making Marta gasp for breath.

Alicia snickered, then let her go as soon as she heard hesitant footsteps behind her.

A short man appeared who was different than the others. He was tiny in comparison and dirty. He wasn't built like the robust muscle-heads that surrounded us. His hair was thin, long, and stringy, as was his face. He didn't belong.

Stopping short just behind Alicia, he gazed at her longingly.

"Sebastian, don't be shy, honey," Alicia said to short man. "Momma needs you now." She reached behind her and held out her hand, and Sebastian took it gently, carefully, as if Alicia was breakable and priceless.

"Remember what we talked about, sweetie?" Alicia cooed. "Could you do that for me now, please?"

Sebastian nodded.

He let go of Alicia's hand, reluctantly, and then reached into his inner coat pocket and pulled out a very long centipede-like insect that wriggled and twisted. The thing's mandibles were protracted and thin, and looked horribly sharp, like small paring knives.

With deft fingers, Sebastian reached into another coat pocket and pulled out another one of the creatures. He then let them run around the palm of his hand as if they were pets.

Alicia cued another one of her posse, this time one of the tall, handsome henchmen. Muscles rippled in his overdeveloped arms as he placed a hand underneath Marta's chin. Marta twisted her head to escape the grasp, but others stepped in to hold her tight. Several hands held Marta's head still and made sure her mouth was kept closed. She was forced onto her knees, so that her height met that of Sebastian.

Sebastian stepped forward and held his bug-infested palm right under Marta's lips. The leggy worms quickly transferred from the hand onto Marta's face where they made a lap, running over her skin and through her hair until they found her nose, and quickly, the long centipedes with their dangerous mandibles disappeared up inside.

Marta let out another noise. It sounded like a whine. But it was more of a terrified scream that was being stifled by the hands holding her jaws shut.

Her gaze dashed around the room, searching desperately for help.

"See, honey, I know a white witch is kinda useless without her words. So I came prepared. My little friend's companions are gonna help keep you quiet while we finish up what we came here to do. Sebastian, please?"

Sebastian snapped his fingers. As the sound echoed through the room—much louder than it should have been—the arthropods pushed up against Marta's cheeks, bulging her skin outwards from inside.

Marta made horrible garbled noises, chokes, and sputters. She shut her eyes tightly, tears still streaming down her face.

With complete synchronicity, all four of the sharp mandibles pierced through her lips. Two upper, two lower, and then clamped down, pinning Marta's mouth closed from the inside.

The multitude of hands holding Marta let go. Marta slumped sideways. The closest muscle-man caught her by the scruff of the neck and held her upright, shaking her with enough force to keep her conscious.

"Oh no, hon, you need to be awake for this," Alicia said before turning her attention to me. "You see, Dati, when Master gives me an order, I gratefully accept and usually relish in the task. All I ever hear from Silenus is how you whine and complain and fight back and give him grief. I mean, after all, you'd think you weren't a demon. This is why you know nothing or have any idea why you've got those clever little minions in you! And why Master chose to insert them into you the most painful way he knew how, because you can't be trusted and must be manipulated.

"See the rest of us, on the other hand...well, we had it much easier." Alicia opened her mouth wide and brought her hand up to her lips, palm up. From the back of her throat, silver spines crawled up and across her tongue until a silvery bug came out of her mouth and sat obediently on the palm of her hand. It was the same kind of parasite that was living in my gut. The spines had left their usual puncture marks, and blood trickled out the corner of her mouth. Her tongue whipped out and licked it up. She glanced at me, winked and smiled, then turned towards Alyx.

"This little devil is for you, honey. I saved it special, and Master, that sly ol' goat, is gonna be so happy to hear that you're now three times the demon any of us could hope to be. Just think, a little Satyr, a little D'Alae, and a little Succubus. Well, maybe Incubus. Anyway that turns out, it just equals sexy!" Alicia stepped forward towards Alyx. "Your daddy is gonna be so proud."

"What do you mean 'daddy'?" Alyx said. With the ire gone, he was now confused. He didn't know what Marta had shared with me, but he knew what was coming, and he started to wrestle against the knots that bound his limbs. Alyx was no longer human and his demonic strength was giving the bonds that held him a difficult time in subduing him.

"Alyx, sweetie, there's no point in fighting. This is gonna happen, so you have a choice. Either you let me just slip my little buddy here down your throat and you swallow it just like I know you can, or we can go a more difficult route."

Alicia lifted her hand into the air and gave a little wave. From the sides of his mother's shop, men stepped in again, and two of them held each side of Marta while the one, who held her by the back of the neck, pulled her head, exposing her neck. A fourth brandished a large sickle with a serrated edge. Alyx's eyes went wide.

Alyx met his mother's gaze. I could see the terror and pain in both mother and son.

"You leave her alone!" Alyx snarled.

"I love it when a man is forceful!" Alicia said mockingly. "Unfortunately, honey, you don't have the ability to tell me what I can or cannot do. So open wide and swallow my little friend, and we'll let your momma go. Fight me, and I'll slit your belly open and shove the fucking insect into your gut, and then I'll slit her throat. Your choice, sweetie. So which do you want?" Alicia said everything with a sickeningly sweet voice, but the undertone was decidedly vicious. She meant every last word.

I couldn't control my demon rage any longer.

"Alyx," I bellowed, my voice filling the room, gravelly and sinister. "Don't do it!" I howled in rage and flung my wings out, hoping I'd knock some of the crew off balance and give me a fighting chance to break our way out of this. I was going to save Alyx, rip Alicia's head off, and beat the mob of men around us to a pulp.

Alicia's men flinched. With my outstretched wings and in fighting stance mode with demon talons and fangs, I was formidable.

Alicia, however, was having none of it.

"I can't kill you, as much as I'd love to. Orders are what they are," she said pointedly to me before turning to her pack. "Make him quiet."

I felt a heavy object hit the back of my head. And then again several more times. I could feel blood trickle down the back of my neck. Blinding pain flashed white light across my eyes. I went down on my knees, struggling to keep my head focused and aware. The beating continued, but not before I managed to grab a man's leg, pull him towards me, and gut him with my claws.

"Enough! Seriously, you people!" Alicia hissed. Suddenly there were enough hands and boots on me to keep me subdued. My rage pulsed within as I struggled and fought back, but there was no escaping from those that bound me.

"Now, Alyx, darling, open wide and let my little acquaintance in." I stood by in horror as Alyx complied. His eyes were shut as the parasite scurried down his throat. I could see the grimace of pain on his face, feeling pain of my own, knowing that the sharp spines of the creature's legs were puncturing the inside of his throat as it crawled down. He coughed, spluttering blood. Alyx appeared to struggle hard not to panic as he waited for the inevitable—another cocoon.

"There, see, that wasn't so hard, was it?" Alicia said. "Now"—she petted his head—"for being such a good boy, you get a reward." She leaned in and gave him a kiss, then whispered in his ear. He started flailing with wide eyes. Alicia glanced up at the figure brandishing the large knife and then directed her glance to the muscled one still holding Marta by the scruff. She nodded.

The large half-circle serrated blade whooshed through the air, the teeth of the knife catching his mother's flesh, slashing through the skin across her neck. Blood sprayed everywhere and quickly flooded down the front of Marta's shirt. A puddle formed around Marta's knees.

I was pinned on the floor, a small rivulet of my own blood running into my eyes and mouth as I started to scream.

Alicia's crew slowly disappeared. Some simply walked away as if nothing had happened, a few slid into the ground like disintegrating shadows, and the monster with the long black hair shifted into the flock of crows and flew away.

Alicia leered at me and said coldly and bitterly, "That is how you follow directions."

Alicia calmly turned and walked down the hallway, her statuesque form disappearing into the blackness as her boots rang out until the chime of the door decreed her departure.

The man with the overdeveloped biceps picked up Marta from the back, carrying her like a limp rag doll, and walked away, a trail of blood following them.

Alyx was losing consciousness. Fine white threads were spewing out of his mouth from the forming Succubus pod. Soon he would be entrapped once more.

Blinding light blurred my vision and my ears rang. I swayed violently and lost control. Dropping to the floor of Marta's office, I fell into the pool of Marta's blood. I was useless, but I wanted so much to do something, anything to help get Marta back, to stop the morphing process, to regain Alyx's trust. But it was all futile. Everything had gone wrong again, and I had been the center of it. I had brought all of this upon Alyx. I had failed him again.

In a half-conscious stupor, I crawled towards Alyx and reaching out one hand helplessly—a rule is a rule—no contact can be made while the cocoon is forming.

Alyx's gaze met mine, and for a second, there was a flash of emotion—a glint from him that said *help me.*

As I lost consciousness, white gossamer wrapped themselves around Alyx, forming his second death cocoon. Strong luminescent threads whipped around him quickly, obscuring his body, but they were also dragging him across the floor, into the corner of the room. As soon as the silken body hit the juncture of floor meeting wall, the body inside inched its way up the wall, defying gravity, until it nestled itself neatly into the corner of two walls and the ceiling.

Sticky strings lashed out around Alyx's body, adhering him to the wall as slithering masses of white spun around what had been Alyx the D'Alae.

I couldn't keep my eyes open.

Alicia walked down the back alley as a flutter of crows' wings descended next to her. When the bird bodies' morphed together again, the monster with straight long hair appeared, and then the image of his monstrosity wavered and morphed until the translucent-skinned, eyeless Mindbender stood beside her.

"Did it work?" Alicia asked.

The demon answered her, but only Alicia would have ever heard it. Its voice rang in her head...

Of course it did.

Haunted

JENAE

"That was the most disgusting thing ever." I gagged while opening Dati's condo door. Caleb was close on my heels, as were the two Shishi, happy to be home. Hemming and Riken followed in behind us.

"I'm sorry," Caleb said, his eyes pleading.

"Never again. Barf."

"Jenae, the boys didn't know what was going to happen..." Hemming started.

"Yeah, but you did!"

"I do believe I told you not to come."

"Ugh." I wouldn't admit to Hemming that he was right. We all had left days ago, after the boys hatched from their Shape-Shifter pods. Their first meal had to be the animal that lived inside of them. The animal's flesh and blood helped the demon animal remember what shape to change into. I should have just left the boys to their feast and hung out with Dati.

A lamp in the corner of the room tilted back and forth until it righted itself. The light blinked on and off a few times.

"Did you just see that?" I asked, pointing to the corner of the room.

It was darker in the condo than I remembered, and now that I was concentrating a little more, I could see rot stains in the shadowy crevices of the rooms, creeping up from the baseboards. The place reeked, just like Mirabelle's place did after she died. The air was stale and felt thick, oppressive.

"See what?" Caleb took my hand.

The scuffed leather sofa skittered several feet across the room.

"Um, maybe that?" I pointed to the couch.

"Shit. That's not good." Hemming's brows furrowed in concern. "Dati, man, where are you?" he yelled into the apartment. The four of us had barely entered the living room when the coffee table slid in front of us, barring our way.

Hemming disappeared down the hall towards Dati's bedroom. I stayed put, especially as the Shishi decided to sit on my feet. They had taken up to perching on my lap when they could, and when that wasn't an option, they were as close as possible. They let out a little whine.

"What the Hell is going on?" I yelled down the hallway to Hemming.

In response, Dati's bedroom door slammed and soft whispering voices could be heard coming from down the hall.

"Ah, Jenae, you might want to move away from the wall." Riken pointed over my shoulder, his pale features made his face easy to see in the darkness. His thin lips scrunched to one side from a mix of surprise and uncertainty.

"For god's sake, what the Hell..." As I glanced over my shoulder, a face stared back at me, masked by a layer of wallpaper. It was as if someone had buried a body in the wall and it had decided now was the time to come out. It stretched towards me, elongating its neck and pulling the entire wall with it. A hand pushed out, trying to grab me, but before it could, I stepped into the center of the room with Caleb and Riken.

The whispers shifted into an eerie moan.

The body melted back into the wall, leaving the wallpaper as it had been, stains and all. The wall rippled and ebbed like water as the body vanished. The tiny waves of wallpaper travelled towards the floor. The baseboards appeared to be moving.

Well, that wasn't correct.

I bent down to take a closer look. A steady stream of bugs, tiny ones, large ones, ants, beetles, spiders crawled along the baseboards as if they were some insect highway.

A pounding noise came from down the hallway.

"Caleb!" Hemming was trapped behind the closed bedroom door, which muffled the shout. A touch of panic escaped from him as his words trembled, "Caleb, where are you?"

I rushed to Dati's bedroom door, Caleb and Riken behind me, and yanked on the handle. It was shut tight.

"Hem, I'm right here," Caleb said, trying to be assuring. He sucked at it.

"Get me out of here," Hemming hissed.

Caleb reached for the doorknob and then pulled his massive hand back. A huge spider had taken up residence on the handle. It reared its front legs and exposed sharp little fangs.

"Dude, what's going on? This whole place is fucked up," Caleb growled.

"Bear down the door. Bust this thing open and get me out. Now!" Hemming ordered. "We need to get the Hell out of here."

Without a second thought, Caleb's arm shifted from a massive muscled human arm into a giant demon-bear paw and began pounding on Dati's bedroom door.

Nothing. The door didn't budge or give. Before we could try again, a hallow moan broke the silence, coming from directly behind the three of us. I turned around to see the walls of the hallway oozing tar-like goo from the ceiling. The liquid seemed eerily like the remnants left from the hatched pods.

Caleb kept pounding.

Another disembodied noise—chattering teeth—echoed down the hallway. Shivers went up my back as the air around us went wintery cold.

Riken turned a pasty white, pastier than normal. His breath puffed out before his face in the cold.

"God, Caleb, move back," I said, preparing myself to perform a spell.

The witch stuff had gotten easier and easier to do. All I really had to do was think about what I wanted to happen, and then let my body take over— but not completely or else all Hell broke loose.

I pushed Caleb out of the way and took a big deep breath. I let everything go silent inside of me and focused on one thing: open the door.

One of the zombie bitches leaned in close. I could feel her dead face close to mine as she whispered in my ear, "*Destroy it, bust it, shatter it...*"

I reached towards the door, letting just the fingertip touch the surface. An audible *crack* sounded. A split ruptured the wood of the door and crackled its way out from my finger, like lightning had struck the door. Splinters flew in all directions as the door crumbled inward and imploded. Pieces flew into Dati's bedroom.

The first thing I noticed was the empty black crystalline pod on Dati's bed.

The second was Hemming lying on the floor, dazed, with a large splinter of wood sticking out of his arm.

"Geez, Jenae!" Caleb elbowed past me and helped Hemming up onto his feet.

The bedroom walls were breathing. Bugs crawled everywhere, and the furniture moved randomly, jerking in every direction.

"You okay?" Caleb asked Hemming.

"Yeah, I'll be fine." He gripped the piece of wood and yanked it out of his flesh. Fresh blood welled up from the wound. "That'll heal. It wasn't deep."

"What the Hell is going on? The whole apartment is like this," Caleb said, indicating the moving furniture.

"Too much of us in one place, too much demonic energy spent in a short period of time," Hemming explained, leading us out of the room. "Alyx's pod is empty, and both you and Riken have hatched here, not to mention Jenae's spell casting." Hemming cast a dirty glance in my direction. "Dati's been living here for many years. Anyone of those things could attract this, but all of it together has basically sent up a massive beacon that says Come."

"What do you mean 'come'?" Caleb asked.

As I walked into the living room, a gargantuan spider dropped from the ceiling in front of me. I squealed a little girlish freak-out noise.

"That is a bucket full of nope. Get me the fuck out, now!" I could handle blood, dead bodies, and lizards, but bugs pushed me past my limits.

In the middle of the living room, a mass of crawling bugs piled into columns that reached from the floor to the ceiling. They splayed out in all directions, skittering above our heads and down the walls. The entire apartment was covered in crawling things.

In the seconds it took to take in the disgusting scene, I was locked to the floor and unable to move. Another pile of insects had collected at my feet, and they were scurrying up my legs.

"Get me out of this!" I screamed in panic.

"I have no idea what the Hell to do! This is beyond me," Hemming said. A gargled scream came from directly above us. I peered up to find Riken strapped to the ceiling and covered in the same swarm. A thick stream of the horde poured into his open mouth. His eyes were rolled into the back of his head, showing only the whites.

"Holy shit!" Caleb said as we studied Riken's body, stuck to the ceiling. "Do something!" Caleb glanced at Hemming, pleading for help, but Hemming appeared lost.

The twisting black cords of creepy-crawlies had wound themselves further up my body, encasing me to the waist.

"Oh my god, get these things off of me!" I swatted and flailed my arms, trying hard to swoosh them away but not crush them. It didn't work. My hands and arms were covered in smashed bug guts.

Caleb did a double-take between his suspended brother and me. "Caleb, help me!" I begged.

Caleb and Hemming, unsure of how to proceed, tried in vain the brush the swarm off of me. It was a losing battle as the sheer volume of insects slowly took us over.

I screamed.

The room swooned and swirled around me. A familiar sensation began to tingle in my skin, but instead of the sensation coming from my hands and feet, where it usually started, I felt it on my shoulders. Was my magic was taking over?

The tingling turned to burning, and flames of fire erupted out from me and danced around my neck.

It was only then that I understood. It was still magic, but it was the amber stone necklace, the one that had erupted in fire and smoked the schoolyard bully. Glowing deep red, it shot out flames, which whipped around in a counterspiral to the black mass of pests.

Hemming and Caleb twirled away from me quickly, fearful of being burnt.

A shriek emanated around the room as the colony of pests that had tried to entomb me retreated and concentrated in a far corner. Riken was still being strangled on the ceiling. He was seizing as he hung above us, making very disturbing gurgling noises.

Directly in front of Hemming, the air shimmered, like heat waves rising off the hood of a hot car in summer. An elaborately patterned sleeve reached out of the shimmer. I recognized the gaudy dress immediately.

An arm and a leg followed, and then hips and a torso too until finally a whole body in peculiar dress stood in front of us. The Kasadya had returned.

His shining black gaze darted around the room, taking in the scene, and then glanced quickly at each of us.

"This was not seen," he grumbled. "We must leave here immediately. Staying does not bode well for any of you, in any timeline."

"What the Hell is happening?" Caleb asked the Watcher. "And can we please do something about him?" Caleb pointed towards Riken.

"The Disembodied have arrived. There are—and *were*—too many of us here, and the bodiless demons can taste it, sense it. They live in the shadows—in the lingering energies we create. They seek to be us. They are far more dangerous than we give them credit for." The Kasadya pointed to the ceiling where Riken's body was pressed up against the ceiling, his mouth still open with a torrent of critters pouring into his opening. "He is being—will be possessed. He is being taken over by *them*."

I clung to Caleb's side and grabbed his massive hand for comfort. "Well, we need to do something." I glared at the Kasadya as if all of this was his fault.

The Kasadya stared at me and nodded.

"Yes." He pointed a long sharp finger at the stone around my neck. "This has and should work. You"—he shifted his digit towards Caleb—"pick her up and thrust her closer to the body there." He glanced at Riken still pinned and convulsing. Froth was dripping out of his open mouth, the horde pouring in. His belly was inflating as the bugs gorged it full. "Take your amulet and shove it into his mouth. The flames must lash out and burn the insects. You must not let go of it."

We did as we were told, but I wasn't particularly happy about getting that close to the insect horde. Gripping the amber stone that dangled from the velvet cord around my neck, I lifted it off of my head, and thrust it upwards towards Riken. Caleb hoisted me close so that I could place the rock where the Watcher had ordered.

The stone was still pulsating and glowing from deep within, but as soon as I shoved it towards Riken's open maw, the protective flames erupted outwards, charring the insects it touched.

A rain of dead bugs descended onto my head. I screamed and flung my hands, trying to get the burnt corpses off of me. As my hand dropped, the protective fire died.

'This is just gross." I made another silly girlish noise, which embarrassed me a little.

"No! Do not stop! Place the amulet back into his mouth now, immediately!" the Watcher said. "Do this now or he's lost to us. He is needed."

I was almost ready to say '*let him die*', but then remembered Riken was Caleb's brother. I flipped my hand upwards as the flames spewed forth and another shower of dead bugs rained down on me.

"Deeper! You must get right into the mouth."

I scrunched my eyelids tight and forced my hand into Riken's mouth. I could feel the licks of fire from the protective flames and the skittering of the crawlers. I shivered with disgust but continued to do as I was told, despite the constant barrage of tiny dead bodies falling into my hair.

Flames thrashed around my hand and penetrated Riken's body through his mouth. Tiny flames came out his nose. A huge spider, cindered and smoking, dropped onto my head. I let out a huge scream, and fire burst forth in a tidal wave, like a backdraft in a house fire.

Riken groaned—which was a new noise. He was regaining consciousness. Without warning, he fell from the ceiling and landed on the fluffy area rug with a dull thud.

Whatever sorts of insects that had escaped the pyre scampered away, in all directions, the room silent but for the clicking of their little legs as they scrambled on the surfaces of the apartment.

"We must leave now," said the Kasadya, while waving sigils into the air with a knife. In a flash movement, he sliced his arm open, coating the blade with his blood, and continued drawing symbols in the air. The shapes dripped in red and shimmered like the air had before. "Everyone must hold on to me as we walk through."

"Wait," I shouted, "I can't leave the dogs." I bent over and scooped up the first Shishi. "Caleb, can you grab the other?"

Caleb bent over and grabbed the guardian beast. It snarled and clamped its square jaw onto his arm. Caleb growled at the Shishi in warning, but he continued to hold onto the guardian. I bit my tongue but was giggling a little. Blood ran down his forearm.

The Shishi jumped out of his arms and ran far enough away to be out of Caleb's reach. It turned, opened its mouth full of pointed teeth and barked a sharp shrill command.

The Shishi in my arms whined, imploring me to stay behind. It did a quick double-take, then jumped out of my arms, running over to its mate and sitting in perfect unison with the other.

"We must go now," said the Kasadya.

"Just get us out of here," Caleb grumbled, as he grabbed my arm and pulled me towards the Kasadya's magical rift.

The Kasadya stepped through the shimmering air, and we were pulled forward. It felt hot, but it was quick. Instantly we were somewhere else. Hemming let out an "*Oh!*" as we spotted Dati sitting at a desk with his head in his hands.

"A little warning on how *that* was gonna feel would have been nice," I spit out, as I grabbed the wall for support.

There was a fainting couch covered in a soft velvety material and a desk with all kinds of things on it. Several filing cabinets lined one wall of the room and an assortment of jars contained interesting ingredients. It reminded me a little of Mirabelle's place.

Riken dropped to his knees and threw up a pile of bugs.

"Dati, where are we?" I asked, fighting a sudden and unexpected wave of nausea.

Dati glanced up to see our little mob, smoking from my flash fire and looking a little cindered and spent.

"Alyx's mother's shop." He was as spent as we were. Actually, he looked like shit.

"It's been a long and strange night, Dati," Hemming said.

"This is not—was not—what should have happened! If it was going to happen, it should occur much later. The timing is wrong," the Kasadya yammered, spewing his unusual speech while pointing at the Succubus pod.

"What the Hell is that?" Hemming blurted out.

"Alyx," Dati said, deflated.

Dati pointed upwards with a bloody hand. We all noticed that Dati cocked his head strangely. His movement was stiff, like when someone favours one leg because he's twisted an ankle. He was injured. But worse was where he pointed to. Alyx wasn't present, but a pure white pod had spun delicate threads high up on the wall, right at the juncture of the ceiling. It appeared silky and was bioluminescent, the gleaming threads cutting through the darkness of the shop at night.

The Kasadya studied the pod and shook his head.

"I have not seen this either. But now that I have, it explains," he said, shaking his head. "This makes all the timelines more perilous. This is one step closer to the end of the world."

Lineage

SILENUS

I stared intently at the wall before me, plotting my script as I examined the cracks in the concrete. I had chosen a home located in an original neighbourhood of the city, as it had once housed a family of witches. The whole structure creaked with age—over a hundred years' worth—and where I was wise and ripened in age, this house had rotted into a decrepit shack.

My human disguise wavered slightly, but I concentrated hard on my dwindling energy reserves and managed to adjust the glamour. I did a cursory glance to see if my devoted Vampyre servant had noticed. He hadn't.

As my plans slowly weaved themselves together, I discovered the effort to pull my lord into the human realm expended far more energy than I had originally expected. But then it would all be so Hellishly wonderful when I achieved my outcome.

Garbled moans from Ivan's captives distracted me from my current machinations. I tried in vain to ignore the sobbing and instead focused on restructuring the sigils I would need to draw on the wall.

"Yes. Yes, this is where that will go," I said to myself. Turning towards the darker half of the room, I instructed the Vampyre, "Ivan, now, as I asked you."

Ivan dragged his body out from deep within the shadows, his head listing. I found it hard to believe that he could have lived as long as he had with the small amount of blood that I allowed him to consume. Apparently, Ivan had the propensity for extreme violence, more so than others of his kind. I didn't see it. He complied better to my commands, better than any others within my horde, yet as a Vampyre—a dirty breed—he could not to be trusted. Vampyres only thought of their next meal.

I beckoned him forward, pointing to the chair next to the large bureau, a desk I had used extensively over the last few years. The surface was littered with notes and parchments, old plans that meant little to me now. One item in particular, though, gave me great satisfaction: a glass jar containing one crushed monarch butterfly. A reminder of Alyx, the leftover token laid upside down, a dried-out exoskeleton with crispy wings. Alyx, my son, displayed aptitudes beyond even what I thought could be possible. He held so much promise.

Ivan slinked across the cold stone basement. His milky orbs glowed with hunger.

I tapped the chair. "Remove your shirt."

Ivan did as I commanded. The dank and shadowy room reminded me more of a crypt than the basement of someone's house, and Ivan's skin gleamed in the darkness. His starvation had emaciated the undead body. I had forbade his feeding until he accomplished my tasks. Vampyres required the right guidance in order to be useful.

The skin sunk in between each of his ribs, and his vertebrae ran down his back so prominently it reminded me of a mountain range separating his body into two equal halves.

He had completed his last task for me, however, and Ivan's reward meant the removal of the last parasite from his torso. After this, Ivan could go free. Our bargain would be complete.

Bending over, I removed a cylindrical glass tube from the bottom drawer. The container held a handful of silvery parasites, which had been removed from Ivan. Like fat little ticks after a bite, they wrestled in their confinement, engorged with the blood from the Vampyre's body.

That might have accounted for his current listlessness. The minions drained more blood from him than I had allowed Ivan to have—a fact I used to my advantage. As long as I dangled the possibility of food in front of him, he obeyed my every word.

Along with the glass tube of scuttling parasites, I pulled out a long length of rope and, of course, my favourite serrated knife.

I placed all the items on the desk in a perfect line. Ivan sat bare-chested in the wooden chair, his torso marred with fresh wounds just below the ribcage. The wounds stretched lengthwise and ran deep. I could only imagine the pain each had caused. Ivan rapped his fingers on the arm of the chair in anticipation.

"Hmmm, no, this isn't right," I mused, studying Ivan, his irises empty of colour. "We should have an audience. After all, it's the last one, isn't it?

Bring my latest request in here, along with the trough." Prolonging the procedure and making him wait, even if just for a few more minutes, pleased me. The added tension the wait created, the expectancy of being free of my parasites, electrified the air with black energy. That sensation invigorated my old Satyr body.

Ivan rose from the chair and walked back into the shadows from where he had come. He made several trips, dragging the trough out first, followed by four very large burlap sacks, each of which wriggled violently as they dropped onto the cold floor.

"Ivan, I do say, you've done excellently. Let's see, shall we?" I stepped over to the four squirming bags and hoisted up the first one, dangling it over the trough.

I ripped the burlap apart with my free hand, exposing a human head, female, with long hair, streaks of grey throughout. The rest of the body I left wrapped, her mouth gagged, but with the utmost care, I pulled the tousled hair out of the woman's face, pushing it behind her ears. Her teary eyes and cheeks smeared with mascara.

"Well, Susan, it has been a very long time. Do you remember? We had so much fun together." I could feel myself becoming aroused, thinking of times Susan and I had spent alone together. I placed her down carefully, so that she knelt close to the large metal trough.

Moving on to the remaining sacks, I uncovered each one in the same way, revealing Bob, the useless husband who couldn't satiate his wife's sexual needs, and two teenagers, one male, one female.

The teenaged boy surprised me by glaring with an intense ferocity.

"Well my, my... now, we have a warrior here. Tell me, son, if you were free right now, would you attempt to fight to save your family?" I cocked an eyebrow.

The boy scowled at me. He gave me no answer, but I could smell the hostility wafting off of him in waves.

"How amusing." I moved my head, flinging it backwards and dropping the glamour from concealing my true self. I sighed with a little relief at taking off the costume, as it were. I ran my hand over the resplendent goat horns that curled away from my head and stomped a furry hoofed foot.

"How about now, child?" My voice had changed as well; it resonated deep and gruff with dominance. That guttural sound always brought humans to a quivering mass of fear.

The boy trembled and paled as I placed my goat-like face inches away from his own, but his angry stare continued. I smelled him. The delicious aroma wet my mouth.

Ivan's foot pumped impatiently. The filthy thing would just have to find some endurance.

"Well, Ivan, I do say, this one seems like an ornery little beastie! I wonder..." Tapping a finger over my lips, I pondered whether or not the boy could be one of ours. Then I grabbed my favourite serrated knife from the desk and cut the sack off him.

I ripped open the shirt, exposing the boy's neck and back. A small whitish scar at the base of his neck and a swirling freckle pattern indicated the boy had been harvested.

"Ah, see, as I suspected. Marked! The boy is ours, Ivan. Ours to do with as we need! Perhaps he is worth more to me than the rest of his family. But of course, this human form will not suffice. You are too weak to do the things I will need you to do for me," I mused, glancing back at Ivan and the jar full of parasites on the desk.

I cocked an eyebrow and tilted my head to the side as an idea formed. "I know just how to make up for that small fault of yours, boy."

Dragging him to the desk, I grabbed the jar filled with the engorged bugs. Once I screwed open the lid, parasites scurried and clamoured over top of each other in a pathetic attempt to crawl up the sides and escape.

I reached in and pulled out a particularly fat and juicy minion. I gripped the parasite at the base of its head, and as I squeezed, the bug's long spindly legs danced in the air as if it were trying to still crawl up the glass tube.

I removed the boy's gag.

"You freak! Let me go!"

I liked the way he displayed his terror though anger. Rage fed the shadows of darkness; it deepened them, made them richer, more sinister and twisted.

"Now, child, do you think you could escape if I did let you go? Do you think you'd get past me and the Vampyre? Would you like to show your family how stupidly brave you think you are?" My lips curled.

"Yes," he spat out towards me, saliva flying and emphasizing his conviction.

I grabbed his crotch and squeezed hard. The boy whined a pathetic little noise.

"Then you have more balls than most. I will use you." I released the parasite onto the youth's cheek.

The bug sat there for just a moment, two front legs bobbing up and down. Gradually, it crawled down the side of his face and sat in the little indent between the collarbone and the neck. It opened its mouth, exposing rows of sharp teeth. Pinpricks of blood welled up on the skin from each of its steps, a tiny trail of red destruction, and then it bit into the boy's neck and stuck its entire head into the wound.

He screamed in agony.

Metal spines dug and tore at the wound, ripping up the skin. Clearly the pain had been too intense, as the boy went limp, falling face-first onto the concrete floor.

The boy's family continued their mewling. Ivan remained in the chair where he'd sat motionless throughout the entire episode.

The Vampyre pod started. Long, wet, sinewy blood-red tendrils spewed out of the boy's neck. Ropes of tissue that seemed like muscle without skin stretched thin to form thick, taut cords. They flailed for a second, wrapping around the youth's body. Within minutes, the human body had disappeared, covered up in several thick layers of glistening sticky dermis. Tendrils erupted from both the top and bottom of what would have been the head and feet. The smaller ligaments anchored the pod onto the floor and attached to the ceiling. The structure pulled itself vertical. The pod pulsated, slowly, like a heart—*beating*—secreting blood, which dripped onto the floor and defied gravity by pooling on the ceiling.

The young teenage girl screamed behind her gag throughout the entire process.

I hated screaming. The shrill noise punctured my ears to the point where it felt like knives piercing my head. I glided over to the human girl and delivered a vicious and loud slap across the face. My thick yellow nails tore her cheek open.

"Silence!"

Ivan sat completely still in his wooden chair, exposed with ribs protruding. He gave no outward appearance of noticing the events that surrounded him. Ivan's stillness belied a state of catatonia. His glassy eyes stared like the dead, focused just above and beyond the warm humans in the room, at nothing.

Certainly, he would have eaten all three of the remaining captives if given the opportunity.

I walked over to him, took the rope, and bound him to the chair. The captives watched every action, their gaze indicating their current level of terror.

As I took my knife, Ivan stiffened, almost imperceptibly, bracing himself against my next action. This would be the last time I would be able to do live surgery on a Vampyre...for now. I took delight in other creatures' expressions of agony. The experience of torture, pain, and humiliation that ran across the ghoul's face as I sawed into him fed my curiosity. I'd have to find another reason to take up the knife and carve another living thing open, soon.

I chose a new spot on the greying Vampyre's abdomen and slowly inserted the serrated blade all the way up to the hilt, then sliced. Ivan clutched the arm of the chair and grimaced through the pain. The wound would heal, thanks to the demon healing, but it would leave a scar. I enlarged the wound to the size large enough to accommodate my fist.

One would have expected lots of blood as I pulled the knife out. Alas, only a small trickle oozed—another sign of Ivan's starvation. Aside from the fact that withholding food made Ivan more compliant, with less blood, the surgery would be less slippery and easier to get a handle on the internal parasites.

I placed the bloody knife on the desk. Bits of Vampyre flesh stuck in the serrated blade.

I squished my callused fist inside the cold abdomen and felt around. It took me a few minutes, but I trapped the last minion between my pinched fingers. It tried to dig further into the body and away from me. The bug didn't come willingly. I dragged the little beastie out from Ivan's midsection, writhing and scraping and clawing.

Ivan jumped a little when I wrenched it free.

As soon as my hand exited the Vampyre's belly, he heaved a sigh of relief and relaxed in the chair. The wound disappeared slowly as the serrated flesh melded back together.

I dropped the last of Ivan's minions into the glass jar, and it joined its other brethren. I spun the metal lid and screwed it on tight, saving the parasites for future use.

"Now that it's done, Ivan, you are free. You have done everything I have asked. You may have him," I said, pointing to the captive father. Ivan flew with such a speed that I almost didn't see him launch himself forward, grab the meat sack of a human, and whisk him away into the darkest corner of the basement.

The father screamed a few times, but Ivan clearly did something to mitigate the noise—knowing how I hated it so. Instead, the sound of a crack and then slurping noises filled the cool underground air. Ivan would have snapped the upper neck bones, resulting in his prey's paralysis, but it would keep the victim alive and conscious.

The Vampyre pod pulsated in time to Ivan's sucking.

I refocused my attention to the remaining two humans, who were trembling and terrified. Their fear saturated the air with the most delicious aroma.

"I have lost one of my parasites, but I have gained a new Vampyre," I said, nodding my head in the direction of the red beating sack of meat that had been the male teenage. "Which means that you really have become useless to me, except for one thing."

I raised my hand with the knife and slashed Susan's neck clean through the jugular. I caught her quick, pulling her head back and let the blood run freely into the metal trough that Ivan had been so good to bring for me.

The girl sobbed violently, her eyes tightly shut.

It took longer than I had patience for, but eventually the blood flow ebbed to a quiet trickle. I let Susan drop to the floor.

"Now see, everyone except you have become very useful tonight." I grabbed the girl's head and pulled it towards myself. "That was your brother?" I pointed to the pulsating meat. "Am I right in saying that your brother is the one who so valiantly wanted to fight his way out of this?"

The girl nodded and then mumbled something through her gag.

"My apologies. So rude of me." I took out the cloth that had been jammed into her mouth and throat. She coughed a few times and then spoke.

"Bradley," she cried and nodded. "My brother Bradley."

"That would mean then, this was your mommy and daddy?"

The girl nodded again.

"Y-Yes…"

"That is simply wondrous. You have shared your family with me, so I shall share mine with you."

I went over to the desk and pulled out a long quill. I bent over and dipped it into the trough, then, with quick actions, began sketching out boxes with lines across the wall. I took my time, drawing with the blood, until the exact numbers of required lineage trees lined the concrete wall.

I heard shuffling, turned away from my penning, and inspected my bound and bagged guest. She wrestled with her binds, her eyes tightly closed.

"Hmph." I waited quietly for her to stop. To her surprise, when she opened her eyes, I glared menacingly, inches away from her face—almost nose to nose.

"Well, there you are. I can't show you my family if you're not watching." I patted her on the head like a puppy.

Dipping my quill in the pool of blood, I returned to my diagram on the wall.

"You see, it started with Astrid, many, many years ago. Astrid gave birth to my first son Charles." I wrote their names in blood on the wall, in the two top boxes on the far left of the drawing, and worked my way down. "Charles, my firstborn, was special. He too, like me, could teleport—although we call it *slipping*.

"Imagine a human who could do such things! Well, I suppose entirely human isn't correct. I needed to create a hybrid. You see, I need very specific participants in order to hold a very special ceremony—a ritual that would bring the dark lord here to your world."

The girl continued to struggle, tears streaming endlessly down her round pink cheeks. The scent of her fear wafted through the air, something akin to incense, and added to the electric energy from the dissection of the Vampyre.

"Charles and I got along very well. But after a time, his attention turned towards the ladies, and one in particular caught his eye. He married a cute little French girl, Geneviève. They gave birth to several children, three daughters. Sadly, none of them retained the gift I had bestowed upon Charles. But, being the gracious son, he gave me one of his daughters.

"Of course, Geneviève expressed her unhappiness about that. Charles had to make her understand. Poor Geneviève, she didn't survive that lesson, but my granddaughter, Celeste, was a lovely child! Once she matured, she and I had our own child together. I hoped mightily that this child would display demonic talents. And alas she did, but she could not slip.

"But even better—she turned out to be a witch! And once a witch is in the family, all succeeding daughters will pass that lineage along.

"And so I could leave that family and simply breed the daughters and wait until the witch of the sixth generation arrived." I wrote in all the names of the daughters, one name in each box. "You see, the sixth in the family line would be born soulless, as they always are. That gives them unending powers but requires that they consume souls for every spell." I jotted down a name in the last box of the lineage. "Now we have our blonde-haired girl, Jenae, our soulless witch. She will be the Soul Door to pull *him* into our world."

I turned to glance at the girl, who had listened to every single word I had said but furrowed her brow and looked totally confused.

"Now you see, there are many other boxes, but a vast majority of my children failed to show affinity towards us. This has been my biggest disappointment. But for those children who developed darker sympathies, being half human would never suffice. I had to find a way to release the dormant demons within them. They needed to be awakened! My D'Alae and his venom helped, but we needed something even more.

"It took me a long time to develop these wonderful little silver minions who would do exactly that, awaken the darkness within them, and which, right now, your brother is experiencing firsthand! You see, you too, child, are one of mine, you and your brother. And as such, you belong to me, and I shall do with you as I need to, in order to bring *him* here. Your brother, he was marked. He showed the balefire, but you, child"—I ripped away the burlap sack and inspected her neck—"you, sadly, have remained human."

"And so, where your brother will serve me for quite some time in his new form, you who has no affinity, you shall have another purpose. You will have the honour of showing me when to complete the ritual so that I can bring *him* here."

And with that, I slayed the girl, let her blood spill into the trough. After I collected as much as I could, I took my enchanted walking stick and began to recite the words and make the symbols, then drew them in the air with her blood.

The blood pulsated, hanging and floating before me. The pulsations of the blood, remembering the beating of the heart, made the symbols come to life.

The dreary basement swirled away as a large landscape appeared before me, and within the picture, my dark demonic children stood at the ready. The moon hung full in the sky, and the trees stood barren. A gentle layer of snow covered the ground. It was the winter equinox.

The girl's blood reacted as it should have. Her blood showed me that *his* time was near.

I was so close to accomplishing my goal.

Tattoo

DATI

I sat on the settee in Marta's office, my head throbbing and still oozing blood, watching Alyx's new cocoon. It had been hours since the white Succubus threads pulled him up towards the ceiling. The white pod glowed faintly.

Once again, the burden of guilt was heavier than I could possibly bear for what I had let happen to Alyx. Marta had been right—I utterly failed to protect him from my world. I had failed Marta as well. How could I possibly apologize to Alyx?

My head hurt from the bashing I'd received via Alicia's minions, but I was wounded more than just physically as I stared helplessly at the cocoon. It made sounds, like the last pod, but this one was reminiscent of paper being crumpled.

The air in front of me shimmered softly, like heat rising off of scalding pavement. A hand reached out from the center of the disturbance. The appendage was clothed in robes from a time long forgotten.

I backed up as the Kasadya pulled himself through the tear in the air, but he was not alone. Attached to him were Hemming, Jenae, Caleb, and Riken, all of whom were a little ashen.

"A little warning on how *that* was gonna feel would have been nice," Jenae spat out as she grabbed the wall for support.

Riken dropped to all fours and immediately threw up a small pile of dead bugs.

Great, another mess to clean up.

"It's been a long and strange night, Dati," Hemming said in response to my surprised face and the gastro contents.

"This is not—was not—what should have happened! If it was going to happen, it should occur much later. The timing is wrong," the Kasadya yammered, spewing his unusual speech while pointing at the Succubus pod.

"What the Hell is that?" Hemming blurted out.

"Alyx," I said, deflated.

"I have not seen this either. But now that I have, it explains," he said, shaking his head. "This makes all the timelines more perilous. This is one step closer to the end of the world."

Everyone ignored the blithering from the Kasadya.

"But that's another pod."

"I've had some fun of my own here," I said, then as quickly as I could, I relayed the events from the moment Alyx broke free of the D'Alae crystalline pod to the encasement in an incubi shell. "Oh, and the best part, Master is Alyx's father," I added, almost forgetting.

Hemming and Jenae were gobsmacked. The Kasadya, who ignored me completely, watched and inspected the pod as threads of various thicknesses continued to spin and weave upon itself.

"I'll explain more later. But right now, we're stuck in Alyx's mother's new-age shop until the pod hatches. Except there's a little bit of a problem with that because Marta has involved the police, and I guarantee they'll be showing up here again soon. We probably have a day, maybe two before they return. He won't be done." I pointed to Alyx.

"That is not as much a problem as you think, D'Alae. There are other issues you have not considered," the Kasadya replied, not taking his attention off of the silky cocoon.

"The ambiguity, god, how I love the ambiguity—do you ever not talk in circles?" Hemming asked suspiciously.

The Watcher demon broke his gaze away from the cocoon and stared at Hemming.

"I see us travelling to the Elementalist—within a few short hours. If we are to be free of your Master's plan and have the parasites that dwell within us removed, we must leave today. And I have a way." The Kasadya grabbed the chair that sat in front of Marta's desk and wheeled it over in front of the ever-spinning threads.

He stood on the chair gracefully and leaned forward, getting close to Alyx—too close. I stood up, ready to pounce, to ensure that he did not touch the pod or interrupt the morphing process. I wasn't as worried that Alyx wouldn't make it through the process—he had already successfully endured the first—but this was also new territory, something I had never seen, and I had no idea what would become of a merging of three different demon bloodlines within one body. What would that do to anyone—or anything?

"Sit, D'Alae. I will not harm your boy. He is needed. You are correct—this place needs to be abandoned and quickly. To do that, I must—will speed up time around him." The Kasadya drew his blade from some hidden pocket within his vest, slashed his arm, and with his own blood, he drew symbols in the air—many of them, in fact. His hands moved quickly as he drew ancient glyphs and marks, some of which glowed red with blood that hung in the air embedded into the script. Others rippled and then vanished. Some became superimposed overtop each other, morphing into one. "All of you should hold on to something. The room may feel, no—will feel *odd* for a few moments."

He had not lied. As he wrote the last mark, the room shifted and tilted slightly. A wall formed just in front of the Kasadya, like a thin sheet of rippling water. The barrier quarantined us from Alyx, but in the corner where Alyx hung suspended in cottony fluff, shadows grew. Light from an unseen sun rose and fell. The pod's threads continued to wind around itself, but they did so violently, as if we were watching everything beyond the water wall in fast forward. The pod grew and shrank, and grew again. One moment, the cocoon was fat and distorted; the next it shrank like plastic wrap, showing Alyx's body beneath the gossamer threads.

"One second becomes many moments; a minute is now a day." The Watcher demon hissed quietly. The faint symbols that floated in front of Alyx's pod faded, and the movement within the confined area slowed, then became absolutely still.

The wall dropped and fell to the ground in a splash that left no trace of wetness.

As the room became whole again, we were jarred by an unseen force, like the moment a foot slams on the brakes of a moving vehicle. Hanging onto something had been an understatement. Lurching in synchronicity, we fell forward towards Alyx's pod, all of us except the Kasadya who was standing still on the chair.

A tear cut through the room, a sound of ripping cloth came from above our heads. I lifted my head to see the cocoon split from top to bottom, and as the fibers began to peel away, a wave of desire washed over me.

I was enthralled by the creature in the pod. I wanted it, had to be near it.

I was captivated as each layer of thread peeled back, slowly revealing Alyx's new form. As the last layer splayed outwards, his wings were the first thing we saw, wrapped protectively around his body. They glistened, slick with sweat. The smell in the room became thick with earthy spices, and it was delicious. It made me think of one thing: *surrender.*

Alyx slid gracefully from the pod to the floor, his wings expanding as he descended. The light in the room dulled and the shadows darkened until it was night and difficult to see, except for Alyx. He glowed.

His body had morphed into a tighter, more muscular version of his D'Alae form. Alyx, being a redhead, already had a light complexion, but whatever pink human tone his skin had once had was now gone. His skin was pure alabaster.

His hair had turned much redder, thicker, with golden highlights. All of his body hair was perfectly tinted the same way, and his wings and tail had a much deeper red cast to them. Small dark-red horns jutted out from the corners that formed the beginning of the widow's peak. Horns just like Alicia's.

He was beautiful.

He was godly.

Bright and pale, dark and sinister, and as much as I would have protected him before, now I would lay down my life for him. And then he softly whispered to me.

Let me feel you, let me touch you. I need you.

Everyone in the room took a step forward. He hadn't been talking to just me. He was addressing all of us.

That made me jealous. He was mine. I was his protector. It was my responsibility to give him everything—and anything he needed.

I stepped closer to Alyx, reached out a hand, and let him touch me.

My entire body shivered with yearning as his fingers wrapped themselves around my hand.

He drew me close. Freshly dug earth with hints of cinnamon and cloves danced through my nose and wet my mouth. It was intoxicating and sensual. I lost myself in his new eyes, they sparkled gold with flecks of emerald. The irises were snake slits.

"Alyx, let them go, use me, take me, I will give you all you need." I offered myself up to him.

Alyx wrapped his strong hand around my face, and his pointed nails dug into the back of my scalp. He leaned in towards me and inhaled deeply. Tendrils of my soul essence floated towards him, like the disappearing trails of a will-o'-the-wisp that evaporates into a haunted forest. As the tendrils rose higher, they caressed Alyx's face until they were absorbed into his skin and up through his nose.

Alyx's massive red wings wrapped around my body with surprising strength as he held me hostage, pulling me closer to him. My feet left the ground as he lifted me up. His barbed reddish tail poised behind him ready to strike.

The others in the room gasped as they were released from Alyx's enthrallment. Now that all of his attention was directed towards me—his prey—he had no use for the others around him.

Alyx had become a very potent and dangerous creature. He had the strength of a D'Alae and retained the wings to fly. He clearly had the incubi charms and sexual energy to ensnare any creature.

I had no idea what talents lay hidden from his father, my Master.

Hemming's deep voice boomed from behind the curtain of Alyx's protective wrap.

"Alyx, let him go. Look at who you are holding. Feasting on Dati is not what you want to do." I could hear Hemming shooing the others out of the room, getting them out of the immediate vicinity to hopefully protect them.

Alyx leered at me, his mouth slightly open. His bright red tongue lashed out, licking his long canines with anticipation of the imminent kill.

I have wanted to destroy you for doing this to me. My need to hurt you is the only thing that got me through the second change. You will pay.

Alyx's majestic voice resonated within my head. The words were terrifying. He was going to kill me.

His wings contracted, pulling me in closer. Alyx leaned in, nuzzling my neck, and inhaled again.

I had no desire to resist. I became completely limp in his grasp. I had hurt him so badly. If this was my punishment, so be it. I was his.

"Alyx!" Hemming said again. "You do not want to do this!" A snarl erupted from behind us, as I recognized the sounds of Hemming pulling the demon wolf to the surface. Bones were cracking and popping.

Lost in Alyx's embrace, I didn't care. I tilted my head to one side, granting more skin surface to Alyx. He inhaled another deep breath as I felt a little more of me let go.

And then we were tumbling, wings flapping, us rolling, snarling, growling, and spinning out of control. The soft paws of Hemming's wolf trotted away. He had knocked us forward, trying to get Alyx off of me.

Alyx's head smacked the hard surface of the back-office floor. He shook his head, and his eyes mellowed, losing the snakelike slits for pupils, his irises becoming a little less gold and a whole lot more green. The violent *I-will-kill-you* look quickly melted from his face, replaced by confusion and embarrassment.

A deep throbbing sensation welled up at the base of my neck, and it stung so badly my eyes blurred and watered.

I reached up to where my neck hurt and found Alyx's barbed tail stuck deep into the crook of my collarbone. I yanked it out, but it was too late.

Alyx pulled his tail back to himself, wrapping it around his leg. He cocked his head to one side, seeming sheepish.

"What is happening to me?" he asked.

The whole world spun. I grabbed for the nearest thing to steady me.

That thing was Alyx. As his poison coursed through my body, the sensation of needles stabbing my veins worked its way down my arm, but it was also disorienting.

"A mirror," was all I was capable of putting together.

Alyx dragged me over to an old mirror that was framed by an ornate wooden carving depicting leaves and twining stems. A snake wrapped itself through the foliage, making a complete circle around the reflecting glass. At the top, the snake was attempting to swallow its tail.

A puffy swollen brand was growing on my neck, in the fashion of a spiral. As it completed the last circle inwards, it ended in a barb, a hook just like the tails both Alyx and I had.

"Oh god, Alyx, you've marked me."

"How?" Alyx's eyebrows arched upwards with shock.

"An Incubus does it with a bite, during sex. Apparently, you've done it with your barb. I need to sit down." I staggered over to the chair that sat below the remnants of Alyx's Incubus pod. The room was still spinning.

As I sat down, the door opened and the others came in. Hemming glanced at me, cocking an eyebrow.

"Well, this is unusually quiet. One-night stand regrets?" he chided, always the joker.

"Worse." I showed Hemming the mark.

"Oh. Well, that pretty much seals that up then, doesn't it?"

"What do you mean?" Alyx cringed in the corner of the room and covered his rather naked self with his wings.

"You've marked Dati!" Hemming chuckled.

"I didn't mean to do it!" Alyx appeared panicked. *Poor boy, his head must be swimming.*

"You've tattooed him with your mark. That means you're connected to him, and he to you. Dati is basically your slave, but the twist is you'll find it rather difficult to not be around him." Hemming couldn't keep a straight face, and he bent over with laughter. "You've just traded one master for another, Dati!"

"Not funny," I said. I wanted to throw up, partly because of Alyx's poison, partly because Master would kill me when he saw the mark.

"Well then, we'll reverse it, or something," Alyx offered.

"Not unless one of you dies," Hemming said, still giggling. "And if I remember correctly, the redder the mark grows, the deeper the connection between each other." Hemming stepped over to study my swollen skin. "And that is about as ruby red as it gets."

Creatures

DATI

"No way! No goddamn way," Jenae said, scowling at the Watcher. "I'm not ripping through space and time ever again."

"But, Jenae, it's *way* quicker," Caleb pleaded.

The Kasadya demon stood silent, but from the look on his face, he was less than patient.

"I cannot—will not be able to get us exactly where we need to go. The Elementalist's wards will prevent any unexpected arrivals. But we will travel—should travel close to where we need to be."

"You hear that? Another puke fest and he doesn't even know where he's taking us. Absolutely not." Jenae crossed her arms.

"I'm with her." Riken's gaunt long features were horrified at the prospect of another dimensional walkabout with the Kasadya.

"My dear, you may be a witch, but you are one letter away from being something else entirely," Hemming said with a deadpan expression. "Then again, the two actually go together rather well."

"Insulting her probably isn't the most persuasive tactic," I said quietly to Hemming with an uneasy smirk, then mouthed the word *magic* to him, while circling my finger around my temple.

"Fine, fine. I'll pull some strings and get us a vehicle. But this is going to take some time." Hemming strode out of Marta's back office and disappeared, his long trench coat billowing out behind him.

Once we acquired a vehicle, the drive took hours. The painted lines of the highway shot out behind us like bullets, but the never-ending road across the vast prairies rarely changed.

Alyx sat beside me. His head bobbed sideways as he fell asleep, resting against my shoulder for a brief second. He woke quickly, then glanced at me awkwardly.

I *so* wanted him to need me.

I had developed new, deeper feelings for him since being stabbed in the neck by his barb. There was a twinge of yearning, an unsettled sense of anxiousness that made me feel lost when Alyx wasn't within my sights. I'd seen that anxiety in small children. It's that first sense of panic when they can't find their parents. That sensation quickly develops into full-blown terror, and I imagined I'd feel the same without Alyx.

Master, on the other hand, would not be pleased at all. There was no hiding the red tattoo. The retribution from Silenus would be epic—mind you, the path we travelled was so defiant, so mutinous, that being marked by another hardly felt like an unloyal act.

We would have to find a way to rest ourselves from Master's grip once and for all.

Alyx rested his head on my shoulder again. I wondered how he felt about us. Was I just a slave to him, or could there be a deeper connection?

I hoped his heart was as bonded to me as I felt to him.

Very gingerly, I inched closer, providing more support, but also allowing our thighs to touch. His heat was calming, and I soon forgot about Master and unrequited emotions from Alyx. For now, this was enough.

From the windows of the minivan, desolate branches of farmyard trees reached towards the sun. The base of each old gnarly trunk lay covered with blazes of gold, tawny yellow, and orange. Those yards slowly disappeared as dark green spikes of coniferous trees became more prevalent, making the fall colours seem brighter, perhaps even happier.

The van progressed through the first mountain pass. Cold shadows wrapped around our vehicle as the sun disappeared behind the massive rock formations.

We stopped in a small town and filled the van with gas as the sun set, casting an ominous red glow across the stone cliffs that surrounded us. I had seen the mountains before, but not often, and it was hard not to be impressed by their magnificence. Their peaks were impossibly high and craggy, heavily iced with gleaming snow caps on the very highest crests.

Jenae returned, clutching snacks from the convenience section of the gas station. The ensuing aroma of sour meat wafted through the van as she and Caleb shared a Pepperoni stick. Alyx and I both turned up our noses at the smell of dead meat.

No one really talked much. Caleb and Jenae snuggled together. Riken brooded in the seat next to the lovebirds. A visage of constant anger had settled on his face, and the shifting gaze indicated that he was thinking to himself, sharing nothing, and trusting no one. He reminded me of most of the demons I've had contact with. Most of us were exactly like that.

The Kasadya raised his hand and pointed past Hemming.

"Here. We will stop here and walk the rest of the way." The van came to a stop on the side of the highway, and Hemming rolled down the window, peering into the night. The beams from the headlights were swallowed up by the forest ahead of us.

"We can't leave the van on the side of the highway. It will attract attention," Hemming said thoughtfully. "We should try and hide it."

"There's an opening in the trees over there. Let's see how deep we can drive it into the forest," Caleb suggested.

Hemming directed the van carefully over the bumpy terrain and into the opening. Branches hit the roof, and one in particular made a horrible screeching noise as a tree scraped against metal.

"Well, that's going to leave a mark," Hemming sneered as if the van had been his. He killed the ignition, and the motor slowly died. With a sigh, he asked the Kasadya, "Okay, now what?"

"We walk." For the first time, the Kasadya smiled. It was a toothy smile, reminding me of a carved pumpkin at Halloween.

The mountain air was much colder than it had been in the city. It smelled clean and fresh, lacking the stench of exhaust fumes, machinery, and garbage that filled the city. There were no city sounds either. In fact, it was deafeningly quiet.

Following the Watcher, we plodded through the dark. The trees were a mob of spires that blocked our every step, yet the Watcher was searching.

It didn't take him long to discover what he was after. A small footpath led away from us, up the mountain and deeper into the dense wood. It was really nothing more than a slight opening in the trees and undergrowth, a trail that the local deer would have used.

"We have—will follow this." He pointed towards the ground. "Be wary. She has protected this. She does not welcome visitors. I am not certain— no, she does not know yet that we are coming."

"Great," Caleb grumbled. His expression of disgust was deep and loud, disturbing the eerie silence of the forest.

Twigs snapped underfoot, announcing our presence to the denizens of the forest as we made our way through the darkness. Lumbering forward, we followed directly behind the Kasadya. Riken, who was caught in the middle, stumbled frequently as we traversed over tree roots and dense underbrush.

"Ouch! Dammit, Caleb," Jenae screeched as she smacked his back.

"What?"

"You didn't hold that branch. God, now I'm bleeding. Shit, this hurts." Jenae sucked in air.

"Let me see," I said. Inspecting the cut on her forehead, I discovered she was indeed bleeding, but it wasn't very deep. "Let's keep going, shall we?"

That's when two red orbs—or what I thought were two red orbs—peered at us from within the woods. But it was fleeting, if anything at all.

Our path forced us to scale up a steep rock face, having to hoist each other up at one point, except for the Kasadya who was impossibly quick and nimble and able to traverse the landscape without any assistance from us, almost like he had walked these woods before.

Even with demon blood, the higher we climbed up the mountain, the more our exposed skin grew cooler. Jenae hugged herself, trying to stay warm. Despite travelling with a brood of demons, she was still human. She had to be feeling the cold night air. We hadn't really dressed well for a backwoods excursion.

The path leveled out considerably after scaling the cliff face. Trees opened up and became a little less dense, and our journey eased slightly. Far off in the distance, I could see smoke rising above the tops of the trees as the land sloped downwards into a large depression in the mountain's side.

An acrid smell tinged the air, and I tensed; one of us was nearby. It was faint, but the air seemed charged, thicker than it should have been. I noticed several of the massive trees that lined the path were dead, their trunks twisted like monstrous corpses in eerie death poses.

"Holy shit. Did you see that?" Caleb pointed ahead of us but slightly off to our side.

"See what?" I asked.

"Eyes. Red ones," he said with a sense of dread.

"Hemming, I think we're being followed," I whispered as I pulled him close. "I saw a pair of them after we crossed the stream."

Hemming stared at me, seemingly stunned. "Why didn't you say something?"

"I wasn't sure," I said, "but I am now. Let's keep moving but be on guard."

"What is it?" Alyx turned to me. There was just the slightest amount of uncertainty in his gaze, and the citrusy smell of his fear gently tickled the inside of my nose.

"I don't know, but we'll be careful. Besides, we're almost there."

As we continued the trek surrounded by dense forest, each of us confirmed when we spotted the red eyes staring back at us. They were always several trees away and disappeared as soon as they were spotted.

As the forest receded, our inquisitive guest became less shy, accompanying our band as we moved forward. At the widest point of the path, we came to an enormous hedge that blocked our passage. Tall and thick, it had been carefully manicured with a rounded arch, and through the opening, I could see a river-stone cottage with a thatched roof. It seemed cold and forgotten.

Jenae screamed.

"I can't lift my foot. It's got me!"

Her eyes rolled white. Caleb roared, his face morphed into a snarling bear muzzle, bones cracking and popping as they rearranged themselves to take on the demon bear form. Caleb's hands were large to begin with, but one swipe of his bear paws would be lethal. He charged towards Jenae's foot.

"No!" Hemming darted in between Jenae and Caleb. He put out a hand, and Caleb stopped. "You cannot touch it."

Caleb snorted. Thick billows of hot breath puffed out his nose like a bull challenging the matador.

Jenae's head listed back as she began to mumble—the air became quiet and still, save for her words.

Hemming grabbed a large fallen stick, thick enough to be a club, and swung. With one deft stroke of the club, an expert golf swing, the hand that had clutched Jenae's foot flew into the air, releasing her.

Realizing she was no longer bound, Jenae calmed and her irises returned to their normal colour. Letting out an exasperated sigh, she approached Caleb, who shifted back into human form. His shredded shirt hung in strips from his waistband, revealing his hairy, muscular chest.

"I'm okay. I'm okay. It just startled me," she said as Caleb wrapped his arms around her in comfort.

But no sooner had she mouthed those words, than the ground started crawling and moving as corpses emerged.

Rotten meat hung off their decaying limbs and torsos. As they ripped themselves out of the dirt, heads with little to no flesh turned to search us out, their eye sockets caked with mud. The entire field where we stood crawled with the dead, and they advanced towards us.

I wasn't prepared for this.

My D'Alae strength couldn't match the relentlessness of the living dead. Keeping them as guardians was clever. They were resilient. The only way to stop them was to take out their arms and legs. Even that didn't *kill* them, but it slowed their advance enough to escape. Their grasp was the killing blow—it would sap the life out of any living tissue.

"Don't touch them, and don't let them touch you," Hemming said sternly.

If an attack on one front wasn't enough, the red eyes that had followed us up the mountain appeared again in the forest. But it wasn't a single pair of eyes. Gathering in masses and floating soundlessly towards us, it seemed like there were hundreds of the creatures.

The ethereal beings came out of the woods and floated above the rotting corpses. All I could make of them were red orbs within shadows.

Alyx crouched in front of us and spread his wings in a guard stance, hiding most of the group behind him. I could smell hints of cinnamon, nutmeg, and fresh earth wafting off of him. He was going off of instinct and using whatever power he had at his disposal, but the heady aroma would only seduce everyone in our group and the creatures around us.

The ground writhed as more limbs erupted out of the ground. I held up my arm to protect my eyes from a spray of dirt and ended up with a mouthful of grit and mud instead.

One of the red-eyed shadow beings moved directly towards Alyx, never slowing. It reached out a dark hand and placed it on Alyx's chest. The hand dissolved into Alyx's torso.

He gasped in shock.

Alyx threw his head back and exhaled torrents of black smoke. His body rose, arms outstretched, until he hung a couple of feet off the ground suspended in midair. The red-eyed monster continued to push a deadly smoulder through Alyx's chest and into his lungs, choking him to death.

I had never seen anything like it before.

I howled. My skin tightened and fangs lengthened as I unleashed my demon and charged the shadow, wings splayed, and tail poised to strike.

The red eyes peeked at me, and then it vanished.

Alyx floated helplessly towards me. I grabbed him as he continued to spew the noxious cloud out of his opened throat. His eyes glassed over, then flipped into the back of his head.

"What the Hell? Hemming, what are these things?" I demanded. But he didn't respond. "Hemming?" I asked, just as another red-eyed monster thrust its hand into Hemming's torso. Black smoke cascaded out Hemming's mouth and down his chest.

Something grabbed my foot. I glanced down to find cadaverous hands gripping my boots, holding me fast.

This was not going well.

I glanced around for assistance from others or for the stick Hemming had used as a club, only to see the Kasadya demon standing in the middle of the fray. None of the creatures were attacking him.

From my peripheral vision, within the arch of the hedge, another creature emerged, moving in fluid steps. Her dress billowed and flowed behind her. The woman carried a staff made of alabaster wood with most of the tree bark still attached to it. A bleached human skull sat crooked, strapped to the top of the stick with thick twine.

The woman lifted the hood of the robe. Within a blink, she hovered directly in front of me.

Her face, covered in mud and wrinkled, glared at me with ebony eyes. Caked hair hung in greasy thick dreads. A beetle crawled across the cheekbone, then disappeared into one nostril.

She slammed the staff down into the mud as she opened her maw and let an airy "Ahhhhh" escape.

Dread filled my soul from the sound of her voice, and shivers ran down my spine, my flesh going cold. As soon as the staff made contact with the ground, a ripple of energy emanated outwards, like a drop of water hitting the surface of a still pond.

The shadows vanished, dissipating like smoke from a campfire. The corpses slowly melted back into the earth.

Alyx, Riken, and Hemming dropped onto the ground, all three choking and wheezing as they tried to get air back into their lungs.

Elementalist

DATI

"What creatures trespass on my mountain?" She spoke with a raspy voice of an old lady.

The Kasadya stepped up to the front. "Mistress Aradia, I have heard of your mastery with Air, Earth, and Fire. We have a need for your talents."

The Elementalist hovered in place, contemplating this.

Her fingers pulled at her chin, and at first, I thought she was thinking, like some people stroke or twirl their hair while deep in thought. I was wrong. She picked and pulled on the skin that covered her chin until it peeled away, and continued the movement until her face had come right off. She folded the skin and stuffed it into a tiny sac she had tied at her waist.

What was left of her face was a mess of bloody tissue, but within seconds, emanating from the ears and jawline, a second skin quickly grew, creating lusciously smooth caramel skin with dark pouty lips. Her cheekbones were rigid and high, which gave her clear blue eyes a sense of severity. Her dreadlocks still hung in dirt-caked, matted strands.

"To control the dead, you must *wear* the dead," she explained as she walked around our group, studying each of us with just a passing glance. "You. Girl. You come here," she commanded.

Jenae glanced at the Kasadya, then at me, holding onto Caleb's hand like a vise grip. The Kasadya pushed Jenae forward.

"Do as you have been asked," he said with disgust for Jenae. "Forgive her, Mistress. She is new and unlearned."

"Come here, child. I will not harm you." She stretched out a hand as if the two were schoolchildren, meeting on the playground for the first time. "Come, don't be shy. Let me have a look at you," Aradia said in a sweet voice.

Jenae and Aradia clasped hands. The minute Aradia's long slender fingers, capped with fierce fingernails, wrapped themselves around Jenae's white trembling hands, Aradia hummed.

"Oh dear, child, so much potential. Do you feel that, between you and me, that pulse, that warmth? Yes, I do believe we'll be good friends." She cocked her head to one side, pulling Jenae close to her side and wrapping her arm around her shoulder. "Come, all of you. I want to see who my new friend has for travelling companions."

Walking through the arch, we followed Aradia and Jenae and passed by a small garden with assorted herbs and tender plants.

Her cottage was just beyond the garden. It was old, made of thick round boulders slathered with mortar to keep them together. Thick and darkened wooden beams framed the door and windows, but the glass in them was so filthy I couldn't see inside. The roof was made of various slabs of wood and patched here and there with fallen trees from the forest around. Moss and tiny ferns littered the surface of the roof, which was why I had thought it was thatched from a distance.

Nothing appeared stable or solid. The chimney was on the furthest side of the cottage, part of it crumbling away.

Aradia opened the door to the small hut and ushered us inside. Surprisingly, we were treated to a wall of warm air as we walked in through the threshold. A raging fire burned in the hearth, and there were candles lit all around the place casting a warm glow, illuminating the living quarters. Trinkets and herbs, bowls and books plagued every flat surface. Something scurried away out of sight as we made our entrance.

There were tall glass pillars in each corner of the room, like old roman columns, but their contents were visible. Each was vibrantly lit from the core and a different colour.

The closest pillar pulsated with the colour of sand, filled with assorted layers of dirt, dried leaves, and tiny rocks, and an enormous slimy worm was pressed against the glass, wriggling its way upwards, leaving a sticky trail behind it.

In the next corner, a pillar was consumed inside with tall flames of orange, red, yellow, and the occasional lick of green and blue. I wasn't sure, but I thought a tiny hand pressed up against the glass, a hand created from clumps of burning embers.

The third pillar had smoke and roiling fog contained within. Shades of purple and smoky grey with hints of yellow undulated inside its confinement, and oddly, it appeared more sinister than the other two.

The last pillar was empty. Well, not quite. There was the odd water droplet inside of it, a trickle running down the inside of the glass. Aradia noticed me studying each of them.

"My sources. Each a different element, Earth, Fire, Air, and alas Water, which is near empty. Each Elementalist has these, they are our tools, and we study them, combine the inherent energies with the fifth element, Soul.

"From this, we can make powerful things happen. But not quite as powerful as what we have here, my dear," she said, nodding in Jenae's direction. Jenae's cheeks reddened with embarrassment, but then she smiled.

"Told you," Jenae said as she elbowed Caleb in a playful way.

"Ha! Careful, child. You are new; I can feel the power in you. I can see the souls you carry with you. That is power! I respect that, and you should too," Aradia cautioned.

"'Souls you carry with you'?" I asked.

Aradia flung her head around to stare at me displeasingly, making one thing very clear. I was allowed in there because of Jenae. She had little or no interest in me and possibly the others. I was but an annoyance.

I glanced at Jenae, waiting for an explanation. I didn't want to displease Aradia, so I kept quiet.

"I'll explain later," Jenae said.

"Yes, later. Later would be better." Aradia squinted her eyes at me, then returned her focus to Jenae. "So, child, tell me: why do you come here with three skin-changers, two demons, and..." Aradia was peering directly at Alyx when she stopped midthought. My back stiffened, and I leaned forward. Powerful or not, I wouldn't let her hurt Alyx.

She sensed my movement and lifted a hand in my direction. Instantly I was thrown back towards the stone wall by a violent wind, and pinned there. The impact against the cabin's stone walls sucked the wind out of me. In that same heartbeat, Aradia was inches from my face, hissing at me. The new caramel skin shrank, wrapping tight around her features, while her eyes turned into burning embers. She opened her mouth, making that awful "Ahhhh" sound again. Her mouth was black and putrid.

"Don't test me, demon. I don't like you and will make short work of you," she hissed, then spun around and resumed her study of Alyx, circling him like a shark.

Her features melded back into a more human form.

"Well, now, boy, I don't think I've ever seen the likes of you." She sniffed him, then glanced at Jenae and leaned in to her neckline and inhaled deeply. "Interesting. Perhaps this group is more intriguing than I first saw."

Aradia scurried around the cottage, pulling together some bottles of dried things, a piece of parchment paper, and then sat at what appeared to be her usual spot: a rickety old stool. It creaked as she sank her slim body onto it, then leaned over a table so worn with use its top was black.

All of us stared in fascination as she placed a drop of dark blue smoke into the mortar that sat before her, then added some sandy grit into the bowl. She picked up her pestle and started to grind, and as she did, she mouthed words, but nothing I could quite make out. Sprinkling some dried herbs, she continued her chant, and then added more of the grit.

She got up suddenly, grabbed a nearby pitcher, and disappeared out the door, then returned far too fast with the vessel full of water. She walked over to the mortar and poured in as much as she could.

We all waited as the mixture swirled, mesmerized. Seconds later, the concoction boiled, but there was no heat source.

Aradia nodded in satisfaction. She took the parchment and carefully dipped it into the water, then poked at it, submersing it until the sheet was soaked.

She took the soggy paper out of the bowl, walked around to the front of her desk, and with an arm, moved all of the items that were on the table off to one side, making room to lay the wet parchment flat on the surface.

"Come," she commanded, and beckoned Jenae and Alyx. Obediently, they moved towards her.

But just as the two approached, Aradia moved past them and sniffed the air again. She stepped towards Caleb and Riken. She cocked an eyebrow and tilted her head, then pointed at the new Shape-Shifters.

"You, too. Forward," she commanded.

Aradia placed herself between the table with the wet piece of paper and the four she had separated. She lashed out quickly, grabbing Caleb's big paw of a hand, and slapped his forearm.

"Open!"

Caleb glanced around at us, confused, but did what he was told. Aradia nodded, then with her free hand, pulled a pin out of her lapel, and stabbed the end of Caleb's finger.

"Ouch, bitch, that hurt," Caleb said, and then immediately regretted his choice of words.

Aradia stared up at him, pupils completely gone, no iris, just the white of her eye. Hissing, she said, "Don't tempt me, boy. I'll make bear soup out of your hide." Her lip curled, exposing blacked teeth.

"Sorry," Caleb whispered and hung his head. Blood dripped from his finger.

Aradia's eyes returned to normal. "Press the paper near the bottom."

Caleb did as he was told, leaving a bloody smear on the paper. Each of the four had their turn, flinching as the pin stuck their fingers, until there were four bloody smears.

Aradia picked the bloodstained paper up, took a knife from the table, and stabbed the parchment to the beam of the window so that all could see.

The blood diluted on the page and rose upwards from all four fingerprints.

Jenae's and Alyx's smears altered in colour as they climbed up the sheet, and then the blood morphed to a solid ebony bar. Both columns stopped growing at that point. They were similar, but not identical.

Caleb's and Riken's continued up, past the top of Jenae's and Alyx's marks. The brothers' blood marks were, on the other hand, identical in shape and colour and slowly traversed from light purple to an odd shade of orange, then shifted to green, and suddenly, the two columns stopped growing and the colour went solid black.

"Well now, that explains the smell," Aradia confirmed.

"Mistress, please, what do you see?" the Watcher asked.

"Well, isn't it obvious?" she said flippantly, tsking afterwards. "These two are brother and sister." She pointed to Jenae and Alyx, then turned her attention to Riken and Caleb. "But these two have shared the womb.

"Although that's not even the interesting part," she cooed. "They are all related. Your father—" She pointed at Jenae and Alyx. "—is their great grandfather—and from the deepness of the black end mark, a rather potent demon himself!"

Jenae, who had been standing as close to Caleb as she could get, shrank away. Alyx stared at Jenae with rounded eyes and mouth agape.

"So the question is—who is really here to visit me? And what do you want with me? I have no quibble with the likes of a demon who makes that black of a mark or who has an interest in creating Daimonion."

Soulless

ALYX

"You're my sister?" My entire life, it had always been just me and my mom, and I had watched as she was ripped from me. But standing right beside me was my sister. *I have a sister.* I wasn't alone in this world. I still had family, *and* I was a big brother.

So much had happened within a short period of time. I had gone from human to demon to ultra-demon. I had lost my mother, gained a slave, and apparently, a sibling.

"I have a sister!" I grabbed Jenae and gave her a huge hug.

"Half-sister," Jenae retorted, then pushed herself out of the embrace. But she gave me a quirky little smile.

"Alyx, I'm sorry—I forgot. Your mother gave me this." Dati pulled a crumpled photo from his pocket and handed it to me.

I examined the blurry picture, and although it had been taken many years ago, it was pretty obvious. Me with red hair, Jenae with her blonde locks, and between us, a dark-haired man crouched with an arm around each of us, a man I immediately recognized.

Silenus.

But the Silenus I had met was the Satyr from the forest glen where I had gone during my meditations. I felt sick. In the picture, he didn't have the horns or the goat legs, but the face...the face was the same. There was no mistaking it.

This demon, this sick bastard, was my father?

"Are you absolutely sure?" I asked hesitantly, crumpling the photo into a ball. Cold sweat beaded my forehead. Dati came closer to me, putting a hand on my shoulder.

"Marta said she wanted to protect you from him," Dati explained. "There are a few more pieces to this, Alyx. That man, he's also our Master. He's the same one who infected us with the parasites that altered you." Dati grimaced. I think he was having a hard time spitting out words.

"Silenus did all this?" I asked, feeling deflated. It was hard to believe that my father was responsible for so much violence and cruelty.

Aradia's eyes widened. "Silenus, you say?" She cocked an eyebrow while examining us closely, her gaze passed slowly between Dati and I. "Do you know who this creature is? Do you know what the beast is?"

"He's a sadist. Even for a demon, he's particularly violent and ruthless," Dati stated.

Aradia snapped her head around to glower at Dati. "Beast, you are so blind. He's no demon."

"I've been enslaved to him for over two hundred years. I think I can safely say he's a demon," Dati said, but Aradia shook her head.

"He is a demigod! He is the Goat Lord; he is Pan—the physical manifestation of sexuality and of all things wild. He is a trickster and has no use for the likes of humans. He has for years wanted only one thing..." Aradia's train of thought ended as she glanced around her one-room cabin. "Let's see, where is that—"

She spun around and, with quick movements, flew through the room, searching in large bottles and behind books. At last, she opened a large barrel that sat near her bed. "Ah, there you are."

Aradia reached in and pulled out a long black snake, which showed its discomfort at being manhandled by attempting to slither back into its hiding spot. She grabbed the serpent by the back of its head and stared directly into its reptilian eyes.

"You will do what I want," she hissed at the snake.

With the snake's head still clutched between her fingers, she approached me. Snakes are cool and all, but they're cooler behind a glass enclosure, not this close. Dati leaned forward, tense and on edge, and I took a step back.

She released the snake's head. Its forked tongue flicked in and out, tasting the air between us. Without warning, it lashed out, mouth open, long fangs exposed, and plunged itself into the side of my neck.

The pain was quick and sharp. I could feel my wings splay straight out behind me, knocking Riken over.

Dati jumped up a second time and took two steps towards me, but the Elementalist raised her hand. A gust of wind blew through the cottage, picking up Dati and throwing him against the wall again with a dull thud while a flutter of loose papers floated gracefully to the floor.

"Demon, I warned you," Aradia said.

I could feel the snake pulsating, sucking blood out of me. My hands flailed, trying to rip the serpent off of me.

"Get it off, get it off!" I clawed at the thing's head. Searing pain shot down the side of my neck and into my shoulder. I hit the thing's head several times, but it did no good. All I could feel was the smooth scales of the snake's head and an odd pulsating sensation.

No one would offer any assistance. They'd all seen what just happened to Dati.

As fast as the serpent bit me, it relaxed its jaws and pulled away. I could feel trickles of blood running down my neck. I lost my balance and fell backwards.

Dati bridged the gap between where he had been pushed to the wall and caught my arm just before I landed sideways.

As the serpent retreated, it wound itself around the Elementalist's arm as if to constrict her, but then it struck for a second time sinking its long fangs into the witch's wrist.

Aradia hissed. The skin near the puncture wound tightened, making her hand appear skeletal. Her eyes rolled into the back of her head as she stood, nodding as if she was listening to a conversation none of us could hear. She said nothing but repeated the creepy "Ahhhh."

Cold shivers ran down my spine, and my tail twitched. That sound coming from her mouth was enough to creep anyone out.

The snake released her and slithered up her sleeve, diving deep into her robe. The skin on Aradia's hand returned to its normal plumpness and her eyes rolled forward. She fixed her gaze on me.

She seemed afraid.

"I did not think such thing was possible. You, boy, you are made for *him*. You are *his* makeup; Satyr, D'Alae, and Incubi. Goat legs and hooved feet, tail and horns, a body constructed to appeal to the *darkest one.*"

"You mean...*the* dark lord? Satan? Why would *he* want or need Alyx?" Dati asked.

"But I don't have goat legs..." I started, somewhat dumbly.

"You're a human imbued with all the talents and abilities *he* needs."

Everyone looked at her, somewhat stunned, and a little unsure.

"I'm sorry, what? I'm made for Satan? Like what...an offering? I'm not being an offering...to anyone, let alone the devil," I retorted angrily.

Aradia said nothing but stared at me intensely, thinking, and then mumbled to herself.

"There is something I know of, something I have, but it's only a partial copy, not the original. I thought that ceremony was lost, gone from this world and the other." As she said *other*, she pointed down.

Scurrying to a corner of the shack where several shelves held an assortment of books, Aradia ran her finger over the old tattered spines, searching, tossing books out of it, leaving the discarded ones in a slowly growing pile on the floor, until she found one leatherbound tome, tan coloured with glyphs on the front that appeared as if they had been etched in blood.

As she opened the tome, a breeze wafted through the room. The fire in the elemental pillar burned a bright yellow as a wave of heat flashed through the room. The flames on the candles became small torches, rapidly melting the wax.

She flipped through several pages until she came to what she had been hunting for.

"This. This is what your Master, Silenus, has been planning. That is why the boy has been created." She gestured towards me. She lay the book down on the bed, and all of us gathered around to see the page.

As we studied the book, a drawing of Satan moved in choppy distorted motions. Despite the animation, I could have been looking at a picture of myself. Only one thing was different: the goatlike legs. Everything else was a perfect match.

The rest of the page contained text, which shifted and rolled across the page, disappearing and merging with other symbols. It would have made it hard to read, except for the fact that it was written in a language I had never seen before.

"This is how to bring *him* here. Very difficult, but it was said that the one who managed to free *him* from Hell would be counted as part of *his* ranks.

"That would mean unending power and immortality. *He* cannot physically move from one plane to another. The seals were put in place to prevent that. If the seals were damaged, *his* soul might manage to slip past those broken bindings. But a free soul would need a body of the same to inhabit once *he* was here."

"Maybe I wasn't clear the first time. That's not happening. No one is going to inhabit me," I said in defiance. Aradia ignored me.

"The only way to do that would be through a Soul Door." The minute Aradia stopped, she mumbled again to herself and glanced at Jenae.

"Girl. You know what this means for you?" Aradia beamed with excitement. She scurried over to a chest she had near the head of her bed, flipped open the lid, and dug around inside. Aradia lifted her hand, holding a large rock. It appeared to be a piece of coal, except it pulsated, glowing white from inside. She walked over and held her rock directly in front of me. "Hold this. Do it. Give me your hand." She grabbed my hand and shoved the rock into my palm.

It felt warm and rough, but it began to glow.

"Pass it," Aradia instructed. I turned and gave it to Dati. The rock went coal black as it passed between us, and then slowly started to pulse again in his hand. But for Dati, the rock only glowed from one side. Dati passed it around so that everyone held it in turn. It responded as it had when I held it, for each person, a bright white glow.

Only Jenae had not held it.

"Give it to her! Now." Aradia could barely contain her enthusiasm.

Jenae placed it into her palm.

Nothing.

No glow. No light. It remained black and dead.

"Your father has done this," Aradia whispered with a cocked eyebrow and a sneer.

"What? Why won't it glow?" Jenae said frantically, shaking the rock.

"Girl, you are dead inside. That is a soul stone; it resonates with the extra spark of life that's in all of us, except you. You have no soul of your own, and that is why you carry the souls of your feasts with you. The souls are attracted to you because they are trying to fill the hole."

"What do you mean I have no soul? How can I be alive if I have no soul? That's stupid," Jenae said with a tinge of fear on the edge of her words.

"Oh, the body runs itself just fine. The soul is what connects you to the other realms and how you pass on to the next life and how you learn life lessons. You will do none of these. There's only one way to achieve such a state in a human. A vile task and malevolent, and yet, very clever, it would never be done easily." Aradia's chest puffed out like she was even more proud to have Jenae in her home.

Jenae, on the other hand, was ashen with terror and clinging to Caleb's arm. She shook her head. It looked like she didn't want to know more.

"Girl, do you know what he has done to create you? Your father, the demigod, had to capture a being of the Light and keep it captive until it bore him a child, a female child. And then that female child would have to bear him another child, and again, and so on, until you.

"He sullied a creature of enlightenment and love through six generations, killing any potential for a soul. A witch with no soul born from the rape of a light creature creates a Soul Door. You are meant to bring *him* here, and you, boy, are *his* host."

"I'm not doing any such thing." A tear ran down Jenae's cheek. Her nails dug quite deeply into Caleb's arm as if she were afraid someone would tear her away from him.

"There is more. In order to bring *him* here, Silenus will require many servants for the ceremony to use the Soul Door. Look, it says: 'Two the same guard back from night, afore and behind mark the way'. Two the same. What are two and yet are the same? Twins, like you two!" Aradia pointed to Riken and Caleb. "But you are not right, you are not identical twins. It says in the book, you must be 'the same'. So there must be others."

"See, Hemming, I told you, we weren't very high on Master's approval list," Dati said. "Yes, Silenus has others that he commands. And Silenus is also making more demons."

"What do you mean? Making more? There is no making of demons outside of Hell."

"Well, he found a way to create Alyx, Caleb, and Riken. They aren't human anymore," Dati argued.

Aradia hissed at him, "But they are not all demon either."

"You mean there's a chance that I might go back to being human?" I leaned forward, thinking there might be a way out of this yet.

"Now why, child, would you want that? And besides, no. You are Daimonion! A mix. Human, yes, a little. Demon mostly, I suspect." Aradia's gaze wandered over each of us.

"But in Hell, the process was the same..." Hemming started but was quickly shut down.

"In Hell, demon flesh is infused with a human soul. Vastly different. These boys are humans, with human souls. The demon flesh is all mixed in," she said, waving her hand in a little circle. "There's no way now to separate, but no, they are not demons. Daimonion, though, yes, and very powerful ones. But how is he doing this?"

Hemming stepped forward and lifted his shirt. A nasty red scar ran just under his ribcage where three of his parasites had ripped their way out of him.

"Silenus infected us with...bugs—let's call them bugs. Bugs that are living off of us, and when they find someone else they like, they rip themselves out of us and bore their way into the other. From there, the lucky candidate gets to change into one of us," Hemming explained. "I have three left in me."

"I have some too," Jenae, still teary-eyed, whimpered out.

"As do I and the Watcher," finished Dati.

"That's how I got to be D'Alae and Incubi?" I asked.

Dati nodded, but there was a hint of guilt and sadness in his face.

"Well now." Aradia's eyebrow was cocked once again, but her mouth was a tight scowl. "Clever little goat-man, aren't we?"

"Aradia, great Mistress, I am told you have the ability to remove these parasites from us?" the Watcher demon asked, but it seemed more like a compliment than a question.

"Aradia, how do we stop this from happening?" I asked.

"I cannot be involved in this or anything to do with you. Silenus is more powerful than you know," she said, spinning away from us. She mumbled again and stiffened. She stood as still as concrete with her back to us as she peered out her dirty window. "Unless...Unless you are all willing to pay a very high price for the use of my magic."

"We'll do anything," I said.

Dati and Hemming's heads whipped around and glared at me with anger plastered on their faces.

"The boy speaks a little too quickly," Hemming said. "What's your price, witch?"

"You must give me all the parasites you have within you," Aradia said. "And then you must let me use the Soul Door." She glanced at Jenae and waited.

"If it stops that bastard and gets rid of the bugs inside of me, then I'll do it," she said. "But I don't know how to be a Soul Door. You'll have to show me what to do. How do I open the door and bring a soul through me?"

"I can teach you what you'll need to know," Aradia said coldly and flatly, her eyes dead and emotionless. "Of course, I'll also need blood and flesh for the soul that comes through the door. And for that, someone must die."

Dissolution

DATI

"You crazy-ass bitch," Hemming said before turning his glare towards the Kasadya. "No way. This is insane. You brought us here for this?"

"I have—was going to tell you there was to be a price," the Watcher demon said.

"Doesn't matter because we're leaving."

"But what about the bugs, Hemming?" I asked, not that I was going to volunteer to sacrifice my life, nor would I even think of letting Alyx give himself up. "Where else are we supposed to go? Think about your son or being free from that malicious bastard?"

Alyx stepped forward, his brows stitched together in thought. Very quietly, he whispered, "Does it matter whose life?"

"I care not. I simply need the blood and the flesh," Aradia said as plainly as "pass the salt" at the dinner table.

Alyx turned towards me with a sly look. His irises were snake slits, shinning gold and emerald.

"What if we were to get Silenus here? He could be the sacrifice." Alyx dropped the idea like a bomb right into the middle of us and watched the explosions of incredulity circle around him from everyone in the room. It was completely absurd. "Seriously, think about it. None of us want him to live after what he's done to us."

"And how do you propose we get him here?" I asked.

"I think, given the opportunity, the temptation to come and collect his Soul Door and his Host would be a bit of a draw. I'm kinda new to all this, but I would bet Silenus has gone to great efforts to create us, right? He doesn't want to lose us." Alyx had an impish smirk plastered on his face. "In fact, if anything, he would want *more* of us. No? Isn't that why he put parasites into Jenae? It's insurance. Create exactly more of her in case she couldn't get the job done. I'm sure he would have stuffed me full of bugs too if he had half a chance."

"Okay, that explains why he would come, but how are you going to get him halfway up a mountain?" Caleb said, growling.

"Slipping," Aradia interjected. "You, boy, you're Satyr, you can slip and bring him here."

"Sorry, what?" Alyx seemed completely confused.

"Slipping, boy. Teleportation... You, beast, you taught him nothing?" Aradia cocked an eyebrow.

"I don't know anything about *slipping*."

"Yes, you do, Alyx. In fact, you've done it," I said, remembering.

"What? When?"

"Yes, you have. At least once. Do you remember when you emerged from your first pod? You had a giant fern leaf in your hand. Where did that come from? It shouldn't have been there."

"The first time I changed? Wait... I went to my glen, my safe spot. The place where Silenus and I met and—" Alyx stopped midsentence, blanched a little, and then quickly picked up the thought again. "And there's a large fern bed there. I had crawled up into it and pulled the leaves over me as a blanket."

"So, somehow, you slipped to your glen. But you must have come back," I said, astounded.

"If I go back to the glen where Silenus and I first met, I bet the bastard would come. Once he's there with me, maybe I can grab him and teleport both of us or trick him into following me."

I was a little proud of him. Alyx had thought of a way around Aradia's price without sacrificing any of us. But there was at least one hole in that plan of his.

"Alyx, you haven't mastered slipping yet. Attempting to drag someone with you can't be easy." I didn't really know the ins and outs of Satyr abilities.

"Well then, we'd better start practicing," he said.

"Mistress Aradia, may I ask?" the Watcher queried.

"You may, Watcher," she replied.

"If Alyx brings the Satyr demigod here, surely you would have the magical abilities to bind him?" the Kasadya asked.

Aradia hesitated, then wryly smiled at the Watcher. "I do, and I can."

"Then with your brilliance, we may stand a chance."

"Why thank you, Watcher."

"So then, if Alyx brings Silenus here, he would then be bound by you and unable to move. Will you also be able to spill his blood?" the Watcher continued.

"I'll do that," I said, curling my lip to expose a little fang. "He has tormented me for the longest, and before he dies, I want to see the look in his eyes as his life drains out before him. I want to watch his face contort when I rip that necklace from around his neck and pocket the soul vial that belongs to me. I will do this. I will end him."

"Hold up," Hemming said. "So, we are dependent upon Satyr-D'Alae-Incubi boy here to time warp, and then for freaky witch-woman to bind him to the spot...assuming Silenus won't slip his own ass out and then what?" He sounded skeptical. "How does the rest of the spell go? How is this Soul Door opened?"

"That part I will teach the girl," Aradia said confidently and winked at Jenae.

"I don't like this," Hemming said. "And what are you going to do once this door is opened? Who exactly are you bringing through?"

Aradia glared at Hemming and finally answered very succinctly, "My sister."

Hemming and Aradia were locked in a staring contest. Hemming broke contact and glanced away.

"I still don't like this."

"What choice do we have? We've already been gone too long. Silenus is going to know that we've travelled outside his territory without permission." I was a little terrified but just a little excited too. The thought of possibly being free was almost uplifting, like we could get away with this crazy plan.

I turned to the Elementalist. "And what are you going to do with our parasites? That was part of the deal, right? You would remove them?"

"I will remove them, but only if I get to keep them," she stated again, coldly.

"That is just fine by me," I said.

No one disagreed.

Aradia had said she could only remove the parasites from one person a day. She said that it took too much magic to do more than that, so we camped out, which wasn't comfortable at all, given that there were eight of us in a one-room cottage.

We had been out in the side yard during the first extraction. Aradia wanted Jenae to go first, and the screaming was horrid. Apparently, getting the vile creatures out was just as painful as them going in. The shrieking had completely destroyed Alyx's ability to concentrate.

"I can't do this with that going on!" he said, frustrated. "It sounds like Aradia is killing her."

Another piercing scream ripped through the air just as Alyx began yet another attempt to meditate. His brows furrowed, and he shook his head from side to side. He stood up from the stone bench we were sitting on.

"Come on, let's get away from here. I can't do this while listening to her scream," he said.

"You know, if you can't find the trigger to make you slip, this whole plan is going to be useless," I said.

"You know I know that, right?" Alyx said as he glanced back at me, annoyed.

We walked in silence for a long time, heading deeper into the forest, until we came to a copse of trees that was dense enough to block out Jenae's screams. We fought our way through the thick bramble of shrub and brush and came across a natural clearing. Together, we sat down on a large boulder. A beam of sunlight shone through the clearing, warming the rock and the area around us.

Alyx glared up at the light. The last few days together I had noted that his facial expressions waffled between rage and awkwardness. Right now, he seemed to be particularly angry, or maybe upset. I wasn't sure.

"Okay, we need to talk," I said.

Alyx immediately appeared uncomfortable.

"Do you remember when Alicia dragged you into your mother's shop, hogtied? You were foaming at the mouth you were so angry, and that rage seemed to be directed at me. You've also morphed not once, but twice, and every demon I know runs off of anger and hate.

"You've been put through Hell. Every time I look at you, I can see the fury in your eyes. I know that hatred hasn't gone away. The demon ire within you is going to burn hot for a long time, so, come on, out with it. I have to be around you. You've marked me, whether you wanted to or not, and now whenever you're not around, I'm anxious and distressed, and I have no idea how you feel. Are you connected to me too because of this thing?" I pointed to the red brand. "We need to clear the air, so...let's talk."

Alyx studied me, his irises shifted to the incubi snake slits. The colours mesmerized me as the iris swirled from light emerald to blazing topaz.

"I am still angry at you, but it's not your fault. The whole thing is nobody's fault except for maybe Silenus. I hate him. Everything he's done to me...to you, to Jenae." Alyx rested his head in his hands. "You know right before Alicia killed Mom, she cast a spell."

"Oh, I remember. It killed me to watch you like that. And then to have Alicia infect you again, and what she did to your mom. I keep saying it, Alyx, but I really am so sorry, for everything that's happened. But I don't know what to do—if there's anything I can do to fix this."

"It's okay, Dati. That word Mom said, that spell—it was a Ukrainian word. It means 'to be still', but it's more than just being motionless. It's more about being calm. Except as a spell, it *forced* my mind to be calm. The anger left me for a little while. And then Mom shared with me everything you had showed her. That glow in the room—that was Mom sharing her vision. I saw everything. Including every moment you sat beside those hideous pods where I was trapped. It's pretty clear you care about me. I should be the one to apologize, not you."

I didn't know what to say.

"So you're not angry?" I asked, incredulous.

"Oh, Hell yes, I'm angry. I'm angry all the time. Sometimes it burns so hot all I see is red and all I can think about is killing anything within my reach. That's not me. How do you deal with this?" Alyx closed his eyes. "Is it going to be like this forever?"

"No. It will subside a little, but it takes time. I can help you, if you want me to," I offered, hoping desperately he would say yes.

"If we get through this mess with Silenus, I'm going to need you to teach me a lot of things," Alyx said. His eyes appeared so sad when he said his father's name.

"He is malicious and cruel," I added.

"He's a sick fuck, Dati. Remember I said that I'd met him in my forest? In my place that was supposed to be safe? Do you know what he did...what we did?"

"Did he...well, he is Satyr. Did he touch you?"

"Yeah. He did. He did a lot more than touch me. I didn't know, Dati. You have to understand; I didn't know he was my father! I wouldn't have let him. I would have killed him. I will kill him," Alyx spat.

"I believe you. I believe you'd kill him, but we have to be careful. He's so powerful. The things I've seen him do over the years, and the things he's made the rest of us do. We're all tainted because of him. You just bring him here, and I will end him. I will do that for you," I said, a burning need to protect him intensifying inside of me. "You just have to get him here."

"I just have to learn how to do this *slipping* crap." Alyx leaned over and bumped me, shoulder to shoulder, a gesture of friendliness. "We have to be free of him. We can do this."

"I'm not as sure of that as you are," I said, "but I like your enthusiasm. You want to try teleportation again?"

"Yeah, let's do this."

"Okay, then."

I sat there, watching him with his eyes closed. His T-shirt was tight, muscles bulging as he wriggled on the rock, trying to find a comfortable spot. Light reddish-blond hair on his arms gleamed in the sunlight. Just looking at him made me feel warm inside, a feeling I had never felt in the three hundred years I'd lived. So many things I missed out on, having served one malevolent being.

Right then and there, I promised myself that once this whole monstrous scenario was over and I was free, I would be exploring all the things I had been forbidden to do. I wanted to know people and not live in fear that Master would slaughter any human who knew what I was. I desperately needed to see other parts of this earthly world and not be tethered to Master's territory. Getting the rest of my soul back and finding a way to heal the two pieces together fell pretty high on a list of things to accomplish. But mostly, the possibility of never having to sully another child made for the most pleasing of thoughts. Well, almost the most pleasing.

Alyx. Thoughts of being with Alyx and being free to do whatever I wanted with him. That was the best possible outcome of all of this.

"Could you stop thinking so loud?" Alyx mumbled. His Incubi telepathy had apparently tuned into me. I had only heard him telepathically once before—just after his emergence from the soft white cocoon.

Alyx cocked his head at me, sporting a wickedly impish grin as he said inside my head, *We could experience all those things together.*

Maybe Alyx's anger at me was really gone—at least for now.

I glanced at Alyx as his smile continued. It was the same smile I'd seen back when I first saw him at his mother's bookstore.

"You know, it's not nice to read people's minds when they think they are having private thoughts," I said smugly, although I was more than willing to share with Alyx.

"It's not like I have a choice. It's almost like you're throwing the words right at me."

I could feel Alyx mentally nudging me, pushing an image into my head of him and me—the two of us, wrapped up in a very strange position—and it made me blush but also made me incredibly excited.

"Why you dirty little demon," I said, but was only too happy to comply with his wishes.

"Ugh, this isn't working, at all," Alyx said opening his eyes and beaming at me. "Now you're the distraction."

"Maybe we're going about it all wrong," I said with a sudden thought.

"What do you mean?"

"Maybe you need a reason to slip... Well, what if you were trying to find me?"

"Still not sure I get it."

"Trust me?" I asked.

"Okay," Alyx replied cautiously.

"Close your eyes, stay out of my head, and let me leave. Then try to find me. Slip to where I am."

Alyx peered at me through half-closed eyelids and arched an eyebrow, with that mischievous grin. "Hide-and-seek. I like it!" He closed his eyes, grinning ear to ear now. "Okay, go."

As quietly as I could manage, I scampered off the rock and broke into a run, disappearing in the forest, dodging trees, and attempting to be as stealthy as I possibly could.

Glancing above my head, I discovered a rocky outcrop: a perfect hiding spot. I ripped off my shirt and scrunched it into a ball, holding it tight in my hands, while flexing my shoulders and unfurled my wings. Muscles that hadn't been used in a long time stretched as my wings flapped. I was unsure if they would hold me up in flight. I hadn't tried flying since Silenus snapped me like a twig.

It took a couple of good beats and some adjustments, but I managed to flap my way up to the rocky outcrop.

The sun beat down on me. I lay bare-chested against the granite slab with wings tucked in close. Like a reptile, absorbing its heat, I kept as flat and hidden as possible. The warmth felt good and therapeutic. Heaving a deep sigh, I relaxed, waiting to see if Alyx could find me.

Time went by, and then a lot of time passed. I started to get a little antsy, wondering if I should abandon the game and go search for him, when I felt a cerebral prod that reminded me of him ever so slightly.

There you are. Alyx spoke in my head.

Out of nowhere, black smoke formed in front of me, wisps and tendrils, swirling and coalescing. The smoke gathered, growing into a small cloud. With a hiss that reminded me of water hitting a hot pan, Alyx's body emerged. It happened quickly, from a gentle puff hanging in the air to Alyx forming right in front of me.

He smiled at me with a wicked grin.

"Found you." He eyed me up, appearing tantalized by my naked torso. "Oh man." He reached out and ran his hand across my chest. "I'll be happy to come find this."

"Alyx, you did it!" I said, grabbing him by the shoulders as my wings flexed straight up.

"Yup, and I think I know how." No anger emanated from him. Instead he was radiant, confident, and beautiful. "It took forever! At first I gave up and was trying to find you, like physically, and looked everywhere. But that was crazy because I wasn't learning what we need to do. So I stopped, thought about where you were, which got me thinking about you, which is when I kind of got all excited. I wanted to be near you. That *want*.... that's what pulled me here," he explained.

"You wanted me?" I asked, surprised.

Alyx's irises turned bright gold. "Oh yeah. I don't like being away from you. There's a pull inside of me when you're not around. It's really uncomfortable. It must be from the Incubus mark."

I didn't want to show it, but I was disappointed by Alyx's comment. I had thought briefly that he had wanted me, and not because of some supernatural branding, but because he liked me.

His smile turned impish. "Um, so are you gonna lose a piece of clothing each time? 'Cause that would make the game even more fun."

"Game it is then." I agreed to the terms, suppressed my disappointment for now, flexed my wings out, and leapt from the cliff, catching the updraft and soared deftly over the top of the forest, gently landing on firm ground but concealed by the trees.

The black smoke of Alyx's slip came within a minute, then the hiss, and there was Alyx, smirking.

"I do believe you owe me a piece of clothing, please," Alyx chimed proudly as he held out his hand.

I tossed him a shoe, one that had been modified to allow for the bone spurs, which broke through each of my heels. Alyx's face registered intense disappointment.

"I get a shoe? That's no fun," he said.

"You're going to have to work for this." I winked at him and took off again, faster and further this time.

We played until the sun went down, which set just in time as I was down to a pair of skivvies.

Alyx could now slip to wherever I was. The trick was to see if he could manage the same task, but with anyone—not just me.

Back at the first rocky outcropping we had started off at, I redressed myself as Alyx tossed me back all the clothing he had collected, playfully miffed we hadn't played out the game to the point Alyx had obtained *all* of my clothing.

We excitedly chatted about the next steps of our industrious and mutinous plan against Silenus.

"I want you to try and find Hemming," I suggested.

"Okay, I think I can do that. You know, you all feel different. You all smell different too, but you feel different to me in my head. You're firm but warm. Hemming is hard and gritty, like sand."

"So go to him. Find him, then come back here to me," I said, not really wanting him to go anywhere.

"Okay. Give me a second." Alyx closed his eyes and dissolve in front of me. Whispers of black trailed away from his body until that hiss sounded...and then he was gone.

Excision

DATI

Hemming was second to have the silvery minions excised from his body. It had been an overly vocal experience for everyone within earshot. I can honestly say, I had never heard Hemming scream.

After the operation, Alyx and I spotted Hemming's demon wolf lurking about the forest several times. Hemming healed much faster while in beast form.

But that had been yesterday. It was my turn to have the parasites removed, and until Aradia sent for me, I spent my time with Alyx. Within the space of three days since discovering the trigger to slip, Alyx had mastered the teleportation talent wickedly quick. He had even developed a snatch-and-grab technique. On more than one occasion, he had erupted in a puff of smoke in front of me, only to pilfer a book I was reading or snatch a piece of clothing, and then combust and disappear.

I encouraged him and wanted him to practice. He needed to become adept with the Satyr ability in order for our devious plan to work. I had my selfish reasons, of course. I wanted my soul piece back, and there was the ever burgeoning possibility of freedom. But more than any of those reasons, I wanted to have some sense of certainty that Alyx would be able to stay out of harm's reach. And having been Silenus's slave for so many years, I was more than fully aware how far Master's reach extended.

Aradia and Jenae spent much of their time together in secret. But to her credit, Jenae used every spare moment dedicating herself to studying spell casting, chants, and symbols. Her grimoire was constantly out, and she pored over the book, absorbing everything it had to teach her.

"Aradia, why didn't my Staunching spell work?" she had asked the Elementalist one evening, taking a break from her studying.

"Bring the book here, child."

Jenae flipped to the spell and set the book down in Aradia's lap.

"Ah, yes. This is fairly straight forward."

"But then why? Why did it not work?"

"How did you get the blood from dead flesh?" asked Aradia.

"I just squeezed some from the steaks that Dati had in the fridge," Jenae explained.

"Oh, child, no. Each ingredient in this book must be made by you in order for the spell to work. Obviously an herb is an herb and a rock can be collected. But blood from dead flesh—"

As she said it, Jenae seemed to understand and her eyes went wide. "I would have had to make the flesh dead and then squeeze the blood from that," Jenae finished.

Aradia beamed a huge smile, "Yes, child! You're a very quick student. Good girl."

I glanced at Hemming who sat across the room from me. We both grimaced.

At least Jenae finally had someone who could teach her the ways of being a witch.

"No, dear, like this." Aradia had shown her yesterday, drawing a rune in the air, which shimmered and then slowly eroded as a gale force wind ripped around the two of them.

Caleb had tried to hang around the two women but was shooed off by Aradia. I felt a little sorry for the big lout.

Alyx might have gotten a hold on his abilities fast, but Jenae struggled to master her magic.

"Oh shit! Dati, duck!" Jenae yelled out. A burning sphere of embers and flame ripped past my head, just barely missing me. It hit the wall instead, resulting in a platter-sized scorch mark. I had to wonder whether she would be ready for the ceremony.

"Sorry." She grimaced.

"All of you, out," Aradia said. "Tomorrow night the moon is full, and it will be the right time to open the Soul Door. Girl, make sure you practice everything I have shown you. If I don't think you're ready, you know what I'll have to do."

Jenae nodded. Her eyes were sad and afraid at the same time.

Once outside, Alyx continued practicing his slipping while I contemplated the best way to finish off Silenus. Hemming hung around Caleb and Riken, keeping the two occupied with learning the ins and outs of shifting.

Caleb had it down pat and was even able to morph individual body parts. Riken's dark shadow of a mood hung close around him, spoiling the session that otherwise should have been fun.

Aradia emerged briefly from her cottage and beckoned the Kasadya into her home. Apparently, it was time for his instructional session. Each of us had been summoned individually, ensuring we knew exactly what to do every minute through the Soul Door ritual.

The Watcher demon bowed deeply before Aradia, and then the two of them disappeared into the cabin. Moments later, I could hear laughing—an odd thing. I'd never seen even a hint of a chuckle, never mind reason to laugh, and Alyx or Hemming always managed to bring a smile or a giggle to most of us in the group.

Having been lost in my thoughts, my attention on Alyx was diverted until I caught a glimpse of him vanishing. The telltale smoke seemed to implode when he disappeared and unfurled outwards when he appeared.

Black wisps manifested behind Jenae and grew like an octopus extending its tentacles.

I signaled to Alyx to immediately cease and desist. Unfortunately, he didn't see my signal. Alyx had never experienced his half-sister's dark spell casting. He didn't know what Jenae was capable of.

Alyx placed a hand on Jenae's shoulder.

Jenae screamed.

Her eyes immediately rolled into the back of her head. I leapt up from the chair I sat in, but before I had taken two steps towards Alyx and Jenae, Alyx flew through the air, telekinetically, on a direct collision course with a jagged rock pile.

Jenae didn't stop there. The air around us immediately thickened and became electric. Sparks snapped and burst all around us.

Alyx's flailing body spiralled towards a stone outcrop. The vapors began to drift off his body, and he disappeared just in time. A breath of a wisp, the last remnants of Alyx's disappearing act, rolled over the rock pile.

Alyx bounced beside me.

"Whew, that was close!" He giggled a little.

"Scaring your sister is usually not a good idea," I warned, but Alyx was still chuckling.

Aradia burst out of the cabin with the Watcher demon close on her heels. She scoured the area until she spotted Jenae. Running over to her, she grabbed Jenae's hands, comforting her and getting her to breathe deeply.

The electrical current, palpable and audible, dispersed as quickly as it happened. Colour returned to Jenae's irises, and in no time, she appeared less witchy and more human.

Hemming let out an audible sigh of relief, then gathered up Caleb and Riken and took them out to the forest for more Shape-Shifting practice.

Aradia turned and stared at me. She gave me a dirty look.

It was then that I was summoned into Aradia's cottage.

"I really do not want to do this. She does *not* like me," I confided in Alyx.

"You don't really have a choice." He grabbed my hand. "I'll stay with you if you want."

I glanced at Alyx's alabaster fingers wrapped around my swarthy and rough skin, and then gripped his hand tight.

"I don't think I've ever held hands with anyone before," I whispered. "Amazing how reassuring it is."

Alyx gave me a smile.

As we walked into the cabin, the Watcher demon passed us on his way out. His gaze shifted furiously as he gave me the oddest look. He was evaluating my timelines, the possibilities of my future. I hated when he used his abilities on me without my permission. The Kasadya grinned with a thin smile that stretched across his face.

A shiver ran across my shoulders, raising the hair on the back of my neck. Like every other demon, I didn't trust him. Not in the slightest.

Inside the cottage, the table had been cleared of all items and was being used as a makeshift operating surface. A folded blanket rested on one end. Aradia tapped the table, indicating where I was to be.

I sat and waited as Aradia pulled together a barrage of items. Alyx never let go of my hand.

"Lay down, beast," she said.

I complied. I really wasn't overly eager about the impending procedure, especially after hearing Jenae and Hemming's hollers. But my desire to be rid of Master's evil little minions meant I was willing to put up with a great deal.

I put my head on the folded blanket. Above me, there were two other sealed glass jars suspended by rope from the ceiling. Each container was squirming with the fattened bugs that had gorged themselves on blood from Hemming and Jenae. I cringed.

Aradia came to the table with a bucket full of items, on top, a glass exactly like the ones that hung suspended above us, but this one was just for me.

"Demon, you expect these things to crawl through your shirt too? Off with it."

I took off my T-shirt and resumed my vertical position. Aradia watched me carefully.

"I don't like you, and I don't like your kind. As far as I'm concerned, you and yours should all be manacled like the slaves you're supposed to be. I am doing this for the boy and his sister. If it was up to me, you'd leave here with these things in you. I don't like you," she repeated.

Great, this really is going to be very painful.

"Look at this, hair everywhere." She made a gagging sound.

Aradia whipped out a knife, placed the blade up against my skin just underneath the ribcage, and dragged the sharpened edge down to my belly button, taking the hair with it.

Using a rag—which was far from clean—she wiped my freshly shaved belly and nodded in satisfaction. I looked like a freak, missing a weird patch of body hair.

Reading my mind, Alyx whispered, "It's okay. It's just hair. It'll grow back."

Aradia grabbed the glass jar and placed the open mouth side onto my newly shaved skin. The mouth had some unknown goo slopped onto the edge and a different deep-red substance plastered all over the inside of the vessel. The slop on the rim was cool as it touched my skin, but it quickly warmed. Then it burned.

That was my first scream.

The edge of the jar burned so hot that it began to sink into my flesh. There was no mistaking why the others had yelled. The pain was excruciating, and the sight of the container sticking out of me made the situation worse.

Alyx gripped my hand tighter.

Finally, the jar settled as blood wept out from the fresh wound it had created. The burning sensation ebbed slightly, but it still felt like someone was holding a branding iron to my midsection.

Aradia sprinkled some herbs onto the flat surface of the inverted vessel. Singing some words in a language I had never heard, she increased the pitch and speed of her chanting until the scattered herbs caught on fire.

The flames licked the surface of the glass and swirled around the vessel for several minutes. If I thought the edge of the glass had been hot when it melted my skin, I was mistaken. The flames swirling around the jar heated up the glass enough for the sticky red substance inside of the jar to bubble and melt. Drips like hot wax splashed onto my exposed and sensitive bare abdomen.

That was screech number two.

The goo hissed and bubbled and burned, blistering the skin. I let go of Alyx, clenched the side of the table, hands morphing into demon claws, and raked the wood. Aradia slapped me.

"If you damage my table any more, I'll stop this and you can leave with the things still in you, with the trap jar still stuck in you."

On each spot where the bloody red wax had dripped onto my skin, silver spikes erupted from inside of me. Fat blood-filled bodies tore and ripped flesh as they exploded out of my torso. Blood burst and splattered the inside of the glass trap. I tried to focus and divert my attention away from the pain, but the ringing in my ears and the fog in my brain damn near had me passing out.

Alyx, staying clear of the demon talons, put a firm hand on my shoulder.

"It's okay, Dati. I'm here. It's almost over."

Having one parasite rip itself out was traumatizing enough. But five of the little Hellions was too much.

The last one extracted itself with a *pop* as it burst through the skin, and scream number three happened. That one went on for a very long time.

"It is done. You tell no one I have these, and you tell no one you ever had them. Take this salve, and you rub it into your wounds. By nightfall, it won't hurt, although if it were up to me..."

"Yes, I know, you'd let me suffer," I finished for her.

"No. If it had been up to me, I would have chained you to the wall and watched when your time ran out. You're a filthy breed."

She yanked the jar out of my midsection, slapped a metal lid on it, and tied a piece of rope around the neck of the bottle, hoisting it up into the rafters with the others.

"Now find the others and tell them to all be here in the cottage by nightfall. The ceremony will be tomorrow night. Everyone needs their final instructions," she commanded, and in a gust of wind, she disappeared.

"You okay?" Alyx asked. "I had no idea you could scream so loud."

"I'll live," I said as I opened up the bottle of salve Aradia had given me. It smelled like rotting meat.

After seeing my hesitation, Alyx took the bottle from me, scooped out some of the salve, then very carefully rubbed the potion into each of the five wounds and into the circle laceration made from the glass jar. He was gentle, but it still hurt like Hell. I clamped the edges of the tables with black demon talons and screamed a final time.

Amulets and Portals

Dati

Alyx and I rounded everyone up that night as the sun set and the mountain air chilled. Our little mob of demons entered into the stone cottage.

Aradia was sitting in her usual spot, reading from a large tome and scribbling notes onto a piece of parchment. The paper was worn and stained but full of script.

As we gathered, shoulder to shoulder in the small room, Aradia closed the book, tucked it under her arm, and reached for a satchel that was lying on the bed. She fished in her bag and pulled out several necklaces, each one sporting an amulet.

"Boy, you will wear this, along with your beast. Skin-changer, you too, and the bear-man." Aradia passed a necklace to each of us, the amulet a crude twig man, like a little doll, made out of wrapped vines. A heavy rock was the chest, and a tuft of dried grass was its hair.

"What about the rest of us?" Riken asked.

"You will wear this. Different, because your beast inside is different. Horses are not predators. Neither is the clairvoyant." Aradia presented Riken and the Watcher a solid amber gem, very similar to the necklace that Jenae wore permanently.

"What about me, Mistress? Do I get one too?" Jenae asked.

"You already have one, child. Yours is much more powerful. You have done as I asked and placed the stone with your grimoire into your sack?"

Jenae nodded.

"Good. Tomorrow night when the moon is full, it will be the perfect time to open the Soul Door." Aradia took a step closer to Jenae and glared into the soulless witch's eyes. "Child, you have done well in the short time you have been here, and you would benefit from spending more time with me. I wish you had had more time."

Aradia held out her hand. The skull-capped staff leaned next to her bed wobbled from its sedentary position, then flew across the room settling neatly into Aradia's hand. She used the walking stick, tapping it on the ground three times, right at the base of Jenae's feet.

"I don't think you are quite prepared yet for what is to come. But this should assist."

In radiating circles from where Aradia's staff had hit, the floor of the cabin rippled, like it was water. Jenae looked confused.

"But, Mistress, I'm strong enough. I can do this without—without... I did everything you told me to!"

"You have, my child. We needed a little more time. Forgive me."

"Forgive you? For what?" I asked Aradia.

She ignored me and continued. From the point of impact where the ripples emerged, the floor turned black, encircling where Jenae stood.

It appeared as if she was standing in black water. Jenae's eyes widened in panic—an emotion we had all seen too often. She attempted to step away from the ripples but only managed to bring her heel off the ground. Strings of black tar stuck to her shoe, then pulled it back into place.

Jenae started sinking.

Caleb lunged to help her, but Riken held him back. I wanted to help, but I wasn't about to interfere with Aradia's magic again—she'd only fling me against the wall.

"But I'm scared, Mistress."

"I understand, but it is necessary."

"No!" Jenae cried, "I'm sorry. I'll do more."

Caleb roared and shoved Riken aside like a domino, toppling over onto Hemming, who in turn stumbled into Alyx. Caleb grabbed onto Jenae and yanked on her, but there was no pulling her out. If anything, the tar swallowed her faster.

The sinking was quick; the black spot on the floor had already consumed her up to her knees.

Hemming, who had ended up in a pile on top of Alyx, pulled himself up only to turn and yell at Aradia.

"What the Hell is going on? Why is this 'necessary'?" But his shouting was in vain. Aradia was gone.

Caleb yanked and pulled Jenae's arm as she whimpered. Her eyes had rolled white, although it didn't seem to help her this time. The candlelight in the room flickered and dimmed quickly as Jenae sank further.

"Come on everyone," I said. "Grab a limb or clothing. Together we should be able to pull her out of this." I moved in to get Jenae out of the sinking hole, Alyx was right behind me.

"Stop!" The Watcher demon put himself in between Jenae and I. "You have not—must not interrupt the process. You heard the Mistress. This is required."

"Screw what is required. The girl doesn't look like she's enjoying this!" I yelled at the Kasadya.

Jenae sank up to her armpits, and the whimpering became a steady panicky whine. Her arms flailed as she reached out and grabbed for anything that would stop her descent. Her eyes were still white, the lit candles in the room erupted into tiny torches, but the rest of the cabin went pitch black.

"The Mistress informed me. The girl has not—is not mature enough in her abilities. The pool will still her mind and remove her willpower, allowing Mistress Aradia to control her completely. It is the only safe way to open the doorway without destroying the girl."

Black sticky goo covered Caleb's arm as he valiantly tried to grab Jenae's body and heave her out of the quicksand tar. Caleb kept up the fight; Jenae lifted her chin, trying to keep her head above the liquid.

The great bear-man was lost. His brute strength was no match. He leaned over and kissed Jenae.

"I'm sorry. What do I do? Tell me what am I supposed to do? I can't—I don't know…"

Alyx stepped in closer to me. Watching Jenae sink and her obvious discomfort and Caleb's inability to assist was gut-wrenching.

A gurgle was all that Caleb got as a response. I was struck with horror as the pitch covered Jenae's nose and slowly climbed over her solid white eyes.

The circular pool rippled a few more times. A bubble rose to the top of the pool and popped.

And then as quickly as the floor had opened up and swallowed Jenae, the floorboards reappeared and nothing was left of the scene, except for Caleb who was still covered in sticky tar. He was motionless. Black liquid dripping off of his arm, making a small mess on the floor beneath him. His mouth quivered as his eyes went glassy and filled with tears.

"I knew we couldn't trust any of these—" Hemming started.

"Careful, skin changer. The Mistress is well aware of your distrust, and she is not pleased. The price for removing the parasites must be paid. You will—must stay the path. The consequences for not paying an owed debt to her would be...deadly." The Kasadya eyed Hemming, and then he shifted his glance towards me, "And she is particularly unhappy with you."

Something didn't sit right within me, a gnawing sense that the debt we owed was far greater than what any of us were prepared to pay.

"I don't like any of this either, Hemming," I said. "Something's not right."

A crackling started from around the windowpanes.

Electric-blue ice crystals formed, covering the pane as if Jack Frost himself had touched it. Beautiful snowflakes of frozen water vapor formed intricate patterns across the grimy and aged windows.

"What the Hell now?" I asked.

"She will—is ensuring that you stay put. She cannot—will not have distractions as she prepares for tomorrow night. You must stay. We have other instructions," the Watcher said as he slid the long blade out from within the gregarious clothing. He made a quick cut across his arm, wetting the blade with his blood. A quick few symbols drawn into the air and a portal began to open.

The Kasadya grabbed Riken and stepped through the shimmering air, vanishing.

Caleb completely lost it.

Roaring in frustration and anger, his face morphed into a bear muzzle. He pounded walls and flipped over furniture. Alyx, Hemming, and I took a step back, trying to avoid his outburst. Caleb raced to the door and reached for the handle, but the ice covered it just as he extended his hand to pull on the doorknob.

Caleb sucked in air as his finger wrapped around the icy handle. His anger went out like a snuffed candle. His face frozen in a grotesque mask of pain laced with panic as the icicles grew up his arm, cementing him to the door. The three of us stood absolutely still as the half bear, half man slowly become encased.

"Don't touch anything," Hemming whispered.

We had been standing with our backs against the wall, but with Hemming's sound advice, all three of us stepped away in unison and stood very still, listening to the ice forming.

"Dati," Alyx asked, "do you notice anything odd about the cabin?"

"Other than it's frozen in ice?"

"No, more like everything is gone."

"What do you mean?"

"I mean the furniture is all here, but there are no books. The bottles and vials and shit are all gone. Look at the pillars. They're empty."

"Oh shit, the parasites are gone too," I said as I glanced up where the glass jars had been suspended above the table.

The jars were gone. All that was left were three severed ropes.

It would seem that Aradia had moved out.

Ritual

DATI

Sleep is an impossible feat when it's forced upon you. I woke up several times during the night, mostly because Alyx had piled himself over the top of me and he was bloody heavy, and also because it was bone-chillingly cold. Despite the demonic hot flesh that always kept me warm, the ice-bound cabin was freezing. I had to rearrange my position just to get comfortable and warm.

The morning sun felt like it took forever to come up. When the light finally peeked through the ice-covered windows, it didn't illuminate any happy faces in the room. In fact, it appeared as if we had pulled an all-nighter. Hair and clothes were disheveled and dark circles hung under everyone's eyes.

There was no food in the cabin or fresh water, and that didn't help anyone's mood levels.

Hours passed by in excruciating boredom, until finally, as the sunlight was receding, we heard footsteps approaching the cottage. As fast as the ice crystals formed, they began to melt, leaving nothing more than water droplets behind.

Caleb thawed as well, leaving him wet and shivering, but no worse for wear otherwise. His teeth chattered together uncontrollably.

"Are you okay?" Hemming rushed over and patted the big bear-man.

I wrapped a blanket from the bed around him. Caleb didn't seem to be particularly appreciative of my efforts, but other than shock, he seemed reasonably fine for a bear previously encased in ice.

The door burst open, and Aradia appeared, glowing white, cleaned, and smelling sweetly of oranges and woodland raspberries. The robes she wore were stunning. Crisp white silk embraced her curvy body. Aradia's dark skin was a sharp contrast to the flowing robe and cape she had adorned, the trim of which was detailed in white stitchery imitating vines and leaves.

"Thanks for a list of instructions, bitch! Don't touch the ice would have been good," Hemming snapped.

Aradia floated over to him, the white of her dress blowing back behind her. She reached up and grabbed him by the throat. Hemming's skin started to darken, then decay, like a rotting carcass.

"I do what I need to do in order to ensure tonight is successful. You do not question me." She let go of Hemming, who choked and spat and sucked in air. The skin around his throat gradually returned to normal.

"Let us go. It is time," she said.

"Wait, we're not going anywhere or doing anything," Alyx demanded. "What the Hell is going on? Where are Riken and the Kasadya demon? What did you do to Jenae, and where is she? Where are all your things...the cabin is completely empty?"

Aradia's skin tightened on her face, and she raised her hand. Sparks of electric-blue energy zapped and bolted from one finger to the next.

"Do you wish to die here and now? Do you have any desire to see your sister again, boy?"

After that display, no one dared defy her.

"As I thought. Now, follow me," she stated as her face returned to normal and the bolts of electricity disappeared.

We filed out of the cottage in a single line. The pit of my stomach turned in anxious knots.

Aradia led us to a side yard where Alyx and I had played our hide-and-seek game. It had been an expansive field, dotted with short grasses and lichens, but within one day, Aradia had completely morphed the area.

Where grasses once lay, there was a circle of stone. Etched into the stone were symbols and carvings and circular indentations where Aradia had instructed each of us to stand.

Jenae was to be positioned in the very middle.

White flowers were in bloom in a perfect circle all the way around the stone, which was odd as it was late fall. There was nothing else in bloom. I had no idea what plant it was, but Alyx knew.

"Sandwort—it's used for protection," he said.

Aradia's magic was indeed impressive. The scent emanating from the white circle perfumed the air around us.

Aradia raised her arms towards the night sky, and a breeze blew up to greet her. The robe billowed out behind her. She reminded me of those frilled lizards that puff themselves up to make themselves appear bigger than they really were. It was a tactic to scare off the enemy.

At her feet, the earth cracked open like a miniature fault line, opening to form a small chasm that encircled the entire stone dais. From within that rift, fire erupted.

Aradia floated over to the center of the circle, the spot that had been reserved for Jenae. With her staff, she tapped the indentation in the stone three times. The stone melted away and was replaced by a pool of black sticky tar.

She raised her arms up again, but this time chanted words, lyrical words.

The pool bubbled and churned, and then the form of a person arose from the middle, black and dripping in the sticky tar. The body continued to rise until it was floating inches above the ground. Aradia banged her stick onto the rock. The sound ricocheted all around us. The figure moved and undulated, stretching as if it were a massive black cat, and as it elongated, the black tar melted and dripped back into the pool. The pitch left no stain or residue; it simply ran off the body like melting wax, revealing a very naked but glowing Jenae.

Alyx whispered, "Jenae?"

She appeared radiant and beautiful. Her hair had grown extremely long, and it had lost the funky die job. She looked less like a rebellious teenager and more like a powerful witch reborn.

She hung there, suspended in air, slowly spinning, her eyes closed and head tilted back.

"What did you do to her?" I asked.

"Jenae!" Alyx cried out.

"Enough!" Aradia hissed. "The pool has stripped her of her will, of her conscious thought, and buried it deep within her. I control her. It is the only way to open the Soul Door and ensure she doesn't destroy us and herself in the process. Now be still!" she commanded to us.

Aradia returned her attention to the naked Jenae and gently placed her staff in the center of her chest.

Jenae opened her eyes, only to reveal pulsating glowing orbs of pure white.

"Now, child. Begin," Aradia cued her.

Unlike the expressive words Aradia had used to open the pool, Jenae mumbled harsh words that were accentuated with tongue-twisting consonants. Despite the angry words that bubbled forth in rapid succession, Jenae's face was serene and calm, as if she was in a state of rapture.

Aradia turned towards Alyx and pointed the skull stick in his direction.

"You, boy, this is your time. Find your father and bring him here."

"You can do this, Alyx," I said.

Alyx smiled at me and nodded. He closed his eyes.

The black smoke drifted off of his body until I heard that hiss.

And then he was gone.

Travelling.

Slip

ALYX

When I opened my eyes, I expected to be surrounded by the ferns and tall trees of my forest glade. But instead, a cold stone slab was beneath my feet and the walls that surrounded me were cracked concrete. Wherever I had ended up, it was dank and it smelled of rot. There were blood stains in several spots, an indication that something gruesome had occurred.

I had no idea where I was, but one thing was certain: Silenus would be near.

A desk sat in the middle of the room, and it was covered with books and papers and assorted items, and a glass jar, filled with bulging silver minion parasites just like what Aradia had taken out of Dati.

Inspecting the wall closer, there was more than just blood spatter. Boxes and lines covered the entire surface, and in each box, there was a name. It was a huge family tree.

Most of the boxes had a large X marked through them. But it didn't take me long to find a box with my own name in it, and directly above was Marta.

Right beside us in the family history was my sister, Jenae. But instead of an X through our box, each was circled several times.

"Welcome home. I see you've found your place," a voice said behind me, deep and raspy.

I spun around and faced Silenus.

My wings spread out, and I could feel my tail twitching.

"That's quite the family tree," I said mockingly.

"Ah, you smell delicious. That would be the Incubus in you. You probably don't even know you've turned on the charm, trying to entice me," Silenus chortled. "I knew you'd be smart enough to understand, to see the glory of all of this work. Tell me, boy, are you not excited? Are you not proud to have been made to receive *him*?"

He eyed me up and down, his grin faltering slightly. "But I see you're not completely ready yet. The Satyr blood in you still needs time to develop. Your legs are still human. That will change in time."

"Great. I have something to look forward to."

"Tell me, do you like the slip? Does it not excite every fiber of your being, knowing that you can go wherever you want to?" Silenus took a step forward.

"It does, Father. It's freeing and exciting." I matched the old goat and inched closer to him.

Silenus's irises were swirling violet.

"Let me show you how quickly I've mastered the ability," I tempted him.

"Ah, a father-son trip sounds so delightful, yet I couldn't possibly leave the solace or safety of my home. Stay, Alyx, stay with me and let me teach you things." A malicious grin spread across Silenus's face.

Two very pale faces appeared behind Silenus as they left the darkest recesses of the basement. Their eyes were winter white with just a hint of blue.

"May I introduce you to Ivan and Bradley, Vampyres in service to me, and as you can see, they are very hungry. I couldn't possibly leave them here without food. You see, Bradley is new, and Ivan has agreed to help me rear him. But new Vampyres require a lot of nourishment. Unfortunately for Ivan, Bradley has had to feed upon him. They are so very hungry." They flanked each side of the Satyr.

I was outnumbered. And I had no idea how to deal with Vampyres. So I had to be smart.

"What a shame. I was hoping you'd want to see how talented you've made me." All of a sudden, my confidence wavered, and I was sure this would end badly. I considered going back there and then, but something stopped me.

Everyone had been freed of their parasites, but for Dati, getting his soul back was of paramount importance. And I had to make sure Dati was okay—he was, after all, marked by me. He was mine to protect.

Silenus had a vial hanging from a necklace. It had to be the one Dati had spoken about.

I could only see one way out of this. Start the slip, and then just as I was about to disappear, I could throw myself towards the Satyr god, grab him, and pull him with me.

"Boys, I do believe Alyx should be shown to the living room upstairs, where we can have a much more civilized conversation. How would you like to take him there?" The two pasty white creatures came towards me.

I had already pictured Dati in my mind, had felt the *want* of being next to him. I remembered touching and feeling his warmth, hearing his deep voice. The tiny tickling sensation ran across my arms and legs. Little tendrils of black smoke began to waft off of me.

"Sorry, Father, perhaps another time." My words hung in the air.

I could feel myself starting to go, the hiss was just beginning.

I leapt forward with a hand extended, hoping to make contact with Silenus, and then it occurred to me, maybe I could tantalize him into following me.

With my Incubus telepathy, I pushed my thoughts into Silenus's head. I pushed them as hard as I possibly could...

Dati and Jenae send their regards, but the D'Alae has been marked and belongs to me.

My outstretched hand was almost completely black smoke.

I could feel the warmth from my father's body. I had gotten that close, but just as I got close enough to put a hand on him...

I was gone from Silenus and the dank. The *want* pulled me towards Dati.

Sacrifice

Dati

Alyx was back on the mountain and standing in the middle of the ritual.

Smoke dissipated all around him as he rematerialized, but his body was lurching forward. He fell facedown.

"Alyx!" I yelled. "Are you okay?"

"Is he here? Is Silenus here?" Hemming yelled out as Alyx jumped to his feet and quickly glanced around.

No Satyr was in sight.

Alyx had failed. My hopes of being free of Master plummeted.

A second hiss sounded around us. Quicker than Alyx had ever slipped, Silenus appeared. Whatever Alyx had done, it had worked. The bastard was standing right there.

I sneered evilly, exposing a fang.

The goat god was furious. His irises were raging violet. His face contorted into a demonic mask. Nothing about him appeared human. Silenus lurched forward towards Alyx on his hooved legs.

Aradia pointed her skull staff directly at Silenus and screamed, "Modus Positus!"

Tree roots broke out of the ground, winding ferociously around Silenus's hooves, twining up his furry legs. Silenus struggled to lift a hoof, his face blood red with anger as the skin shrank so deeply, the face became nothing more than a skull. His goat horns elongated, and he let out a howl that shook the entire forest.

Aradia spoke a new word in a whisper.

"Immobilibus."

Every one of us was instantly locked into place.

What was Aradia doing? She wasn't supposed to freeze everyone!

Aradia elegantly glided towards Silenus, leaned in, and whispered into his ear. I could just hear her.

"Well now, goat lord, not so much a god, are we? Looks like your children have turned against you."

Silenus gritted his teeth, and through locked jaws, he spoke. "Aradia, you bitch, what did you do to them?" Spit flew from his mouth.

"Oh, Silenus, they came to me, child. They have no idea; they are but infants. They couldn't possibly compare to either you or me in age. But I must say, I am very impressed with your work. Really, I am. So many generations of raping and pillaging. So much manipulation and child-rearing! I wouldn't have had the patience! It must have been exhausting, and all to try and bring Satan here. So close, beast, so close. And yet," Aradia said as she caressed Silenus's demonic face, "not close enough. If you don't mind, I'll be taking over now."

Aradia's hands weaved in oblong circular motions parallel to the ground. Tree roots erupted through the ground close to Silenus's feet. Rearing up like cobras, pointed and sharp they lunged forward, piercing through the meat of each leg.

Silenus roared again. It sent shivers of absolute fear through me. I'd never heard him that angry.

Red streams flowed down from Silenus's leg wounds, and as his demigod blood hit the stone dais, steam rose.

Aradia motioned again with her hand, and with that simple gesture, I was free from Aradia's spell.

Aradia focused intently on Jenae. Jenae was chanting words that were unintelligible and gesturing wildly. Aradia then glanced sideways towards me, "Demon beast, do what you said you would."

I took a couple of steps, unsure. Was it a trap? What other tricks did this witch have planned?

"What are you waiting for? Do it!" Aradia commanded. She held up her hand and clenched her fist.

It felt as if someone had grabbed loose skin from the center of my chest and dragged me forward. As I moved, my hands morphed into demon claws. Aradia deposited me directly in front of the tree-root-caged Satyr.

Silenus's face was purple, he was so enraged.

Very carefully, I grabbed the vial that hung from the necklace Silenus always wore. With a quick jerk, the chain snapped, freeing the vial. I gingerly placed it in my coat pocket.

"That is mine," I said through gritted teeth, but in my hand, I finally held the one thing that guaranteed my freedom. I felt safe, secure in knowing that I was once again in possession of the one element that would make me whole again. "I am no longer bound to you. I will never do another task for you. I am not yours to command."

Grabbing a tuft of hair at the top of Silenus's head, I held my ex-master's head back, exposing the goat god's throat.

Silenus struggled in vain.

Using a razor-sharp claw, I stuck one pointed tip into the soft flesh just below the jaw and sawed. Blood spurted out, soaking the front of the goat and coating me.

As the blood gushed from his throat, I finally felt relief, a calmness I had never experienced.

I was free.

As soon as I returned to my position on the dais, Aradia's spell took hold and once again and I became immobile.

Blood from the sacrificed goat god pooled on the stone platform and found its way through the carvings that had been etched into the surface by Aradia. The channels ran in towards the middle of the circle, where Jenae floated.

Silenus's swirling violet irises dimmed as his life spewed onto the rock beneath him. He convulsed within the tree roots that wound tightly around him. A thick pool of the Satyr's blood collected in the center of the dais, underneath the airborne witch.

Hemming, Caleb, and Alyx stood motionless like grotesque garden statues, still trapped within Aradia's spell.

Jenae stopped chanting.

She was glowing from deep within herself. As if someone had turned a light on inside of her chest. Her heart beat slow and steady, and with each beat, the light became a little brighter, until it was brilliant and blinding.

The spirit light revealed the four souls Jenae had been carrying with her, each one positioned perfectly in a circle around her. Their faces were demented, tortured, and inhuman. A scream arose as each of them shrieked like banshees. Their scream slowly subsiding as they dissolved into wisps of light and were absorbed into Jenae.

I didn't think it possible, but the light coming from within Jenae got brighter—so bright I couldn't look in her direction.

But just as I turned away, Jenae's heart stopped beating and the light from within her dimmed.

Everything was deathly quiet and dark.

Light erupted in a nuclear wave, and Jenae was at the nucleus. As rigid as we were, the energy that should have sent us reeling coursed through us like an electrical current, sucking the air out of my lungs.

And then everything went black. There was no sound.

It was pitch black. Empty.

And then the heart beat again, *thump - thump.* The glow returned but dimly.

Glancing back towards the epicenter, Jenae was stretched out, spread eagle, but she had become translucent. I could see right through her, and yet I could see everything in her, bones, and veins and organs.

From within the hollow of her pelvis, something stirred, a shadow, tinted red, which slithered within Jenae.

Red shadow hands grasped onto Jenae's hip bones. A head and shoulders pulled their way up. Clawing and climbing, the inner shadow slipped and wound its way up through the chest cavity, compressing itself as it shimmied through the narrow throat.

A second body existed within Jenae, twisting and turning, scrunching its way through the translucent soulless witch. It was like watching a panicked rat scrambling through crevices too tight for it to get through.

Jenae's head snapped backwards and her mouth opened. The red hands poked through her open mouth.

It didn't seem possible and it defied reason, but the hands pushed and pulled until half a body was protruding from Jenae's open mouth.

And then the red shadow flopped onto the stone dais right a Jenae's feet, falling right into the pool of Silenus's blood. It lay still for a moment.

Jenae slumped forward but remained suspended in the air.

The pool of the goat god's blood slowly began to disappear as the shadow filled with the slain demigod's essence.

A snaking writhing noise came from behind me, and I turned to see the roots and vines that held Silenus disappear back into the ground.

Aradia mouthed more words and flicked a finger.

I gaped in fascination as Silenus's body rose off the dais, sailing past me towards the ethereal being that was full of his blood. I'd never seen such demonstrations of magic, and it was terrifying.

Silenus's body and the soul that Jenae had summoned hovered close to each other, then began to spin, one around the other, like a moon orbiting the earth. As they spun, flesh was torn off of Silenus in minute strips and flecks, almost too small to see. But within seconds, all the skin and muscle were gone from Silenus.

Flesh and tissue swirled violently in circles as Silenus's body was torn apart and shredded.

The shadow spirit reached out towards the floating mass of tissue that had been Silenus, and touched the tiniest little piece. The entire floating mass responded.

In a swirling whirlwind of bodily fluids, the corporeal being began to form, made from the remnants of Silenus. Little pieces of bone fragments flew into place, creating a new skeleton. Internal organs filled in the cavities, followed by muscle and sinew and tendons and skin.

The goat god was gone, his blood, bone, and tissue used to create a new life.

And she was voluptuous, with dark swirling locks cascading over olive skin. Her hips were wide and full, her breasts perky, skin supple and delicate. She smiled, and her teeth gleamed white and perfect.

She was an enthralling beauty.

The woman took a step down from where she had been floating and spinning, placing her bare feet on solid earth.

Jenae, no longer transparent or glowing or of use, fell to the ground.

Aradia removed the cape part of her robe, unwinding it so that it appeared like one long piece of flowing white material. She flung it towards the naked woman.

The material undulated in the dark night and wound its way towards the newly formed body. The stranger stretched out her arm to accept the dancing sheet. As soon as she touched it, the silky material wrapped itself around her curvy frame until she was covered.

A robe formed out of the fabric donated by Aradia. But where Aradia had stitching that imitated swirling vines and falling leaves, the stranger's robe was decorated in dancing white flames.

The beautiful woman glanced down at the empty pool of blood, the place where her existence had started. Bending down, she dipped her finger into a small remaining puddle.

She stuck her finger in her mouth and savoured the metallic taste. A scowl crossed her face.

"Really, Aradia, you gave me the blood from a goat?" She sounded disappointed, if not a little disturbed.

"No, sister, not just a goat: a Satyr. *The* Satyr, Silenus, the Pan god," Aradia said proudly.

"Oh, well then, that is different! Thank you for extricating me." She walked towards Aradia, embraced her, and gave her a long kiss of thanks, on the lips.

"That exile was particularly unpleasant and long. Where's Magdalena?" she asked.

"Siofra, my dear sister, that is where I need you and your talents the most. She's still being held prisoner. We should leave now. We need to continue our work."

Aradia turned to us. "You've done well, beasts. But I have no use for winged demons or skin changers like you. But brilliant young witches who are Soul Doors, now that's particularly delightful, and a talent I can use many times over."

Aradia reached into a small bag she had tied at her waist and pulled out a handful of sparkling sand. Some spilled out as she opened her fist and blew.

The granules of grit blustered into the night air towards us and then swept over, covering us in glitter.

The amulets that Aradia had given us came to life. The arms and legs of the little wicker man grew and spun so fast that before I could raise an arm in my own defence, I was encased in twigs and roots.

I peered through the cage of branches and switches to catch Aradia leaning in close and whispering secret words to her sister.

"You've arranged for a ride?" Siofra said. Her voice was soft and soothing. She stood next to her sister, took a deep breath, and then stretched out her palms.

A flapping noise could be heard from above. I peered out through my cage to see giant leathery bat wings gracefully carrying a large dark horse. It landed gracefully, almost silently beside the two sisters.

"Well done, Aradia. Where on earth did you find such a beautiful creature?" Siofra asked.

"That, sister, is a very long story."

"Well then, one you should tell me all about!"

"In time. In time." Aradia nodded at her sister, indicating that there would be plenty to say.

The winged horse stepped closer to us. I could see the flesh, half-rotted and exposing the beast's skeleton in some places, others displayed shiny wet muscle tissue.

"Riken, what are you doing? Help us!" Caleb said. I could hear the desperation in his voice.

The horse pawed the ground. It moved closer to the bear-man and huffed out a long breath of air from its nostrils.

Grey smoke billowed out, tumbling in swirling little currents as it fell towards the stone dais. As it hit the rock formation where the ritual had taken place, it spread out, never dissipating, it wound its way towards Caleb, but as it progressed, anything living it touched curled and shriveled.

The poisonous gas found Caleb, ensnared. The bear-man panicked and tried to push his cage, roll it out of the way of the oncoming vapour. When that didn't work, he resorted to pounding the inside of the wooden restraints—to no avail.

The breath encircled Caleb, winding its way up, and as it did, the huge beast-man's skin began to shrink in on itself. His bulk decreased, his body became frail.

Caleb slumped to the bottom of his enclosure. He was thin and gaunt.

The horse, satisfied, backed up carefully towards Aradia and Siofra. They climbed onto the rotted stallion.

"Behold, the Horseman of Famine has found his ability and purpose!" Aradia said and then cackled.

Siofra held out her hands, and flames shot out from the center of her palm. Her eyeballs became flaming orbs.

The crackling from the fire was deafening.

Fire snakes twisted and turned, creating funnels of inferno in random spots around us. Writhing ropes of hot flames scampered forth, encircling Jenae, forming a fire tornado around her, carrying her gently towards Aradia and Siofra.

Riken, the horse, beat his giant wings, taking off, while the blazing tornado followed behind. Siofra controlling Jenae's swirling storm of flames in one hand, released a huge fireball from the other. As the horse drew them up high into the night, carrying Jenae engulfed in a personal pyre, a giant billowing mushroom cloud of smoke and fire erupted on the ground in front of us.

The heat and intensity of light was so great that the casing of wood that held me in my spot shattered. The blast rang in my ears as the explosion flung us backwards.

The monster hedge that surrounded the yard caught me and broke my fall.

Smoke clouded my vision and stung my eyes, tears streaming down my face as I called out for Alyx.

"Where are you, Alyx? Hemming? Caleb?"

I could hear someone coughing.

Beating off a small ember that had caught my shirtsleeve on fire, I stumbled towards the sound. My sensitive demon ears were ringing.

It was Alyx.

He was caught up in the hedge several feet away. I pulled him out of the shrubbery. He was covered in soot and one side of his face was blackened. But he wasn't burnt or too badly damaged.

From across the field, I could see Hemming attempting to stand up, his face covered in blood from a gash on his forehead.

In the middle of the field lay a half-morphed, emaciated demon-bear.

Alyx and I went to collect Caleb.

He was a shell of the great beast of a man he had been. Alyx and I cradled him gently and carried him away from the field.

"Jenae!" he croaked out. "Riken, why?"

I held him a little closer until Hemming caught up with us. Hemming's gaze said what I would not in front of Caleb. We too were stunned from the turn of events, but more importantly, we were concerned for Caleb's well-being.

"What is the Horseman of Famine?" Alyx asked.

"One of the four horses of the apocalypse. Death, War, Famine, and Pestilence," Hemming said.

"What the Hell did we just do?" Alyx turned and said, wide-eyed at the destruction around us. Smoke rose from our clothes.

"Nothing good," I replied. "Nothing good at all."

The Return

THE KASADYA

Dati's condo will do—has done just fine, thank you.

Riken and I were sent—are off to find a suitable living quarter before Siofra was emancipated. I returned briefly to the mountain and informed Aradia of our chosen spot, then came back to make arrangements for their arrival.

"How ironically wonderful," she responded.

The saturation of rot and evil has already deeply permeated into the walls, and the hordes of the Disembodied that have taken up residence are numerable. It was—is a perfect spot for my new Mistress.

Aradia and Siofra have afternoon tea in the living room by the window, to discuss their next moves. The original furniture, we disposed of and replaced with more suitable refinements. After all, Aradia and Siofra are goddesses in their own right. They should have—will have only the best.

The look is quite stunning: elegance and decomposition go together rather well. It was—is far more functional if not even more comfortable.

The paint on the walls continues to peel and has become separated from its various coats over the years, making the walls appear as if they have— had the pox. Stains of mold and rot add to the dark and sullied ambience. It's settling and easing to the soul.

"Watcher, come here. We have need of your clairvoyance," Aradia beckons.

Siofra, being of like mind to the element of fire, always has numerous candles lit and a fire burned—is roaring in the fireplace. Snow will fall soon, and so the additional heat is welcome.

Riken has become thinner since we parted from his brother. He also had—is refusing outright any food that is placed before him. He was always distant and contemplative, which is just fine, as it means no arguments. He sits in one of the Claremore chairs, slouched over, brooding, ignoring the others in the room.

"We must free Magdalena," says Siofra. "Tell us, Kasadya, what do you see?"

As much as I will assist my Mistress with anything she asks, I don't like using my abilities. They trouble me, and it is dizzying to watch so many possibilities. The only way for me to keep—have kept some semblance of sanity is to ensure that there is as much chaos surrounding me as possible.

With chaos comes opportunities and possibilities, in fact, too many options. So when there's a certain level of disorder and confusion, the visions I see are blurred to the point where nothing is decipherable, and it shuts down, and I have quiet.

That level of anarchy hasn't erupted just quite yet.

I bow my head at Aradia's request.

Peering out the windows past Aradia and Siofra, my gaze focuses on the air in between. It begins to shimmer and dance, as if the colours that were—are in front of me are suddenly disorganized and jagged. Like someone has shattered—is shattering a mirror image of the room and put the glass pieces together all wrong.

And then the shards fall away, and the scenarios begin…

"I see you and Siofra and the woman of air, Magdelena, sitting in this room all in white robes as they flow outwards and the sky is dark with demons. You cast humans off the building, and as they fall, the Disembodied possess them. You have unleashed the first wave of the end of times. The Earth has not yet rendered, and the darkest one has not yet come.

"Aradia and Jenae both dressed in red gowns are veiled and bound, but tears of blood stain your faces. There are mountains of dead beneath your feet. They are your soldiers. You have been conquered and the pyre that you are being pulled towards is awaiting your flesh.

"There are five women of incomprehensible power; earth, air, fire, and water merging with the fifth element that is soul. The Earth opens and releases beasts, demons, and dragons. Mankind trembles; blood is spilled and ancient rituals open the gates. The angels fall. *He* comes to Earth on the back of the leviathan.

"I see pain and sickness. I see famine and death. War and strife cause havoc amongst all of mankind as the four horsemen and their mounts perch on a hilltop made of corpses. The land is desecrated and bare.

"I see a winged demon and an angel. I see my sister Kasadya Cerys, all in white. She aids them in their quest to beat the beast and—" I stop.

"And what, boy? Why have you stopped? So far, we are ahead, more possibility exists that the world we want is the one we shall have. What is this last possibility?" Aradia demands.

"I cannot say. The vision has blurred. It is not clear," I lie.

What I see is only what might happen. Nothing is certain. Every action can change all outcomes.

There is a cry from down the hall. Jenae is stirring again.

"Ugh, that girl," Aradia says.

"Watcher, attend to her. Keep her silent. We have work to complete here," Siofra says.

As I entered—was entering the spare room, Jenae spins slowly in circles from the chain that hangs from the ceiling. Her manacles bind and cut the flesh around her wrists. Her eyes are permanently white now, as she possesses no willpower of her own anymore. She is a tool for Aradia and Siofra to use, and they have. The Shishi stood—were still standing immobile on each side of Jenae, and have proved to be difficult to deal with as they are both loyal to the girl.

Jenae's grimoire was—is encased in a pillar of glass on the opposite side of the room. It too has given my mistress much difficulty being separated from its owner. Occasionally, the book will flutter about within its enclosure, attempting to find a way to be closer to Jenae.

Every now and then, the girl had—will have moments of lucidity.

Dirty hair hangs unkempt and matted, covering most of her face. The white gown that Aradia has put her into is soiled and filthy.

Cages line the periphery of the room, and the guests contained within make—have made various assortments of disturbing noises and outlandish requests.

"Quit taunting the girl, Watcher. She is drained. If you don't tend to her wounds soon, she will die," says the pudgy old woman whose cheeks are always ruddy and who smelled of jasmine and vanilla. She has been here the longest. "You let me out. Please, let me help her." Her accent is thick and old-world.

"Quiet, Healer, your talents are not—have not been requested."

Jenae swings her head towards me and glares even though her eyes hold no irises or pupils. She should not—cannot see. She smiles wickedly, and it sends a shiver through me when she speaks.

"I see a winged demon and an angel. I see my sister, Kasadya Cerys, all in white. She aids them in their quest to beat back the beast and—" She copies me word for word, and then she finishes. "The demon who found freedom shall heal his soul. His companion, an angel made from demon flesh, shall best you all."

About the Author

J.P. Jackson is an IT Analyst by day working in the health industry, but at night, when the monsters come out, he writes. Demons, shape-shifters, and a host of non-human entities converge around the computer as disturbing tales are shared and recorded.

Twitter: https://twitter.com/Canuckbear88
Facebook: https://www.facebook.com/jpjacksonwrites/
Goodreads: https://www.goodreads.com/user/show/46056760
Tumblr (18+ only): http://canuckbear88.tumblr.com/

Nephalem

The Apocalypse, Book Two

Into the Light

DATI

It took hours to stumble down the side of the mountain in the dark, putting as much distance as possible between us and the destruction we had played a part in creating.

We climbed into the van that had brought us here days earlier with Hemming taking the passenger side, his head wrapped in strips of clothing. The blood steadily dripped from his head wound, but he would recover, eventually.

The vehicle seemed particularly empty with Jenae, Riken, and the Kasadya demon missing.

No one said anything. What could be said?

Caleb was distraught not having Jenae next to him, not to mention losing his brother. His emaciated frame shook with anger, his eyes red and puffy.

Alyx took the seat behind me, and as we pulled out of the forest, tree branches scraped the side of the van. Alyx laid his hand gently on my shoulder. It was an attempt at comfort.

Pulling onto the highway, I couldn't help but think: Silenus is dead. I'm free.

The soul vial was tucked away in my pocket. I would never allow it to leave my possession, but now I had to find a way to mend the two pieces of my soul back together.

Most importantly, Alyx was still with me and, by all accounts, wanted to be as close to me as I did to him, despite the Incubus brand on my neck that marked me as his and forced us to be together.

It had been a long night, and we all wanted to be as far away from the mountain as possible. Even though Hemming and I were free from Silenus, we had a whole host of other problems now, the least of which would be healing Caleb.

Aradia and Silenus had known each other and, it would seem, had been rivals. The Kasadya had lured us into Aradia's hands. Aradia had seen a way to free her sister Siofra, using Jenae and her Soul Door. But in return, she had stolen Jenae from us.

Somewhere in the mix, Riken had been taken as well, but something told me that his disappearance with the Kasadya meant that he had willingly chosen to go with them.

The sky was lightening as the sun began to rise, but despite the impending brightness, everything before us was just grey.

In the middle of the highway, a bright light shone, blinding us as it grew in intensity. At first, I thought it was another car, until we almost drove into it. I slammed on the van's brakes and swerved the vehicle sideways. The van came to a halt with a lurch. Hemming smacked his head on the window beside him, then gave me a dirty look.

"Everyone okay?" I asked.

There were grunts of discontent, but no one had sustained any further injuries.

The light was still shining brightly as we got out of the van. It was as if someone had punctured the air in front of us and shone a floodlight through the hole.

A tiny ball of intense white light the size of a marble, at half my height, in midair, floated in the center of the road.

The four of us inspected it. Caleb, weak and unsteady, hung onto me for support. Hemming walked around the light and inspected it from the other side.

"There's no light here. I can see you, but you look as if you have a spotlight on you, but there's nothing here." Hemming walked back around to stand behind us. And then a familiar thing happened.

A delicate hand pushed forward from the center of the light. The appendage was covered in a fingerless white lace glove, followed by a large billowing white sleeve. The material was silky, shiny, and the cuff was over-exaggerated and trimmed in pure white fluffy feathers.

In unison, we took a step back.

From within the light, an arm with ornate clothes appeared, followed by a shoulder, until a small-framed delicate young woman stood before us.

The elaborate sleeve was part of a well-tailored and tight-fitting jacket that had a massive stiff collar, also trimmed in feathers. The girl's bobbed platinum hair was streaked with white highlights; the ends were tipped in pink.

A black tattoo seemed out of place jutting out from under her lace-trimmed blouse. It ended in a strange hieroglyph just under her ear, which was pierced multiple times, each hole occupied by silver hoops of descending sizes.

I knew exactly what she was. We had another Kasadya on our hands.

"My name is Cerys," she said cheerfully but succinctly. "It took you long enough to get here. But now that I did—will have, you came—you're going to have to come with me."

"We are done dealing with the likes of you, Kasadya," I said.

"I'm watching—have seen what you've been doing. The whole lot of you have really screwed things up. And so now, you're going to help—have helped me restore some balance," she said authoritatively.

Her voice was perky. She was determined and straight to the point, but her gaze bounced back and forth, evaluating each of us, seeing the various timelines and the options that lay ahead of us.

When she stopped evaluating, she took two steps forward, placing herself in the middle of our mob of demons.

Another blinding white light surrounded us.

It was warm.

Also Available from NineStar Press

www.ninestarpress.com